THE SPICE GATE

THE
SPICE
GATE

A Fantasy

PRASHANTH
SRIVATSA

HARPER Voyager
An Imprint of HarperCollins Publishers

HarperCollins books may be purchased for educational, business, or sales promotional use. For information, please email the Special Markets Department at SPsales@harpercollins.com.

Harper Voyager and design are trademarks of HarperCollins Publishers LLC.

FIRST EDITION

Designed by Jennifer Chung
Map design by Virginia Allyn
Title spread image © Bolbik/stock.adobe.com
Chapter opener and backmatter chart images © Orange Sky/stock.adobe.com

Library of Congress Cataloging-in-Publication Data has been applied for.

ISBN 978-0-06-326683-4

24 25 26 27 28 LBC 5 4 3 2 1

*To my grandparents, and the infinite
worlds they carried in their frail bodies*

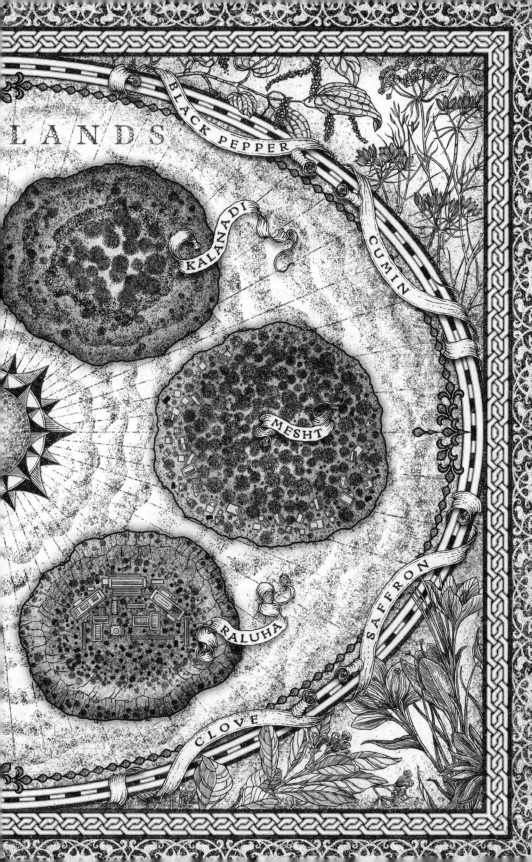

DRAMATIS PERSONAE

In Raluha

Amir: A Carrier
Karim bhai: A Carrier, also a servant of Suman-Koti, Minister of Silks
Kabir: Amir's brother
Noori: Amir's mother
Hasmin: The chief of the chowkidars
Orbalun: The thronekeeper of Raluha

In Halmora

Harini: The rajkumari of Halmora

In Illindhi

Fylan: the commander of the Uyirsena
Makun-kunj: A guardian of the Spice Gate, the twin of Sibil-kunj
Sibil-kunj: A guardian of the Spice Gate, the twin of Makun-kunj
Kalay: An acolyte of the Uyirsena
Kashyni: The stewardess of Illindhi, one of the Five Chairs
Mahrang: One of the Five Chairs, the high priest of the Uyirsena
Munivarey: One of the Five Chairs, a scientist
Shashulyan: One of the Five Chairs
Alinjya: One of the Five Chairs
Madhyra: The thronekeeper of Illindhi

DRAMATIS PERSONAE

AT THE AFSAL DINA IN JHANAK

Rani Zariba: The thronekeeper of Jhanak

Ilangovan: A pirate and renegade Carrier

Sekaran: A pirate; Ilangovan's right-hand man

Raja Silmehi: The thronekeeper of Talashshukh

Rani Asphalekha: The thronekeeper of Kalanadi

IN VANASI

Bindu: A merchant

IN AMAROHI

Rani Kaivalya: The thronekeeper of Amarohi

CHAPTER

1

*A man who offers you tea without ginger is more miserly than
one who doesn't offer you tea at all.*

—*Morsels of a Bent Back*, Volume 1

Amir stood within the ring of erected stones encircling the Spice
Gate in the midst of the saffron fields. The spicemark burned
on his throat, sensing his proximity to the arch. Karim bhai
shuffled next to him, stoic as ever, hair ruffled, beard unkempt, age
wrinkling his forehead. He held a pinch of turmeric in his hand.

Amir counted the others. Forty Carriers in all. Twenty each to Vanasi
and Halmora. Squatting beside tilted sacks or perched on cartons filled
to the brim with saffron, cardamom, and rhubarb, and vials of honey and
crates of rosewood. Jhengara, the accountant, whistled an old tune at
the front of the queue, a stack of papers beneath his arm and an anxious
tremble that was visible twenty feet away.

Amir shivered.

Because no amount of experience could settle the nerves when it came
to walking through the Spice Gate. Not for the first time; not for the
thousandth.

It loomed ahead like a monstrous archway upon a pedestal, dressed
in gray marble and ancient stone, its base withered and swamped with

creeping vines that twisted around the pillars in a gnarled choke hold. But what caught Amir's attention as always was that swirling tempest beneath the arch, a veil like a melted mirror that held a storm within its prison.

The soul of the eight kingdoms ran through its crevices.

A soul I want no part of.

"Salaam," Karim bhai greeted one of the chowkidars. The guard waved a pike in their direction, its tip grazing Amir's elbow. Karim bhai raised his hands in supplication and continued. "If you'd be so kind to tell us what we're waiting for?"

The chowkidar shrugged and moved away. Amir clenched his fists but prevented himself from prodding the chowkidar further. There was added security by the Gate today, and Hasmin, the chief of the chowkidars himself, stood by the Gate's arch, casting a derisive frown at the column of Carriers waiting to sift through.

Amir whispered in Karim bhai's ear, "Don't tell me that now, of all times, they got a hunch about Ilangovan prowling Vanasi."

He was careful to temper the tension in his voice as he mentioned the most wanted man in the eight kingdoms. Karim bhai sounded far less anxious. "They can pursue him all they want. But make no mistake, in those Mouth-cursed towers, I'd no sooner find a dropped cardamom."

It ought to have allayed Amir's fears a little. But as a bowler of Raluha, as a gatecaste Carrier of the eight kingdoms, his fortunes, like those of Karim bhai, flickered like a candle about to be extinguished.

And there's never been enough wax to begin with.

Ilangovan was a source of light for Amir and the gatecaste. Amir just needed it to hold steady a while longer. Or, better yet, go shine somewhere else, far away from Vanasi. Of course, Amir was not certain if Ilangovan was even *in* Vanasi—no one could ever really know where he'd be when he was not in the Black Coves; the renegade Carrier was as much a spirit as a pirate. But there was one thing Amir *was* certain was in Vanasi: the Jewelmaker's Poison.

And much as he desired to meet Ilangovan, now was not the time.

In fact, the time would only come if he could get his hands on the Poison, and it would be a gatecaste irony, where one desire was upset by the appearance of another.

No—he would get the Poison. It *had to be* in Vanasi. He'd sacrificed three fortnights' worth of spices to be certain. He'd climbed enough vines, delivered enough contraband, and crawled on enough rooftops to know that the Jewelmaker and his elusive Carnelian Caravan were supplying the Poison to the denizens of the upper levels of Vanasi's bramble-choked towers. And all Amir needed was *one* vial.

Karim bhai must have sensed the trepidation in his voice, the vacancy in his eyes as his thoughts plunged into darkness. "Ho, pulla. Are you sure you're up for this?"

Amir blinked. "What? Oh, yes—of course, yeah. What do you mean, bhai! I *have* to do this."

He immediately regretted those words. Making it a compulsion sounded insensitive of Karim bhai and the other bowlers, who harbored no desire to upend their fates. Or at any rate put their lives at stake for it.

But Ilangovan had. He had broken free.

Karim bhai chuckled. "So much for not wanting to be like your father. You remind me of Arsalan in more ways than one."

"Is that what you think I am? Delusional?"

"It's not very far from reckless, pulla. The line between them blurs as you get more desperate."

Amir forced himself to not think of his father. He raised his head stiffly, to regard the mountains looming beyond the Spice Gate, and the dense hold of trees hugging their bellies. Beautiful and treacherous, the stench of death in the air and the promise of darkness. No, he was nothing like his father. Unlike Appa, he had a plan.

"The Jewelmaker is in Vanasi," he said. "I am certain. I will have the Poison in my hands before nightfall, bhai."

"By the Gates I hope you do."

"Don't worry about me," said Amir. "Just give my letter to Harini."

Karim bhai, who had begun cleaning his teeth with a bristled leaf, clicked his tongue. "She's going to be upset you're not on the roster for Halmora today."

"I have explained it all in the letter. Just ensure she reads it."

"I will do what I always do: deliver. But remember, pulla," warned Karim bhai, "if the thronekeeper of Halmora finds out his daughter is reading letters sent to her by a bowler of Raluha, things will get ugly real soon, and this whole dream—of joining Ilangovan, of getting your mother and Kabir to the Black Coves—it disappears."

Amir had thought about this possibility too many times to be truly bothered by Karim bhai's warning. "She's not like the other thronekeepers."

At that, Karim bhai laughed. "If I had a peppercorn for every time the abovefolk thought that of themselves—"

"No, she truly is not. It's not her saying this but me. I trust her. Ten years of carrying, twenty years in the Bowl. Do you think I do not know the thousand ways the abovefolk discriminate against us? Do you think, after the lashes, after the stink, the seclusion, I would consider opening my heart to one of the abovefolk, to a *princess* of Halmora, if I was not certain?"

"You're certain of a lot of things today, pulla." Karim bhai continued chewing the leaf, massaging his teeth as he did so. "I fear for these assurances you've got going on in your head. It reeks of having control over one's lives. And we? Pulla, we're not the ones in control. We're not bred to be certain of anything except the pain of passing through the Gates."

Amir wanted to argue further—and the Gates knew he was tired of repeating his arguments to Karim bhai day and night as the years rolled by—but at that moment, the line of Carriers began to shuffle ahead. Jhengara the accountant's tune intensified as a signal for the Spice Trade to begin. Hasmin's eyes trailed each Carrier as they picked up the sacks and lifted the crates to place them over their heads. Amir swung his own sack over his back and staggered ahead, his head low, his gaze fixed on the back of Karim bhai's feet, the coarse, fissured skin, the garb of dirt, only a feeble image of the end of the day shimmering in his mind.

At one point, Karim bhai stumbled, and Amir groaned. A whip fell on the old Carrier, and he dropped the sack with a wince. Karim bhai lowered himself to the ground, wheezing, one hand twisted to massage his back, and the other pulling the dropped sack closer to him. Amir's eyes widened as Hasmin loomed behind the old Carrier, a snarl on his face that he had come to loathe.

"Ho, that wasn't necessary!" Amir protested.

Yet Hasmin ignored him and, like a predator patiently enjoying the struggles of its prey, watched Karim bhai pick himself up, and the sack with him. Karim bhai almost fell again, teetering against the weight of saffron. Any temerity, any social capital Karim bhai had built over five decades of carrying, vanished in that moment as he enslaved himself to the tenets of his duty. That's all that remained once stripped of the brittle comforts to which the bowlers had clung to. That frenetic moment of picking the spice-laden sack and hoisting it upon their shoulder—that was the only permanence. That, and the aroma of spices that surrounded them, of course.

If not for the sack on his back, Amir would have stood erect, with his chest out, and glared at Hasmin. He'd have spat at him if there were enough saliva in his mouth.

Fortunately, he could do neither.

Remember, you need the Poison. Keep your mouth shut.

For a moment, Amir wondered if Hasmin would grab him and shove him to the ground. Or perhaps, cup him under his chin and crush the bones of his jaw.

Wishful thinking.

What Amir got was, instead, a projectile of mucus right in his face. All the wealth of a hydrated body, conjured in that working of tongue and cheek muscles.

Hasmin would sooner parade naked in front of the bowlers than touch one of them. But whip them? Spit on them?

That he did without compunction.

Amir, who needed both hands to cling to the sack, felt the spittle

5

dribble down his cheek and along the line of his throat where the spice-mark rested, and could do nothing about it. Even looking the chief of the chowkidars in the eye could be seen as an act of defiance.

Jhengara's tune ended. A whistle from the Gate broke Hasmin's glare. The second signal had arrived. Carriers shuffled ahead. Hasmin spat once more, this time so Amir had to sidestep the wad as it smacked into the dirt at his feet. The chief bellowed for the Carriers to maintain their line. A low breeze wafted in the scent from the saffron fields, stalks swaying, bulbs frolicking.

The rest was clockwork. Amir trudged on, not trying to be too eager. Usually, he would scurry to the end on all the duties—all except Halmora, when he'd always be excited to meet Harini. With those other deliveries, he'd hope against hope that, by the time his chance came, Hasmin would hold him back; announce that there had been a mistake, that the Carriers who had been ferried ahead were sufficient to complete the trade. That he, Amir, could return home, no harm done.

But in his ten years of carrying, he had never been blessed with such fortune.

Now, though, he wanted to get through. *Needed* his fortune to keep Hasmin from holding him back. Once Karim bhai sprinkled turmeric on the veil and disappeared through the Gate to Halmora, Amir took a deep breath and a step forward, his head spinning as the swirl beneath the arch shimmered with a steady thrum. A thrum that hammered into his bones. A thrum he wanted to stop screaming in his ears.

He adjusted the sack of saffron and hoisted it higher over his shoulder. It was amazing to think that such tiny strands or ground bits of a seed could weigh so much, but stuffed into a burlap bag until near-bursting, it was enough to bend the strongest back—which Amir could hardly claim to have. He gritted his teeth but said nothing as Hasmin poured some of the powdered leftover nutmeg on Amir's extended palm. His key through the Gate.

His mind wobbled. He was not sure if the scent on Hasmin's person was of orange or ginger. Amma would know.

The jumble continued, the Gate making it hard for him to focus. A lash fell on his back. He yelped. One of the chowkidars screamed at him to keep moving.

He swallowed hard and stopped a retort from escaping his mouth. The gatekeepers were only doing their jobs, yet in the presence of Hasmin, they appeared like extensions of him, like poisonous tentacles tethered to a heartless monster.

"I better not discover that you have strayed from the spice trail," Hasmin growled, low enough for Amir to hear, then nudged him up the steps. Hasmin's shadow eclipsed any warmth Amir might have felt as the Gate's essence vibrated in his chest even louder.

Amir climbed the seven steps to the Gate, panting as his sack threatened to drag him down. When he was within a foot of the arch, he opened his fist and cast the nutmeg into the veil. The mirror shimmered violently, jerking and shuddering, dispelling a wave of heat—like masala thrust into boiling water—before transforming into a rippling shade of golden brown. It pulled the air toward itself, like a vacuum.

The Gate worked. Amir had no choice. He lifted his chin and stepped through, giving himself to the spice god, and as always, the great Gate tore him apart.

THERE WAS NOTHING LIKE IT. MOONFALL AFTER MOONFALL, AND that weightless, evanescent folding of himself was still something that stole Amir's breath. The spicemark on his neck singed and flared like a wound that was being tortured with fire whips. His consciousness strained in that flicker as he glided through layers in space. That's what Karim bhai called it. Space. Emptiness. Impossible, inhospitable—unknowns separating two far-flung kingdoms. And a tether in between.

Amir's younger brother, Kabir, had questioned him a hundred times about it in curiosity over the years and all he could manage to tell the boy was this: *Imagine yourself being pulled and pressed at the same time, from all sides, until you can no longer feel any sensation but pain—a harsh, searing pain. Your ribs, folding. Your flesh, compressed, like a ball of tamarind to be boiled. And before the realization of that impossibility sinks in, you're on the other side, in a new land, denying that it had ever happened. Only the pain remains with you, lingering in the screaming shadows of the mind's trauma, never to be forgotten.*

Amir sucked in the air as that memory now swam inside him once more. He found his body struggling to accommodate this new intake of breath. Pain clogged his pores, and he ended up panting. He dropped the sack. The agony of passage—that he was used to. But why was every muscle on fire? He stayed there, kneeling, oblivious to the shifting footfalls around him.

Without Karim bhai, Amir suddenly felt alone. The other Carriers were similarly pained, and their glances spoke of that same wonder, as to why the Mouth was tormenting them more today. Was this punishment? Did the Mouth, in some inexplicable way, discover that Amir had switched his name from the Halmoran roster to the one heading to Vanasi by bribing Jhengara with a pouch full of cumin seeds? Had he inadvertently caused harm to his fellow Carriers?

As with each time through the gate, however, the pain dimmed. His eyes ceased to water, and the surroundings came into view.

The Spice Gate at Vanasi grew on a mound of earth, overlooking the fourth tower. The Gate was less haggard than the one in Raluha. Amir craned his neck, standing in the midst of the twisted vines, and gazed at the nine towers that surrounded the Gate. They were, each, at least three hundred to five hundred meters wide, and twenty stories high, piercing the sky like crooked fingers of stone. No two towers looked alike, but they were all unmistakably in the grasp of the forest they sprouted from. Bridges spanned overhead like cross ropes, connecting the towers at every few levels. The pathways were swamped by the movement of carts, wagons, and people, hanging markets and banners that children swung down from to move between levels, steps and ladders, and wooden mechanical lifts operated by pulleys that gave Vanasi the look of a constantly stirring jungle. And through it all, the vines and trees weaved a tapestry of nature, impossible to untangle.

Amir inhaled sharply, forgetting for one moment the pain at the fringes of his shoulder and down his back. The distant smell of nutmeg assaulted his senses, but Vanasi was more than nutmeg. The shadows within the towers spoke of strange secrets, of alchemy and spells and the abodes of reclusive chroniclers, astrologers, and mantravaadis whose rooms reeked of ink, coffee, and sacred ash, and whose windows were curved into the roofs so that they had a clear view of the night skies with stars that shone upon Vanasi brighter than on any other kingdom.

Sweet, leathery, almost balsamic was the fragrance of ghaliyah as it permeated through the forested floor of Vanasi. Amir stood to pick up his sack and followed the other Carriers toward the third tower.

No kingdom among the eight smelled as rich as Vanasi, except perhaps the perfume market of Talashshukh. The smells engulfed him here amid the chitter of birds, the sound of crickets, and the crush of undergrowth beneath his feet. The sun beat down on the Carriers' necks, and Amir, feeling quite small and insignificant, craned to glimpse the tower through its myriad windows. The tower dwarfed everyone else, too, and for Amir, being amid these imposing towers of Vanasi, this was as close to being an equal to the abovefolk as he thought he could manage.

As they entered the third tower, Amir cast the net of his gaze toward the crowd of people for any hint of the Jewelmaker and his elusive Carnelian Caravan. They would have with them a vial of the Poison for him. He only had to find his contact.

There was always a singular trail for the Carriers from the Gate to the place of deposit. From there, they'd carry back to Raluha fresh sacks, laden with mace and nutmeg, or crates filled to the brim with bottles of perfume, with aromas ranging from camphor and musk to mastic and the enigmatic khaoulan. Occasionally, there'd be bags filled with astrology charts and spellbooks, and pages of religious scripture that were only reluctantly handed over to the Carriers, who—by virtue of belonging to the gatecaste—were forbidden to read them. Today, as they climbed the stairs of the third tower, from the opposite side came the rooters of Vanasi, the gatecaste equivalent of the Raluhan bowlers. Different names, similar fates. Amir exchanged nods with a few of the rooters he knew by face or name, and to the others he gave a perfunctory smile, a shared suffering that did not require words but merely the ghost of a sigh or the gentle scuttling aside to allow passage for the other person, a nicety invisible to the eyes of the abovefolk.

Once they deposited their sacks and crates, Amir and the other Carriers had an hour in which the Vanasari accountants and merchants counted the arrivals, wrote in their ledgers, and prepared for the return consignment to Raluha. In that time, most Carriers simply rested their backs against the walls, their eyes closed, their breaths shallow and blue. Many slept.

Karim bhai and Amir alone had been the exceptions through the years.

There was always a letter to deliver to someone in another kingdom, a secret correspondence, a gift or a curse, medicines and books that the kingdoms would otherwise tax on import. No end to the list of objects and services that people wished to trade beneath the gaze of the throne-keepers, and to them Karim bhai folded his hands, bowed, and offered himself as the shadow merchant who had an ear even among the ministers of the Raluhan palace, a station few bowlers could lay claim to.

And because Karim bhai would often not manage to carry all these surreptitious objects of another's desire by himself, Amir would accompany him, cursing under his breath every additional step, every warren or tower they crawled into. There would always be an additional pouch of spice on offer, or a trinket to steal, anything that would make his family's life more respectable in the Bowl. And more, the vagaries of the eight kingdoms laid themselves bare in front of Amir during these forbidden expeditions, and if not for one of those, Amir would never have met Bindu.

Today, as ever, the habit worked as a boon for him. He slipped out of the granary, tied a shawl around his throat to conceal the spicemark, and made his way across the bridge to the fifth tower: to the hanging market.

The bazaar was a series of circular bridges of wooden planks that wound around the tower like bangles around a wrist. Tethered to the bridges were platforms of shops, wrapped in nets like cocoons, suspended beneath rafters like lanterns. Amir, terrified of heights, clung to each pole and rafter, or occasionally grabbed someone's arm with his eyes shut while he navigated through the crowd at the lip of the tower. He didn't have much time.

Bindu, the woman who had tipped him off about the Jewelmaker during Amir's previous visit to Vanasi, ran her shop of cheap perfumes in one of these concentric rings around the fifth tower. There was no short-age of distractions along the way. For Amir, who could smell every herb and condiment in the air, it took that little bit extra to make a beeline through the chaos of haggling and soaring voices to where Bindu kept her shop.

When he reached her stall, though, she was not there. Instead, a small boy sat on the swollen folds of the net, looking cross and betrayed while tossing a ball of tamarind in the air and catching it. He made a face as though his time were being abused.

Amir squeezed beneath the rafter and perched beside the boy. "Ho, where's Bindu?"

All around them were hastily assembled shelves of perfumes and attar, the wind doing little to dissuade the fragrance of frankincense, myrrh, and sandalwood from leaving the shop. The tantalizing scents almost deflated what little energy Amir had left after Carrying. He wouldn't mind sleeping here for a while.

"Not here," said the boy.

"I can see that. Do you know when she'll be back?"

The boy frowned at the shawl around Amir's throat. "Who are you?"

Amir licked his lip and examined the boy. Nothing extraordinary. Bazaar-bred of Vanasi, the kind who could look at a nutmeg tree and tell when the pericarp was ripe to split open and fall.

"I am from the Carnelian Caravan," whispered Amir, narrowing his eyes, pursing his lips, and looking straight at the boy condescendingly.

If the boy was skeptical, he did not show it at once. He continued fiddling with the tamarind ball, tossing it up and catching it even as he returned Amir's cold stare. The next moment, however, he flung the tamarind at Amir's face and screamed, "Akka, run!"

The tamarind smacked Amir on the nose. He'd have fallen backward if not for the shrouding of net that caught him. He turned in time to see a shape hurtling across the wooden planks on the market gangway, brushing past a host of bodies.

Amir cursed and shot a glare at the boy, who was grinning widely, revealing sparkling white teeth. Pulling himself out of the shop and back onto the plank bridge, Amir made his way through the crowd, through the haggling and the bargaining, the breeze whipping against his face and flicking his hair aside. Bindu had disappeared into the narrow crowd of shoppers on the bridge.

Amir hurried after her, fearing the worst: that she had kept the Poison for herself. His fear of heights dwindled in those feeble moments as he imagined returning to Raluha empty-handed, his future laid bare, his brother, Kabir, following him through the Spice Gate in a moonfall's time, a sack bowing the little boy under. He dashed across the planks, each step a wager against slipping through a crack. But the hanging market of Vanasi had not killed a haggler in fifty years. He doubted he'd break the record today.

He pushed past jute sellers, past shops that sold wholesale herbs and spices, past karuveppilai hoarders and potato merchants, past a sea of carrots and sundried chilies. He then climbed three ladders to the next level—nearly bumping his head upon the feet of a descending woman, to whom he apologized profusely—to where the bazaar opened up to sprawls of books and scrolls, shrugging off shopkeepers screaming discounts in his ear. His eyes were trained on the flickering figure of Bindu ahead, in her black salwaar kameez, a wick against the sky as she dashed past where the market swerved into the tower, where in the shadows there came alive lanterns and candles of a hundred shapes and sizes.

Beneath that light, Amir stopped to catch his breath. The pain along his back magnified, and he clutched the pole of a shop's tent, which annoyed the shopkeeper, who began to harass Amir to buy the bronze astrolabe swinging in front of his face, his gaze apparently constituting a contract to purchase. Amir had to duck to avoid the shopkeeper's lunge, and once more chased after Bindu inside the tower.

She was heading toward the stairs, Amir realized, and along that way were the Vanasari guards. They wore gray, like the towers they patrolled, with large, angular helms that swayed with each step. They held batons in their hands and a permanent suspicion in their eyes. Amir wagered even being in their vicinity would lure them all to him. He'd be reported to Hasmin, and even a whiff of that singular threat was enough to deter him from going down that path. He couldn't give up, though, so he slipped between two shops instead, past empty wagons and community homes stacked along the tower's inner walls, and was quick to spy a second stairway built into a stone arch, a narrower one used by the servants and rooters.

Feeling right at home, Amir skipped down after a column of stragglers, past a family of seven trying to catch their breath, and down to the lower level, the door to which swung open once more into the winding bazaar around the tower. The breeze hit him hard, and he dashed across the wooden gangway, teetering precariously on a plank that leaned half into the open, and past sprawls of cabbages and beetroots and white pumpkins cut up in quarters. He leaped upward, caught the foot of a ladder, hoisted himself up, and climbed ten feet to land on a platform. The flooring shifted tremulously beneath his feet. He regained his balance and glowered at a shopkeeper who cursed him for being reckless.

Sorry, chacha, let me tell you another day how desperate I am.

At last, he rounded a bend, slipped beneath a plank, and scurried down three ladders to the lower level, where, precisely at that moment, Bindu was dashing toward him from the opposite side. She skidded to a halt in front of him, and Amir lunged to grab her. Together, they rolled on the narrow pathway along the side of the tower. People shrieked and jumped aside, and the shopkeepers yelled and hurled abuses at them. Amir stood, grabbed Bindu's salwaar, and dragged her aside. He pushed her against the slab of an empty shop and, aware of dozens of eyes on them, managed a weak grin.

"I am a thief by nature, Bindu," he gasped, each word revealing a stitch in his ribs. "Must you make this difficult? I thought we had a deal."

Bindu coughed, her silver hair wriggling out of its bun. Her chest heaved. In that spoiled state, she looked no older than Amir, although he knew her to have at least a decade on him. She pushed his hand away and bent to catch her breath.

"They're gone," she managed.

Amir thought he hadn't heard her properly. "I'm sorry?"

"They're gone," she repeated, pulling herself up, her hands on her hips, her gaze darting left and right. The onlookers had resumed shopping. The market had returned to its bustle.

"The Jewelmaker?"

Bindu raised her palm to cover Amir's mouth. "Shush, will you? Gates, you're a loud one. Not here. Follow me."

Amir held her hand. "Don't try to run away this time."

He followed her out of the market and back inside the tower. They crossed two bridges to reach the second tower, nearly a mile away from the third, where he was due to return in a few minutes. He couldn't afford to be late, not unless he wished a lifetime of recrimination from Hasmin and the end of any hope he had of escaping Raluha with his mother and brother. He conveyed as much to Bindu, who did not appear to be bothered by any of it. She appeared quite defeated herself, and Amir wondered what had transpired for a Vanasari local to be scared out of her wits.

Bindu led him into what appeared to be a carpenter's workshop, where a lone man was polishing a cutting board. Bindu gestured to him to leave, which he promptly did. From one of the windows inside the workshop, Amir spied the first and the third towers and, in the distance below, one-half of the Spice Gate's arch, beckoning him.

"The Jewelmaker's gone," she stated with a finality.

Amir allowed the words to sink in. He had hoped he'd misheard her in the market, that perhaps the wind had played tricks on his ears. "What do you mean he's gone?" he sputtered, his heart racing. "He isn't . . . you know, he's not *there*, per se, ever, is he? He's a shadow, a thing that many people imagine. How can he be *gone* if he wasn't properly there?"

Bindu placed a hand on his cheek. "I mean he has decided not to supply the Poison anymore, thambi. Not him, nor the Carnelian Caravan that runs on his command."

Amir chuckled. "That's not possible. Don't lie to me. Is it more saffron you need? Or perhaps honey? Tell me your price, Bindu ka, and I'll give it to you."

Bindu inspected the surface of a worktable, then turned to Amir. "As we speak, the upper levels of the ninth tower are in an uproar. Raja Jirasandha and Rani Ugrannia have summoned the ministers, the guilds, and the rooters' representatives. Since nobody knows what the Jewelmaker looks like, and his caravan has all but disappeared off the face of the eight kingdoms, nobody knows what to do except scream into each other's faces. The Poison, after all, is a bigger addiction than the spices. So, no, thambi, I am not lying. I stand to gain nothing by it."

"Do you think it's him?" Amir asked desperately. "Ilangovan?"

Bindu burst out laughing. "The Jewelmaker? No way! I have met Ilangovan, although briefly. Do not pay heed to such rumors. Besides, Ilangovan has not been seen in Vanasi in a long while now. He is content at the Black Coves. It is harvest season for coriander, after all."

"It doesn't make any sense," Amir muttered. "Why would the Jewelmaker disappear?"

Bindu shrugged. "Perhaps that was the point, you know?"

"What?"

"To be senseless. To test how addicted people would get to a drug that would allow anyone not born branded by the spicemark to painlessly pass through the Gates. And then snatch it away from them without warning. A great joke?"

"I don't know if it's a joke or not, but the Poison is not for everyone. People like us, the bowlers, the rooters, we could never afford it, could we? I haven't been able to buy a *single* vial. Nobody in the Bowl has."

Bindu looked offended. "Ho, this is not exclusive to you gatecaste. Very few can afford the Poison, even outside the Root. Ever see me go buy a vial? I'd have to sell my shop and sell my ma's bangles, and even then I might not get one. When was the last time someone other than a royal or a minister's family member ever drank the Poison and used the Gates?"

"But this was supposed to be my chance. You were my contact, and I had enough spice and . . ."

"And you're a Carrier. A Carrier asking for the Poison. Do you even hear yourself, thambi? You're whining about something you never possibly could have had."

He bristled at "whining," and at the implication that she had always been leading him on. "This isn't even for me—I'm not asking because of some fancy desire to travel the eight kingdoms. Gates know I do enough of that."

"Then what do you need it for?" She looked at him shrewdly. "Or rather, who do you need it for?"

Amir bit his lip. He stiffened suddenly. "My business is my own. I paid you to give me information on the Jewelmaker. Is that why you ran? You finished off the saffron, didn't you?"

"It's saffron," Bindu conceded at once. "What do you expect me to do, hoard it? I'd be robbed the first night here. Every sack you lot brought from Raluha goes into the eighth and ninth towers. The bazaar gets pittances. Just a ghost of it, a shade of it on our palms."

And the rooters and the bowlers, even less, he wanted to say, but held his tongue.

"I expected you to hold up your end of the bargain."

"I did what I could—I gave you information about the Jewelmaker. That information is that he's not here."

Amir slumped against the wall, holding his head in his hands. He had wasted the saffron from his allowance. The bits and pieces of other spices he'd received as payment from Karim bhai for those little secret expeditions, those he had squirreled away to pay Bindu to help him. He was a thief, and it was a bitter feeling being robbed. He felt suddenly powerless, a rage clotting in his heart against the system. He felt as though he deserved at least a little for things to go his way. Some meager compensation. A pinch of luck.

That wasn't the bowlers' lot now, was it?

"So . . . that's it?" he moaned. "The Poison's gone? Perhaps the Jewelmaker will return, perhaps in a fortnight, perhaps a mooncycle? He has to!"

"And if he does, I'll let you know," replied Bindu. "But right now, the market runs dry, thambi. Not a single drop. The afsal dina is in a week's time, and the thronekeepers have already begun to scour their last reserves to travel to Jhanak for the harvest and the feast. You'd do better to forget whatever it is that you think you need the Poison for."

"You must know if someone has a vial," Amir pleaded. "Just one vial." *For my mother*, he added under his breath.

Bindu shook her head. "Ever since the Jewelmaker's disappearance, Jirasandha conducted raids across the nine towers, including the Root. Weeded out every last drop of the Poison that came in as contraband and smuggled them into the ninth. And even that has not been sufficient. Everyone's furious, and it doesn't help that Ilangovan's menace in Jhanak has only worsened. The thronekeepers need more Poison if they're to send guards to bolster Jhanak's navy and nab the damned pirate. But even that plan is now down the drain. At the afsal dina, the thronekeepers will gather in Jhanak to find a way to solve this problem once and for all."

Amir looked away, through a window, swallowing any rebuttal that rose up in his throat. He wished to defend Ilangovan, but he knew he'd only make matters worse for himself. He had worried that Ilangovan, who was known to smuggle the gatecaste out of their plight, was here and had ruined everything. But now he wondered if it would have been better if the smuggler *had* been in Vanasi, so that Amir could have seen what the man could do to help his family. Instead, Amir had trusted Bindu and the elusive promise of the Poison—clearly that had been a mistake. To believe in what Bindu was saying now felt like a mistake too. For deep down, he knew Ilangovan would never be caught. He had provided haven to runaway Carriers for four decades, eluding the Spice Trade's venomous arms and defying their will at every turn.

And even though Ilangovan's methods had often been questionable, Amir did not think he could find a better home for his mother and Kabir.

And yourself. You deserve it just as much.

Bindu must have seen the despair on his face, the hopelessness haunting his eyes. She sighed, emitting a low whistle. "Gates, you must really be desperate if you can manage that expression on your face. What is it, a lover from another kingdom you wish to sneak into Raluha? I've heard there are daayans among the Kalanadi women luring Carriers like you."

"No, not a lover—"

"Ah, you know what, it doesn't matter. Gates know I've paid for my curiosities. And this whole Poison game is an upper-caste scandal, and I don't mind seeing bowlers like you swigging a vial down your throats every now and then, so mayhaps I'll part with this little whisper that floated into my ears earlier today."

Amir perked up. Of course there was an exception. It was Bindu he was talking to, the thrift rani of Vanasi, from whom nothing that transpired in this aesthetic regime was hidden. A daughter of Karim bhai in spirit. A liar, for sure, but a liar who sold lies he was eager to hear.

"Who?" Amir asked, his chest swelling up.

She kept her face plain and unyielding. And slowly, one arm extended toward Amir, the palm open. "If you're a thief by nature, Amir of Raluha, I am the Vanasari rat of bargain."

One finger curled in invitation.

"Then fulfill your previous bargain! I don't have any more saffron,"

Amir snapped. It gladdened him for once that he was not bluffing. Be it bowlers or rooters, or any of the gatecaste among the eight kingdoms, the obsession with spice escaped few. What began in the ornate palaces and the marble-decked households trickled down to the bazaar, and from there to the thin, barely stitched pockets of the lowborn. Seven levels of the hanging market in the tower of Vanasi was not sufficient to fill the bellies of one kingdom. They needed more; they always needed more.

"Empty your pockets," she commanded him.

Amir was stunned at her audacity. She had the temerity to question him after consuming his own saffron for nothing, and yet there was little he could do in that moment except obey her. *If she isn't lying . . .*

He emptied his pockets.

A single rolled parchment fell out.

A gift for Harini he had forgotten to hand over to Karim bhai along with the letter.

Bindu picked up the parchment and untied the ribbon before he could snatch it back. She opened it, and her eyes widened. For on the parchment was a painting of Raluha as seen from the eyes of a vulture. Replete with the saffron fields, the Spice Gate in its blooming midst, the great vale of settlements shaped like a bowl, the palace to the north, the stone manors and marble halls to the west, the market along the slopes, and at the bottom of the valley, the Bowl itself. The home of the gatecaste.

Bindu stared at it, at a loss for words. She licked the dryness off her lips and blinked. A moment later, she folded and pocketed the parchment.

"Give it back, please," said Amir. "It is a gift meant for another."

"Do you want your whisper or not?"

"I do, but this cannot be the price."

"The painting will fetch entire jars of spice," Bindu argued, wonder laced in her own voice, at the ease of the argument. "So very few in Vanasi know what Raluha looks like. These saffron fields . . ."

"Ho," cried Amir. "Look at your face. I doubt you will sell this."

You know you will. You have in the past, too, to earn a few extra spices for Amma.

19

Bindu smiled sadly, and Amir wondered if he was finally seeing her true face. "No, I will not."

Amir clenched his fists and took a deep breath. Bindu's thin smile did not waver. Amir slowly smiled in return, as though this were a game that they would never tire of playing, this ridiculous stench of barter, this inheritance of the bazaar that ran in the blood of every man, woman, and child of the eight kingdoms. He did not doubt the wealth of what Bindu was holding in her hands.

And thus, he conceded it.

"Okay, you have a deal. Tell me now. Who has the Poison?"

"I cannot say for certain," Bindu replied, "and you will certainly not hold me accountable, but word in the bazaar is that the Jewelmaker ceased his supply after Rajkumari Harini of Halmora duped the Carnelian Caravan for a barrel full of the Poison five days ago."

CHAPTER

2

*Each daughter of Kabuliyah sat on one side of the weighing
scale, the other balanced by sacks of cardamoms and groundnuts.
And when the weights matched, the dowry for the wedding
was decided.*

—Jannat Munshi, *Shaadighar:
Criticisms of a Raluhan Marriage*

The Bowl sagged in a life of its own. Its breathing was labored
and rattled, often mingling with the sounds of its occupants: the
bowlers—and among them, the Carriers—who snored louder
than the roosters, and for longer than the bells clanged each morning
from the Mouth's temples. Kabir swore Amir snored like a pigsty, and no
amount of crushed elaichi in water made it go away.

"Ho, did you give the painting to Harini?" Kabir asked the following
evening after Amir had returned from Vanasi, his voice low, one eye beyond the curtain where Amma cooked dinner with one hand cupping her
round belly. The aroma of spices was faint, and Amir hoped the Bashara
would refill their jars next week.

He gave a faint nod to his brother, the spasms in his back stinging his
bones. He winced, tracing a hand as far down his spine as he could and

stretching his shoulders. "Yes, yes. She loved it. Said she'd hang it in her bedchamber along with the other paintings."

Kabir's chest heaved, and a grin formed on his lips. "I'm going to paint more. Do you think the other thronekeepers might like them too?" In the semidarkness of their home, Amir glimpsed the spicemark on his brother's throat. He shrugged noncommittally. "It doesn't matter. Just draw because *you* like to. I'm sure someone will find it worthy of hanging in their bedchamber."

The thought seemed to please Kabir, who scampered to the shelf to pick out a fresh sheet of parchment and ran out of the house to begin his new work. Amir, too tired to chase after his brother, sat and leafed through his other paintings. Raluha was not the only focus of Kabir's art. He had, in his boundless eleven-year-old imagination, conjured even the Outerlands beyond the kingdoms. The mountains that could be seen from the saffron fields, the clouds hovering over them, the forests and the darkness they heralded beyond the fences. He had drawn rivers sparkling beneath the sunlight, burbling through thick jungles, and—

Amir paused, his hand shivering at the next sheaf of parchment he came to. It showed an enormous beast, covering nearly the entirety of the paper, a black thing of malice that seemed to tower over a village. Kabir had liberally blackened the painting and left two crimson pinpricks in the heart of that darkness for eyes that glared at Amir through the parchment.

Heedless of his own words, he folded the painting and went after Kabir. He knew where to find him.

The Bowl came alive in much the same way Jhanak's fish market did in the evenings. Nobody liked to sit inside their homes, not like the abovefolk. An hour of opinions and gossip, an hour of salves being applied to soothe troubled spines. The air stank of stale ginger, and the trickle of sewage was a permanent fixture along the fringes of the Bowl, like the steady passage of time, an endless riot of decadence amid the dim, flickering lanterns, while the Raluha above glowed like fragments of a golden moon.

The one thing it rarely smelled like was, ironically, saffron. No, only one yellow thing trickled down to the Bowl, and it wasn't the kingdom's spice.

Amir hated how content many of the bowlers looked. The sound of laughter stopped him in his tracks as he glimpsed Veni and Madhuri exchanging quips while sitting on a ledge. Beyond them, half a dozen men lounged outside a chai stall. Damini, who had tied a cloth around half her face, was sweeping one corner of the lane and with a swerve of her hip breaking into an awkward dance, her lips moving in sync with a song.

Or perhaps this was what it meant to live, and Amir had gotten it all wrong. That his desire to escape Raluha and join Ilangovan and his band of pirates in the Black Coves was as delusional as Karim bhai had claimed.

He found the object of his ire lying on a jute cot in a lungi, one leg across the other, a beedi between his lips, wispy clouds of smoke shooting out from an "o" at the center of his mouth. Kabir sat beside Karim bhai, sketching beneath candlelight.

"Go back home," Amir told him. "Amma needs your help."

Kabir looked pained. "But I just started drawing. Give me some time."

"Now, Kabir," Amir growled. Beside him, Karim bhai chuckled, removing the beedi from his mouth to reveal betel-stained teeth, and prodded Kabir to heed his brother's instruction. When Kabir was gone, Amir shed what little patience he had. He unfolded the painting stowed beneath his tunic and shoved it into Karim bhai's face.

"You're teaching him to draw the Immortal Sons?"

Karim bhai gave a nonchalant shrug, his eyes darting around the edges of the parchment. "Someone has to. It is better they fear from a young age what waits for them beyond the fence in the Outerlands. It is how we'll have fewer runaways like your father. Walked right into death's open maw, didn't he?"

Amir pulled the painting away and tore it to pieces, letting the bits rain on Karim bhai's head. "It is enough to know the Outerlands as impassable. There's no need for this religious hogwash peddled by the abovefolk to add flavor to it. I don't want Kabir to be a slave to such stories, bhai."

"You talk as if you haven't been getting money or spices from selling them. And what do you tell the poor boy, ho? That you're gifting his works to the people of the eight kingdoms. *Gifting.*"

Amir had, on several occasions, sold Kabir's paintings. Amma's addiction to ginger and cumin had grown to a point where she was willing to starve in their absence. Of course, Amir never told this to Kabir. His brother had *one* thing going for him, and Amir did not wish to ruin the flavor of this passion by making it seem like a profitable endeavor. Not when, soon enough, Kabir would be forced upon the spice trail. Would his callused hands be willing to paint after that? The thought made Amir shudder.

Karim bhai took another drag of the beedi before stubbing it beneath his sandals. He bade Amir to sit beside him on the cot, then swatted a mosquito on his arm. "There was a time when your father was not a slave to such stories, either, pulla. Instead, he got too curious. Would creep to the fences and wonder what lay beyond. He was a fearless one, your appa. Hated being told what to do, and where his station lay. There's always folk like that from the Bowl, who, once they start climbing out, don't want to stop. They don't know how to."

"I can't imagine why," replied Amir scathingly, thinking of Ilangovan.

"It's not unwise, then, to say your prayers. To remain bounded by the scriptures."

"Scriptures that exclude us as humans." Amir spat on the ground. "We're worse than slaves, bhai."

Karim bhai emitted a gentle *tsk*. "Gah! We all make a big deal out of it, don't we?"

"Easy for you to say," Amir barked. "You get everything you want at the feet of your dear ministers."

"Ho, pulla, and you don't? Last I checked, we were two shadows prowling the eight kingdoms, not one. You may not walk their halls, but you carry their scents just as much as I do."

Amir was incensed. "I did it so I could save up for the Poison!"

If Karim bhai was offended by the remark, he did not show it. "I do my bit for the Bowl while walking the gilded palace, pulla. Fifty-five years I've served the palace, since I was your brother's age. Who do you think convinced Suman-Koti to sign the accord to permit bowlers to open their shops in the bazaar? Who do you think urged the Minister of Grains to increase the spice allowance for families whose sons and daughters were Carriers? If Orbalun is considering reserving even a single seat upon his council for a gatecaste, it is because I have sat at his ministers' feet day and night, groveling, stitching myself to the shadows, delivering gifts and personal messages to distant kingdoms unbeknownst to the Spice Trade. I have planted myself between the abovefolk and you lot so that I take the first blow when I can."

"You don't have to," Amir pleaded with him. "You can come with me to the Black Coves. To Ilangovan."

Karim bhai clapped, bursting into laughter. He laughed for what seemed like a long time, until the skies darkened, then sighed and descended into coughs, clutching his chest, sputtering in smaller bursts of cackles. He placed a hand on Amir's shoulder and leaned against him, chest heaving. "Do your thing, pulla, and let me do mine. The Mouth has blessed me with the spicemark in this life, and I intend to see this duty through."

"Ho," Amir complained. "Do your duty, all right. Deliver all the letters the abovefolk give you. But don't deliver mine, is that your way?"

Karim bhai shoved him off the cot. "I waited an entire hour at the doors to the palace. Harini never showed up. Nor her father, nor her guards. The palace was naught but quiet, pulla. Don't blame me. Karim bhai never fails to deliver a letter."

Amir's train of thought—and frustration at Karim bhai's argument—snapped at once. His heart skipped a beat as Harini swam back into his thoughts.

What did she need all that Poison for? Or had Bindu been lying merely to get away from Amir? She couldn't have possibly known any feelings he had for Harini. And it seemed improbable that, of all the thronekeepers and their scions, Bindu would have taken the name of Harini out of thin air to spin such a tale.

Equally as curious was why Harini wouldn't receive Karim bhai. Was she angry that Amir had not come himself? He'd promised her, after all. Either way, he had too many questions that needed answering, none of which this old fool of a Carrier smoking his beedi and scratching his beard could give.

"I need to go to Halmora," Amir said flatly.

Karim bhai smiled, lighting up another beedi and exhaling a puff of smoke into the stale night air of the Bowl. "You're lucky, we have carrying duty to Halmora in five days. I checked Jhengara's roster, and your name is on it. We've been chosen to bring back a hundred pounds of turmeric, for the maharani's Bashara."

A hundred pounds, he thought wearily, touching the mark on his neck. *A blessing and a curse.*

HASMIN WHIPPED THE CARRIERS INTO A STRAIGHT LINE. HE barked incessant orders and was in general a pestilence that afternoon. Amir was tempted to rile him up further, just to show his spine wasn't fully bent, but was held back by Karim bhai.

"I can't just let him go about—"

"Of course you can! Hasmin knows how important today's duty is. If anything, he's being more restrained than usual."

"Gah!"

"Look at how he glances about. He feels the eyes on him."

"Eyes?"

"We are going to Halmora to help fulfill the Bashara."

"I couldn't care less about the Bashara, bhai."

"Ignore the significance of the Bashara at your own peril. Not for nothing did the Minister of Silk himself remind me to count the sacks. And who do you think put Suman-Koti in charge?"

"Orbalun?" Amir made an educated guess. Trust Karim bhai to constantly measure his closeness to the maharaja of Raluha at every opportunity. In this matter, though, Amir conceded the right of pride to the old Carrier. The Bashara was a sacred ritual, one that celebrated the future of the kingdom. And for Carriers, it meant an additional spice allowance for their families, and perhaps even a day off. Amir did not care for the former, but the day off . . . ah, the temptation was sore.

"Ho." Karim bhai nodded. "The Bashara cannot start without the maharaja smearing the Mouth's idol with turmeric."

A hundred pounds of it, Amir thought bitterly. *That should cover the Mouth and then some.*

Coming from the Bowl, Amir never understood this incessant thirst for rituals the rest of Raluha had. Bowlers liked to keep things simple. A quick prayer, a song or two, and then out flowed the barrels of toddy. The palace, on the other hand, swam in the quagmire of a hundred customs.

Not that he'd been spared learning about the Bashara: Amir's mother had not held back on any of the ostentatious details. She spoke of it like a song: as the queen went into labor, all the labor would go into serving the queen. Nine crones from the merchant quarters were to ascend the palace on the eve of the birth, muttering *bashara* under their breath. Adorned with pearl necklaces and gems encrusted with strips of amethysts, the crones would calm the queen in her torment and screeching agony, pasting turmeric on her cheeks, putting garlic and pepper in her mouth, and smearing saffron on her hair. A nutmeg, if she behaved. They would then dip her feet in rosewater pestled with sandalwood and dried ash and sing verses from the song of the unborn. From the doors at the end of the wetchamber the priests would ring bells until the baby slithered out, and the runners would dash to the restless thronekeeper—Maharaja Orbalun—with the good news.

It was all a little too much. No—it was a lot too much. But he was going to meet Harini, and on most days the mere thought of a moment with her was enough reason to suffer Hasmin's whips and barks, even though it was in service of wasting spice on a baby.

"Remember, not more than an hour," Karim bhai warned as the line began to move, the Carriers ahead flicking pinches of turmeric into the veil and disappearing through the Spice Gate. "You got lucky with the Vanasari guards, but the Haldiveer are not so frugal in their security."

"I'll be in and out before they know it."

"I'm not so sure, pulla." Karim bhai lowered his voice. "Something is amiss."

"What do you mean?"

"Could be nothing, but I brought Suman-Koti a letter from Halmora yesterday. A letter written by a Meshti minister. He demanded to escalate a trade inquiry into why Halmora had given the Meshti Carriers only a quarter of their agreed-upon turmeric."

"A quarter? But—"

"Ho!" Karim bhai whispered gravely. They were close to the Gate. "Halmora has been desperate to sell their turmeric. It's always been a demand issue. Why are they withholding it now? Unless there's been a production choke, which is unlikely. The forests around the fort teem with turmeric plants."

"What does this have to do with anything?"

"It's just strange, ho, is all. And the Spice Trade abhors strange," Karim bhai said. "I'm just asking you to be careful, pulla. Whatever you do, be back in an hour. Today is not like other days.

"And Halmora is nothing like Vanasi."

This conversation seemed overly dramatic, and Amir wanted to chide Karim bhai for his superstitious nonsense, but they could not continue speaking, for Hasmin was upon them like a storm. It wasn't like they had ever stopped walking—Karim bhai lumbered up the seven steps, Amir on his trail. But the senapati still snuck between them and stopped Amir with the tip of his pike.

"You . . ." A sardonic smile crept across his face. "You think I don't know what you're up to?"

Amir blinked but did not avert his gaze. He exerted a grimace as the sack wore him down, but he remained standing on the first step, watching

Karim bhai disappear through the Spice Gate. "I don't know what you're talking about."

Hasmin pushed the tip deeper. The uneasiness spread through Amir's skin, a cold, gnawing feeling. But even worse was the premonition of the words to come. Hasmin towered over Amir in that fragile moment. "Word always reaches my ears. Don't think I don't know what happened in Vanasi, and who was responsible for the mess in the hanging market."

Amir shivered on the inside, but outwardly he remained stoic as ever. "I have absolutely no idea what you're talking about, Hasmin kaka." He made to dodge the pike and resume his climb to the Gate, but Hasmin stopped him again.

"Your brother turns twelve in six moonfalls," he whispered. "All his days of gallivanting across the Bowl, scribbling on parchment, are coming to an end." The smile lingered on Hasmin's lips, and Amir wanted little more than to whirl the sack over his head and smack Hasmin with it.

"Try it," Hasmin said, obviously seeing the violence in Amir's eyes, which he now averted, knowing confrontation would get him nowhere. He seethed, though, hearing his brother's name on this vile man's lips. "If you stray from your duty again," Hasmin threatened, bringing his face closer to Amir's, who, pressed by the weight of the sack, could barely shift, "or if I hear one more word of a Raluhan mishap on foreign soil, your brother will wake up tomorrow a Carrier."

Amir gulped and nodded. The words pummeled him, churning his flesh, invoking the kind of rage that had thrust him headlong into this ploy to get himself and his family out of Raluha in the first place. Yet he leashed his anger, that bubbling fury, and gripped the ends of his sack tighter, his beaten knuckles straining, letting the rage guide him forward to Halmora. To Harini. To the Poison.

Somehow he managed to pull himself away from Hasmin.

"Kaka," he said with false cheer, "it's the Bashara. Don't want us to be late with the turmeric, do you?"

Saying this, he brushed past the chief, who persisted with his smugness. Amir flicked a handful of turmeric into the veil. His heart was buried by thoughts that could have been nightmares, and in that sea of saffron, against the frolicking bulbs, he conjured Harini's face in his mind and stepped into the Spice Gate.

AMIR SUCKED IN A DIFFERENT AIR AS THE MEMORY OF HARINI faded, even if for a moment. For his body was breaking down. His insides roared as though they had been imprisoned inside his body and demanded to be released.

His eyes struggled open. Afternoon had transformed into the death of evening. The sound of thunder filled the sky, trailing a residue of the fading light. A gentle drizzle pattered down. Around Amir, a score of Halmoran warriors—the Haldiveer—stood on alert, their faces like painted leather shields, hair pinned back like horsetails, and a hairband of golden feathers tied together with a string of bones and tusks. They looked more and more frightening as the day melted into night.

Few places demanded caution like Halmora, the turmeric empire.

Like Amir, the other Carriers struggled to recover from the passage through the Gate. Karim bhai was hobbling, his grip on his sack slackening with each step. Amir's own muscles heated, his back spasmed, and something with thorns uncoiled in his head.

Gates, it has never been this bad before! He realized he'd had the same thought after going through the gate to Vanasi and wondered if he always thought this. But no, this was different, as it had been the time before. It was worse.

What is happening?

It didn't bother the Haldiveer, though. Since they did not bear the spicemark, they couldn't possibly know how traveling through the Gate felt, let alone how it might feel different. Their change in attire did not conceal their spite for the gatecaste, a trait they shared with the saffron-garbed chowkidars of Raluha and with the guards of each of the other six kingdoms.

Amir looked beyond the warriors, where a narrow trail led down through a forested slope into the great palace fort snuggled within an endless jungle.

The Halmoran qila.

Firelight sizzled under fluttering canopies of the market and from hollow windows of the fort, reminding Amir that neither the darkness nor the rain deterred the trade of spices.

"Keep moving," one of the Haldiveer barked.

Karim bhai dropped his sack and clasped his quaking hands together. "Please, saheb. Just give us a moment."

The Haldiveer closest to him remained tight-lipped, but his companions grimaced in disapproval. An unrest prevailed in the air. Amir thought he would collapse before he reached the granary. Forcing his feet to hold his weight, he allowed himself to dream of the comforts of home. Of Amma's sambar, infused with garlic, tamarind, and heeng, floating in a well of rice, awaiting to be slurped. Home, however, he imagined, was one among the distant specks of stars spattered on the sky. Although for all he knew, the Gates bridged the farthest corners of the world, making home even farther away.

The rain intensified. The fleeting moment of rest ended. The Haldiveer rushed to whip the Carriers into picking up the sacks before covering the goods with poncho bags. It left the Carriers soaking in the rain as they hobbled toward the fort-kingdom.

Amir snuck up beside Karim bhai. "Why is it hurting more?"

"How would I know?" Karim bhai whispered back. "But it does, and they won't give us a break."

"They seem to be in a hurry to get us to the granary and back to Raluha."

Less time to meet Harini. If anyone ever calls me lucky again . . .

A pair of the Haldiveer on horseback came riding beside them, and the conversation died. Worry crept into Amir's mood. *Strange times,* Karim bhai had said. And it seemed as if that was indeed the case, the more he thought about the news Bindu had shared. No kingdom among the eight had ever withheld the spice they were producing. Could Harini be aware of this? She'd always hated politics, or at least stayed away from them while her parents oversaw the Spice Trade. And yet, it was *her* name Bindu had spoken, and not those of Raja Virular or Rani Bhagyamma.

What if Harini was in trouble? What if the Jewelmaker had decided to reclaim his lost Poison?

If what Bindu said is true . . . no—you still don't know that.

The problem was, Amir didn't seem to know anything.

His heart rate spiked. What little patience he had fizzled out like a headache after chewing pepper. He had to find Harini. If she truly believed in what they shared, she'd give him at least one vial of the Poison and tell him what was going on.

He had bartered his entire monthly spice allowance—and a painting—for this one opportunity to meet again with her, and he was not going to squander it.

If he was caught, he'd be at peace knowing he had tried.

But if you're not . . .

The Haldiveer led them down the trail and into the great walled fort through the portcullis. The air was alive with murmurs. Nobody said a word out loud, save the odd command directing them toward the storehouses. The itch of impatience awakened in Amir once they were inside the fort proper. Each step was an invisible obstacle he had to kick through on that dirt-strewn path that spiraled around the palace, hugging the mound upon which it sat like a sagacious thronekeeper. Sand-baked walls, now flaky and wet, flanked them on both sides, and the scratches on them were window slits, revealing decadent homes and cave shops. Amir knew the hidden alleyways by heart, including the ones that burrowed into the qila cellars and the deep vaults where Harini claimed the older thronekeepers had once bred fire-lions for pit fights and for punishing disobedient Carriers.

In the past, using Karim bhai to distract the others while Amir slipped away was a simple task. Harini would wait for him in the cellar in her dusk-colored paavadai, smelling of amber and chive, sniffing a strip of cinnamon with a grin that revealed her broken tooth. They never had much time, and Amir had made the most of every heartbeat. Each moment seemed to race toward that end where he would tie himself back to the tail of the Carriers' procession, his sweat glossed over by layers of Harini's perfume.

He never believed at first that it was happening. That Harini, the scion of the Halmoran Empire, was down in the cellars with him, from where they would stalk into the palace gardens above, dig their nails into the soil, sift through the mud, and laugh to themselves. She talked to him about her palace, her family, her walks into the wilderness, sitting on great boars or horses, mimicking the sound of birds and crickets until her father's men chased the rabbits and the deer all the way to the edge of the forest, where the world ended and the unknown Outerlands began.

Amir always questioned her motives and avoided that vacuum in their conversation that would prompt her to ask him about *his* life, and he would have nothing to talk of but his brother who would be a Carrier in a year, and his pregnant mother due any day now. Not to mention those who lurked above Raluha's Bowl, stamping on their heads, calling them gatecaste as if they had some kind of choice in the matter, and crushing their lives in squalor.

Amir had, long ago, exhausted his trunk of dreams, those initial weeks when he couldn't stop blabbering to Harini about the other kingdoms—about Amarohi, with its waterfalls and white clouds, where the great bridge of cloves spanned a gorge so deep that his guts threatened to spill out. Of Talashshukh and its marble halls and libraries and endless bazaars fragrant in ginger and nutmeg, of Jhanak and its bustling port, its drunk merchants and taverns streaming with ale, cinnamon, and meat. Of drowning the pains of the Gate in a mug with Karim bhai and the others, learning songs from the sailors who brought back fish in barges or on canoes. Harini basked in his words, and even though her family would occasionally purchase the Poison from the Jewelmaker, she herself was never permitted to use the Gates.

If it was indeed true, was this why Harini had duped the Carnelian Caravan for the Poison? If so, a single vial would have sufficed. There was no need to antagonize the Jewelmaker over her desire to see the other kingdoms.

But he felt in his gut that something was off. *There's something more.* Which was yet another reason why he needed to find Harini.

The everlasting jungle around the qila shook, the timber creaking, the leaves whistling against the rain. Normally, the Haldiveer held back, or sent a few men to surround the granary, which made it easy for Karim bhai to distract them and for Amir to escape. This evening, however, over three dozen Haldiveer flanked them. There was no way he could detach from the sacred spice trail. He'd have to try his luck on the return journey. Cursing, he adjusted the sack on his back and lumbered behind Karim bhai and the other Carriers.

The routine was simple.

Except . . . tonight it wasn't.

Because, as the fort came into view, all at once the hundreds of candles and torches—even the firelight seeping through windows—blinked out of existence. The entire fort-kingdom of Halmora plunged into a rain-soaked darkness.

Amir could see only the faint outline of Karim bhai ahead of him, and beyond, shifting shapes and layers of blackness stirring. One of the Carriers barged into him from behind, and Amir nearly fell.

One of the Haldiveer's steeds neighed loudly and launched itself on its hindlegs. Another guard bellowed for silence. The remaining Haldiveer rushed to light the torches along the spice trail once more, while apprehensions abounded as to what sorcery had caused all of the firelight in Halmora to be extinguished at once. Amir could make out the back of a column of riders as they stripped away from the trail and dashed off to the qila's main keep.

The Carriers stood near the entrance to the granary, whispering about the sudden darkness as though nothing could be more ominous on the eve of the Bashara. Karim bhai dispatched a quick prayer to the Mouth and urged Amir to do the same. The rain drowned out even those feeble mutterings.

Amir had no interest in prayers. His eyes, instead, had lifted toward the palace.

He fixed his gaze on the westernmost tower that broke out of the keep like a twisted finger. Harini's chambers. A lone light flickered in the highest window amid that sea of darkness, and his heart skipped a beat.

Karim bhai wandered ahead with his sack, trying to communicate with the Haldiveer. After several minutes, he lumbered back, looking as if he'd seen a perichali in the dark.

"What is it?" Amir asked him, wiping the water from his eyes with one hand, the other still clinging to his sack of powdered saffron.

Karim bhai took a deep breath. "There's a problem."

"I can see that," Amir answered impatiently. "Or, rather," he said, blinking furiously to adjust to the darkness, "I can't."

"The turmeric . . ." Karim bhai bit his lip, water clogged in his unruly beard, lines of strain deepening on his forehead as he tried to summon the right words. "The turmeric, pulla," he stuttered. "It is not being with-held. It's stolen."

Amir's jaw dropped. "That's impossible. How? *Who?* Is it the Jewel-maker?" His suspicions may have been right after all. The Jewelmaker had come to reclaim the Poison Harini had taken from him.

He watched the huddled group of Haldiveer frantically awaiting further instructions. "They won't say," Karim bhai muttered. "They're as confused by this as we are."

In that instant, the eyes of all the Carriers and the Haldiveer were transfixed on that high window—Harini's bedchamber—as though the answers to their prayers lay in that fragile, flickering flame.

The moment lingered in a rain-swept silence. Amir glanced from tower to tower of the qila and its numerous smoky windows, now like hollow borings of something undesirable.

Then, slowly, the windows released something. It looked like fumes at first, but then the smoke assumed color. Red like blood, and then saffron, yellow, violet, green, and white. Like the ghost of a thali meal.

The fumes breathed a shade darker than the night before being consumed by the rain.

Within seconds, the entire qila was shrouded in a fog of color.

No. Amir swallowed, and the hint of cinnamon oppressed his nose through the rain.

Not color.

Spice.

If there was one thing he was grateful for in that moment, it was that every pair of eyes, including Karim bhai's devout ones, was glued to the palace.

It was, therefore, rather simple for Amir to drop his sack, slip off the sacred spice trail of Carriers, and squeeze into a narrow fissure between the walls, the memory of Harini's scent drawing him into her decadent home.

CHAPTER

3

*Too err is human. To forget to add spices for lunch is a
non-bailable offense, with punishments ranging from seven
years to death.*

—*Spice Trade for the Uninitiated*, Chapter 6: Sins

The weight of the great fort pressed down on Amir heavier than
a spice sack as he slunk through its narrow caves and passageways.

The flickering light in Harini's chamber in the tower continued to
cast a shadow in his mind. The silence, the gloom, the rain outside, and
the clouds of spice—they foretold an endless night.

Harini had never snuck him into the palace proper. They would
always roam the periphery instead, in shadow beside the walls, along
the dense gardens, down the slopes, or even the cold, wet heights that
could be reached by secret staircases springing up within an abandoned
tower, from where they would count the treetops of the endless jungle
that surrounded Halmora under moonlight.

Tonight he was alone. Tonight he was terrified.

He passed scullions and servants like a gust of wind, pretending to
be in the fort on business. But even if his mannerism and stride had ac-
quired a shade of royalty, his attire, wet hair, torn tunic, and the ungodly

time of night worked against him. Above all, the brand of the spicemark on his throat blared like a warning.

A pang of sudden longing hit him: he wished he had Karim bhai for company.

Calm down, he told himself. All he had to do was find Harini and unpeel the layers of this strange night. He wanted the Poison, but he also wanted to see Harini. This gnawing feeling of suspicion made him queasy.

As for the Poison, even if Bindu's claim was a lie, Harini would still have a single vial to spare. She had always spoken of wanting to steal one from her father for herself. All royals had a secret stash over and above what they reserved for the occasions needed to visit the other kingdoms, like the afsal dina.

For the first time that evening, hope bubbled in Amir's heart.

Just one vial. For Amma.

And that was the key to everything, wasn't it? That he couldn't leave Amma behind like his father had all those years ago. Karim bhai was wrong. This would always distinguish Amir from his old man—the fact that he was scouring the ends of the eight kingdoms for the Poison to ensure that Amma would not be left behind. That, wherever he sought a new life, it would be *with* Kabir and Amma, and her child yet unborn, by his side.

A new life with no more carrying, especially for Kabir.

Each step he took was a reminder of that necessity. His bones rang with the echoes of pain, of the price of passing through the Gates. Kabir could not be a party to this agony. He himself couldn't anymore. All these years, watching his brother grow up in the Bowl, Amir had never fully appreciated how soon Kabir would be dragged into service for the eight kingdoms. And now, mere months away, guilt coursed through his blood. He ought to have acted sooner. He ought to have seized a vial of the Poison long ago when he'd had the chance and left the Gates and the Trade and the Mouth far, far behind.

Amir despised the Mouth! The spice god. How could Karim bhai, in his infinite devotion, not see it? How could the other Carriers not see it? How could they not want for themselves a better life than the dregs of the Bowl, not want to flee like Ilangovan had all those years ago? Or even Appa, who had decided death in the Outerlands was preferable to the pain of passage?

Scriptures, scriptures, scriptures! Amir had had enough. If he could, he'd have saved every bowler in Raluha. But as it happened, even saving his own family demanded that he stretch the limits of his life. And with no guarantees.

The echoes of scriptures in Amir's mind manifested as whispered rituals and twilight hymns for the Mouth. The sound seeped out of the walls of the qila, and briefly Amir thought he was not in Halmora at all but in the middle of the Gate, neither on one side nor on the other but in that abyss where the Mouth was said to reside.

Murals of the Mouth adorned pillars, jasmines sprinkled at their bases and little shrines built into alcoves where lamps burned ensconced in glass vases.

There had been a time when Harini had joked to Amir that if he ever moved to Halmora, into her family, half his life would wither away in attending rituals. Decked in silk veshtis with sacred ash on his forehead, sitting with his legs folded beside her father while he performed a series of endless homams that invoked the blessings of the Mouth in exchange for fumes of turmeric and rosewater, and words of subservience and eternal devotion.

Spice dreams, all of them! He could never be allowed into the Halmoran household. Not him, not his family. No matter the gilding they put on him, there was no way to erase the sins of his prior birth, or the impurity coursing through his blood in the present one. The scriptures of the Mouth ensured it was a path closed off to him forever.

What remained instead was only a blurred future in the Black Coves beyond Jhanak, living under the sprawl of Ilangovan's reign. An outlaw who was once a Carrier himself, Ilangovan could keep him and his family safe, if not comfortable. Hundreds of gatecaste who had fled from their kingdoms lived under his care. It couldn't just be fireside tales—the fact there were paintings and slogans declaring his banditry and piracy across the eight kingdoms was proof that he was real, as was his protection.

If Ilangovan and his fellow outlaws could escape their bonds, so could Amir. It wasn't the embrace of Harini, but it would have to be enough.

This goal felt far away, though, and at present, the silence of Halmora ate into him. What had happened? Where was the pomp and fanfare of the Halmoran palace that could be heard from a mile away even at twilight?

At one point, he was certain he was lost. This was not the way to Harini's tower. Had his sense of direction truly failed? Perhaps he ought to double back.

He heard footsteps. He quickly slipped into a passageway leading out of one of the numerous tributaries of the qila. Ahead, the rest of the way was partitioned with a silk curtain. *Might as well!*

He brushed through to the smell of cinnamon and honeysuckle, and to the feel of a carpet beneath his feet. Murals on the walls spoke of traditional Halmoran feasts. He picked up a few grapes from a basket on a side table and ran his fingers over the flame from the lamps. The warmth seeped into his skin, calmed his nerves.

At the end of the passage, a chamber greeted him, half its candles smothered, the other half giving off a dim light from a table where spilled grapes and half-filled wineglasses lay abandoned. Across from the entrance he spied a window screened by mesh. Was this chamber supposed to lead to Harini's tower? He couldn't be certain. He sneaked across the threshold anyway.

No doors. Nor a staircase. Instead, plush diwans lay rolled beside the window, with upholstered mattresses and cushions. Empty goblets of wine and more plates of fruit lay strewn nearby.

Voices from beyond the window lured him to it. He laid a knee on the diwan and peered through the shrouding.

The darbar below was strangely empty. The court hall was resplendent with banners, diwans, and . . . offshoots of trees. Amir was agape. He had never seen the Halmoran court. Vines and creepers were one thing, but here whole branches were breaking through the windows and the walls like an extension of the jungle, slithering inside unhindered. Long tables like birch rinds took up most of the room in the center. Lanterns the shape of mushrooms hung from the branches running under the dome. Fireflies swam beneath them or around the pillars in hundreds, lighting up the space with a hypnotic flicker.

Amir blinked in surprise at how empty the darbar was. He had heard stories from Harini about the feasts held every night. The silence was mesmerizing, and he stood there forgetting for an instant that he had to find Harini. Then his eyes caught the dais directly below, with a throne of oakwood and amber, like a large toadstool. Someone stood beside the throne, one hand over its arm as casually as one would stand beside a friend.

Harini.

His heart staggered as he squatted upon the upholstery in what he now recognized as the queen's vantage, and peered down. Harini had tied her hair in a severe black bun—a style she had sworn never to adopt. It hurt the roots, she would say, and made her look old. In addition, she wore her mother's antimony necklace; that hideous rock that made it seem as if her throat had been ripped out and she had spilled blood the color of ash. She had hated that too. A talwar lay strapped to her robe. Harini never carried sharp objects. It disturbed Amir to see her bedecked in everything he knew she didn't believe in. He paused, trying to restitch his memories, wondering when they had turned into something unrecognizable.

Also unrecognizable was the woman facing Harini. An air of calmness hung about her, as though impervious to the tension that gripped the rest of Halmora. She wore her hair loose, long black curls that extended to her waist. Her face was small and oval-shaped, like a nutmeg, with a certain amused curiosity, as though she were observing a play or a dance.

She wore a robe unlike anything Amir had seen, either in Halmora or Raluha. In fact, he'd wager nobody from the eight kingdoms ever wore a robe so hideously multicolored, a lehenga with a pallu tied around the waist as a cummerbund, and a yellow-green bandana on their forehead, the latter of which reminded Amir of minstrels who stalked the docks of Jhanak.

". . . and what am I supposed to tell them?" Harini asked the stranger, casually drumming the rosewood of the throne's arm. Amir had no doubt that this position—this *dominance*—was new for Harini, and that whatever she was doing caused her as many jitters as those that shook Amir, watching from the secret chamber above the darbar.

Where was Raja Virular?

"Be delicate," the stranger replied. Her voice had a hollow darkness to it. "And ask your men to not overlook a single place. Fylan is not prone to defeat."

"I saw he was wounded. Rather badly. I'm sorry."

The stranger waved her hand. "It would cause him nothing more than the slightest hindrance. He will ensure the stolen turmeric is returned."

Harini shook her head in frustration. "You should have warned me something like this would happen. You . . . you have no idea how much I've risked for *your* ambitions. My own parents are locked in my bedchamber. The people sense there's something wrong. Already the Spice Trade Council has decided to overlook any irregularities in the supply, and they make no efforts at glancing at our accounts. And you don't know Orbalun . . . he senses trouble even beyond the Gates, squatting in his throne all the way in Raluha."

The woman's eyes widened. She strode up the dais to the throne and grabbed Harini by the shoulders. "Harini, Harini! You must calm down, all right? Nothing is lost, even now. We are close, so close. Let's just stick to our plan."

Harini detached herself from the throne, and the woman's grasp, and paced the dais. Amir was troubled at the unrest on her face.

"Okay," Harini said resignedly after a while. "Okay. I'm just . . . terrified of getting this wrong."

"It's natural," the woman said. "We have a narrow window to work with, and we cannot lose focus. I promised you I'd help you, and that's what I'll do. First, tell me, what is the latest on Ilangovan?"

Amir froze in his position in the queen's vantage.

Harini faced her companion. "We have his routine charted. It's only a matter of getting in now."

"Good, good. Remember: it must happen during the afsal dina feast. That's when I expect the release."

Amir scratched his stubble. Release of what? And what could happen during the afsal dina feast? And had Harini said her parents were *locked* in her bedchamber?

Gates, was Harini finally rebelling against her parents and the Spice Trade? Amir smiled despite himself.

She took a deep breath. "Yes. Just . . . don't keep pushing it, okay? The more I stress out, the closer I am to making a mistake. Just let me . . . *breathe*. I need to do this with a calm head. You know this is new for me."

"And for me," said the woman. She was facing Harini now, her back to Amir so he could only speculate that she was smiling. "But we have planned this well, and as long as we time this to perfection—which we have—nobody needs to die."

"Except, someone *might* die today," Harini hissed. The coldness in her voice sent a shiver down Amir's spine—that she could speak so casually of death. His own smile faded. She might as well have been discussing abandoned drumstick skins after a meal.

"Fylan is strong," the stranger countered. "He will survive. And if he doesn't, we will honor him for his sacrifice when the time is right. But that time is not now, Harini. You must focus," the woman repeated. "You cannot be swayed by people or any outside forces. Yes, there will be revolts. Yes, the other kingdoms will oppose what has happened. In time, however, nobody will have a choice but to adapt. And you will already be in front of the race. For how the turmeric empire suffers now, you will never have to see that suffering again."

Amir's head spun in dizziness. Revolts in Halmora? A race to adapt?

He was looking to escape from the order of the world he was trapped in, and yet he could tell that the two women below were far ahead of him.

After what seemed an age Harini nodded, and even with that acquiescence, Amir sensed the residue of reluctance on her face. Still, she rushed to the stranger and embraced her, tears dripping from her eyes. Amir was unable to process what was happening. Confusion and frustration, and even a bizarre fascination, warred within him, his pulse racing in his neck. Whatever ploy Harini and the other woman had hatched involved not just the theft of spices, and the antagonism of the Spice Trade, but also something to do with Ilangovan. Gates, he wanted *answers*!

"The people will ask about the missing turmeric," said Harini. "The priests will demand it for the Mouth's temple."

The woman laughed at that. "Come, Rajkumari. Are you telling me that the sages of your kingdom who have preached penance and austerity would suddenly demand the whereabouts of wealth?"

"And the people?"

"It will be a test," the stranger conceded, and she raised her head almost proudly.

Then, saying no more, the woman left, her footsteps echoing in the darbar. After several minutes of complete silence, seeing that Harini remained by the throne by herself, Amir gathered the courage to approach her. He traced the route he had taken, instead choosing passageways he knew would lead to the darbar. The door he chose opened behind the dais, the court hall looming against him. He found Harini slouched on the throne, her head in her hands.

"Harini?" he called, rounding the looming, opal-encrusted golden chair.

Harini sprang up, her eyes widening. "Amir! You scared me to death. Gates! What are you doing here?"

Amir's chest welled up at the sight of her from up close. He'd not seen her for over three months. He was afraid he'd forgotten the contours of her face. *Like that could ever happen.*

"Carrying duty, what else?" he murmured. "And I . . . er, wanted to see you."

Harini made a move as though wanting to rush to embrace him, but stopped herself at the last breath. Slowly, she shook her head, throwing a quick glance back at the great iron doors at the opposite end of the court hall. "You must not be here, Amir. The Haldiveer will return any moment."

Of course, a gatecaste was not permitted inside the darbar.

"Then let's get out. To the gardens."

Harini bit her lip. "I . . . I can't, Amir. Not now . . . I have some things to do."

Amir took a deep breath. "I have not seen you in three months. Hasmin . . . he ensured my name never came up in the roster for Halmora. I wanted to tell you, and of course neither I nor Karim bhai know how to read or write well, so it took me a while to find someone who could. But Karim bhai could not find you three days ago when he came with my letter. And so today I . . . somehow . . . *is everything okay*, Harini?"

His shoulders ached in that instant, and a grimace of pain twitched across his face.

"Of course everything is okay," she replied, without missing a beat. "And I've missed you, Amir," she said, her fingers grazing his cheek. He didn't realize it, but he leaned into that touch, unconsciously needing it. When she pulled it away, he almost recoiled, as if slapped. "It's just . . . things have been busy here. My parents, they . . . you know how it's been with turmeric these days. The Spice Trade Council has ignored our pleas."

"I've heard," he lied. He'd heard the opposite, which made her dishonesty all the more strange. He looked around at the darbar, the amalgamation of stone, forest, and gold still a source of unceasing wonder in his head, before his eyes rested on the bun atop her head, and the antimony necklace. "So, are you in charge of the trade, now? I thought you hated all this throne-keeper business."

Gates, must you sound so passive-aggressive?

Harini laughed, and it was in this momentary heartbeat where Amir shed his confusion and reveled in her laughter, the sound of her unrestrained voice. It bore him into the past, to nights when they had little to worry about beside being seen by the Haldiveer.

Harini took his hand in hers, an act that meant more to him than everything that had occurred over the past few days. "Is this what is bothering you, Amir? My parents are unwell, and the priests have been clamoring for a conference. They won't listen to me, not if I go in my usual attire. I know it feels like I'm rushing you, but listen to me, you really need to leave. If the Haldiveer find you here—"

"But they won't, will they?" Amir interjected, slowly pulling his hand away, and taking a step back. "Not if they are busy looking for the stolen turmeric."

Amir's own breath was as loud as fireworks in that silence. A shrill breeze blew through the windows, and the leaves along the branches wide as trunks sizzled. In that whistling night, Harini appeared to deflate. "How did you hear—*Amir*, did you eavesdrop on me?"

"I didn't mean to. Honestly, I just came to meet you, and I got lost a bit. I wanted to—"

"What did you hear?" Her voice dropped to a flat monotone.

"Nothing that I truly understood. Harini, please, you must tell me what is going on. Did you really trick the Carnelian Caravan out of a barrel full of the Poison? You could have visited me in Raluha if you had the Pois—"

"*What?*" Harini sounded flabbergasted, and Amir gulped. "Who planted that thought in your head, Amir? Where have you been hearing these things?"

Amir took another step back and raised his hands in apology. "I'm sorry. I did not mean to assume or accuse. Truly. You must forgive me, but . . ." He paused. Harini had always known that Amir sought to be done with carrying, to go somewhere he could disappear, and the memory of the Bowl of Raluha would all be but an illusion. He had given her enough hints of his plan to join Ilangovan, how desperate he had gotten over the last few months now that Kabir was close to joining duty. At one point, he'd feared provoking her ire if she discovered Amir had plans to join a violent outlaw and his band of pirates and mercenaries. Now it didn't matter. As the choices melted away in the face of vanishing time, Amir could not afford the luxury of lies.

In fact, he had, over the last several days, considered asking her to join him.

"But what, Amir?" she pressed on.

Amir swallowed a mouthful of saliva. *Here goes.* "I was in Vanasi looking for a vial of the Poison when I . . . when I discovered that the Jewelmaker had ceased his supply. And word . . . word in the bazaar is that you swindled him out of a barrel."

"That is absurd," Harini shot back. "I wouldn't even know where to look for the caravan. Besides, what did you want the Poison for?"

"What do you think?"

She looked at him, her eyes softening just slightly. "To get your mother out of Raluha."

"Yes," he whispered, glad she remembered. "It's what I've always told you about but never acted upon."

"So why now? There couldn't be a worse time, Amir."

"Exactly because of that: time. Hasmin has threatened to put Kabir on the trail within a month. And when I heard you had the Poison, I came right away."

"So, it's the Poison you came here for, is it? Not to see me?" She narrowed her eyes. "Based on a rumor in the Vanasari bazaar?"

Fell right into that, didn't you?

"No, I don't mean that," he stammered. "I came to meet you—of course I wanted to see you! But I also need the Poison, Harini—I won't lie to you about that. And with everything that seems to be going on, some answers would be helpful here. The Jewelmaker is missing, there is news of the turmeric being stolen, and you're here, decked in throne-keeper clothes. What is truly going on?"

"And I already told you—nothing. Just Spice Trade business."

Yet Harini averted her gaze. She began pacing the dais, her hands clasped behind her back. *Gates, why does she have to look so stern?*

And why can't I leave this alone?

"Then who was that woman? She didn't sound like she was from any guild or the Spice Trade."

He did not intend to interrogate Harini. But he also desperately hoped that she was not like the other abovefolk. There had to be at least one who wasn't . . . right? His trust could not have been for nothing, and this—this was their test. Of friendship.

Or love.

She remained silent for a while, only staring at him, at his struggling countenance, as though he had betrayed her.

"You should not have come tonight to the qila, Amir," she said.

"But I am here. And is this what I get? Not an answer but a dismissal?"

"I didn't know you were coming today."

"I don't really have a choice when I get to come, Harini," he said, and then sighed. Gates, but he did not wish to argue. Not with her. "Look, I'm here to see you. But I'd be lying if I didn't say I also really need the Poison. Not more than a vial, I promise. I have given away my month's spice allowance. The Jewelmaker's gone, and Raluha and the eight kingdoms run dry. I have tried every other way, and you're my last hope." He was surprised at the flow of words, at the seemingly endless supply of desperation buried within him that poured out onto Harini's lap. "I would never ask anything of you other than what we feel for each other if it weren't so important—you know that."

"I do know that," she said, her own chest heaving. Harini, however, was also shaking her head, the coldness manifesting in her eyes and seeping down her face to her tongue. "I don't have any Poison to spare, Amir. I am sorry."

She was lying. He could measure the timbre of her voice, the way her lips quivered to utter that falsehood. And her eyes spoke the loudest: they looked askance for a fleeting instant, unmasking her.

Amir did not wish to ask her again, so instead said, "It's the stranger you were talking to earlier, isn't it? You wish to give her the Poison and take her with you to Jhanak for the afsal dina feast."

Harini emitted a deep sigh. "I don't know how much you heard, Amir, but you do not understand—"

"Then tell me," Amir pleaded. "I am tired of making assumptions and jumping to conclusions. Tell me the truth, and I'll leave."

Harini clenched her fists. She rounded the throne and leaned against the seat's edge. Her gaze was fixed on one of the windows, unseeing and ghostly. "I can't."

He was gutted.

"Believe me, I wish I could, but this—whatever is happening is bigger than what we feel for each other. You must trust me on this, Amir."

"And Ilangovan?" he prodded, unable to stop now that he had begun, his heart a thousand shards in his chest, each piece ricocheting in a different direction. "What do you plan to do with him?"

"What is he to you?" she retorted, and then the realization seemed to dawn on her. "Wait, is *that* where you plan to take your family? To the Black Coves? Amir, he's a criminal."

"He's a hero. He's someone countless Carriers and gatecaste across the eight kingdoms look up to."

"For all the wrong reasons," she hissed.

"They're wrong because they could upset the balance of power. Your power. They upset your sense of justice." Amir shook his head. "But that's neither here nor there . . . I thought you cared what happens to my family. I thought you knew how unjust our lives were. Merely saying out loud that the discrimination against the gatecaste needs to stop does not make it go away, Harini. Something needs to be done!"

Amir was red-faced, veins throbbing, ready to explode.

Harini rushed to clamp a palm to his mouth as she threw a glance at the doors again. It was then he realized he had been shouting. "And I need you to trust me, Amir. Ilangovan cannot be the solution."

He wrestled her hand away, even as he savored the musk on her skin, and lowered his voice.

"Are you going to arrest him? Have you ever wondered why he's looting the eight kingdoms for their spices? Why he chose this life?"

The beauty faded from her like the light of a sun at the edge of dusk. She appeared to have a thousand words on her tongue that were tethered to whatever promises or deals she had made not to utter them. His heart softened, making him momentarily regret the harshness of his words.

Where was the woman who blushed when he poked her dimple with a finger? Where was the gentleness, the tender touches to blooming chrysanthemums and the patience with which she would wait for the earthworms to climb a mound of mud and slither onto her thumb? Where were her desires to escape into the forests and become one with the wilderness? Tame the wild horses, swim in the river, build a hut alongside it where she would store all her spices in little wooden boxes that her grandmother had given her . . .

And above all, where was the woman who wanted all of this for the bowlers and the rooters, and the easters of Halmora? Who bribed the Haldiveer to allow Carriers additional minutes for rest after passing through the gate, who smuggled pocketfuls of spices to Amir to be shared among the others, who had once sworn that as she was inducted into the trade council, she would upend the system?

What did those ideals amount to now?

"Amir, I want you to listen to me," Harini began. "For a year now, turmeric has been the least desirable of all spices. Ever since the alchemists of Vanasi proclaimed how it is ineffective against many ailments, people have reduced its consumption. Our yellow-tongued Mouth is not an accountant, Amir. Because if it were, our people would realize that Halmora is being taken for a fool. Our coffers empty only by the grace of those who smear it on the idols in the temples in each of the eight kingdoms and for rituals like the Bashara. My father thinks so long as we're devout and remain true to the Mouth, we will not face any trouble. But the truth is, turmeric is no longer the Mouth's own spice. And if nobody buys turmeric, Halmora is staring at a crisis. We will not have enough to buy the spices from the other kingdoms. The people will revolt. You know how it goes. This qila cannot stand an uprising."

"What does this have to do with Ilangovan?" Amir asked. "Without him, the coves would cease to exist!"

Harini once again remained tight-lipped. When she spoke, Amir sensed the trepidation in her voice, as though she were speaking only in half-truths. "Amir, you're not understanding what I'm try—"

Amir raised his hands in supplication. "I . . . I'm sorry I came here today. I am sorry I asked you for the Poison. I'm sorry I tried to obtain a better life for my mother, and that I tried to save my brother and possibly my unborn sibling from a life of pain and servitude. I . . . *thought* I loved you, you know?"

Something akin to tears formed in Harini's eyes. Let her cry! He wasn't finished.

"I did, even when I came out of that hole up there and stood in front of you. I was on the verge of giving myself to you, considering myself fortunate for having someone like you in my life. I don't know what it is that you're plotting with this stranger. You claim to not be able to tell me, and I do not even know whether I can trust you on that, Harini. Trust came so easily until today, but somehow, I am unable to at the moment. All I can think of is that if I don't get the Poison and get my family out of Raluha, I will have failed them. I would then be no better than my father."

He joined his hands in a pious goodbye and began to head toward the servants' door.

"Amir, wait," Harini called.

He stopped and turned.

If there indeed had been tears earlier, Harini had wiped them off her face. A glassy look prevailed now. Amir wanted to believe her. But he also knew that she had the Poison. He could always tell when she kept things from him to prevent him from being hurt. A trait of the abovefolk he could neither fault nor forgive but something he had grown to live with.

And with Harini, it took on the added flavor of affection, for he truly believed that she cared for him.

Gates, it is a heart, not a furnace.

He considered whether to ask for the Poison one last time.

The moment passed. He knew she would not part with it.

"I implore you again to trust me," she said. "There *will* be a better life for you and your family, I promise. Away from the Bowl, away from Raluha."

Amir shrugged, stunned at how cold his own body could be. "Perhaps, but I cannot afford to wait, Harini. Gates know we've waited long enough. I'm tired of people acknowledging problems and doing nothing about them."

"And us?" Harini's lips quivered. "What did you think would happen to us once you joined Ilangovan?"

Amir smiled, and it sapped his reserves. "It doesn't matter now. Looks like I'm not going anywhere."

And then he was gone, running through the empty passageways, through the dark and silent qila of Halmora, the walls and the air like a brooding sepulcher. The conversation replayed in his head over and over— where had it all gone wrong? Or perhaps it had been wrong from the start. To harbor hope of anything evolving between him and Harini . . . it was a fool's dream. In the end, Harini was the scion of a thronekeeper, and he, Amir, a lowly Carrier of Raluha. That was the truth, and he had been given a reminder of it in the darbar. Harini would do what it took for the betterment of Halmora, even if it meant discarding Amir and his life.

Amir blinked and snapped out of his despondence. He had stopped in his tracks, lost in thought and . . . just lost. The labyrinth enveloped him, shrunk him to the size of a speck. He'd forgotten about the spice trail. What if he didn't make it back before Karim bhai and the other Carriers left for Raluha? He hastened his step, clawing his way out of the qila.

At one point, he caught the scent of rain. The corridor expanded into a kitchen of sorts, which was, once more, oddly empty. From the windows, he heard the sound of rain. Where were the cooks and the maids? The grim-faced tray boys who'd catch Amir gallivanting with Harini in the gardens?

The path meandered to meet the great staircase that dipped in spirals around the walls and toward the front doors of the qila.

The doors themselves stood on a raised platform, with a wider berth of stairs expanding downward into the now-drenched courtyard.

Amir braked hard and came to a standstill, the rain pattering over his head.

Ahead, on the staircase, a man stood panting over the slain bodies of a dozen Haldiveer, holding a silver scimitar in one hand and pressing the other to his bleeding gut. A stream of color hovered about him like thick smoke, engulfing the stairs and the guards sprawled at his feet. The cloud of spice drifted up the walls of the palace and down the steps, ensnaring the banisters, slithering into the windows, and wrapping themselves around light posts as though it were alive, purple tendrils crawling out of a russet heart.

At the sight of Amir, frozen under the torch suspended over his head, the man's eyes widened, and Amir's did in kind. He then ran toward Amir, his weapon aloft.

CHAPTER

4

The sanctity of the Spice Gate was secure in the fact that no amount of weather and assault could make it look worse than it already did.

—NARESH PARAGAM, *THE FACE OF A SPICE GOD*

Amir had time only to unfreeze, turn, and dash back to the kitchens.

Lightning tore a rift in the skies, bathing the staircase in bluish-white light. Amir caught a quick glimpse of the man's dark skin, a violet robe with armor that was sliced open, revealing deep gashes. He was wounded, mortally perhaps, but he was still coming after Amir, and that was enough to keep him running.

If this man had stolen turmeric, it was a capital crime under the laws of the Spice Trade. To be caught stealing spice was to be resigned to the rotten-most depths of imprisonment, where they tortured you until your sense of smell was but a strange memory, where your mind that once understood taste was now bereft of sanity. He had known a few who had suffered that torment and could only wonder now at the fate that awaited his pursuer.

At the moment, though, Amir was more worried about his own fate as he scampered into the empty kitchens, a thin cloud of flour and the smell of fried vadas from earlier in the evening still hanging in the air. His heart galloped in his chest.

Ten strides in, the man with a gash in his gut caught up with him.

Amir had always prided himself on his speed. He would often race the other Carriers up and down the Bowl and would beat them soundly. Needless to say, he cursed himself as he hurled forward like a boulder falling from a cliff and crashed into a vat filled with smaller vessels that spilled out in a menacing clamor of steel.

The man's knee found the small of Amir's back a moment later. Amir's scream cartwheeled through the corridor, and he hoped it would attract attention. A garrison of Haldiveer would be a lovely sight! Though, having witnessed the slaughter on the steps, he didn't harbor much hope of rescue.

Only when the blade of the man's scimitar flashed beside Amir's face, and from the corner of his eye he glimpsed the water dripping off its serrated edge, did he quieten. In fact, he could barely breathe. His cheek was crushed on wet stone, and whatever his mouth could conjure in that moment did not sound like praise of the stranger's strength or an admission of defeat.

Ignoring Amir's struggle, the stranger turned Amir over and tore the top of his tunic, revealing the spicemark in clear candlelight.

"Wh-What do you want? Let me go!" Amir managed.

"Silence," the man hissed. His labored breath battered Amir's face and his wet fingers uncurled from Amir's throat. From the spicemark. A searing tingle spread through Amir's body as the man's finger brushed against the imprint.

The man pulled away suddenly and slunk back into the shadows of the nearest wall of the kitchen, clutching his belly and emitting a low moan.

Amir straightened himself, stood up, and staggered back a few steps. But he did not run. Fear clogged his head and froze his feet in place.

The wounded man wore a healer's robe tucked into a quilted armor and sewn into gauntlets around his corded muscles. The cracked mail and the telltale gray of the robe made him seem like a thunderous cloud whose desire to rain had ebbed.

It was apparent that he was dying. Blood gushed out of his hands. He tried to stanch the wounds, where the mail had been torn apart. His lips were paan red, and flakes of blood peppered his beard. The only skin that could be seen was a thin strip of forehead, upon which was etched a symbol—an eye within a circle within a diamond.

"You're a Carrier," he mumbled to Amir. Each syllable seemed to drain a bit more life from him.

Amir nodded, hoping that his reluctance to run away would not prove to be his undoing. "Very perceptive of you."

The man coughed up some blood. "My name is . . . Fylan. I'm of the legion of the Uyirsena of Illindhi."

Amir stared at him. He had never heard of Illindhi before, nor of any legion, or Uyirsena. This man showed every sign of being under the influence of the saeveroot, tripping on a hallucinogenic adventure.

Fylan coughed. More blood drooled from his mouth. Every syllable he uttered seemed to take minutes off his life, but the urgency of his situation did not merit the conservation of speech. "You're a Spice Carrier," he said again. "And that is your boon."

"A curse," Amir corrected promptly.

"Then I'm afraid I'm going to add to that curse, because what I'm about to ask you can be done by no one else. Please . . . do not . . . walk away."

Amir had always dismissed many of his life's situations as acts of fate. Fate had thrust him into the role of a Carrier, and fate decreed that he lived with Amma and Kabir, scavenging for the most meager of spices. It was fate that his father had abandoned him and his family, fate that his mother had decided to bear a child with another man in the Bowl, a man she could not even identify. Fate that the woman he loved and desired to be with was keeping secrets from him. And now, since the same fate had given him permission, for once, to make his own choice, he obeyed this strange man.

He chose to not walk away.

He took a few steps closer until he could smell the dying man's flesh. Fylan's eyes drooped, and only the last vestiges of life kept his head from rolling forward.

"Closer," Fylan croaked, and again until Amir stood over him in that dank kitchen, a sense of wonder pulling him nearer even as he prayed for someone to show up and take away the powers of decision-making from him.

When Amir squatted in front of Fylan, the wounded man smiled, teeth coated in blood. His hand let slip the scimitar he was holding— it clattered to the floor—and moved into the inner pockets of his robe. A second later, the hand emerged, clutching a medallion. The string was adorned with beaded agates, and it threaded into a small jar at the center, containing what looked to Amir like silvery sand. It was too difficult to tell in the darkness.

Fylan gestured that Amir should take it.

For a moment, Amir hesitated. Then he obeyed. Or rather, chose to obey. Again.

Feels good, doesn't it?

The medallion was as light as an idli in his hands, as though the beads were only an illusion.

"Please, you must help me take this to Illindhi."

Amir was willing to wager half his earnings on his saeveroot speculation. The man must have loitered in the poppy dens for days to be in this state of fractured confusion where his physical prowess remained undimmed even as his mental faculties melted away.

"Listen," Amir said, praying for Karim bhai to materialize from one of these walls to continue this conversation, "I don't know what you're talking about. I don't know where or what this Illindhi is. You . . . someone was talking about you earlier . . ." And then, as his thoughts drifted and he reclaimed them, Amir asked, "How do you know Harini?"

Fylan continued, ignoring Amir's question altogether. "In Illindhi, you must speak to Madhyra. To no one else but Madhyra. And give this to her. Tell her Fylan has failed, but there can yet be hope. Tell her *not* to send the Uyirsena."

The onslaught of unfamiliar names rattled Amir's thoughts. "Okay, you need to really slow down."

Fylan had slowed down too much, though, having stopped speaking altogether. Instead, he took the time to stare at Amir, who shirked away, gaze focused on the gaping wound and the incessant gush of blood that had pooled around the kitchen floor where Fylan lay. Amir had witnessed healers in the Bowl give up for less. Fylan gestured weakly to the medallion in Amir's hand.

"What you have in your hands," Fylan mustered, "is olum. It is the most sacred of the spices. It can be . . . man . . . manipulated to produce any of the other spices, and it must be returned to its home. To Illindhi, the ninth kingdom."

The earth seemed to open beneath Amir and swallow him whole. A spice he'd never heard of. A *ninth* kingdom? A thousand thoughts unspooled in his mind before he trained his mind's eye on the distant horizon of the Outerlands bordering the forests of Raluha. The silhouettes of the mountain, and the promise of an endless wilderness beyond. He shook himself out of the dazed vision. *Who are you kidding?* A ninth kingdom! *Preposterous.* It lay even beyond the periphery of his imagination . . . and possibly his belief.

Amir stared at the spice within the vial attached to the medallion. *A spice that can transform into any of the other spices*—was this man even telling the truth? Amir shuddered at what his thoughts were telling him, almost a seditious hiss in his ear: *If he is, there would no longer be a need to use the Spice Gates. Where you grew the olum, that is where life would be.*

Amir's head spun, and he thought he was going to collapse from the burden.

"I . . . don't have the strength," Fylan whispered. "Can . . . not . . . explain. Please go . . . for the sake of us all."

From a distance, Amir heard the sound of the Haldiveer. Not anywhere close. But they would be soon. Which made him question why he still stood there, listening to a deranged man's rambling on his deathbed. He ought to be rejoining the spice trail and Karim bhai. And yet, an unseen force kept him rooted to the spot. It was as if a terrible injustice would be committed if Amir were to walk away and let this man die alone. Perhaps Amir could give him that little gift of company during his passage. He had seen the wounds. This man had minutes, perhaps seconds. And in his desire to offer comfort, perhaps he could draw out a few more answers. He was distraught, sunk beneath the weight of what he held in his hand, the potential truth of it. *I have to know.*

"Why should I believe you?" Amir managed at last, aware of how his voice had begun to waver.

Fylan sighed, closed his eyes, and opened them again. "I . . . do not know you. No reason . . . to lie to you. Please . . ."

"You had a companion . . ." Amir began, remembering the strange woman's words in the court hall. "Someone else is here, isn't she? She . . . she wants to go to Jhanak and—and—Ilangovan . . . What do you know about that? Can you tell me? I can then help stop her. I can inform the Spice Trade and they will put an end to all this."

Fylan's eyes widened momentarily, then nearly closed again. He shook his head frantically. "Do not . . . tell *anyone*. She is . . . luring them. The Uyirsena . . . cannot be released. She will . . . destroy . . . them."

Destroy whom? Amir's head throbbed. There was that unfamiliar word again, spoken with a disturbing darkness by Fylan's sputtering lips. The Uyirsena. Was this whom the stranger had earlier mentioned releasing? Amir stood once again and paced in front of Fylan, rubbing his knuckles. Gates, what was he doing? This was insane! He was already late; Karim bhai wouldn't be able to delay the Carriers for much longer. He was moments away from being caught by the Haldiveer, and punishments in Halmora were far worse than those in Raluha. Amir would probably never see his home again. He had to leave.

"Okay, look . . . Fylan saheb . . . I don't know what to say to you, but I can't help you, ho? This . . . this is not what I do. I don't know if you're telling the truth or not. This . . . this is way beyond what I can handle.

I was here because I know Harini, and I was hoping she'd give me a vial of the Poison. But guess what? My luck is rotten, it's a bowler thing, to be sure. I'm—I'm sorry—I need to head back home. I hope you understand."

Fylan struggled to sit up. Then, with an abrupt surge of passion, he lurched to grab Amir, bringing him close to his face. Amir could smell the blood pouring out of wounds that would never heal.

"The Poison . . ." Fylan whispered. "Illindhi is where it is made . . . caverns full of it."

Amir blinked.

He did not even struggle out of Fylan's grip. "You're lying."

"I . . . told you. I . . . have no reason . . . to lie." Fylan's breath was now coming in deep rattles. He was running out of words and the sands of time melted in his heart. Swollen, dying eyes gazed at the medallion in Amir's hand, at that little jar with the silver spice. "You must take the olum to Illindhi . . . tell them, *beg* them . . . not to send the Uyirsena."

He then stopped again to cough before releasing Amir. Slowly, he began to unwind the turban around his head. It took an age to unwrap, revealing a mop of hair that fell back to his shoulders as he handed Amir the purple cloth. It was wet with the smell of spice.

"Wear this around your neck . . . talk to nobody in Illindhi but Madhyra. Give the olum to her. An empire counts on you . . . All nine do."

All nine. Those treasonous words again.

Confusion flooded his head. Amir almost let the medallion slip out of his hand. He wiped the sweat off his forehead. None of what Fylan said made any sense. *No, no, no.* He had to rejoin the spice trail. He had failed in his mission to procure the Poison, and now he had to get home. It was the least he could do for his family—show up.

It took the utter silence in the kitchen for Amir to understand that the tender string that had until then held Fylan's head up had snapped. Fylan had floated through the Lip of the Mouth long before he, Amir, had planned to reject the man's entreaty once more.

A deep breath. A sigh. Amir wrapped the medallion's string around his fingers. Outside, the sound of rain drummed like a pulsating rhythm from the skies, punctuated by voices.

A fresh troop of the Haldiveer forced a gulp out of him. They would clear the bodies outside first, near the staircase, sprinkling pepper on the corpses as a bargain for the fallen ones to be let into the Fields of Cinnamon. And then they would make for the gaping door of the kitchens, lured by the flicker of light, and would come upon Fylan and him.

Against the feeble light of the torch in the vault, he stared at Fylan, at his motionless figure that would never rise again. It didn't matter that Amir hadn't known him longer than a few frantic minutes. Standing in the midst of that shadow, witnessing his breath leave his body was a reminder of why Amir despised the conditions of his life. That life could be snatched from him while he withered as a slave of the eight kingdoms while his own desires lay buried. If ever there came another opportunity to do as he wished, he would grab it. But right now, he settled for home.

He pocketed the medallion and ran across the kitchen, away from the sound of the warriors. Out into the rain and darkness where he was only a trick of the moonlight, a hurtling shadow desperate to rejoin the tail of the body it belonged to. The Haldiveer were busy poring over the slain bodies of their companions, and in the distance, Amir heard shouts and commands. If there was one thing he was certain of, it was how well he knew the passageways in and out of the fort and onto the spice trail. Each time a journey to meet Harini inevitably resulted in this mazy dance, and today he prayed it'd be no different. With the relentless rain, he chose to slink down a dirt pathway that smelled of cow dung, leading into a canal dug beneath the fort. This in turn led through an underground passage to a sluice that opened into the fringes of the jungle outside the qila. If he could wade through the accumulated water, there would be no way the Haldiveer would follow him.

Once he rejoined the trail, it would only be a matter of sharing a load with a fellow Carrier grateful to ease their own burden.

Amir's heart raced as he hobbled through the canal. A war raged in his mind between two forces—one that believed Fylan and one that did not.

The part that did not believe choked the part that did, drowning Amir in the years that had passed, the failures that had accumulated, reminding him of what it meant to place his trust in people outside the Bowl. He knew of the foolishness of hope, of how bowlers like him were lured into the world with the promise of a reward for the goodness of their service, of honor to be bestowed upon them by the Mouth, until they were stamped upon and toyed with and dragged around, spat on and whipped, had their spines broken until day melted into night. The comforts the night brought would be lost in overcoming the pain of the day, and before they knew it, it would be day again and the cycle repeated, and repeated, and repeated . . .

He had seen himself fail to procure the Poison over and over again, all so he could get his family out of Raluha. It was not enough merely to abandon the Spice Trade like his father did. He could not take the easy way out, could not leave his family behind. Not in the Bowl.

Yet even with his doubt, even after his conversation with Harini, Amir knew better than to bite on fruit that should never have been offered to him in the first place.

He would return to Raluha. He'd try again.

And if Fylan is right? A cavern full of the Poison . . . and all you need is one vial. A trickle of it down Amma's throat for a painless passage . . .

The conflict dragged Amir out of the sluice and onto an ominously empty trail. As he clambered up a slope toward the Spice Gate with the rain having dimmed to a cold drizzle once more, he realized with dread and shivering silence that the Carriers had already returned to Raluha without him.

CHAPTER
5

A chest of gold and a jar of cloves hold the same value in my eyes. Without the latter, there is no motivation to hoard the former.

—MISHURA VARDHAN, *ALL THAT GLITTERS*, CHAPTER 4

Amir stepped out of the Gate into the saffron fields of Raluha, stopping just short of Hasmin's outstretched spear. His back spasmed in pain. If he'd been carrying a sack, he wasn't certain if he'd have survived the jolt that stretched his muscles and clamped his heart. Breathing became difficult. He thought he heard a sizzling voice in his head, like too much mustard allowed to fry in a chetti of coconut oil. The voice clung to his skull and threatened to claw out of his head.

The Spice Gate had once again dismantled everything that stitched his body together. A fire burned within, more ferocious than ever, and Amir wondered if death would be kinder. But he was alive . . . for the time being. Hasmin's eyes seemed to harbor every intention to change that.

Behind Amir, Karim bhai stepped out of the Gate and let out a low moan at the sight. "Hasmin kaka, you'd promised." Amir heard his friend's voice like a sound from a deep well.

Slowly, he raised his head. Hasmin clicked his tongue at Karim bhai, the trail of his khaki turban swaying in the evening breeze.

"Did I?" he asked mockingly, with a gentle tilt of his head.

"Yes, we had a deal, kaka!" The voice was clearer. Karim bhai came to stand beside Amir, one eye resting on the pike, his hands folded in submission. "I gave not two pouches but an entire fortnight's black pepper, kaka, to the Haldiveer to bring Amir back to Raluha. He had already been imprisoned for a day. You must honor your word and let him go."

Karim bhai himself was panting, clutching his arms and hobbling with difficulty. The Gate had torn him as much as it had Amir, and yet the old Carrier, for his age, stood without a grimace, while Amir thought there was a saw hacking away at flesh below his thigh at that moment.

Gates, please make it stop!

Half a dozen chowkidars stood in a semicircle behind Hasmin, their pikes erect, on alert, as though Amir and the stuttering Karim bhai were perfectly capable of overcoming all of them with their unspoken machinations.

Hasmin did not lower his spear. Amir waited for the pain from the Spice Gate to evaporate like it always did, minutes after passage. And yet, today the pain persisted, threatening to be endless in its torment. Hasmin straightened his weapon.

"Why?" was all he asked; his eyes bored into Amir.

Amir coughed up a response. "I . . . I got lost. You may ask the other Carriers, but the lights went out across Halmora, Hasmin kaka, I promise."

"And you walked blindly into a wall of blood, did you?"

Hasmin's eyes lowered to Amir's tunic, which Amir had forgotten was stained with Fylan's blood.

"It . . . I . . ." he stuttered in response. *Shit!* Would Hasmin even believe him if Amir told him of the circumstances that delayed his return? Would Hasmin believe him if Amir spoke of a ninth kingdom and a spice that could be manipulated into producing any of the others?

One look at Hasmin's controlled fury gave Amir his answer. Silence would be worth a nutmeg today. And a day of a nutmeg was one worth cherishing.

"And you," Hasmin barked at Karim bhai. "Pick up your sack and get out of here."

"But kaka . . . what will you do with him?" It came so naturally to Karim bhai to feign servitude, that cautious meekness of bowlers that alone could satisfy the egos of those who lived above them. Times were, Amir hated Karim bhai for that pantomime. He didn't believe the gate-caste ought to be bowing to these people, no matter their station. Yet Amir was one man, a Carrier at that, who had little going for him but his weekly struggle of passage. From where he stood, and where he lived, he knew he couldn't change a single thing, not in stubborn old Raluha.

Hasmin spat at Amir's feet and nudged Karim bhai toward one of the chowkidars with the tip of his spear. "What will I do with him, you ask? I will do what I should have done a long time ago."

Amir was alarmed. "You can't take me to the Pyramid! You're not allowed to arrest Carriers. It says so in the—"

"I am not going to arrest you," Hasmin snarled. "Or take you to the Pyramid. I promised Karim that I would let you go, and that is what I will do."

Amir narrowed his eyes. Something did not add up. A generous Hasmin was an anomaly, a thing that couldn't be fathomed except in the strangest of dreams.

Hasmin smiled, a grin of malice that quickened Amir's breathing even as the Spice Gate's passage dimmed the pain in his body. The chief of chowkidars growled at Karim bhai. "Leave us."

Karim bhai did not need to be told again. He glanced at Amir, emitted a deep sigh that Amir understood only too well—a tacit exchange of emotions between bowlers that conveyed that the day had gone to shit and that the night would be no better, but that tomorrow was a new day and would hold the promise of a better one if you could make it until then.

In a blink Karim bhai was gone, limping down the fields toward the bowl-shaped Raluhan valley, surrounded by swaying bulbs of saffron.

The sun had nearly set, the horizon a vermilion stroke that made the saffron fields appear more beautiful. The breeze softened, and a pinch of cold hung in the air, making Amir want to hug himself for warmth despite the blood on his tunic and the weakness in his bones. All he could do, though, was stare at Hasmin.

"The queen had a failed Bashara," Hasmin said. "The child was still-born."

Amir gasped, although a part of him had foreseen this. The queen had had failed births in the past, and this may well have sealed the fate for Maharaja Orbalun's lineage.

Hasmin, however, was not done. "We did not have enough spices to conduct the rituals earlier today, thanks to you."

"But kaka, the Halmorans—"

"Had withheld the turmeric? Had stolen it? Does it matter? The heir to the throne is dead, and the kingdom is in mourning."

Amir could predict how the abovefolk would twist the facts to blame the bowlers for this outcome. While he empathized with Orbalun, he had little patience or sympathy for those Orbalun ruled over. Inevitably, there would be a few public lashings, a shaming or two, and a bazaar ban for a day or so. What this meant for Amir—

"Empty your pockets," Hasmin said.

"I have nothing of value," Amir replied promptly.

"I will be the judge of it. Go ahead, don't make me ask again."

Amir dug his fingers into every cranny of his attire, fishing out a handkerchief, a tiny sash of crushed ginger, a comb, and an empty water flask. Amir splayed his hands confidently in completion of his task.

Hasmin scratched his beard. After a moment, he summoned one of the lower-caste chowkidars and ordered him to frisk Amir thoroughly. Hasmin, of course, would no sooner assume full responsibility for the failed Bashara than touch a hair on Amir's body with his own bare hands.

"Don't leave a single stitch."

The chowkidar was meticulous. Within seconds, he found Fylan's medallion trapped between the crumpled band of Amir's pants and his waist. The chowkidar returned to Hasmin with the medallion, the vial of olum embedded in it. Hasmin squinted at the vial and traced his fingers along the metal of the medallion, an eyebrow gradually rising as though the item's worth had dawned upon him.

"What is this?"

Amir gulped, stretching his cheeks to buy a feather's time. The lie scampered out of his throat. "It's a friend's. From the Bowl. Given to me as a mark of good fortune."

Hasmin chuckled. "A metal so finely polished? In a bowler's hands? Tell me the truth. Before I decide to stick this spear into you and report you as an accident of duty."

An empty threat. Deep down, Hasmin knew his own helplessness. Killing a Carrier—or even arresting one—was forbidden, according to the rules, given how few they numbered in each kingdom and how important it was for them to report for duty for the sake of the Spice Trade. Only in exceptional circumstances and for grave crimes did a thronekeeper permit the *incarceration*—and never the execution—of Carriers. Amir felt insulated, but he also knew that his fortune was very close to drying out. If not him, Hasmin would take out his anger on another bowler, one who did not have the spicemark etched on their throat.

Maybe Amma.

"It's nothing," Amir replied. "Just a fistful of sand that I found in Jhanak. The medallion, as I told you, is a friend's."

Hasmin chuckled. "Sand, is it? Looks like spice to me." He twisted the vial until it came out of the medallion. Opening it, he inhaled sharply. A second passed, then a minute. Hasmin stoppered the vial once more and fitted it back into the medallion.

Amir knew Hasmin was dallying, and each second stretched, taking Amir further and further away from the Poison. Surely, Hasmin couldn't have known what Amir carried in his pockets. It had to be a test. His true punishment awaited now, and Amir feared to what extent Hasmin would go to satiate his passions.

His fingers curled around the medallion, and he pocketed it with a finality. Raising his head, he smiled at Amir. "Well, I'll keep the 'sand.' You can leave."

Amir blinked. The sun had fully set, and in the time it took for the last vestiges of light to disappear and for the stars to come forward like a blue, pinpricked canvas overhead, Amir failed to wrap his head around what Hasmin had said.

"I-I can go?"

Hasmin nodded. "Absolutely. You will go home, and in four days' time, for your next carrying duty, you will report to this very place, along with your brother."

The mask that concealed Hasmin's face truly came away in that semi-darkness. The plain shadow around his eyes belied the emphatic joy in them, the culmination of a sadistic plan Hasmin must have itched to execute. All he needed was an excuse, and Amir had just given one to him on a platter.

Amir wanted to bury himself in the saffron fields. Instead, he clenched his fists and gave Hasmin a stiff nod.

"A chowkidar will be sent to your home to ensure . . . a complete family attendance," Hasmin added.

With a satisfied sigh, the chief of chowkidars twirled his fingers over his head as a signal for his companions to depart. Hasmin shifted his pike from one hand to the other and joined his comrades as they ambled toward the valley, leaving Amir swallowing the last of his saliva and utterly unable to process the plight he'd just brought upon his family.

THE BAZAAR CAME TRULY ALIVE AT NIGHT. UNDER SHIMMERING stars and the pale glow of the moon, merchants gathered beneath their canopies or opened the locks of their stone dens. Out spilled dynastic dealings and modest fillings in crates of sugar, zedoary, and galangal;

barrels of honey and oil; perfumes of musk and camphor, aloes and sandalwood; wagons loaded with sealed boxes of ivory and cheap pearls; tortoiseshells from the coast of Mesht; ginger dolls from the byways of Talashshukh; incense, skins and ebony, and costsusts and nards from the mountains beyond Jhanak; and iron from Kalanadi.

Nobody asked or cared on whose back these sacks came riding through the Spice Gates. Only that they were here, laid out under the canopies and the moonlight on the winding trail of the spice bazaar. And if Amir cared to venture into the narrower alleyways, he was certain to be dragged into poppy dens stinking of saeveroot or wine cellars where they served boar's tail and fish and pottage and whale meat hooked off the coasts of Jhanak, beer and mead, and crones who gave the wicked eye before they rummaged in their nets for arcane parcels of panther skins and furs and chains of lapis lazuli from Vanasi for the lovers who wished to glimpse each other's bodies in the dark.

It required courage to wander in the night bazaar, for both your coin and your sanity were at stake. Tonight, Amir's mind was on edge, and it raged with the torment of multiple truths crashing in from so many directions, all the while suffering the residue of the physical toll imposed by the Gate. He wandered the market with the shawl around his throat almost in a stupor. A failed Bashara did not stop people from crowding the bazaar, but the air was glum, and in the distance the lights in the palace had been extinguished—much like in Halmora—making the bazaar look like a constellation of fragrances and footsteps beneath the stars.

And in the argument of bargains, Amir heard the usual recriminations from the abovefolk. Nothing he hadn't heard before. The echoes of those words were already imprinted on his skin.

As he squeezed into the throng, he realized he wasn't the only one being oppressed. Even among the abovefolk, there remained a hierarchy, this denigration that manifested not always in abuses and exclusions but in gentle displays of superiority.

Amir had time for none of them. He followed the sound of a tambourine rising from the vale. Surely not a feast in the Bowl! In the wake of a failed

Bashara? The upper castes would be livid. He smiled despite himself at this small rebellion.

The lower he sank into the Bowl, the more clustered the houses became, the scabbier the bricks, the more scattered the firelight, the louder the dogs, the more clogged the drains, and the more the stench of garbage and burn piles grew.

Familiar, the smell of home.

The bowlers had gathered where the mud roads and the wide steps met—in a square near the bottom, around a great campfire. It was the birth of a child in the Bowl, and celebration was due. There was enough firelight to balance the darkness of Raluha's palace in the distance above, and enough music to silence the sounds of the bazaar.

Karim bhai stood at the center of the circle, singing a song as people swayed around him as though he were the Grand Ustad himself. He loved to sing, and he loved to sing to an audience. All the energy carrying sapped out of him emerged in his voice, and it set the Bowl aflame in a way that few people could rival.

The other Carriers were present too, all of them resting their backs on benches or against the mud bricks of their homes, feet sprawled on their verandahs, lazy smiles, and betel-stained grins. Grandmothers stood beneath rafters, squinting at the figures dancing by the fire.

An entire portion of the square was reserved for food. Amir imagined there was biryani, but it'd be a bland variety. He did not wish to have one without nutmegs, bay leaves, and cumin, whose rations to the bowlers were the least among the spices. On the other hand, there'd be tamarind rasam, crushed pumpkin, and pongal with diced jaggery. And buttermilk. It wasn't a bowler feast without buttermilk, infused with turmeric, pepper, and the rarest of rare coriander leaves—smuggled to Raluha by Ilangovan—with chilies crushed and seasoned atop. Did they have enough spices this time, though? He doubted it. It'd be bland, but it was comfort food.

Amir resisted the temptation and instead brushed through the crowd, hollering at those who hollered at him, winking at those who winked at him. In the flickering firelight, nobody noticed the bloodstains on Amir's tunic. He found Kabir among those who were dancing, a much shorter eleven-year-old scampering through the more adult crowd. Amma was on the other side, sitting on a stool, flanked by Panchavarnam didi and Gulbega didi and a dog that slept beside her feet. One of Amma's hands cupped her bloated belly, the other rested behind her head as she grinned at the dancers. The fire and heat made her sweat profusely.

She smiled when Amir approached, rubbing her glistening forehead with her wrist. He gave her the slightest shake of his head, which snatched the smile from Amma's face. He hated himself in that moment for evoking that reaction in her. After Appa had left them and disappeared, all Amir had wanted was for her to suffer less. He'd stayed silent while she overcame the loss in her own way. He would leave his home, dragging Kabir with him to Karim bhai's house anytime Amma wanted to indulge in the fleshier pleasures. And now a consequence of that grew in her belly, and even she couldn't say who the father might be.

To her, it didn't matter.

Amir only prayed it was a girl. It was rare for a girl to be born with the spicemark.

"What took you so long?" Amma asked, her voice rising over the music and the chatter.

He couldn't bring himself to tell her what Hasmin had decided for Kabir, or what he'd undergone in Halmora. "Just strolling down the bazaar," he said. Amma inclined her head in an exhausted nod, but her eyes told him a different story. What Amir understood from her was this—*It's okay, we will try another day. I know you will find it eventually. If not, go ahead, you and Kabir. I will remain here in Raluha.*

The thought stung him. Before he could say anything more to Amma, however, Karim bhai swept Amir into a sweaty embrace and dragged him aside. Someone else had taken up the singing. "Apologies, Noori," he said. "I am going to borrow your son for a bit." He grinned at Amir before growling into his ear, "Come along, you little rat, we need to talk."

Amir frowned but did not resist, allowing Karim bhai to lead him away. When they were a safe distance from the party, deeper into the Bowl, descending the mud lanes running beside the sewage, Amir finally asked Karim bhai, "Where are you taking me?"

Karim bhai stopped and shoved Amir against a wall. He unwrapped his toweled turban and whacked Amir with it. "Where am I taking you? To ask you about the blood on your filthy person. If your mother sees it, it is not you she scolds but *me*. I get the brunt of your stupidity all the time, naaye."

"And you do a fine job of defending me." Amir ignored the expletives. "What's the problem?"

"The problem is I want to know whose blood that is, and where in the eight kingdoms you disappeared to yesterday within Halmora! If I hadn't begged Hasmin to be sent back to retrieve you, you'd have rotted the rest of your life away in the Halmoran prison."

Amir sighed. "I didn't *disappear*. I went to meet Harini."

In the dark of the Bowl, amid the distant sounds of drums and tambourine, Amir told Karim bhai everything that happened from the moment he left the spice trail. At no point did he stop, and there was little he concealed. Karim bhai was the pillar upon which Amir had leaned all these years. The bulwark without whom Carrying would have destroyed Amir long ago. After his father had abandoned them, Karim bhai had come, bringing Amir and his mother a week's worth of vegetables and rice, and although he did not have much spice to spare, he had given Amma his entire allowance of cumin and mace. She had immediately cooked a great bowl of biryani for Karim bhai and the neighbors. More than that, for Amir, Karim bhai was the one who'd helped ease him into the tormented life of a Carrier. Who'd warned him of the pain of passage, who'd offered him salves and potions and bribed the accountants and the chowkidars with every resource he could muster to protect Amir during the most difficult of carrying days.

Despite the grizzly old man's eccentricities, despite his fanaticism, Amir couldn't imagine a life without Karim bhai—either on the spice trail or in the Bowl.

And so, Amir held nothing back, knowing he could trust this man implicitly. When he was done, he straightened himself, the blood on his tunic suddenly clearer, more meaningful.

"Did you know," Amir whispered, his eyes frantically searching the lane for eavesdroppers, "that there might be a ninth kingdom? And . . . and a spice that could become any spice?"

Karim bhai, who was still digesting the enormity of Amir's tale, slowly shook his head. The man had surrounded himself with conspiracy theories, myths of the Mouth he had once desired to tell his children, but *this* even he struggled to grasp.

"Do you know what this means?" he asked, his voice pitching low with fear. He paled, like he'd seen an Immortal Son of the Outerlands and returned alive to tell the tale. Fear in a man like Karim bhai sent shudders through Amir.

Amir's voice was a faint whisper in the dark. "I have a vague idea. Let's just say I do believe what Fylan told me. Let's say it is true that there is a ninth kingdom. If so, its secret could—"

"Destroy the Spice Trade," Karim bhai said. His fingers curled into a fist almost involuntarily. "Think about it, Amir. There are eight great spices. Eight kingdoms, each to grow one spice. A perfect balance. The . . . the people are fallible, be it us in the Bowl or the abovefolk. They— we—are addicted to the spices. The balance thrives on this dependency. Give and take what is rightfully yours. Why is no one thronekeeper superior to the seven others? Because there is absolute equality. They are all vested with the power to send Carriers across the Spice Gate with spices, messages, and goods to another realm—a realm that cannot otherwise be reached through the Outerlands."

"And now . . ."

"With a ninth kingdom bearing a spice like olum . . . that balance stands to shatter."

A weight settled in Amir's chest. "The one who controls olum will have leverage over the others. *Gates!*"

Karim bhai placed both his hands on Amir's shoulders. "Not just leverage, Amir. It could lead to war."

"War? What is that?"

Karim bhai scratched his head and made a face. "I . . . don't know how to explain it. Suman-Koti has told me this story a dozen times while I made baths for him. Ministers, I tell you. But ho, ho, okay—don't look at me like that, pulla." He scowled at Amir's judgmental expression. "As I was telling you . . ." It took him a moment to gather his thoughts. "Ho . . . legend has it that there was a time when conflict between two kingdoms over the supply of spices had reached such heights that the Jewelmaker made the Poison freely available. Word in the bazaar was he wanted the royals to meet and settle the conflict. The kingdoms, however, fed the Poison to armies of their soldiers and fought a terrible battle across Gates. Soldiers wearing helms like the faces of the Immortal Sons you can only see in paintings and wielding blades like their teeth. The end was ugly. Thousands died. It's said the Jewelmakers of lore have since tightened their reins on the supply of Poison. But . . . if this . . . this olum comes into the eight kingdoms, it could cause big problems, Amir. I don't think the ministers of the palace, and even Orbalun, would be happy to know there's someone from a ninth kingdom sitting in Halmora, offering her magic spice to Harini. I say Harini alone, for I don't think Raja Virular would stoop to agree to this blasphemy, even in that terrible economy."

Conflict over supply. Amir recalled what Harini had told him in the palace. She had feared the eight kingdoms were losing their desire for turmeric and preferring other spices. If Harini had access to olum, she wouldn't need to bother buying spices from the other kingdoms anymore. But it would also lure every thronekeeper to Halmora in a bid to claim olum. What did she want with Ilangovan, then? If she had olum, she wouldn't need to bargain with anyone. A piece of the puzzle was missing—at least one piece, Amir surmised. He scratched his own head, the scope of the issue meddling with his sanity.

What did Amir really stand to gain by bothering himself with the problems of thronekeepers anyway? He admitted he was tempted to join in whatever Harini and the stranger were cooking up in the darbar of Halmora. But the moment had passed; he clearly hadn't been invited—

his conversation with Harini had proved as much. No, he would always be beneath their squabbles. He would always be a *bowler*. Only one goal could remain—and that was to escape the Spice Trade and join with Ilangovan.

But to do that, he needed the Poison. It always seemed to come back to that. One vial. One simple little vial. No, not simple, especially not for a Carrier.

It was settled, then: he'd have to go to this Illindhi, if such a place truly existed. There he'd find what he needed. *Caverns full of it.* Was this how the Jewelmaker had once supplied all that Poison to the warring kingdoms? It stood to reason. Gates, he was buying into this theory sooner than he'd have liked.

Because that's what desperate people are forced to do. Latch on to whatever they're thrown and let it drag them in. He glanced ahead at where orange flickers rose from the scene of the bowlers' feast. Kabir was there. So was Amma, and in a few days, there would be another child in the house while Kabir would struggle to lift the sack over his shoulder and not crumble each time he passed through the Gate. He'd have to be disciplined; avoid the whips, turn a deaf ear to the slurs. He'd have to conceal within himself the temptation of the bazaar and learn to save what little allowance the Spice Trade Council provided Carriers. Be it saffron or cardamom or ginger or pepper, Kabir would have to value them in a new way. All the while massaging the pain that would flood his body. All the while going from a boy to a man.

No matter who won, the bowlers would lose.

A dreadful silence folded around Amir and Karim bhai as they both soaked in the sounds of the feast. "Pulla . . ." Karim bhai finally said, as if seeing Amir's thoughts, "if I know you like I think I know you, I'd say you've decided to go to this . . . this Illindhi, whether you believe in it or not. Ho?"

Amir nodded weakly. "I have no choice. But that bastard Hasmin has the vial with the olum. I don't know how I can get it from him."

Karim bhai slipped into a contemplative state. After a moment, he said, "There is a way."

Amir grabbed Karim bhai's tunic and stared into his eyes. "Tell me. Anything."

Karim bhai sighed. He detached himself from Amir's grip, glanced along both sides of the long, wide steps that descended into the dark Bowl.

"You must once more become what the abovefolk claim you already are."

"What is that?"

"A thief."

CHAPTER

6

*A Talashshukian was evidence that formal education was often
not as important as a day spent in the foundry.*

—*MORSELS OF A BENT BACK*, VOLUME 2

Amir stood outside the Pyramid with a bucket and a mop in his
hand. He wore a loose, stained tunic, and a lungi borrowed
from Karim bhai that was too large for him. A thin, reedy
chowkidar approached him from the gates. He concealed his trembling
hand and put on an impassive face.

"Ho, Carrier! What are you doing here?" called the chowkidar. "Get
out before the chief sees you."

Amir did not move. "Kaikeyi is sick, saheb. I have come on her behalf
for cleaning."

The chowkidar inspected Amir from head to toe before permitting
him through the gates. Amir gazed up at the Pyramid as he walked in.
It was the ugliest building in Raluha. Various types of brick and stone
arranged in a haphazard manner, with deep, sunken windows, and barbed
scaffolding that climbed the walls like creepers and tendrils. At the top,
embedded into the wall itself was a great clock, whose hands appeared to
be rusted pikes, rotating on a dial that resembled a peacock's head.

In a twisted way, it fit that Hasmin was in charge of this place. It was nauseating to stare at, and Amir decided to be on his best behavior in front of the chief of the chowkidars, striding in with his cleaning paraphernalia.

Inside, Hasmin lounged on a chair, his feet stretched up on the table in front of him, his hands knotted behind his head. He muttered something incomprehensible when he locked eyes with Amir. The chowkidar standing behind him sniggered.

"Saheb, where should I begin?" Amir asked.

The inside of the chowkidars' jail looked fairly respectable. Benches and tables, glass almirahs, a spice box on every chowkidar's desk, with pockets for saffron, mace, and saunf. Amir scoffed. A nice way to conceal the dirt beneath the surface.

The true evil of the Pyramid lay underground, in those dank cells clad in darkness. He had visited them once, albeit for a very short period of time when he'd irked Hasmin during one of the Carrying duties. Hasmin, of course, had been forced to gnash his teeth, stop himself from assaulting Amir, and respectfully release him under the law of the Spice Trade Council.

But Amir had seen enough of what lurked beneath in shadow to never want to go there again.

Hasmin presently stood and rounded the table. He came to stand within a foot of Amir and gave an ugly frown. "Why must it be you all the time?"

Amir gulped. "Kaikeyi is sick, saheb."

"Of course she is," he said with a sigh, and thrust a parchment into Amir's hand. "Do you see what this is?"

Amir squinted. He couldn't read very well. A minute of scanning told him it was a list of Carriers for the duty to Talashshukh in three days, sealed by the minister of silk, Suman-Koti. He spotted his own name and Karim bhai's. His eyes roved down the list until, at the very end, he saw Kabir's. His heart skipped a beat. The little corner of his heart that had hoped Hasmin had been idly threatening to unleash his anger disappeared in a blink. Here was a genuine need to be vindictive, and Hasmin had achieved it.

Amir returned the parchment, his hands trembling. He couldn't lose his cool now. Not here, when everything hinged on how he'd temper his emotions. This was a moment for truly being what the abovefolk expected the bowlers to be—submissive.

Gathering his composure he removed a small wooden box from his pocket. He flipped the lid to reveal a golden-brown spice.

Hasmin's eyes widened and the parchment sailed out of his hand and landed on the table. "Is . . . is that heeng?"

"Grandmother-crushed," Amir offered, as though he had completely forgotten seeing Kabir's name on the list. "A traditional mixture. Amma thought I should compensate you for . . . the trouble I caused yesterday."

The Pyramid lay at the mouth of the Raajapaadhai, a lane of marble, muffled voices, and silent whips squatting in the shadows of the Palace of Raluha, where the trimmed bushes appeared like rectangular sentries with sharp pikes. Places like this, the word "grandmother" held a magical allure. There was something authentic and enigmatic about anything wrung out of a grandmother's coarse, wrinkled hands. Made them appear nostalgic and valuable, as though an old woman's tears dribbled onto it to improve its texture.

Heeng was also the only ingredient the abovefolk condescended to desire from the Bowl.

Amir hid a smile. Hasmin lifted the box from his hand and inspected it closely. A homemade dash and sprinkle of diced coconut, salt, turmeric, and chilies—crushed in a mortar with an ancient pestle passed down through Amma's generations and left to haunt the farthest corners of their living quarters. Did Hasmin truly sense the pinch of heeng? That sacrilegious spice that the abovefolk craved?

Few could resist the allure. Although abovefolk did not like to admit it, spice *was* an obsession, and he, Amir, was the deliverer of their desires. He, who stumbled on the spice trail with twenty pounds of cloves on his back knowing he wasn't permitted to sniff a single bud. His head lowered, and from the rims of his eyes, Amir watched Hasmin sway.

An urge to urinate flooded his body, and Amir controlled it with a tight lip, a heavy blink, and a long and deep breath.

The chief of chowkidars took an age to close the lid on the box and lay it gently on the table. There was a conflicted loathing in his eyes that Amir cherished. For the abovefolk never touched food made by the bowlers. But heeng, ah, heeng was the beautiful exception. Hasmin slowly chided, "Very well, get out of my sight. You can start with the floor above. Then the toilets."

When Amir began to move, Hasmin tapped his baton on Amir's shoulder, his frown deepening as though he had changed his mind. "Mabali, over here."

The chowkidar who had frisked Amir by the Gate came running to Hasmin. "Yes, saheb!"

"Search him," said Hasmin. "Thoroughly."

After a minute of patient scanning, the chowkidar stood and shook his head.

"He's clear, saheb."

Hasmin coughed and flicked his hand for Amir to disappear.

Kissing the air of fortune, and cursing the increasing pressure to relieve himself, Amir grabbed the bucket and the mop cloth and scuttled toward the staircase winding up the Pyramid before Hasmin could think of another reason to stop him.

Rows of almirahs greeted him on the first level. They were filled with records and documents. Alcoves and glass cabinets abounded along one stretch, stuffed with ceramics, spice jars, and glassware. They were flanked by mounted heads of beasts rumored to be from beyond the Raluhan borders. Every inch of those borders was marked with barbed fencing and manned at intervals by sentries as vile and beady-eyed as Hasmin. They were boundaries Raluhans weren't permitted to cross, be they bowlers *or* abovefolk. *Why would anyone?* But then Amir winced at the thought, trying not to dwell on his father's crime of desertion. It wouldn't do to become distracted now.

A dampness prevailed in the air, mingled with an effusion of sandalwood and saffron. A few chowkidars scurried about with a hasty impatience, saffron turbans taut over their heads, maroon scarves flapping behind them as they rushed here and there.

On one side of the cluttered floor, Amir spotted three offices, one of them larger than the other two, which he supposed belonged to Hasmin.

The doors were locked. Karim bhai had been certain they'd be open. A pair of chowkidars walked by, avoiding Amir altogether.

All right, he had to be patient. Find a way inside, or perhaps just start cleaning until a thought would pop in his head.

At that moment, however, he'd crossed a threshold. Unable to resist his urge to pee, Amir dragged the bucket to the opposite side of the corridor, to where the toilet was. Leaving the mop outside, Amir stumbled in.

At first glance, the room was larger than his home. More marble than all of the Bowl put together, albeit old and stained. Several toilet pits lay on one side, separated by vertical stone privacy flats. But Amir's eyes had already steered away.

What he saw made his heart do a somersault even as a treacherous stink assaulted his nose and summoned a gag.

In one corner, squatting in a pool of shit, was his neighbor Damini. Damini, who had been dancing while sweeping the streets of the Bowl, now in a pose that could evoke none of that boundless grace. A face, all of twelve years old, stared openmouthed at him, her face warped in sweat. When she brushed the sweat away, she seemed to realize that some of the feces she had been gathering with her hands now soiled her forehead and trickled down her nose. They were not hers.

Hasmin and his chowkidars' feces were a golden brown, much like the spices they dealt in.

Amir gritted his teeth at the sight of Damini, whose one hand lay halfburied in an effort to unclog the toilet. They needed the bowlers for this.

Summoned from the bottom of Raluha, eternally fated to serve, constantly reminded of their place. Karim bhai had told Amir he'd find her here, but nothing prepared him for the bile that now rushed up his throat.

He pulled up his towel and walked over to her, his hand outstretched. "Take it," he said. "And keep it with you."

Damini did not complain. She took the cloth and nodded. "Thanks, 'na. What are you doing here?"

"I . . . uh, came to clean. And to pee, of course. Do you mind looking the other way, Dami? I will be quick."

When Amir was finished, he exhaled a long, slow breath. He glanced at Damini, swabbing the floor with her mop that had already turned brown. He couldn't look at it for longer than a moment, and yet she was one of his. A product of a society that wanted the bowlers only to clean their toilets, unclog the sewage, beat the drums at funerals, shepherd the goats on land owned by the abovefolk, and work at the tanneries. And of course, lest he forget, the greatest of jobs—to suffer the incomparable pain of walking through the Spice Gate.

What did the bowlers get in return? A place to squabble together in, at the base of Raluha, ostracized from the rest of the kingdom.

Perhaps this was why he, even though everything in him told him he was being foolish, could not resist the desire to believe in Illindhi.

He would go and bring back a handful of the Poison for as many bowlers as he could manage. His desperation would take him there, if not the pleading of a dead man. Damini wouldn't have to do this anymore. They'd all seek refuge with Ilangovan . . .

A bell tolled in his head. Amir was wasting time.

"Dami," he said, "can you give me your hairpin?"

Damini frowned, but after a moment of hesitation plucked the pin out of her hair and threw it at Amir. He caught it and inspected the tip. It'd work. Thanking her and apologizing for wasting her time, he grabbed the bucket and scampered out of the toilet. He picked up the mop, spilled some of the water on the floor, and began to clean.

Cleaning was a chore. Amma did it all the time at home, but theirs was a small place with barely enough floor space to use the broom. The Pyramid's floor, on the other hand, was a den of dust. And Amir had to tie Fylan's turban around his face to cover his nose and mouth to keep from choking.

At all points, there was always a chowkidar or two nearby, making it impossible for him to make a beeline for Hasmin's office. Karim bhai had warned of this as well. He'd have to be patient. He moved as he squatted, slowly closing the distance to the door. At one point, he was squatting right opposite the door, cleaning the floor beneath a desk. A chowkidar sat on the other side, having his lunch. Amir could smell the drumstick in the sambar, the aroma of curry leaves, and the beetroot cooked with diced coconuts and chilies.

The chowkidar was staring at him, his hand poised halfway between his dabba and his mouth. A second later, casting Amir a look of disgust, he stood, picked up his dabba and stormed away.

Amir almost wanted to thank him. He wheeled around, jamming Damini's pin into the door's lock. Not all bowlers were thieves, but Karim bhai hadn't been entirely righteous when he made it seem as if this would be Amir's—or any bowler's—first criminal foray. Living in the squat inevitably led to learning a thing or two about the forbidden art of stealing. Amir's fingers quivered, but he gripped the lock firmly, wiped his sweat, and focused.

Within a minute, the lock clicked and came free. Amir slid open the door, slowly in order to avoid a creak, and slipped inside, shutting it behind him.

Hasmin's office was cluttered with heaps of parchment, files, and cupboards overflowing with recovered objects and artifacts. A mural of the Spice Gate hung on the wall opposite the door, beneath which was a platform for an incense stick and little vats of turmeric, sacred ash, and kumkum. A window lay open on one wall. Sunlight streamed in, from right off the edge of Raluha's Bowl, in beams of motes that sprayed on the large table in the center. It was a beautiful view, and one he had no time for. Amir proceeded toward the desk and opened the first drawer.

The medallion and the vial of olum sat on a piece of parchment. Careless, effortless—just like everything Hasmin did. A luxury he could afford in his station.

Amir twisted the medallion and opened the vial. The unfamiliar aroma of olum—neither too sweet nor too pungent, yet with a hint of bitterness that ran up his nose—ensnared his senses. He replaced the little cork in the vial and breathed a sigh of relief.

A hiss escaped from his lips suddenly at the cold touch of metal on his nape.

"I see you've made yourself at home."

Amir's breath caught in his throat. Clutching the medallion, he rotated slowly as Hasmin's face—and the sword he held to Amir—came into focus. Veins bulged on Hasmin's forehead, eyes bloodshot and wide, and without his turban, his hair that fell to his shoulders made him seem like an intoxicated saeveroot addict in the night bazaar.

"Not a word," Hasmin growled as though predicting a defense clambering up Amir's throat but getting stuck where the tip of the sword grazed his skin. "You will place the medallion back inside the drawer, and you're going to come with me. I am going to lock you up in the lowest, darkest cell that I can find, and let there be a man in Raluha who holds the law against me, and he will be disposed of. Do you understand? Nod if you do."

Amir's chest heaved with every breath. Sweat trickled down his face, and a flurry of thoughts raced in his mind. So, this was how it ended. His great plan, his dreams, his desires. Why did Hasmin have to be the one always standing in his way? At the end of all lanes. He could almost picture Kabir stumbling through the Gate, crushed on his first journey, and with how much more it hurt these days to travel than ever before, fury cloyed its way down Amir's arms.

Slowly, he nodded.

At that moment, a horrible stench filled the doorway. Hasmin's entire face seemed to expand with his cheeks, and his other hand rushed to cover his nose as he drew the sword back and wheeled.

Damini stood there, holding a bucket of shit-colored water and the mop cloth she'd used to unclog the toilet drain and clean the overflow.

"Saheb, is there anything else to clean?"

Amir's fingers, sensing an opportunity, closed around the medallion. Before Hasmin could realize that he had taken his eyes off his prisoner, Amir shoved the desk against the chief of chowkidars with all his might and dashed toward the window. A clamor behind him—from the sound and smell, Amir surmised Hasmin fell right on Damini, who dropped the bucket, scattering shit-water all over Hasmin and his office. By the time he regained his footing, Amir was already squeezing through the window.

The ledge sloped downward and dropped more than twenty feet. Behind him, he heard Hasmin shout, "He's trying to escape, the thevidiya! Seal the exit!"

Amir lowered himself, stretching his arms to hold the railing along the ledge. He measured the distance again. He had no choice. With Amma's name on his lips, he let go.

He landed on his feet, but one of his legs buckled and he felt a slight crack behind the knee. Pain shot up to his pelvis, but drowning out the pain was the sound of half a dozen pairs of feet running toward him. Wincing, he pocketed the medallion as safely as he could. The main gate of the Pyramid lay open for him, and so Amir ran, the pain lancing up his leg and reducing half his steps to hobbles, but adrenaline and fear urged him on.

As he approached the gate, the lone chowkidar manning it wheeled with a jolt of surprise. Amir crashed into him, tackling him to the ground. The guard attempted to wriggle free, but Amir slapped him once and then delivered a punch to his gut that pushed a gust of air out of the man's mouth.

Assaulting a chowkidar. Just one more crime for Hasmin to use against you . . . Not that he lacks enough already to imprison you for a hundred years.

Amir scrambled up and away into the main road that hugged the valley side. The throne road stretched north, the marble lane of manor houses and trimmed gardens. At the end of the lane, the Palace of Raluha gleamed over a pedestal of rock and mountain, sunlight bathing it in gold.

Amir smirked and chose the other way. Karim bhai stood there smiling, and behind him stood a hundred bowlers. They had flags in their hands and slogans on their lips. The previous night's celebrations had died with the moon, and today was a new day—a new day to raise their voices against the masters they were tethered to. He knew by heart a litany of their demands—cleaner water, better spice allowances, redistribution of land, justices for forgotten crimes by the abovefolk against the bowlers, and more—all of it organized by people who wielded more clout in the Bowl than Karim bhai. And yet Karim bhai stood among them, as part of a solution he did not believe in. A hundred years of marching in the abovefolks' neighborhoods had not yielded half as much as Karim bhai had secured prowling in the shadows of the ministers' feet.

As Amir approached, they began to march along the throne road.

Amir limped toward them and merged into the crowd as they passed by the gates of the Pyramid, their chants cacophonic.

Hasmin and the chowkidars skidded right into the belly of this gathering. Hasmin looked confused, as though he could not tell one bowler from another. Amir glanced back and smiled with a smug satisfaction. He hadn't been spotted disappearing through the crowd.

Today, for the first time, Amir found the protests to be worth their weight in cardamoms. The pain of falling from the Pyramid's window now enveloped him. It threatened to collapse every bone in his body. He dragged himself up the valley's lanes until the saffron fields emerged, bathed in the afternoon light. The bulbs frolicked against the hillside wind. A sea of purple and saffron, with patches of wild grass and distant foliage.

Beyond the foliage lay the thick, barbed border fence interspersed with armed sentries and an emptiness of moors that stretched beyond it to the horizon. If he squinted, the hint of a sprawl of mountains, like scratches on the sky. The Outerlands.

Amir ignored the looming vision and made his way toward the Spice Gate in the middle of the saffron fields. A few chowkidars stood on alert around it, their pikes upright, their gazes unwavering.

Amir fished out the letter with Minister Suman-Koti's seal, which had been handed to him by Karim bhai. The letter would state Amir's purpose of visit, of how he was an emissary of Suman-Koti, of fisheries and silk, and that this medallion, currently in possession of this Carrier, was to be handed over to Minister Devanangal of Kalanadi on an urgent summons. Karim bhai, ever in the service of Suman-Koti, and never too far from his shadows, had managed to stamp the royal seal on an empty piece of parchment before returning it to its complacent master.

Amir threw a nervous glance behind him at the rim of the Bowl while the chowkidars inspected the letter. He was careful not to appear jittery, but Gates! He couldn't help the fidgeting of his fingers, the raking of his hand through his hair. So much rested on these fragile moments, these otherwise inconsequential events.

At last, the chowkidar flicked his finger at the parchment, tsked in reluctant satisfaction, and handed it back. "You can go."

Amir passed him and climbed the steps to the Gate's pedestal. The chowkidar hollered, "Ho!"

Amir froze. "Yes, saheb?"

"You're forgetting the black pepper." His hand was outstretched, a pinch of milagai tul on his palm. A low breeze swished over their heads, and Amir considered it as a good omen.

He exhaled. "Oh, right. Sorry." He received the black pepper from the chowkidar and climbed the steps to the Gate just as a shout rang in the distance. Amir whirled to glimpse half a dozen chowkidars dashing toward the Gate, and in the lead, unmistakably, was Hasmin, his baton aloft.

Amir's heart thundered in his chest. The veil beneath the arch swirled like a tempest, inviting him inside. The gray stone, enigmatic and un-breakable, stood poised to envelop him.

He dropped the black pepper he was holding. The chowkidar screamed at him. Amir, instead, opened the vial in the medallion and poured the olum into his palm. The guard screamed his name once more, raising his pike and climbing the steps.

This had to work. This *had* to work.

Amir had never prayed to the Mouth in his life—he'd cursed it a lot. It wouldn't hurt, he supposed. He cast the olum into the Gate and, as the chowkidar's spear thrust toward him, leaped inside.

CHAPTER

7

*In the Great Abstinence tournament held during the afsal
dina in Kalanadi, eight thousand men and women competed
for who could go the longest without consuming a single spice—
not even salt—in their meal. A gatecaste woman won the
tournament on the eleventh day. She was awarded a barrel of
black pepper by the thronekeeper. She promptly emptied it into
the drains, complaining that, by then, she preferred the taste of
a spiceless meal.*

—Mukund Vati, *Peppersona*

A sepulchral voice clattered in Amir's head. Like a thousand
cloaks ripped to shreds and left to scatter the skies like a
murder of crows. Amir was trapped in a storm, a dome of
lightning overhead. Something sizzled and pulsated beneath his feet.
He was not on steady ground. It moved, rose and fell like the heaving
chest of a man who had eaten too much for lunch.

He teetered as if on a tightrope. Then the bottom opened up.

He did not fall.

A rift appeared, cracks running along the surface until they widened
and Amir could see the blackness within. And a shape to that blackness.
His world had ended. He had died and this was where the dead went, he

thought, for nothing else could explain what he was seeing. Or perhaps only bowlers came here. To this indeterminate end that was devoid of air, life, or light.

What there was, though, was the fragrance of spice. It rose through the rift like a million censers were burning beneath. Saffron, cumin, cardamom, turmeric, ginger, clove, pepper, nutmeg, and everything else he could put a name to.

And finally, a voice.

HELP ME.

It was the groan of a mountain, the dense hiss of a jungle, the swirling tempest of an ocean. And yet those words, in the timbre of such impossible vistas, entered his head like a whisper.

Amir couldn't fight against it as the nothingness around him suddenly changed. His feet left the not-ground he'd been floating on, and . . .

Dawn.

Amir felt queasy. He thought he had landed on his back upon a flat piece of rock. He expected the usual jolt of pain to shoot through his body, forbidding him from making the slightest movement. But no, there was no pain. There was only consciousness, and before he opened his eyes, his hand wrapped around the medallion, its icy touch reminding him of what he'd passed through.

What had that voice been? And what had he seen while passing through the Spice Gate? It was odd; clearer than a dream, yet there was an illusory quality to the vision. Was someone asking for his help? Could it be another Carrier? Could Carriers communicate with each other through the Gate? No, that couldn't be right. The passage never lasted more than a blip—a snap of your fingers, the click of a tongue. The only thing he would normally remember was the immediate pain of emerging, not the passing itself.

Something brushed against his cheek. Wet and sloppy, like a donkey's kiss. He tried to sit straight. His limbs disagreed. His eyes had been shut all along. A minute passed, then several. It felt like the right thing to do, just sit there, unaware and in blissful rest.

He couldn't sit like this forever, though. Was he even alive? He opened his eyes, and immediately a gust of wind shut them.

Voices ahead. He scrambled to get up, but a hand like a boulder shoved him down again.

Amir tried once more to open his eyes. He could see. The sky was pale; the clouds were shaped like corn kernels and, much to his terror, were closer. The wet whack on his cheeks returned and with it the brush of wind through his hair. High wind.

Behind him, the Spice Gate loomed, ancient and withered, an eerie sound accompanying the wind as it lashed against the stone, knifing into its cracks but giving up against the veil.

The sky occupied almost all of his sight. It was as if he had been transported to a haven among the clouds, but his body was not prepared for it. The cold bit through his tunic and he gnashed his teeth. He had nearly decided to creep through the Gate once more, then realized that he did not have any saffron on him.

He had no way to return to Raluha.

Another hand on his shoulder. Amir wheeled to face a stocky, bearded man, with a turban wound over his head. He'd woven a woolen blanket around him, maroon and dotted. Most of his forehead lines converged in a frown and he held a sickle whose gleaming tip rested inches away from Amir's face.

Before Amir could utter a word, another man, equally barrel-shaped, with a bush of frothy hair on his head, appeared from behind the first, armed with nothing but a piece of black cloth. He knelt beside Amir. "Gates, why is trouble always in the shape of young, ruffled men!" He was shouting to be heard over the wind.

In an instant this second man waddled a step forward and wrapped the cloth around Amir's eyes. Amir tried to scream, but the curve of the first man's sickle grazed against his cheek, and that was enough to silence anyone. The bushy-haired one wasted little time in blindfolding Amir while he belched out a few words.

"You don't understand," Amir reasoned blindly, groping toward them.

"Ho, ho! What are you doing? No, you must listen. I'm just here for the Poison. I was sent by—aaargh!" The man tightened the knot behind Amir's head, yanking his hair and hurting his scalp. Any further attempts to lift his hand were thwarted when the sickle-holder bound Amir's hands in rope.

"Is this Illindhi?" A rush of air escaped his lips.

A moment's silence. "Why, yes, it's Illindhi, of course. If you sprinkle some olum on the Spice Gate, where else do you expect to appear? You are on the tallest peak of Mount Ilom, where all who take this path arrive."

Amir gulped. The tallest peak. It felt unnecessary to convey his terrible fear of heights; he silently thanked them for the blindfold.

"Makun-kunj, do you wish to read out the young man's rights?"

Apparently the swordsman was named Makun-kunj, and Amir heard the rustling of a piece of parchment. Makun-kunj coughed before orating in a loud, gruff voice, "Pursuant to the decree of the Raz Illindha Maharsh Sevak, Chapter Eight, Verse Fourteen, narrated by Shat . . . Shatru . . . Shat . . . I don't get this. Why couldn't someone named Bil or Jun or Dev have drafted this?"

"Shatrughan Saalan," the other man corrected patiently.

"Oh, yes. I remember. It's been a while and my grasp of the old tongue weakens. What now? Four thousand one hundred and twelve years, if we go by the scratches on the cave. I daresay there will be quite the fanfare around this . . . Sorry, where was I? Right. Pursuant to the decree of the Raz Illindha Maharsh Sevak, Chapter Eight, Verse Fourteen, narrated by Shatrughan Saalan, House of the West Mouth, you are found trespassing upon land that you cannot trespass through. You will be stripped of all spices and weapons and will have your eyes blinded for the duration of your stay. You will be given a chance to explain your trespassing to the Chairs. You have the right to seek a Defender, and if you are unable to procure one, the Chairs' honorary members will ensure that you are provided one prior to the hearing. Any questions?"

"Yes—I—"

"Good. Sibil-kunj, let's drag him down, shall we?"

The wind swept through Amir's hair, knocking him back as he tried to stir. Sibil-kunj and Makun-kunj were not gentle handlers, and anything Amir said was either ignored or interrupted, if they heard him at all over the wind. Both of them stank of unwashed tunics, though there was a hint of clove on one of their breaths as they hissed beside him. Amir tried to stand erect, but his body was desperate to fold, like a piece of parchment kept rolled for too long.

Stumbling along for an unknown amount of time—it was strange how time did not feel the same when you couldn't see, Amir thought— something finally shifted. Through the blindfold, he sensed a darkening presence ahead, like the mouth of a door. The frail light of the open sky disappeared as he extended the next step, afraid of losing his footing.

Steps. Steep and slippery. "Careful, now."

Amir was not sure if it was Makun-kunj or Sibil-kunj who spoke.

"Only a hundred of them."

Amir groaned. "Listen, you are mistaken. I have been sent here by Fylan."

This halted the footfalls. Although Amir could not see, he sensed his captors' eyes narrowing at him. "Pray, what did you say?"

"I said, Fylan sent me."

"Did he say Fylan, Sibil-kunj?"

"I believe he did. Do you think we should ask him?"

Amir called upon his patience. "Ask me what?"

Silence for the next few seconds while he teetered at the edge of a step, sensing the hollowness beneath him and the dank walls around him, as though he were in a vast cylindrical shaft, drilled into the mountain.

"What is he like?" Makun-kunj asked.

Amir's eyebrow nearly escaped the blindfold's rim. "What is—*what*?"

"He is always elusive, isn't he, Sibil-kunj? Oh, we would wait for his patrols in the night, and we would have our little wagers over what we would wear. He looked at me once, he did. Never at you, Sibil-kunj, ha! Never at you."

"But he did talk to me," Sibil-kunj countered, helping Amir down a step. Overhead, he could still hear the whirl of the wind as it blasted across the opening.

"He borrowed a pipe from you, is all. I was there. He never raised his eye." They began to tug Amir lower, and each step delivered a fresh stock of fear.

"And yet, my privilege stands above yours," Sibil-kunj said. "I would much rather have his voice than his eyes. It is more . . . personal."

"The eyes do not lie. But the mouth can. And will."

"The mouth can express the depth of one's heart. The eyes, however . . ."

Amir coughed to interrupt their banter, lowering his foot onto the next step in trepidation. "Did you say four thousand one hundred and twelve years? You know, earlier?"

Another moment's silence. "Well, you're the first one since then whom we've caught," Sibil-kunj said. "The other one, well. He comes and goes, but we are instructed to leave him and his kind be. Not that we *could* do anything if we wanted to. He always . . . scares us."

Their voices echoed through the hollow space. Amir took a deep breath and threw a more direct question at them: "Do you mean *you* have been around for that long?"

Amir dreaded the answer. Impossibilities somersaulted in his stomach. Sweat clinging to the kerchief spilled out and soiled his cheek. Four thousand years? What was this place? Who were these people? What had he gotten himself into in his desperation?

Makun-kunj pressed Amir's shoulder. "What do you mean, *that long*? Are you presuming to call me old?"

Amir hesitated, placing the question in the repository of absurd thoughts he had been entertaining over the past several hours. If he wanted answers, he'd have to be more respectful of all that now frightened him. The horror of age would have to be tempered.

"No, of course not. I was just curious."

The deeper they descended, the stiffer the air became. If this was Illindhi, he was not impressed. Already he felt deceived, and his arguments were worth a pail of filth. Neither Sibil-kunj nor Makun-kunj were interested in anything more than Fylan's biceps and mustache, and lent their rapt attentions only when Amir started to describe the battle on the stairs of the Halmoran palace.

"There was never a doubt," they exclaimed in unison. "The Uyirsena themselves train under his tutelage. He is a shadow, a force of nature that cannot be opposed or harmed. He is sculpted in iron, molded like a hammer is forged in the bellies of the deep caves, and there is nothing that isn't accomplished once he has set his mind to it."

"He's—" Amir paused, the word "dead" hanging at the cliff's edge of his lips. He pulled it back. Perhaps it could wait.

"He is, indeed. A warrior," he muttered instead, resigning to be the hider of truths, the keeper of secrets.

He recalled Fylan's warning that the Uyirsena were being readied. Fylan had trained them, and if what Amir had witnessed outside the palace of Halmora was any indication of the kind of warrior he was, he shuddered to imagine what an army trained under him could accomplish. Karim bhai had spoken of armies—of thousands of soldiers marching against another army, with only one aim—to kill. The thought sent ripples of unrest through Amir. Was that what awaited the eight kingdoms? Was that the price of knowing the secret of olum?

Amir, once again, had the queasy feeling of something he couldn't fully comprehend. Although perhaps he wouldn't need to. It wasn't his problem. What he had was a nudge from a stranger, a pinprick of hope after being certain he had lost everything in the forested courtroom of Halmora, and an overwhelming desire to not be imprisoned by Hasmin.

More than anything, the Poison was within his grasp, and he was not going to let the opportunity pass. Only three days in which to return to Raluha, he reminded himself, before Kabir would be conscripted for his first day of duty.

At one point, Amir thrust his foot forward, expecting the next step, and found flat ground. They had reached the bottom. Amir attempted to grasp for some support but remembered with a moan that his hands were tied.

A grinding noise ahead. The sound of scrunching twigs. The shifting of stones. In the utter darkness, he lent his ear to every syllable of sound.

The two guards led him across a flat path riddled with pebbles, through what must have been the heart of the mountain. After a point, it began to get hotter. Amir experienced a churning in his stomach, a heap of bile threatening to rush out.

"Am I a criminal then?" Amir asked, swallowing the urge.

The guards took a moment to respond. "We're not certain of the nature of your crime yet. The Chairs will wring out the truth from you, make no mistake. But you are different, we must admit. You claim to know Fylan, and that alone gives you the benefit of the doubt. Don't you think so, Sibil-kunj?"

"But a ruffian he looks and seems. And maybe that's what we had to be, Makun-kunj. Ruffians. To fall under Fylan's gaze."

Amir shook his head, wondering if there was ever a conversation that wouldn't circle back to Fylan between his immortal fawns.

"Maybe because I know Fylan, you could at least cut my hands loose?" he asked. "I promise I won't run away. I doubt I'll get far even if I do."

Sibil-kunj's breath tickled Amir's nape. A long minute later, Amir's hands were released after an unscrambling of knots. He sighed in relief. "Thank you."

"Trust comes only for a few, intruder. You would do well to remember that."

They forged on. Ahead, something gave halt to Amir's steps. The ground began to tremble, slowly at first, and then with greater urgency. He heard the sound of scraping stones, of sediments from the ceiling dirtying his hair, and in the deep distance the faint murmur of thumping footfalls. When he touched the stone walls, the vibration of the mountain hummed within him. The beating of drums.

A horn echoed through the cavern.

Neither Makun-kunj nor Sibil-kunj seemed to be bothered by the disturbance, muttering between themselves. But if you were over four thousand years old, Amir supposed, not a lot would irk you. The thought of four casual millennia being shared between these two continued to stifle his hold on reality. *Four thousand*. Amir had thought Karim bhai, well over sixty, was old.

He heard voices following the horn. Not a conversation, but a collective, harmonic thrum of words. It echoed across the distance with some ferocity. The sounds emerged from farther ahead and below.

Within minutes, the voices were accompanied by footfalls, a synchronized march of several columns of people. Amir heard the grounding of pikes and the stomping of boots. Someone was shouting orders. Several someones.

Unable to resist, he let Makun-kunj and Sibil-kunj take a couple of steps ahead before he raised his blindfold and gazed down.

His jaw dropped.

Sprawled beneath the narrow bridge they were now standing on, occupying an enormous cavern was . . . a group of warriors of a size he'd never imagined. *This* was an army? When Karim bhai had spoken of war, Amir had assumed there to be a crowd of people. Perhaps a few hundred.

Down in this hollow mountain, there had to be at least a thousand men and women, their bodies covered in saffron armor and mail, with gauntlets on their wrists; swords, sickles, and axes in their hands; marked helms on their heads; and boots on their feet. There was a frightening discipline to them, a pulverizing coat of synchronization in the way they moved—*trained*—in tandem. It was their stomping that shook the mountain. The tips of their weapons glistened against the strange firelight in the cavern, not emanating from torches or candlesticks but from *behind* the walls, through cracks and crevices, slits and holes. The light seeped out in shades of blue and orange, a miasmic glow that darkened and brightened alternatively like a throbbing, pulsing cabochon.

Clinging to the sides of the cavern were beasts of a kind Amir had never seen. They resembled dogs, but they were five times the size of any mutt Amir had encountered in the Bowl, with sharp claws and drooling, saw-toothed mouths that seemed in perpetual hunger. They were tied to icy spikes of the cavern jutting out of the floor with heavy chains, and they rested on their haunches, their bodies heaving. Were these the thornwolves Karim bhai spoke of, rumored to haunt the Outerlands? One of the Immortal Sons . . .

Amir gulped and averted his gaze. *Just stories, just stories.*

Against the glow of the light within the walls themselves, Amir watched the Uyirsena of Illindhi train for battle, the air filled with their stomping and war cries.

Make no mistake, this is an army trained to kill.

"Their time is coming," Makun-kunj said prophetically.

"They will make their mothers and fathers proud, and of course the Mouth," Sibil-kunj said from a few feet ahead. "Not every generation is given this chance to Cleanse."

"Cleanse?" Amir asked, teeth clattering and a rush of piss waiting to be released that he barely held in.

"The Uyirsena are bred for one purpose, intruder, and that is to preserve what we are and how we choose to be. They are trained to exterminate."

He froze in his step. "Exterminate whom?"

"Ah." Makun-kunj clapped his hands, nudging Amir ahead once more. "The Chairs would be better suited to answer that for you."

Before Amir could respond, the ground underneath began to sway, and Makun-kunj—worried for Amir—clasped his hand and shrieked. "You lied!"

Amir had forgotten to replace the blindfold. Following a slap to his face, Makun-kunj retied the kerchief around Amir's head. For the rest of the journey, Amir complained little, instead filling his mind with the prospect of the monstrosity he had just witnessed setting out for the eight kingdoms. This was what Fylan had *not* wanted, what he had begged for Amir to go to Illindhi and prevent. If Fylan had wished to keep the stranger in Harini's court from leaking the secret of olum, why would he be so insistent this army not be sent to stop her?

Once again, the gaps in what Amir knew overwhelmed him. He was floundering in darkness.

When his feet landed on roughhewn stone once more, Amir heaved a sigh of relief, knowing he was no longer on that narrow bridge. Within moments, the sounds of the Uyirsena dwindled as Amir, Makun-kunj, and Sibil-kunj burrowed into another opening, the darkness scattering out of the blindfold replaced by the orange flicker of torches.

By the time Amir smelled open air, and the warm breeze that carried the scent of trees and flowers, his feet had numbed, his back was on the verge of detaching from the rest of his body, and his throat ached for anything liquid. He broke down and crawled in the dark to whatever mound of stone he could find on the slopes outside the mountain. There he lay, panting, massaging his thighs, and rubbing his knee. Makun-kunj and Sibil-kunj stood nearby, permitting him his blind recuperation.

Maybe all of this had been a mistake. Amir had hoped to be rewarded for his courage in the face of the unknown in carrying Fylan's message. Instead, he had not only lost his sight but was making his way to some kind of hearing where he could well be sentenced. How was this any better than being dragged by Hasmin into the Pyramid's prison? All told, he was as foolish as fools came.

He tried to regard the slope through the blindfold, imagining the fresh colors of the sky and the earth, presently mingling and morphing within the cloth, in layers of darkness. And slowly, as he sat up, he heard the sound of hoofbeats and the tumble of wheels, and with it came the unforgettable aroma of saffron and mace.

The chariot seemed to stop at the foot of the mountain. He heard someone jump out of it and stride up the slope to where he lay, where they exchanged a few words with Makun-kunj and Sibil-kunj in a tongue Amir did not understand. He could smell a heady scent of honeyed sweetness with a floating hint of pungency, as though the breeze were battling an old foe.

The figure approached him, a third shadow, and crouched beside him.

When their hands grazed his face, Amir winced. Their touch was soft, laden with promise. It smelled of musk and honey, and a deep lacing of nutmeg. A hint of aloe in the face and shikakai in the hair. There was something else about the hand that he could not weave into a word. His memory choked and shut down. Instead, his mouth opened of its own accord, sensing its role to play, and absorbed the magical taste of water as it swam over his tongue and down his throat. He gulped until he could drink no more.

"Come," said the voice. Dreamlike, the word enveloped him in her intentions. *A woman's voice. Could this be Madhyra?* She placed a hand on his nose, a piece of cloth—one that reeked of the opium saeveroot—and he at once tried to jerk away. Her hand was firm on the back of his head, though, and he felt her suck the consciousness out of him.

"We need a lot of answers, Carrier, unless you wish to remain in Illindhi forever."

It was all Amir heard before he submitted to the black.

CHAPTER

8

*Show me a home with an empty spice jar, and I will show you
the djinn that has haunted their daughter.*

—*A Spirit Through Each Window of a Dreary Town*

When the cloth came off his eyes—when Amir woke up—the
brilliance of the light blinded him. He found himself curled
on a floor, the touch of it unfamiliar but slick, recently
washed, with a natural, earthy smell. It emitted a silvery glow along the
edges of the marbling as though someone were shining dazzles of moonlight from beneath. His head pounded, so he left that mystery to another
time and was on his way back into the state of unconsciousness he had
been drugged into.

Lights flickered in front of his eyes, keeping him from falling asleep
once more. Blinding lights. Not one. At least four. No, a dozen. A hundred. Glued to a membrane running along the walls in a circle like a great
cummerbund for the chamber he was in. Pale blue light sprayed out of
glass carapaces, the peripheries embedded with rubies and topazes.
Mirrors were spaced between them, so that wherever he looked, he saw
his own reflection, the ruffles of his hair and the vacancy in his eyes.
Not quite what a man who came to help should look like.

A cavern full of the Poison, Fylan had said. But where? Could it be where the Uyirsena are training?

Two suits of armor stood near a door, their faces resting under candle-light, armed with a spear and a sword. Above, the gnarled wall tapered to form a dome, the keystone bathed in darkness, and for a moment it looked to Amir like he was inside a great tree.

A cough. Murmurs from ahead. *Above.* "Rise, Amir of Raluha. You are in the chamber of the Chairs."

He struggled to stand. Bones cracked and revolted against the attempt. He felt like he had swallowed a cow and was then asked to run. With an effort, Amir managed to crane his neck at the dais in front, a series of six rock protrusions that jutted out of the floor like gigantic fingers of a hand. Atop each of them, surrounded by embroidered drapes, he glimpsed silhouettes, faces and bodies leashed to the shadows, their arms resting on what appeared to be cushions and diwans. The contours of the figure at the center, however, seemed familiar, and he couldn't help but inhale, expecting a flow of honeysuckle and musk up his nose.

With a groan, the rock pillar shifted ahead. Only a step, almost a trick of the eye, but he swore it did. The woman's face emerged from shadow, revealing her in a stark violet gown and a pruned bottom, with lemon leaves creeping out to envelop her ankles. A crown rested on her head, diaphanous, like a molded froth of lather, the wings clipping her ears. Her eyes seemed darker, dabbed in mascara, while her lips re-mained guarded, as though they would open to speak only to the most privileged.

Amir squinted to look behind her at the five other pillars and the silhouettes upon them. He must have seemed like a pitiable creature to them, barely able to stand, throat parched and every joint in his body aching and on the brink of yielding.

It was rather annoying how Karim bhai had overstated the whole affair with messengers and how they were treated in other kingdoms.

"Can I get something to eat?" he asked, and because he could no longer tolerate this treatment meted out to him, he added with a sneer,

"A plate of bisibelle bath, perhaps?" His voice bounced off the walls like a threat. He avoided looking at himself in the mirrors, but they were everywhere, portraying him in cracked and distorted forms, diminishing him to a boneless figure.

The woman not in shadows said, "You already ate." Her voice, on another day, could have been a remedy for the worst ailment that afflicted him.

Amir frowned, puzzled. "I don't remember eating."

"We fed you a meal while you were unconscious the last two days and then delirious for one. Suffice it to say, any hunger you feel now is merely a lack of awareness in your head. A trick of the mind."

Amir's heart thundered in his chest. "*Three* days?"

It meant . . . *Kabir!* Amir scrambled up from where he lay on the floor, the panic surging. "Wh-Why did you keep me unconscious for so long?"

"The Chair," the woman replied, "had to convene in your absence and discuss your intrusion. You fail to realize that you are the first outsider in Illindhi for a long, long time."

Amir's mind raged. All he could imagine was Hasmin leading Kabir down the saffron fields, loading his back with glassware or victuals or saffron stalks or jars of honey then sending him through the Gate . . .

A grumble in his stomach shook him away from that dreadful thought. A trouble that was no less pernicious than the others—that of having eaten several meals without the knowledge of them. And, rather importantly, not knowing what he'd eaten.

Amir took a pause before asking, "You are Madhyra, aren't you?"

"No," she replied, and Amir wished he could reclaim his educated guess.

"My name is Kashyni, of the Circle of Leaves. I am the stewardess of Illindhi, ruling in place of our thronekeeper, Maharani Madhyra."

A thronekeeper? "Where is Madhyra? F-Fylan told me I should speak to no one else."

A hint of discomfort rippled within the other silhouettes. A whisper sliced the dark air between the pedestals like a scythe's blade. Kashyni sighed, glancing to either side at her elevated companions before refocusing her gaze on him.

"She is a traitor," she said coldly. "Who took our olum and crossed the Spice Gate into Halmora, threatening to reveal its knowledge to the eight kingdoms. It is after her that we sent Fylan—to bring her back, or if that did not succeed, then to kill her. Where is Fylan?"

A flurry of thoughts clattered into Amir's head, jumbled into a knot, and came out, bruised and tattered, like several drunks stumbling out of a tavern together.

Thronekeeper. "But—"

"I ordered Fylan to give Madhyra's name to anyone whom he trusted to carry a message back were he to fail. Only then could we separate Madhyra's spies from our own. And she has quite a few, as many in the eight kingdoms as in Illindhi. I now repeat, where is Fylan?"

Amir gulped. "He's dead. He asked me to come to Illindhi before he died."

Silence on the pillars. Amir shifted uncomfortably beneath them, awaiting the Chairs' proclamation. Perhaps, his purpose would hold more sway now that he had arrived to fulfill a dying man's wish.

And to get the Poison, don't forget that.

Kashyni was the first to break the spell of quiet. "It was not entirely unforeseen. We have prepared for this contingency."

Amir didn't know what to make of that, and—more—had no desire to interrogate them on their workings. He'd already landed on the wrong side of bewilderment, and this quest for normalcy was a dying breath, one he did not wish to waste on people who weren't even looking at him.

A second silhouette—to Kashyni's right—moved to adjust themselves and spoke. "He looks barely twenty."

"When I was twenty, I had pulled far greater stunts," a third silhouette said with a giggle from a pedestal to Kashyni's left, a little farther behind.

A fourth shadow—twice as far away from Kashyni to the left—chuckled. "Your stunts were academic, Munivarey. I don't remember you plucking up the courage to pass through the Spice Gate and out of Illindhi."

"Oh, I dreamed of it! Only, I wasn't permitted. Don't you put this on me, Shashulyan. Kashyni, back me up! How can you just sit and listen to this?"

The softer but rickety voice of the second silhouette spoke up. "This is ridiculous. Whatever are we considering? The boy needs to be sent back to his homeland at once."

Amir could have snapped his neck with how vigorously he nodded at that. Was she the one who would defend him?

"Ho," agreed another Chair, and Amir was losing track of who was speaking. He sensed a commotion as murmurs exploded into more flickering shadows and bobbing heads. The rickety voice beside Kashyni persisted. "He could have chosen not to bring Fylan's words here, but he did. We would have been floundering in the dark if not for his decision. Has anybody thought of that? This is an insult and is unfair. The Chair stands for justice."

Amir watched Kashyni lift her palm to her forehead and close her eyes. The others were, however, relentless.

"Send him back? Armed with the knowledge of Illindhi? This would be the beginning of the downfall of the realm's greatest kingdom. As if Madhyra wasn't doing enough already."

"Look at him, Shashulyan! He's a child."

Shashulyan snarled. "Alinjya, it is not a question of age. The Spice Trade is at a risk of severe imbalance. The first and only law of the land is that there is absolute status quo in the trade. It ceases to exist if we reveal ourselves. Our purpose is to bring Madhyra back, or even kill her if we must. Without *anyone* knowing. And yet now, there is another who can very well go back through the Gate and talk. Clove's breath, it's preposterous that we're even considering it."

"But we *are* considering it. Who would believe him, should we send him back?" replied Alinjya. "He would be like a naked suckling, his words carrying as much weight as those of a blabbering drunk dragging himself down the street having forgotten his way home. Haven't we witnessed enough deranged souls in the past who were spared by the Uyirsena? What have they amounted to if not to become delusional prophets?"

"What then, once Madhyra's truth begins to spread? This boy's words will serve to corroborate a bubbling rumor. Do you not foresee how this can magnify and come back to bite us? I'm sorry, Alinjya, but this time, my morality forbids me to participate in this discourse. The Chairs were raised to prevent this from happening. For centuries, we simmered under the surface, biding our time, waiting for the inevitability that someone out there would leak our secret to the realm. Years of silence and darkness. And when it finally is the time for our purpose to be fulfilled, you wish to be reckless and abandon the very principles of the Chairs? I cannot stand for this. And Kashyni, I do not expect you to either. The boy cannot be sent back."

The giggling male voice, the man named Munivarey, squabbled for attention, silencing Shashulyan. "Leave him to me, Kashyni," he said. "Maybe I can scrub something off him before you decide to drop him down the Mouth in a coffin of peppers. If he is indeed a Spice Carrier, then I wish to record his experience and his sensations at the very least."

There was a sudden whip of silence that made Amir aware of the fact that shadows had eyes, scrawny blobs of reduced darkness pointed at him. In that inescapable moment, the hairs on the back of his hands stood erect.

When he thought it couldn't get worse, a fifth voice, belonging to the greatest of the shadow dwellers away from Kashyni, came forth. It stirred like a beast awakening from a slumber. The voice was melodious and deep.

"People fail to realize that curiosity is often the greatest of all sins. The boy is not here because he was commanded."

"You do not rain your judgment upon this person because he was *curious*, Mahrang," Alinjya said.

The baritone-voiced Mahrang ignored her, his silhouette like a dark loaf of bread. "Until today, we were lesser than a figment of his imagination, an impossibility. Eight kingdoms, never nine. His innocence goes only as far as fate placed him on those palace grounds, and for Fylan to plead a request of him, inches away from his death. There, this man's innocence dies. Beyond that, his choices have been born out of an inclination to do something few would do in his place. Do you disagree?"

"But," argued Alinjya, "we stand to gain from his choice."

Amir wanted to buy Alinjya all the saffron enameled garlands from the streets on Raluha and stuff her mouth with all the vadas Amma could conjure. This faceless one who fought for his freedom. He stole a glance at Kashyni, who seemed intent on bringing about some order to the discussion, but she was left clutching at the tails of words and their ghosts.

Mahrang leaned forward in his chair, and for the first time Amir saw his chin fall under the candlelight, a beard wriggling beneath thin lips. He addressed Amir. "Why are you truly here, child of the Mouth?"

Child of the Mouth? He didn't know what that meant, and wasn't sure he wanted to. But it didn't seem like his situation could be any worse. *In for a pinch of spice, in for a jar . . .*

He took a deep breath and gazed up at the shadows, at the pinpricks that were eyes.

"I . . . I came here because I need the Poison."

Murmurs dribbled across the Chairs once more. Amir could sense the tension on the pedestal, and Kashyni's stunned face peering down at him. Was she disappointed in his purpose? Did she feel cheated? Amir did not care at that point. What he wanted was the Poison, and he'd delivered Fylan's message as payment for it.

"Fylan told me to stop you from releasing the Uyirsena," he added as an incentive to bolster his case.

"Did he now?" Mahrang growled. "He swore by the laws of the Mouth. And he disobeys them now? Tell me, what reason did he give for recommending this course of action?"

Amir gulped, his cheeks hardening. "H-He said Madhyra was . . . luring you, and not to fall for her ploy. H-He said she was counting on you to send the Uyirsena."

Mahrang's shadow writhed. "Manipulation!" he bellowed, his voice echoing across the chamber. "Lies." But even Amir sensed a certain trepidation in Mahrang's voice, as though his mind were fighting two battles.

"He sounded quite serious," Amir said softly, with folded hands, careful not to look up. "And in his defense . . . he was dying, saheb. He had nothing to lose."

Just like you.

Kashyni lowered her head and closed her eyes momentarily, as though she had not yet recovered from the news of Fylan's death.

Alinjya clapped her hands. "There! See reason, Mahrang. Fylan was the best of us. Why would he send a Carrier of the eight kingdoms if he did not truly think we must hold back? As a servant of the Mouth, it is preposterous to assume that he would do anything to jeopardize it."

Shashulyan, who had initially wanted Amir to be apprehended, spoke again. "Madhyra is well aware of the laws that govern the Uyirsena. She is our thronekeeper, after all. She knows how long we must hold back before the Uyirsena can be released. Knowing this, if she has overstayed her time, it could be that Fylan is right, and Madhyra *wants* us to send the Uyirsena. But for what purpose? Is it bloodshed she seeks? Is this the kind of woman we have been serving beneath? I refuse to believe so."

Mahrang scoffed. "Does it matter? She betrayed the Mouth. We knew her intentions since the day she met that wretched man, Sukalyan. I warned you, Kashyni, that such a day might come, and yet you stood for keeping Madhyra on the throne."

Alinjya offered, "It is possible she has had trouble with the recipe. Kashyni, you are certain she did not get a single ounce of coriander leaves?"

"Not a pinch," Kashyni confirmed, her voice reduced to a pitiable murmur. "I had the warehouses guarded by the Uyirsena themselves. If Madhyra has to convince the eight kingdoms of the powers of olum, she will need to harvest the coriander leaves on her own."

Coriander leaves. Amir had heard of the rare herb, even tasted it on one occasion—the previous Bashara. And if Madhyra had to harvest any decent quantity of it, she'd have a hard time doing it in the eight kingdoms without attracting attention. Yet, the thought gnawed at the back of his head. He was forgetting something . . .

"All the more reason why we must dispatch the Uyirsena *before* she succeeds," Mahrang countered. "Are we to sit back and watch while she flounders in strange territory with our secret? Our scriptures stipulate one mooncycle to allow our allies to recover the knowledge before it is spread. We're at the cusp of that mooncycle now. You're asking me to put all of Illindhi at risk."

Kashyni took a deep breath. "Fylan *must* have had a reason. I know my husband."

This explained her silent suffering. Always an ill omen, the bowlers would say, to carry the news of another's death to the families. In some distant, crude way, Amir supposed he could sympathize with Kashyni. If he thought about it, Fylan had been the only one who'd actually gotten Amir closer to the Poison, even if it was to serve his own means.

Kashyni wiped a tear from her face and stiffened to reclaim her role as the chief of the Chairs. "He must have figured out what Madhyra was truly planning, if these were his words. Sending the Uyirsena would be . . . the religious move and as per the law, but if we can avoid it, we must. It is the lives of tens of thousands of people at stake, Mahrang. Of the balance of the Spice Trade itself."

"I agree," Alinjya said. "Unless Fylan knew what Madhyra was up to, why would he specifically ask us to *not* send the Uyirsena? We're missing something, Mahrang, and it would be on all of our consciences to commit to such an atrocity only later to realize our haste."

"Hear, hear," Munivarey giggled. He alone Amir couldn't place on this spectrum in terms of what he truly wanted.

A word, however, rang in his ears, knotted itself in his throat. *Atrocity.* "Wait—what do you mean the lives of tens of thousands of—"

"Carrier," Mahrang said, raising his voice, interrupting Amir. "It is the Poison you seek?"

Amir found himself faltering. "Yes, but—"

"Then you shall have it."

"But what did you mean by tens of thous—" Amir blinked. "Wait, *what?*"

Mahrang leaned forward on his pedestal, his chin appearing once more in faint candlelight. From the corners of his eyes, he regarded his companions on the Chairs. Kashyni appeared ready to defy him, as did the silhouette of Alinjya. The broader silhouette of Munivarey appeared ambivalent.

"If Fylan truly believes we can harbor hope, I will respect his belief. But I will not sit back and wait for that hope to manifest. Hear me, Kashyni. I am not going to sit here while the Mouth is threatened by a traitor, even if she is our thronekeeper.

"You, Carrier," Mahrang continued, almost prophetic in his voice. "If you truly need the Poison, you shall have it."

Amir's head shot up. Something akin to a bubble rose in his chest, and he thought he was floating, soaring, *smiling.* Gates, was this what good news felt like?

Mahrang inclined his head forward further. "But first, you will go back to the eight kingdoms and stop Madhyra." And quietly, he added, "For the sake of us all."

A shower of pins rained on Amir, pricking the bubble, sending him crashing down.

Immediately, a clamor of voices rose among the Chairs. Alinjya was furious. Munivarey's laughter was loud and boisterous. Shashulyan was irate, and he raised his hands as though he'd had enough of the day.

When the argument simmered down, Amir decided he would never get a chance to speak if he didn't break his way into their circle. "Listen, saheb, please." The clamor ceased. Mahrang looked down at him. Amir's insides squirmed, Mahrang's words still pounding in his head like a hammer. "I can't do this. I may be a lowly thief, but for certain I'm no killer. I . . . I just want a vial of the Poison for my mother, to take her and my brother to the coves beyond Jhanak and live out the rest of our lives. I care little of this . . . this ninth kingdom, or olum . . . or what your thronekeeper plans to do. I care little of war. Please . . . just give me a vial. That's all I ask."

Mahrang leaned in deeper, and his entire face came into view. He had a pale, coarse face, like a Meshti miner's, with high cheekbones and a crooked nose, and eyes sharp as a sword. "You wish to abandon your duty as a Carrier?"

Slowly, realizing lying would not gain him anything, Amir nodded.

The murmur of voices rushed back. Mahrang raised his hands to silence them. "You disrespect the Mouth with your words, Carrier. You shirk from what you are born to do. The warriors of the Uyirsena and I— we have dedicated our lives to guarding and serving the Mouth. It is our purpose, as Carrying is yours. And yet . . . and yet . . ."

Amir wanted to speak, but Mahrang once again put up a hand and stopped him. "I will permit you your little indulgence away from your duties. I will permit you to forsake what you were born for, and never be a Carrier again in your life. However, you will have to stop Madhyra. Bring her to me, alive or dead, and buy your freedom and the freedom of your family."

The protests blurted out of Amir's mouth before he could contain his passion. "I *cannot*. I . . . I am not a part of this . . . this problem you have. I am not a soldier, saheb. I am not one of those warriors training in that mountain. I don't know how to fight, not like Fylan did, not like anyone. I am only a man who wants to give his people a better life. Or at least, my family."

"You will not be alone," Mahrang offered as a bargain. "An acolyte of the Uyirsena will accompany you, to aid you in your quest."

Having seen them train, Amir wondered what it'd be like to walk beside one such warrior. It did not entirely erase his reluctance. His hesitancy was only confirmed when Mahrang continued. "They will also see to it that you do not expend our secret to the eight kingdoms. If you do, you and anyone the secret is uttered to will be killed."

The blood drained from Amir's face. A paleness engulfed him and sank into his voice, so what came out resembled a pleading croak. "This is . . . unfair. I came as a messenger, and with a request that you can easily satisfy. *One* vial of the Poison. Just one."

"You will be rewarded with a barrel of it should you wish," Mahrang argued passionately. "Do this task on behalf of the kingdom of Illindhi, and much will be yours."

Amir scoffed. "You make it seem like I have no other choice. The Jewelmaker will reappear sooner or later, and then I will have found my way."

Munivarey's giggle was almost instantaneous. Alinjya silenced him. After a tense moment that threatened to stretch infinitely, Mahrang's voice cut the pervading silence like a knife—but not in anger.

Rather, it came in derisive mirth.

Amir looked around, unsure what was so amusing, when Mahrang spoke again. "I thought you would have understood your situation, Carrier, when you witnessed the light glowing off the caverns of Mount Ilom, where the Uyirsena train. The Poison is made here. And I?" He leaned forward. "*I* am the Jewelmaker."

A strange ache scourged Amir's heart, as though hope were something tangible, like a vein within his chest, and it was suddenly yanked out and cast aside.

Mahrang smiled, though there was little warmth in it. "*I* stopped the supply to the eight kingdoms after Madhyra escaped from Illindhi. And you're at *my* mercy if you ever wish to lay a hand on the Poison anywhere in the eight kingdoms."

Amir's world collapsed on itself. Mahrang . . . the Jewelmaker. It suddenly fell into place. How else could one build this terrible army in the mountain if not with the money earned from selling the Poison across the eight kingdoms. Nobody knew the Jewelmaker's true identity. He'd always been a shadow, a ghost riding the caravan at the front, encased in a cloud of spice. The eight kingdoms had been the Jewelmaker's—Mahrang's—puppets, and he their silent puppeteer.

Above all, this meant Harini had not duped the caravan for the Poison. She was not the reason the Jewelmaker had ceased its supply. Of that, at least, she was innocent.

With so much whirling around him, the one thought Amir had was that he ought to apologize to her for suspecting her of colluding with the Jewelmaker.

Mahrang spoke again. "The way I see it, *Carrier*, is that the Chairs and I are armed with three options. The first is that the Uyirsena leave at dawn tomorrow to the eight kingdoms as per the laws. Their minds are tethered to the Mouth. They will know of anyone who is privy to the secret of olum and Illindhi, and they will plunge their blades into the throats of each of them—man, woman, or child—in order to cull Madhyra's ambitions."

"You're killers," Amir gasped. "That is genocide."

Mahrang did not pay heed to his cries. "Our second choice is that you accomplish the task you have been given. If you succeed, there needn't be any bloodshed, and the knowledge of Illindhi shall have been preserved. You will be given the Poison—as reward or payment—and you can do with it what you wish. If you fail, I will give no longer than a fortnight, at the end of which we will dispatch the Uyirsena nevertheless to complete what you had begun.

"Our final choice is to respect your assessment that you're no warrior, and that you do not wish to go up against Madhyra. However, that would mean we cannot send you back to your home. Instead, you will remain here as a citizen of Illindhi."

"'Remain'? You mean I'll be imprisoned here."

"However you wish to see it. You could choose to be an upstanding citizen of Illindhi, but for all purposes, yes, you will never see your home again, nor your family. You will never be allowed henceforth to leave the kingdom. And the Uyirsena, as before, would be dispatched at the end of a fortnight, in consideration of Fylan's dying wish.

"There is one choice that keeps the Uyirsena here in Illindhi forever. One that prevents what you call *genocide*. The choice, Carrier, is yours."

"Why does it have to be me?" Amir argued.

"Because," Mahrang explained patiently, as though it were not already obvious, "you're the only Carrier we have at our disposal who is armed with the knowledge of Illindhi. We cannot ask anyone else. Besides, you should be proud. No outsider who knows of Illindhi has ever lived to tell the tale. You will be the first . . . if you succeed."

"He's a child, Mahrang," Alinjya said once more. "A boy no older than twenty, and, as he admitted, possesses no fighting ability. You will send *him* to stop Madhyra? A thronekeeper? Unreasonable! Since when have the Chairs resorted to such foolishness?" She turned in her seat. "Kashyni, your silence disgusts me."

Kashyni scowled. "Do not mistake my silence for cowardice, Alinjya. What would you have me do? Blindly heed Fylan? Yes, I trust him. I trust him enough to consider his pleas. Madhyra wanting us to release the Uyirsena on purpose sounds farfetched but plausible, though for what reason I do not know. Can she be so cruel? I . . . do not know. But I agree with Mahrang. *Someone* needs to act. And the choices given to this boy are all we have. It is a fair judgment, and I have nothing further to say on this matter."

Shashulyan sounded irate. "You all keep speaking of choices, but there is no choice! He *cannot* be allowed to leave Illindhi. He is consumed by the knowledge of Illindhi, and we plot to send him back to the eight kingdoms, armed with this secret? You are fools to even entertain this, as surely he will be our downfall sooner than Madhyra."

Mahrang was scathing in his reply. "If he stops Madhyra for us, he has earned his release, Shashulyan. Not before. And he now knows what the consequence shall be if he chooses to let the knowledge of Illindhi and olum slip. The Mouth *always* knows. What say you, Kashyni? You must make the final proclamation."

Shashulyan threw what appeared to be a towel and disappeared into the darkness. The towel floated down from the pedestal and landed a few feet away from Amir.

Kashyni took what seemed to be an age to respond. When she spoke, Amir could tell she had made up her mind. He recalled the smell of musk and sandalwood, and the soothing, honeyed voice of hers that now resonated through the Hall of Chairs.

"If the Carrier so accepts, he will be sent back to the eight kingdoms, under the conditions that Mahrang, of the Circle of Swords, and the High Priest of the Uyirsena, has specified. Carrier, do you accept?"

Amir, in that moment, experienced a strange sensation of being not too far from the Mouth. The Mouth that he had dismissed as his guardian, as the entity the other bowlers prayed to with fear, without whose invocation not a single grain of spice would trade in the markets—it was that presence he felt around him there, in that chamber, or perhaps beneath it. Gates, could the Mouth really tell who knew about Illindhi and who didn't?

He was certain, however, it wouldn't take a keen eye for Mahrang and his Uyirsena to tell that *Harini* knew. Kashyni was aware that Madhyra had gone to Halmora. Harini would be the first one the Uyirsena would sink their blades into. A weight settled in his chest. And after Harini? How much longer would they take to discover he'd told Karim bhai everything?

More, if Amir declined Mahrang's offer, he would remain here, in Illindhi, for the rest of his life. And from the way Mahrang was staring at him, Amir was not hopeful of an escape.

By now his brother would have crossed the Spice Gate and realized what Amir had meant all those years ago about pain. He would stumble and fall and raise his head as a whip lashed his back and a scar traced his spine, the blood congealing as the days passed, and never be soothed by the slurs that he'd surely receive from the mouths of the abovefolk. Hasmin wouldn't care if it was Amir or Kabir. The whips and the slurs would fall just the same, as long as the spices made their way through the Gates.

And Amma . . . his father had abandoned her all those years ago, and now Amir—by the virtue of his own choices—would be doing the same. She'd give birth to a child who would be taken care of by Kabir as he, Amir, had raised his little brother.

And how many years did Karim bhai have to live that he would watch over Amir's family?

If there was faint solace, it was in those narrow, sharp eyes of Mahrang's that had spoken nothing but the truth. Of all he'd learned today, he was certain: Mahrang wasn't lying, neither about the consequences nor the promised reward. If Amir did what was asked, Mahrang would truly give him the Poison and release him and his family from their burden. Of that bleak possibility Amir was sure, and the thought clung to him like a blanket on the coldest of nights.

He gazed up at Kashyni and Mahrang, and at the still-unknown faces of Alinjya and Munivarey.

Finally, he said, "Yes. I don't seem to have a choice, but let's assume for a moment I do. So . . . yes."

Alinjya withdrew into darkness, followed closely by Mahrang, until only Kashyni and the squat silhouette of Munivarey remained. A giggle ensued, forcing Kashyni to glance sideways at her companion.

"Does it mean I get him until he leaves?" Munivarey asked.

"Whatever for?"

"Well, the false gate isn't going to work by itself, Kashyni. And I'd much rather not waste the opportunity."

Kashyni sighed and waved her hand. "Go. Take him."

Amir squinted at the Chairs. "Wait . . . take me where?"

Munivarey burst into fresh laughter and clapped his hands. "Excellent, excellent! Are you ready, Carrier?"

Amir did not know what to say to that, so he stayed silent, numb, the two silhouettes contorting as they retreated deeper into the shadow of the Chairs.

Without warning, the floor upon which Amir stood opened beneath him, and he dropped into emptiness.

CHAPTER
9

We are what we are addicted to.

—Old Vanasari proverb

The last time he'd experienced blackness in Illindhi, he'd lost three days. He worried that he was about to lose the same amount of time, if not more, as his fall threatened to be endless. Amir's arms flailed beside him, and his cheeks flapped in the current of air as he fell. The passage wound like a burrow, only down at first, then sideways and even up at one point, air gushing out of the earth and propelling him toward the ground. When he tried to stop himself, the burrow ejected him out of a wall and spat him out like a sauce with too much garlic.

He landed on his back, then rolled to a standstill. He was on one side of a large cavern, nearly as large as the one the Uyirsena had been training in. A black dome loomed above him. Faint light shimmered from the walls. He limped closer to it, drawn by its power. Pale blue, like the reflection of sky on water, blinking, flickering, undulating light as though the stone of the walls held sapphires within them that had burst like starlight and oozed out of crevices in faint liquid, as if the pores of the mountain were bleeding this perplexing cerulean blood.

Amir was staring at the Poison.

His heart skipped a beat at the realization. He glanced around. Nobody else in the vast cavern but him; an insect in a forest. He felt dwarfed as he took in the walls of the mountain, the throbbing light, the blue spill that cast everything else in miasmic shadow.

A shape caught his eye in the center of the cavern. Something like a malformation of stone. Amir limped away from the walls and toward this shape. The light scattered across the floor like a vast honeycomb of different colors. Slabs and thorny shards of ice and black metal jutted out of the ground in their hundreds near the walls and grew toward the shape. They broke from the ground and hung from the ceiling and gnashed at each other like angry teeth. An eerie forest of shiny black and pointy pillars nestled in a wider circle of shards of ice. Orange and yellow light radiated from them, dimmed by the wider and brighter blue light of the Poison.

Closer and closer he crept toward the shape, then he froze in his tracks as the shape materialized into clarity.

A Spice Gate.

Excitement frothed up within him. This Gate did not have any of the ancient carvings or inscriptions on its arch. The molten mirror within sizzled and cracked. The base tapered in loose stone and sinuous roots into the ground, gnarls and vines wrapped around it in imitation of the one nestled outside Halmora.

The antiquity of this structure was diminished, somehow. It lacked a *life*, the pulling sensation Amir would typically feel as he stood beside any of the other eight Gates. He thought he was looking at a fake, like gemstones and garnet rings he'd nick for cheap in the night bazaar in Raluha. Yet what was it doing in the heart of this cavern, deep inside this mountain?

At the lowermost step to the gate were several glass cages. The closer Amir got, the queasier he felt. It seemed he was staring at what his own insides would look like. Gathered in bulk, torn, molded, and left to slap against a glass rib cage like gooey tentacles. There were at least a dozen cages filled with these lumps of flesh and bone. Upon closer inspection they were tethered to the roots of the gate, like multiple hands to one monstrous body.

Was this the gate Mahrang used as the Jewelmaker? Was this how he distributed the Poison to eight kingdoms? No. It couldn't be. At every other Gate, Amir sensed the echoes of the Mouth, an eerie whisper inside the veil that he had once attributed to the wind and later to something he realized the other Carriers feared and prayed to.

But if the Mouth truly touched the other Gates in some gnarled fashion, it had left this gate alone. There were no eerie whispers, and even the little connection to the Mouth Amir felt in the Chamber of Chairs had all but dissipated in this vast cavern.

He inched closer to this false gate, thoughts of the Mouth running wild in his head, Mahrang's words beating against his skull.

Not just the Jewelmaker, though. His father's words also surfaced. He had raised his son to look for a pinch of truth in even the strangest of stories. *Nothing truly emerges from darkness, Amir. The kernels of truth gather and gain the appearance of lies in the face of political necessity. But they're never fully lies.*

Even now, the idea disagreed with him as he stared at this dead gate: the Mouth—and within it a spice god, garbed in a veil of saffron—seated on a throne whose apex resembled a star anise, holding the reins of all of the Spice Gates, keeping them *alive*.

In the Bowl, the Mouth was a being to be feared, a force that kept them chained to their fates, their pasts, and the threads of their social limitations woven into the tapestry of an unquestionable scripture. If Appa had been right, then even the usage of the word—the "Mouth"— had to have started somewhere. And here in Illindhi—if this was where the Mouth truly originated—Amir found himself amid those kernels of truth that had mythologized and seeped into their lives in distant Raluha and across the eight kingdoms.

Even as the bowlers feared and prayed to the Mouth, Amir had found the pain of passage prevented him from the devoutness the others shared. But he had not shied away from embracing the myth. He had come to imagine that when he died, he'd be led past the Gates into a Great Kitchen, with a roaring fireplace and meat grilled in skewers and spits, and biryani cooked in a great vat, and the fragrance of spices engulfing him as he was welcomed into death. A life of suffering for a while of spices and dreams, until rebirth. A fair exchange, the bowlers would say.

Except the gatecaste don't get to be reborn. You're the once-born, remember?

Amir had never fully wrapped his mind around this thought, but he couldn't resist basking in the imagined pleasures that would await him one day after a lifetime of carrying.

The longer he stared at the false gate, the more he was certain that there was a real Mouth, which touched the other Spice Gates, which had people like Mahrang and Fylan as its servants, and which, knowingly or unknowingly, was capable of orchestrating this worldly passage between the eight . . . no, nine kingdoms.

He climbed the steps to the false gate, his heart racing. On the last step, he halted, his hands on his hips. He did not have any saffron to spray upon the veil, stir the gate, and take him to Raluha. And as for the Poison, even though he was currently surrounded by it, he had no inkling how to harvest its light into a vial. There was so much he did not know, and that ignorance—itself almost certainly the work of the abovefolk—kept him trapped by these Gates.

One hand on the stone pillar, another shaking on his hip. His hand traced down the stone, through the artificially created crevices that lent it the appearance of something ancient and unbreakable.

A touch wouldn't hurt, he supposed.

The platform quaked.

The molten veil beneath the arch shot out a ray of sparks as Amir's hand came in contact with what he could swear was dead. The sparks arced over his head and landed behind him in the cavern.

Amir tried to back away, but a voice from *within* the gate called to him, and involuntarily, he found himself taking a step forward, into the veil. He heard the voice, not in his ears but coursing through his body, as though carried by his blood. A voice not too unlike what he'd heard when he had sifted through the Gate to Illindhi.

A prick in his body. A swooping sensation. Amir could taste it. The heart of a meal. A biryani in the Bowl for lunch. All of a sudden, he was lifted off his feet, dragged by whatever was powering the gate and into that swirling vortex of air and spice.

The next second, the cavern disappeared. In a flash of images, Amir was transported, not to one but all the Gates at once in repeated blinks of an eye. Halmora, at the periphery of the forest, from where he could see the silhouette of the palace. Jhanak, where he could hear the rush of waves and the rocking sails of moored ships. Mesht, Vanasi, Amarohi, Kalanadi, Talashshukh, and finally, Raluha. The familiar scent of saffron wrapped around him, reviving his decayed memories, nudging him to fall from the gate and rush toward the land of his home.

It ceased, and Amir was once again yanked back by the gate's failing power.

DARKNESS. A FLICKER OF LIGHT. MOVEMENT IN FRONT OF HIS EYES. He had not emerged in any of the eight kingdoms. Nor had he returned to the cavern. He was floating in emptiness, the gate stretching horizontally above him while he stared into an abyss below, surrounded by specks of dust and saffron. The droning voice intensified, as if in that abyss was a great drum whose beats were akin to the beating of a gigantic heart.

The abyss blinked.

Recognition coursed through Amir's veins. He was surprised to see that the Mouth was in torment. A god-beast of a size Amir could not comprehend, which Mahrang and his cult of warriors prayed to, was quivering in its slumber, aching to silence what was trying to break it. Amir wanted to scream, but no sound came out. He could only stare and assimilate. The Mouth was the god and the god was the Mouth, and the abyss, every inch of it layered in flesh of a deep russet, with bone and hide that heaved with each breath.

And Amir floated in the midst of it, like swallowed prey, watching from the edge of a gate that served as the beast's maw. Perhaps this is why they called it the Mouth.

Help.

The voice clawed into Amir all at once like a hundred needles piercing his skin.

You must stop her.

Only once the pain dimmed could he think. Stop who? Madhyra? Could this be an illusion, a false feeling of importance that the Gates fed into the minds of Carriers? Why else would the Mouth be asking *him* for help? And if it was truly doing so, why could it not be less violent? Torturing Amir with needles of pain was hardly an incentive.

And as though the Mouth had heard his thoughts, the pain forced a gasp out of him and ceased. The voice died down in his mind and released its hold on his body. A scent of cinnamon assaulted him, the sweetness plunging into his nose as a mild compensation.

Gah. He'd never liked cinnamon that much.

Amir's limbs were frozen in that space hovering above the Mouth, which expanded and shrunk with each breath. From the pockmarked hides glued to the surface of the vast, dark space, rotten aromas emerged, tainting the fragrance and clouds of spice now circling Amir. *This? This is what the eight kingdoms worship?* Bile rushed up his throat, and he wanted the misery to end. Wherever he was, whatever this was, and whatever it was that he was staring into, he only prayed for it to be a nightmare to be washed away by the cool breeze of a Raluhan morning and the barking of a street dog.

A child of my bosom, a feather of my wing, a morsel of my meal. Save me.

It all happened in an instant. No time to register, let alone allow the fear to envelop him.

Then just as the fear came, it went. Within seconds, he was yanked upward and through the gate, jolting into a vertical position. Light from the shards inside the cavern instantly blinded him. He teetered backward and fell out of the gate, onto hard ground.

Munivarey stood over him, all laughter and wonder etched on his face. "Mahrang was not wrong."

Amir was panting as he straightened himself and regarded Munivarey. He was shaped like a matka, round and stuffy, with a mop of hair on his head and cheeks blossoming like oranges. His face exploded suddenly into a grin as their gazes met.

"What . . . was that?" Amir gasped.

"You tell me," Munivarey said, his hands on his hips, still grinning. "You were the one who got curious."

Curiosity is for those who have the luxury of exploration. For you, it has always been a desperate leap of faith into the unknown.

"I . . . I was in the Mouth," Amir mumbled, eyes staring into the distance at the cold shards of gleaming black and the red light spattered between them. "I saw it. Whatever . . . was inside it."

"The Mouth," maintained Munivarey, although a twitch of his lips belied the incredulity he wished to conceal from Amir. "You certainly carry the whiff of its odor. The god that lies within the Mouth and is the Mouth."

"The spice god?" Amir asked. "Is that whom I saw? What do you mean the god *is* the Mouth?"

"I find it beneficial to keep the semantics vague. Research purposes, of course." Munivarey pressed his hair down with his palm, then combed it to one side with his fingernails. He was still grinning emphatically. "To believe in a god of spices extracts from us a certain spirituality. It diminishes once you realize that the being you pray to—which runs the Gates—is real, and not something the, ah . . . eight kingdoms . . . consider beyond such mortal planes of existence. But of course, arriving at such a conclusion requires a thorough understanding of formal litera-ture. The scriptures exist to corroborate this spiritual relationship between human and Mouth. They legitimize the social structures in place, this deification of transcendence. Otherwise, it becomes impossible to conduct a religion with . . . an accountable deity."

Amir raised his hands. "I . . . understood *nothing* of all of that. And I'm not sure I want to anymore. Though I did wonder how . . ."

"How you managed to use the gate without the spices or the Poison?" Munivarey asked.

Amir gave a faint nod. "I thought the Gates do not work without them."

Munivarey scratched his beard. "There's a reason this is called the false gate, which meant until today, anyone here in Illindhi even using the spices and the Poison did not trigger the veil. Can you tell me why you could?"

Amir had suspected the answer himself as he floundered helplessly in the maw of the Mouth. "Because there are no Carriers in Illindhi. No Carrier has passed through this gate until now."

Munivarey's nod was barely perceptible. He pointed at the glass cages surrounding the platform. "The feces are old."

"Excuse me?" Amir thought he had misheard.

"Fecal matter," clarified Munivarey, throwing another glance at the *things* that wriggled within the cages. "I would advise you to keep your distance from them."

Amir had no other intention. Merely looking at the tangles made him nauseated. He hobbled around Munivarey, the tingles in his arms and legs a residue of his experience inside the gate. Munivarey appeared content, as though overcome by the excitement of having a guest at his home.

"Until today," he agreed, "the false gate did not work. Nothing more than a little research of mine, if you wish. Nowhere close to empirical. But it *could* work. In principle. All it, and I, lacked was a soul."

"A soul?" Amir asked, stopping short of the steps, soaking in the flickering blue light of the cavern.

Munivarey replied, "A purpose." He waddled toward one pillar of the gate. He placed his palm on the stone and took a deep breath. "The Mouth, Amir of Raluha, built the Spice Gates. They are far too complex to have been built by anything else. Think about it. They span leagues, oceans. And yet, they have a uniting spirit."

"The spices."

"Indeed. The spices. Something as simple as household spice has been running our world since consciousness took birth."

Had Amir not been plagued by a dozen piercing thoughts, he'd have perhaps found all of this fascinating. Except now all of it baffled him. "What do you want me to do? Why did you insist you have me before the Chairs sent me back?"

Munivarey gave one of his irritating giggles and clapped his hands, and in that instant, Amir was yanked away from the seriousness of it all. "Nothing anymore. In your haste, you already accomplished what I have struggled with all my life. You just made the false gate work."

"But I merely—"

Munivarey gestured maniacally at the glass crates of tentacles. Amir swore one of the limbs moved. "It is common knowledge among the historians and anthropologists of Illindhi that the first Spice Gate was built upon the peaks of the Ilom, the mountain from which you actually emerged. The ones in the other eight kingdoms were mere extensions, something . . . the Mouth might have determined as an afterthought. But they did not just start working on their own—something triggered them. How did a Gate merely respond to another by the sprinkling of spice? How did space expand and contract in the blink of an eye, physically transporting you to another realm, tens of hundreds of miles away? So many questions, Amir. So many!

"But to lead every unanswered question to the bank of the Mouth is boring. It makes me give up on life's mysteries. Not now. Not anymore." Munivarey was speaking as if for an audience, his body seeming to grow in stature as each word tumbled out of his mouth. Finally, he looked at Amir with a knowing smile. "The Mouth controls the Gates across the realm almost independently. Of course, it would be impossible for me to get the Mouth to work *this* gate by myself. But its feces are the closest link to the Mouth's own body."

Amir recalled once more the swooping sensation of having been close to the Mouth when he was in the Chamber of Chairs. "So the Mouth is indeed here. In Illindhi."

"In the ancient tongue, and in the scriptures, the Mouth is known as Elluvar, that which is born out of a single sesame seed. From there, the name and the realm of Illindhi came into being. Of course the Mouth is here. It lies beneath the mountain. It lies beneath all of us."

Amir eyed the remains uncertainly. Surely, even this knowledge of the Mouth's existence did not merit digging up these feces.

Munivarey must have sensed the discomfort bubbling inside Amir. "It is the only part of the Mouth that flows out of the mountain and into the moats. The farmers in Illindhi gather the waste from these trenches, then preserve and process it into what we call olum. Which is then manipulated into behaving like the other spices using different techniques. It is our deepest secret, one Madhyra has taken to the outside world. But the Mouth—or at least this gate—appears to awaken when these fecal remains come into contact with the veil. It is perhaps associative, just as the Mouth's spit seeps into the mountain's caves and stones, and secretes as raw, unprocessed Poison. These things come from the very intestines of this beast that swims under the ground. Your precious creator."

Amir ignored the hint of derision laced in the last three words. Munivarey raised a finger to his temple, as though to correct his own claim. "I believed the feces served as a reasonable substitute for the powers the Mouth possesses and exhibits on the other Gates, the true ones. I only lacked one ingredient."

"The soul," Amir offered, again not quite understanding what Munivarey was talking about, let alone why he was telling *him*.

Munivarey's grin seemed plastered on his face. "Your soul."

"So . . . now, I can just . . . leave? This . . . this gate works?"

Munivarey shrugged. "Only one way to find out. However, I believe

Mahrang will arrive here shortly. He will be bringing your companion from the Uyirsena. I'm afraid you cannot leave until then. Especially since you have no spices to direct your travel through the gate."

Amir eyed the Poison running along the walls. Munivarey smiled. "That is unprocessed. Mahrang has scores of acolytes working day and night to make it usable for the Gates. As you can see, we are in the business of temptation."

Amir soaked in the blue light of unprocessed Poison. He was surrounded by it, enough for not a vial, not a jar, but a lake of Poison. He had enough to transport every bowler who was not branded with the spicemark out of Raluha. And if he came back here enough times, he could rescue the gatecaste of every kingdom.

A savior complex. Wonderful! The last thing you need when everything around you is crumbling.

"It's . . . unfair," Amir said, at last.

"What is?"

"All . . . all of this. Everything that's happened to me. And your great judgment for me being a messenger."

Munivarey took a deep breath as he rotated to view the entire cavern. "The Mouth has never excreted so much raw Poison. This cavern is usually dark, and I have to bring candles. But of late, the light glows bright. It is curious."

"What is curious?" Amir asked, frustrated at the lack of empathy toward his own plight.

"Legend has it that the Mouth secretes more of the Poison when it is afraid. When it prepares for a Brahmai."

"A Brahmai?"

"The Cleansing. What was being debated by the Chair. You would be naïve to think that this was the first time a secret as vast as this has leaked out. We speak of humans, Carrier. Humans. To keep a secret defies vanity. Brahmai, in the ancient tongue, means illusion. Each time the secret slipped out of our grasp, the warriors of the Uyirsena drank great vials of the Poison secreted from the Mouth and set out to nab every man, woman, and child who fell under that knowledge. They put swords to their throats. It is annihilation—as you said, a genocide. When the dust settled, it was as if there had never been a secret. The ones who survived either went mad or their stories melted into fables and myths, the images in their words illusions of what we did over the ages."

"But what is the need for such violence? To protect"—he gestured frantically around the cave—"*this*? It's just a kingdom, like Raluha or Halmora."

Munivarey frowned. "If only. In a world of absolute parity, it is but the weakest tether that keeps everything from descending into chaos. Everything hangs by a thread, and that thread is Illindhi. Even if you were not a thronekeeper bound in vanity, even if you wanted to remain quiet, nod your head at those who held the secret, there *will* roost a cloud of fear. Of anger. Of desire. Make no mistake about it. Fear of the one who might just tear away from the circle of unity and tiptoe toward the Spice Gate with an army, setting out to conquer Illindhi and the reserves of olum rooted in its soil."

"Again—so what?" Amir blurted out, recalling a similar concern on Karim bhai's face when he had told him of the ninth kingdom. Could they both have a point?

"Don't you see?" Munivarey reasoned patiently. "With olum in your grasp, you would be able to strategically dominate the other kingdoms. The Spice Trade is as much a political entity as it is an economic one. Olum negates this political equilibrium, and in turn makes you vulnerable.

"That is what Madhyra aims to do. People always desire that power, and it is impossible to keep them away from that enchantment once they hear of it. If not you, someone else will fall under its spell. And with them, the whole Spice Trade stands to collapse. It is vital that the balance is maintained. For humanity's very survival, and for the sake of the Mouth that governs us, who holds us to that promise. We all fear what will befall us from the Mouth should we fail. Our fear is our purpose, here, and we take it seriously. That is why Illindhi must remain a secret. It is why it is also vital that the spirituality of the Mouth must endure. And for that, olum cannot slip into the outside world, Amir. Not now, not ever."

Amir chuckled, then burst into laughter.

Munivarey, so prone to laughter himself, looked affronted. "You laugh at this?"

"I just find it funny how a bowler has been dragged into this. All this talk of balance and equality, but do you even realize how much inequality actually exists *out there*? Your precious balance comes at a price. It has built a social hierarchy, which is poisonous from head to toe. A legacy of abuse where I stand at the bottom, cast aside, and yet seemingly all-important now to the survival of all that you hold dear." He shook his head. "Each time I think the fate of our kind cannot get more twisted, life surprises me."

Munivarey sported a sympathetic expression, but deep down, the academic in him grew fascinated. "I'm afraid I do not know what 'bowler' means, but I presume you mean yourself and the other Carriers. The gatecaste. You are said to be the Mouth's Children. The chosen ones who travel through its feces, so that all that is left of it is purity, with which it blesses the nine kingdoms. And that is why the kingdoms have suppressed your kind for so long, as reinforced by the scriptures. It is a question of purity."

Amir had not known that. Did Karim bhai know this? Of course he must. He'd read the scriptures more times than anyone else. Without the knowledge of the abovefolks, of course. And Amma? She'd have known too, Amir supposed. Down in the Bowl, there were only a handful like Amir who scoffed at the scriptures, who found it in themselves to view the eight kingdoms the way Ilangovan had.

The realization of his purity—or the absurd lack of it—hit him like a wave, threatening to lift him off his feet and carry him in its torrent. He'd always assumed the abovefolk hated the bowlers because of the jobs they worked—the tanneries, the sewage and the waste gathering, the pigsties, the crematoriums and the death drums, the daakiyas and the bookbinders, the shepherds and the leaf blowers, and lest he forget, the Carriers. But no, the jobs were not the cause, they were the consequence. He'd gotten it all wrong. By passing through the Mouth's own excreta, the Carriers, and by extension the bowlers, were a part of the world that had been deemed a necessary impurity, with whom association never went beyond whipping them across the Gates.

The Mouth had to know. That its so-called children were being tormented this way. If it knew who harbored the secret of Illindhi, surely it could sense this injustice. Surely . . . it encouraged it.

Amir's breathing intensified. He suddenly felt small, inconsequential. Even with a purpose as large as the world in his hands, the fact that he was this neglected creature, this abused and impure facet of nature, stung him like a hundred bees.

An urge thus rose in Amir, to tell Munivarey what he'd heard when he'd been transported into the Mouth. It had asked Amir—its own child—for *help*.

You do not know what for. If it is Madhyra the Mouth wants you to stop, be certain of it. Do not be a fool and blurt out something to this mad scientist that would keep you imprisoned here.

No, he'd keep it to himself. He was far from the truth that rippled across the eight kingdoms, but that would have to be dealt with another day. Today, he'd go back. Simper and scrape and do whatever he needed to in order to get the Poison. And then . . . it wouldn't matter. Not the Gates, not the kingdoms. Not his impurity. He'd be on an island off Jhanak, safe with his family, living a life in the Black Coves among people like him.

And that was something to look forward to.

Two figures entered from the opposite side of the cavern. As they approached Munivarey's false gate, Amir recognized one of the figures as Mahrang. He was tall and garbed in a long, saffron robe, with a red turban wound in thick layers around his head. The Jewelmaker was carrying a shamshir in his hand.

His companion was a girl much shorter than him. Her hair was tied in an oily braid down to her elbows. Her eyes were a chestnut brown, and she had high cheekbones and a broad nose that stood prominent over a mouth so thin and stern, Amir doubted she'd ever open it to speak. Buckled to a strap on her waist was a scimitar quite like the one Fylan had carried. Amir gulped. The violence the weapon had inflicted on the Haldiveer sparkled fresh in his mind.

A good day to keep the number of words you utter to a minimum.

Munivarey chortled to break the ice. "Ah, Mahrang. I see you've brought a . . . worthy companion to our dear Carrier."

"A necessary addition," Mahrang said. He regarded Amir with a certain distaste, as though, given his choice, he'd have thrust Amir into the deepest prison and allowed him to rot. His eyes were fixed not on Amir's face but on his throat, on the spicemark. "Carrier," he said, the baritone voice burying into Amir's senses. "This is Kalay, an acolyte of the Uyirsena. She will accompany you at all times, and you are expected to heed her words before you take action. You in turn will guide her on the lay of your land and make no attempt to misguide or betray her. She will not hesitate to kill you."

Amir absorbed these words and gathered the courage to take a step forward in order to shake her hand. Kalay gave a quick glance at Mahrang and made a hasty salute, which made all of them uncomfortable.

Mahrang said: "At any point, if you choose to abandon your mission, remember that the Mouth will know. I *will not* hesitate to dispatch the Uyirsena at that moment. And believe me when I say that everyone you know or care about will fall under their blade. You are all that stands between them and the bloodshed they're born for, and *that* will be on your conscience."

Amir gulped all of his saliva, held back his tongue, and offered a weak nod.

Mahrang brought forth the shamshir he'd been carrying. "This is Alkar, forged in the Mouth itself, imbued with its holy scent. A weapon used by every warrior of the Uyirsena. Go and put an end to Madhyra," he said as casually as one asks to take a pot off the fire once the broth has sufficiently boiled. "Finish this before the Uyirsena smear their foreheads with blood."

With trepidation, Amir lifted the shamshir from Mahrang's hands. Much against his fear, it was as light as a stick of cinnamon. Steel clanged against steel in his imagination. Back in Raluha, he had always kept a handy knife, a small chaku stuffed into the fold of his sarongs and pajamas. He was never the reckless sort who wandered out of his house after the sun set looking for a beef or a brawl. But being a bowler *and* a Carrier meant Amir was often the victim of assault from not just the abovefolk but also from among those who lurked in dark corners of the Bowl awaiting his passing, hoping he'd have a pinch or two of something valuable to spare.

A chaku, though, was one tool. A broad, curved shamshir was far beyond what he had ever lifted. There was something peculiar about the sword, however, that made it *fit*. His skin tingled as it came in contact with the hilt, as though the millions of pores on his palm were absorbing the particles of the iron; a glint on the pommel against the harsh light of the sapphires as he turned the blade over in his hand.

Forged in the Mouth itself, imbued with its holy scent.

He imagined what Hasmin would say if he saw Amir wandering around the Bowl or any part of Raluha at all wielding a shamshir. A sudden urge to laugh rose in his chest. Amir smothered it with a soft chuckle and averted his gaze from Mahrang. At that moment, Kalay removed a water flask from her hip and swung to take a sip. Clear blue liquid streamed into her mouth.

The Poison. She frowned, catching him staring at her as she closed the lid and concealed the flask beneath her robe. "Don't even think about it," she snarled, her voice flat yet silvery.

Amir raised his hands in defense, much against his instincts as a thief. "I'll be a quiet guide."

"Remember," Mahrang addressed both of them. "You have a fortnight. Tomorrow begins the afsal dina, a week during which Madhyra will not be able to plant or harvest the olum and transform it. However, that should not mean that she will not be spending her time gathering resources. You must stop her before she can convince the eight kingdoms of olum's potency. And you, Kalay . . ." He narrowed his eyes at her and exhaled slowly. "Do not fail me like Fylan did."

Kalay went down on one knee, crossed a hand upon her thigh, and bent to touch her forehead to it. "I won't, aiyya."

Mahrang blessed the back of her head and raised her. He kissed her forehead and applied what looked like a saffron tika between her eyes with his thumb. It rose on her skin like a candle flame. Mahrang extended his arm and dropped a fistful of olum on Kalay's palms. To Amir, he gave little vials of saffron, cumin, cinnamon, turmeric, black pepper, nutmeg, and cloves. "For the Mouth," he whispered.

"For the Mouth," repeated Kalay, who opened her own vial of cinnamon.

Amir narrowed his eyes at the cinnamon in her hand. "Aren't we going to Raluha?"

"Madhyra will be in Jhanak," Mahrang said. "The kingdom of cinnamon. She will be attending the feast of the afsal dina. It is where all the eight thronekeepers will be gathered."

Amir wanted to argue. He had a pinch of saffron in his hand, and he was itching to go home, even if it meant dodging Hasmin and his chowkidars through the narrow lanes and the bazaar. Kabir would have left for duty already, and he, Amir, had not been beside him. He'd promised his brother he'd take him far away from Raluha before his first day as a Carrier. And if he couldn't, he'd at least stand beside him as he stepped through the Gate. They'd share the pain and the whippings, and perhaps even the good times of walking through wondrous kingdoms that were ever so different from Raluha.

Wishful thinking. There's nothing to romanticize about Carrying.

Gates! And here he thought he could slip away. Kalay, with her silvery voice, however, did not let her eyes leave him. In the end, he settled for a resigned nod, fearing that the longer he dallied, the more he was prone to forcing Mahrang to change his mind. He would at least be in some part of the eight kingdoms. Home would be only a pinch of saffron away, and there'd be one less of these Illindhi murderers around to stop him then.

"I told you it'll work," Munivarey said from behind them, gesturing to the false gate. He appeared to be addressing Mahrang.

Mahrang scoffed and muttered something that sounded like "infidel." Amir did not pay any heed to their argument. The day had passed like a dream, and yet, suddenly it had overturned his future. He had a chance, albeit a bleak one, and he would not let it pass. He'd do whatever it took for his family.

He followed Kalay up the steps and they stood side by side in front of the arch.

"You first," he muttered.

Kalay shrugged, threw the cinnamon, and disappeared into the veil. *Feces*, Amir reminded himself. *You're going to be walking through an extension of a god's shit.*

Amir swallowed, threw the cinnamon, and dived into the gate.

CHAPTER

10

It is always goats that are sacrificed, never lions.

—THE ROOT TO THE TOWER

You have pledged yourself to me. That is good. You will be remembered, Child.

Amir was floating inside the Mouth once more. He watched the great mound of flesh around him blink and stretch. He winced at the strain on his own consciousness.

"I don't understand what you want me to help with."

Stop her. Kill her.

Amir found the rush of violence from the Mouth's words manifesting as a storm that battered against his floating body. His back arched, and his feet tingled in pain.

"Then stop hurting me!"

Silence. The Mouth darkened, as though invisible lights within the enormous maw of the beast had suddenly been extinguished, leaving Amir in complete darkness. Darkness but for two lines like the rim of the sun along the horizon, which were the half-opened eyes of the spice god.

Stop her without the truth.

"The truth? . . . I don't understand."

You will not feel pain anymore. I have blessed you. But remember this—she has set out on a lie. Conquer the lie, but do not allow the truth to sway you. Stop her without the truth. For her truth is not ours.

AMIR STEPPED OUT OF THE SPICE GATE PAINLESSLY FOR THE FIRST time, as if he had walked through an ordinary door. The absence of pain was a new sensation, and Amir did not know how to respond to it. He stared at his body as though expecting some part of it to suddenly tingle or lose sensation altogether. When nothing happened, Amir decided to inhale all of Jhanak in a lungful of breath.

He was never fond of heights. The air in high places was untrustworthy. The ground beneath his feet even more so. But each time he emerged from the Spice Gate in Jhanak upon that narrow outcropping of land poking out of the earth like a crooked leg, he overlooked the ocean—even if for a flicker—and forgot what it was to be afraid.

For there was much in Jhanak to look upon from that ridge. It stole his fear and replaced it with a sense of calmness and awe.

Jhanak had been erected against a great mountainside, sprawling across its foot. Homes and markets built into caves, its palace trying to carve itself out of the very mountain it lay ensconced in; its turrets and towers great basaltic pillars crawling out of the cliff. On the other end, the city's carpet of settlements and lanes swept into the bay, into a wide port where more than a hundred boats lay moored with a cluster of sails fluttering overhead, squabbling for space. The jetties and piers were alive with shouts of sailors and haggling merchants with too much cargo on their decks. A perpetual rabble of chaos reigned on those salty streets. Karim bhai had quipped that Jhanak was full of folks so stupid that if they wished to do evil, they wouldn't know how. The air was loaded with vapors along that unwholesome coast, and it contained nothing worthy but the little twigs of cinnamon roosting in everyone's pocket and in their batters and pies.

So different from Raluha, yet so similar. Threads of memory unspooled in his mind, and he bade them cease.

The sound of waves crashing against the rocks filled Amir's ears. The tang of seawater clamped his senses. The wind whipped at his nape, tossed his hair, and forced his lips to twitch until he smiled and took a deep breath.

Beside him, Kalay was breathing slowly. Her eyes were closed, her arms were splayed wide, and the jute satchel she carried with her flask of Poison and other spices billowed against the sea breeze. Had she felt the Mouth's presence in her head too? Or was it just him? What was certain was that she had not felt pain. The Poison had excised it from their bodies, leaving passage to be something . . . cherished. She didn't seem to be fazed. Rather, she was perhaps even enjoying the view. There was the hint of a smile on her lips, something Amir assumed she was not capable of.

An aura of childishness fluttered about her as she regarded Jhanak and the coast it slouched on. She seemed different from what he'd seen of her in the cavern earlier. As though she'd been itching to be rid of Mahrang and his company, and just . . . pass. To finally leave Illindhi. It didn't escape Amir that, like most Raluhans, she too had never seen the ocean before.

"How can you curse being a Carrier?" she asked Amir when she caught him watching her.

Amir's smile waned. "Because in a few moments of arriving I would be whipped down the sides of this cliff, pushed into an underpass, and made to lumber my way to the granaries. All the while carrying a load that would burden a mule, let alone a man. I can't remember the last time I stood here for longer than a minute and breathed this air, since I'm usually gasping in pain and exertion upon exiting the Gate. Fancy a try?"

Kalay quirked her head at him, but before she could respond, half a dozen Jhanakari guards jogged up the crag toward them. Kalay stepped beside Amir and whispered in his ear. "Listen to me. You and I are both merchants of the Carnelian Caravan, and we come bearing a message from the Jewelmaker. Wear this scarf and hide your spicemark."

Amir hesitated but did not deny that it was a fair thought to conceal their identity. In a way, they were not being dishonest either—he was certainly working for Mahrang, even though his pay would be in the form of not having him and his family murdered. The alibi made sense, too, since only the now-absent Jewelmaker could secure for himself—or a merchant of his Carnelian Caravan—entry into Jhanak on the eve of afsal dina, especially with weapons on display.

Amir was once again witness to just how precious—and powerful— the Poison was.

Amir wound Kalay's scarf around his neck and bowed as the Jhanakari guards came up to them. He was secretly glad that this was a new retinue and that they had never seen him before on Carrying duty.

The chowkidars were hard not to look at twice. They were tall, slender men and women with hair as white as grated coconut, perched over faces as dark as milkless tea. Their helms had a cinnamon stick poking from a slit carved into the metal.

Kalay whipped out a letter from the folds of her robe and proudly handed it over to the foremost thin-faced guard while casually eyeing the whole group with curiosity. So much about all of this was new—and Amir couldn't help but remember the first time he'd arrived in Jhanak, or any of the other kingdoms. The strange faces, the stranger aromas.

The chowkidar's eyes widened as he read the letter, and immediately a flurry of conversation transpired among his retinue.

Minutes later, the foreman straightened. "The seal of the Jewelmaker is intact. We're honored to . . . have you back."

Kalay nodded professionally and snatched the letter from the man. "Thank you. The Jewelmaker sends his regards." Gone was her silvery voice. It was now low and monotonous, and frighteningly cold.

The chowkidars stepped aside amid excited whispers, cutting a narrow trail between them for Kalay and Amir to pass through. Amir didn't have to pretend. He looked naturally every part a humble, servile acolyte of the caravan.

He kept at Kalay's heels and tightened the dupatta around his neck. When they were upon the spice trail that led to the granaries, having seen the back of the Jhanakari chowkidars, Amir heaved a sigh of relief.

"That was close!"

Kalay appeared to be unsure, her eyes never focused on one place. "There are too many guards."

"What did you expect? It's the afsal dina. There will be royals from the other seven kingdoms, and the entire city gets drunk, and there is a feast that lasts all night. You need a lot of security if you want to send fewer people to the Whorl."

"The Whorl?" Kalay asked, pausing in her tracks. From her tone, Amir could tell that she did not ask out of ignorance, more out of surprise.

He stepped to the edge of the narrow pathway leading away from the ridge and pointed to the sea.

"It is the barrier in the waters," he said. "You cannot see it from here; it's quite far from shore, but ships that go to the Whorl . . . nobody returns alive. It is believed impossible to cross, a treacherous part of the ocean."

"All the more foolish to attempt to go there," Kalay said. She sounded curious now, and Amir sensed that there was more to the woman than just being a servant of the Mouth.

"Not by choice, of course. The Whorl is for the Neverknown Sailors," he muttered. "The condemned. Thieves, crooks, and killers convicted of various crimes, armed with nothing but oars and a sail. The Jhanakari court sends them deep into the ocean. If they are to prove themselves in the eyes of the Mouth, they must cross the Whorl as punishment. And salvation, if they are lucky. A moonfall after the criminals depart, they are remembered and their belongings are burned as a sacrifice to the Mouth and the Gates. That's why you see the Jhanakari Gate garlanded with all those pieces of cloth. Banners of the Neverknown Sailors are raised across the city on that day."

"You make them sound like martyrs," Kalay said, sounding critical of this practice.

"What's a martyr?"

Kalay rolled her eyes. "Never mind. Has anyone crossed the Whorl?"

"Nobody. They fail. Always. Like they fail to cross every other part of the Outerlands beyond the eight kingdoms."

"You mean the Ranagala," Kalay said, the realization eliciting a sigh.

"But I understand the different realms have different words. The ancient tongue seems to have been forgotten in these parts. It must mean that the Whorl, too, is an aspect of the Ranagala."

"So you know about the . . . Outerlands, or whatever it is you called it?"

"It is all the realm of the Mouth," Kalay replied.

Amir's heart skipped a beat. "So, can anyone . . . survive the Outerlands?"

At that, Kalay laughed. "You just told me nobody has crossed the Whorl. That should answer your question."

The rising bubble in Amir's chest subsided. He'd hoped against hope that a stranger who bore knowledge Amir was ignorant of could perhaps be aware of the secrets of the Outerlands. That his father *may* have survived his reckless escape from the borders of Raluha.

If he did survive, though . . . ten years is a long time for a man to find his way back home.

"Besides," Kalay continued, "the Ranagala is sacred. It is forbidden to the people. And to prevent vanity, the Mouth has ensured it cannot be survived. The terrain around Illindhi is impassable."

"A pity." Amir bit his lip, forcing himself not to think of his father. It always evoked an uncontrollable rage in him, the kind he usually treated by walking away, into silence, into darkness—a choice he did not have at present. So, he clenched his fists, closed his eyes, and inhaled sharply. "It's a pity," he repeated, his voice controlled. "There's much that is beautiful about the eight kingdoms that is forbidden."

A glint played in Kalay's eyes. Not for long. He was certain she'd been on the cusp of asking a question, to implore him to tell her more. She did not give in to her curiosity. At once, her opaque, pitiless expression returned, akin to the one she wore in Munivarey's cavern.

They walked in silence as they entered the city proper, the wind nipping at their skin. The sounds of the market and the streets enveloped them, and Amir was inexplicably certain that the conversation they had abandoned would continue some other time.

"Where do we go now?" he asked instead. "The palace? If Madhyra is here, then so is Harini. She must have found a way to bring Madhyra into the palace."

"Who is Harini?"

"The rajkumari of Halmora," Amir said, keeping as straight a face as possible, although his heart somersaulted in his chest. Dandelions in his mind swayed in time with the breeze of his breath, and the salt glazed on his lips desired the taste of her skin.

Kalay narrowed her eyes at him. "Are you certain that is all she is to you? The princess of Halmora? Your eyes conspire against you, Carrier."

"My eyes do nothing but look ahead along the path," he maintained. Yet if Amir could gaze into a mirror, he knew he was bound to see his cheeks turning red. "She was also a . . . friend. Not so much anymore, or maybe, I don't know. Enough, ho! Are you going to interrogate me all day, or will you tell me what we must do?"

He envied Kalay's ability to maintain a straight, impassive face. "The feast will be tomorrow night," she said. "We must find a way into the palace before that."

Amir held her back. "Wait! If the feast is tomorrow night, then the harvest ritual will begin . . ." He glanced at the sun above their heads. "*Now!*"

Kalay jumped at his touch. She softened at once, almost guiltily. "The palace looks vast. If there is a chance they are already inside, we must go there."

Amir smiled. "Oh, but they won't be. The ritual demands all the thronekeepers to be present in the fields. Come, you wouldn't want to miss Orbalun's dance."

"*Dance?*" Kalay sounded mortified, but she was too late, as Amir was already dragging her along the street, and this time, she did not protest his touch.

Sure enough, the people of Jhanak were ambling up the lanes. A sea of white hair, some turbaned, some with bandanas like the guards. Over half the city had emptied out of their homes, crawled out of their dens in the docks, and begun to lumber toward the great paddy fields to the east. The mountain to which the palace was pasted tapered eastward into a plain rising away from the sea, and a wave of soft, sweet straw greeted them like a floral exhibition. It smelled of the land and of damp soils. A release from everything that was clamped tight.

Amir kept an eye out for any of the Haldiveer, as though that would be evidence enough of Harini being around. Thoughts of Madhyra and her spice conquest dug a trench at the back of his head and curled into a ball to remain there for the rest of the hike up to the rice plantations. The road curved upward to meet the slope of the hill before dipping into the terraced fields. Most people gathered along the escarpment, which was barricaded by a fence and a row of Jhanakari chowkidars who only let a select few down to where the ritual was to be held.

Amir pushed through the crowd, Kalay's scent of sandalwood in his nose, until he reached the railing. He squinted through the fence at the plowed land, where, at the center, a huge square had been tilled and left barren for the thronekeepers, their immediate families, and their personal guards to stand on.

Seven thronekeepers stood in a circle, distinguished by their attire. Amir recognized Maharaja Orbalun among them in a sharp purple kaftan. He had a face with keen eyes, which Karim bhai swore would notice in a hair's breadth if something was wrong on the best of days. The same couldn't be said for his cheeks, bloated and swollen, as though in grief or anger. Amir could speculate on the reason for that—the failed Bashara. Orbalun had lost a child.

Perhaps Amir was used to expecting people to look like what they stood for. Which was why the sight of the thronekeeper underwhelmed him. Maharaja Orbalun looked . . . diminished in front of the other six royal figures.

Of the eighth thronekeeper, there was no sign. Neither of Raja Virular nor of Rani Bhagyamma. And certainly no sign of Harini. The Halmoran contingent—as a whole—was absent.

"She's not there," he muttered as much to Kalay, who squeezed beside him, casting a stern look at a local for trying to shoulder her aside for a better view.

"But it is the afsal dina," Kalay said exasperatedly. "In Illindhi, it is a day when the entire Mandala is expected to be present for the prayer to the Mouth."

"I am *aware*. But look around: she's clearly not here, is she? No, and I wouldn't be surprised if your own thronekeeper is responsible for it. Not one to follow the rules, either, that one?" Amir muttered, and Kalay stiffened at the reminder that her thronekeeper had crossed too far beyond the threshold of their scriptures to be justified in criticizing the scriptures of others.

With a gentle smirk, Amir returned his gaze to the cleared area for the abovefolk. He eyed the thronekeepers once more, and then the ministers behind them in lesser attire, and farther behind—the chowkidars and charioteers in sweat-stained livery, forming a circular shield.

With a groan, Amir spotted Hasmin among them.

What a waste of the Poison!

The chief of the Raluhan chowkidars kept a straight face, eyes only for the pit around which the thronekeepers of the seven kingdoms stood, each with a sickle or a plow, a hoe or a spade in their hands, waiting for the burial of the tools.

Amir seethed. *So pious and dutiful that you're willing to sacrifice an eleven-year-old boy to a life of torment and servitude.*

Kabir would have begun his duty as a Carrier. Perhaps, at this moment, in Talashshukh, trailing the other Carriers through the cobbled lanes filled with teahouses and sheesha mahals.

At the end of the ritual, the presiding priest stood, dusted his garb, and made his way to the thronekeepers. One by one, with the blessing of the priest, the royals descended into the pit to place their tools upon the consecrated plot of land. Orbalun was the last to lay his spade over the others before retreating. The priest placed a sickle above Orbalun's as a symbol of Halmoran cultivation and signaled the completion of the ritual. Now, nobody in the eight kingdoms would be permitted to harvest any spice until the end of the week.

In consonance with Orbalun's retreat and the placing of the final tool by the priest, a symphony of ululations ensued from the Jhanakari populace. Their sounds carried across the terraced rice fields like a wave. Amir much preferred the silent hand gestures of the afsal dina in Amarohi, or even the seed-casting ritual of Halmora, where a rain of seeds preceded the ritual dance.

"Each year, the afsal dina is held in a different kingdom," he explained to Kalay. "Only in Jhanak are they this loud, this . . . unruly."

Kalay, however, appeared to not be listening. She had closed her eyes and was . . . praying. Her lips moved in incomprehensible verses, and when the hymn ended, she opened her eyes and touched the fence they had been leaning against, then tapped her forehead thrice in reverence.

"In Illindhi, the people travel beneath the mountain, to the rim of the Mouth," she said. "Where they cast their farming tools into the Mouth as a gift on the eve of the harvest festival. Over the following fortnight, they forge new ones."

"Such respect," Amir replied scathingly.

Kalay, however, had lost interest already. She was thinking of Madhyra, he could tell.

And you're thinking of Harini.

What were the two planning? The Mouth's words echoed in his skull. *She set out on a lie.*

When the ululations ceased, Amir's attention returned to the field. "Look." He pointed to Kalay.

The priest's voice rose above the breeze, and at his gesture, the royals spread themselves into a wider circle, then faced the person beside them, dividing into pairs. One of the higher-level ministers was summoned to fill in for the absent Halmoran thronekeeper. Orbalun formed a pair with the thronekeeper of Kalanadi, a tall, sallow-faced woman wrapped in deerskin with hair that fell to her waist in tight curls.

At a gesture—as was the custom—they began to dance. Orbalun did not appear to be in the mood for it; he dragged his feet too wide or bowed too low, while the Kalanadian thronekeeper engaged him with a sense of excitement. She was far more agile, far quicker, and far more willing to submit to Orbalun's breezier version of the steps. When he held her waist and spun her, she twirled like a cyclone under his arched arm, feet never buckling over the muddy ground. Amir imagined dancing with Harini, perhaps more privately, and swallowed what little saliva rested on his tongue.

The dance must have lasted only a few minutes, for the Jhanakari locals groaned and complained when it ceased. Almost immediately, cheers rose from the same people as the thronekeepers bowed in their direction, joining their palms together in gratitude.

Kalay squinted at several other figures squatting a few yards away from the ceremonial pit. At a whistle from the chowkidars, the figures rose and lumbered forward. Turbans wound over their heads, a stained towel thrown over their shoulder and a loose tunic on top of a lungi that flailed against the tangy breeze.

Carriers. One from each kingdom—once more, except Halmora—to receive the blessings of the thronekeepers. Amir adjusted his shawl around his throat, the spicemark seeming to writhe beneath it. One of the older Carriers stumbled as they walked, then regained their footing and rejoined the other Carriers.

Involuntarily, Amir's hand raised to grip Kalay's shoulder, his breath caught in his throat. He had just recognized the man who had stumbled. The man who now knelt opposite Orbalun and removed his turban. The mop of familiar gray hair falling to his shoulders, bristling against the breeze.

Karim bhai.

"They must be in the palace," Kalay said, ignoring Amir's excitement. "Come, we must try to get in."

Amir waved her away. "It will be swarming with chowkidars. We should wait for Karim bhai."

"Who?" Kalay frowned.

Amir pointed at the field. "The Carrier who is kneeling in front of Orbalun. I know him. He can help us. He's the most resourceful man in the eight kingdoms." A bubble of relief expanded in his chest. After the last several days of strangeness and incredulity, here was something that was familiar, with a fragrance of home. Here was his oldest friend . . .

The Mouth always knows.

Amir instinctively grabbed Kalay's arm and began to drag her through the crowd. Each body he brushed past, each face he looked at . . . *No, no. Don't think about it. It cannot work that way.* Yet could he be certain? Was he jeopardizing everyone's lives by simply *being* in their presence? He shut his eyes and elbowed through the throng, Kalay in tow, until they were safely away, no more jostling but nevertheless breathing heavily, standing on the road that led toward the docks.

When she wrestled away from him, he was taking long, deep breaths. He squatted on the dirt track stampeded upon by a thousand Jhanakari less than an hour before.

"What was I thinking?"

"Speak plainly." Kalay scowled, massaging her wrist where Amir had held her.

Amir dug his fingers into his hair. "Karim bhai . . . he knows. I told him about Illindhi."

Kalay remained tight-lipped. Amir shut his eyes. He'd feared the worst, and her silence confirmed it.

She adjusted the satchel's thread running across her chest. "That is why the palace is our best choice."

This time, Amir did not resist. A dreariness engulfed him, weighing him down by the responsibility he suddenly shouldered. Moreover, he was hungry, and he itched to abandon the entire plan, hike down the lanes to the docks, sneak into one of the inns, and swig a mug of ale. Complement it with some salted peanuts and kara sev before diving into a bowl of meen kulambu and rice. The true Jhanakari experience, which the bowlers barely got a taste of during their duties. And here he was, not on the Spice Trail, but on his own, chasing a ghost. A different whip was at his back, albeit a whip wielded by Mahrang and his bloodthirsty army. Time, like always, wrapped its thorny coils around him.

Perhaps this could end tonight. They'd find Madhyra and this would all be over and he—and his family—would finally be free.

And perhaps, if you look far enough into the sea, you'll see where you will live out the rest of your life.

He hoped Kalay would take care of apprehending Madhyra. He was merely her guide in this endeavor. Each minute stretched endlessly in the thought of using the shamshir given to him by Mahrang. He fought imaginary battles in his mind over and over, and even in those, he did not emerge the victor. Even in his most delusional of daydreams he realized his own incompetence.

Kalay had better be up for it!

It was evening by the time they climbed the rugged trail toward the palace. With coins dug out from Kalay's pouch, they purchased new clothes for Amir from an emporium in the sea market, a traditional Jhanakari chogha in black with little fake sapphire mirror beads on it, and a pajama that flourished around his ankle, concealing most of his chappal, its leather now tearing.

Kalay complained she was uncomfortable in a sari, so she chose a thin chestnut salwaar kameez and veiled her head with a translucent blue dupatta.

Blending in, it was easier to maneuver, especially once they'd escaped the crowd from the ritual. Behind and beneath them, the city sprawled in myriad colors, a cluster of cone-shaped houses and settlements, all the way to the docks, where the many boats were silhouetted against the striking orange of the sun as it dipped westward along the watery horizon.

At the entrance to the palace, the chowkidars stopped them again. Once more, Kalay flashed her letter and offered the Jewelmaker's regards. And once more, amid animated murmurs, they were allowed to pass, although the guards did request their weapons, which they stored in a room close to the gate. Amir was secretly glad to part with the shamshir, and Kalay the opposite. She continued murmuring to herself, as though concocting a plot to retrieve her weapon later.

The palace of Jhanak was wholly different from the experience of weaving through the Halmoran qila. While Harini's home was brooding and lonely, the stone castle of Jhanak hugging the mountain had a festive air. Lights everywhere—lanterns on cross-ropes, candelabras, chandeliers beneath domed ceilings, glass-encased candles ensconced in walls, and even artificial fireflies strung up on invisible threads and suspended from the roofs. Servants scurried about singing songs, chattering and laughing, carrying plates of laddoos, jelebis, jamuns, and gujiyas topped with nuts and sprinkled with cinnamon. The air was rife with cinnamon most of all, brimming with its haze and sweetness, a lush fragrance that reminded Amir of a feast in the Bowl when a pair of thieves had stolen a sack full of cinnamon from the granaries and had gathered everyone at the bottom-most square. And even though cinnamon was not his favorite spice, he couldn't resist being enthralled by its aroma.

Kalay was not as captivated by the sights and sounds as Amir, but the fragrances seemed to catch her attention just the same. They stopped a few servants to grab what confections they could sweep into their arms, then found a dank corner to stuff their bellies. Kalay did not eat much. She had something on her mind, for why else would she avoid most of his questions? Her curiosity upon entering Jhanak had dimmed, and she was more acolyte than wanderer now.

Remember who sent her.

Tonight was a lesser feast, an occasion to commemorate the burial of the spades. The following day, after abstinence, would be the real pomp. Amir had been a kitchen servant dragged in by Karim bhai for the afsal dina held in Raluha the previous year. He'd never entered the darbar, but he'd smelled enough perfumes and heard enough music to imagine what transpired beyond those great iron doors.

How would the thronekeepers react, he wondered, if they discovered a ninth kingdom? Who among them would, as Munivarey prophesied, upset the balance of the Spice Trade and chase after olum?

Or has one already done so?

There was a lot Amir did not yet know of what transpired in Halmora, but could Harini—who had never been proud of her heritage to begin with—have been swayed by Madhyra? During the times Amir and Harini had spent together, she had often spoken of desiring to travel the eight kingdoms, a craving for the Poison she had never been permitted by her parents to drink—and now Amir began to wonder if it was this longing that had drawn her to him.

It was an unkind thought, he realized, and shook his head as if to clear it. *You went to Halmora with the intention to use her as well— remember that.* This feeling . . . it was not good. This relentless barrage. Of half-baked hypotheses. Of foreboding strange ideas and possibilities. Of people not being who he thought they were.

Now that he came to think of it, Harini *had* been happy on seeing him in the darbar. Surprised, sure, but he'd also seen a genuine joy on her face, a contrast to the countenance with which she had spoken to Madhyra moments earlier. A reminder of where her heart lay, even if Amir, since then, had come much to doubt it.

He wasn't sure if she'd be so happy to see him now.

It didn't bode well to think of Harini in the same vein as the other thronekeepers and their spoiled, privileged children. Even if she was ultimately serving the people of Halmora—in her heart, she was still who Amir thought she was.

Amir and Kalay reached a domed antechamber separating the corridors from the Great Hall. A retinue of Jhanakari chowkidars stood in conversation with a turbaned man in Raluhan attire. At the sight of him, a wave of panic flooded Amir.

It was Hasmin.

Amir wheeled around and covered his face with one hand, grabbing Kalay with the other.

"What?" she snapped.

Amir began to walk back the way they'd come. "Don't look back, just keep walking," he muttered. "Hasmin, that chowkidar, he knows me."

When he'd nearly reached the bend, Hasmin, who had probably gotten only a fleeting glimpse of Amir, shouted, "Ho! You there, halt!"

Amir, however, had no intention of halting, especially now that Hasmin was accompanied by some of the Jhanakari chowkidars he also recognized. These particular guards knew him for his scrambling detours to get a closer glimpse of the docks and perhaps wet his lips with some ale. While they condoned Karim bhai, who always had a way with people of other kingdoms, he, Amir, always found himself on the end of whips and lashes. He didn't relish that today and so increased his pace, Kalay nearly jogging to catch up with him.

"What are you *doing*?" she growled.

"Just keep walking."

When Amir glanced back, Hasmin and three of the Jhanakari guards had detached from the retinue and were coming after him. Amir began to run.

"You! Stop!"

The servants scrambled toward the periphery with their plates and glasses of wine as Amir and Kalay dashed through the space. He had no idea where he was going, only that he had to get away from Hasmin. The image of the chief's face in his office in the Pyramid burned in Amir's mind. There would be no room for forgiveness or escape this time. Amir had broken the most serious, and unspoken, law of the Spice Trade: he'd deceived one of the abovefolk in charge.

It'd make sense to escape and try again the next day. Today was definitely not a possibility; not even the excuse of Amir being an enigmatic member of the Jewelmaker's caravan would play in front of Hasmin. Already, locating Harini and Madhyra had proved difficult, and in a palace of this size, as tall as a mountain, where would they find two women who didn't wish to be found? With a contingent of the Jhanakari chowkidars behind them, no less. The thought numbed his feet but also kept him running.

Hasmin was getting closer. Amir and Kalay rounded another domed antechamber, scurried through a half-open door, rushed along another passageway lit with scintillating candles, and dashed down the stairs, the air rife with cinnamon.

Amir glanced up to see the chowkidars behind them. "Run, run, run!" he shouted. Kalay's scarf around his throat fell off as he ran.

At the landing, Amir and Kalay separated. He scampered left; she ran right. By the time the separation dawned on him, the chowkidars behind had already split off also, with two of them, including Hasmin, chasing Amir. He bolted without a smidgen of care for people in his way.

Ahead, another curved hallway emerged, the walls strung with paintings and murals hanging against a faded tapestry of the Whorl. A dense cyclone across the ocean, creating a seemingly bottomless fissure beyond which no ships could sail. A lone galley straddled that line between water and abyss in the painting, and Amir conjured the remainder of its fate in his mind as he dashed past. An Outerlands wonder he had no time for.

A great bronze door appeared ahead, polished and gilded. *Gates*, he thought, *that's a door made to keep people like me out of it.*

So be it.

In that moment, Amir decided there was little difference in breaking one rule versus a dozen and rushed headlong toward the door just as the door itself groaned open.

Amir crashed into the first person to walk through the doorframe. The collision led to a soft landing for him, though the same could not be said for the person he fell into. From the fold and brush of silk against his skin, Amir knew he'd just physically assaulted a royal. He was attempting to scramble to his feet when Hasmin's hands grabbed him from behind. He was scooped up, even as he skidded to regain balance. *Did Hasmin just . . . touch you? This has to mean—*

With Hasmin's nails clawing into his skin, the sense of disbelief turned profound and washed over him. He had collided with none other than Maharaja Orbalun.

The thronekeeper of Raluha lay on the floor, weighed down by his mantle of silk and silver, almost chuckling. He was declining help from the thronekeeper of Jhanak, Rani Zariba, a tall, thin woman with a neck-lace of lapis lazuli and a golden nethi chuti that was brighter than all the lights in the palace. Behind Zariba, the rest of the thronekeepers Amir had seen at the ceremony stood in shock (*still no Harini!*), their families, ministers, and their personal retinue of chowkidars rallying to safeguard them, equally perplexed at this turn of events.

"Zariba, is this the extent of your security?" one of the thronekeepers—a thin, wiry man in Vanasari attire—raged. "We have an assassin caught outside the royal chambers. So much for snatching away our weapons at the doors."

Amir gave up struggling with his captor. He lay limp as Hasmin flipped the baton he was carrying and pummeled one end of it into Amir's gut. His stomach convulsed, all the breath rushed out of his mouth, and the brilliance of the light around them muddled in his head.

"There will be no need for that," Orbalun said, helping himself up. "It was an accident."

"You wouldn't be saying this if there was a chaku in your gut, Orba," Rani Asphalekha of Kalanadi, whom Orbalun had earlier danced with, rebuked.

Hasmin joined his palms and performed a deep bow. "Apologies, huzoor, but this man is a Carrier. He is not permitted in the palace. I will take him and leave him outside."

All of a sudden, Amir felt more than fifty eyes on his throat, followed by the uncomfortable feeling that being an assassin was perhaps a better option in these circumstances.

Orbalun dusted his robe and smiled. "I would like to think I'm no-where near as diabolical to my populace as to be deposed by an assassin, Asphalekha. And as for you Senapati Hasmin, I would be a fool if I couldn't recognize a Carrier by his mark. I'm well aware of this young man's position. It does not change the accidental nature of our collision."

"But huzoor—"

"Didn't you hear him?" Rani Zariba barked at Hasmin. "Get out of here. And take him with you. Leave him outside."

Stiffening at the reprimand, Hasmin's head jerked between Orbalun and Zariba, as though he had trouble judging the extent of his loyalties. However, Zariba's glare was absolute, a countenance that would have prompted even Amir to obey any instruction from her.

Before Hasmin could act, however, a commotion broke out behind the thronekeepers. Some of the ministers and soldiers parted, with shrieks of barely contained disgust as a tiny, stooped figure nosed ahead.

Karim bhai appeared just as disheveled as he was on a day of Carrying, his beard even more unkempt, offering a stark contrast in the midst of all the glitter and silk.

The only difference now was that he was no longer bare-chested. Instead he wore a gray shirt over a white dhoti, which all but screamed *abovefolk*. It'd be plain for anyone who could look at Karim bhai that he was utterly discomfited by it.

Karim bhai rushed to Hasmin, who had begun to drag Amir out. "Dei naaye," he called out to Amir loudly, with no consideration whatsoever of who he stood among. "We thought you were dead."

"I . . ." Amir began, dangling beneath Hasmin's clasp, his head tilted awkwardly backward. "I'm not?"

A more urgent thought rose to the surface, which he could not hold back from asking. "Karim bhai . . . *Kabir* . . . did they?"

Karim bhai nodded weakly. "To Talashshukh."

Amir concealed with difficulty a deep desire to hurt Hasmin. He didn't know to what extent, or how. Only that Hasmin, who held Amir like one holds a dead rat picked from the gutter, had to pay. He glared at the chief of the chowkidars, who merely shrugged, as if to say, *I told you this was his—and your—fate.*

"What is the meaning of this, Karim?" Orbalun demanded, having gathered himself and shrugged off the fawning touches of half a dozen ministers.

Karim bhai turned and fell at Orbalun's feet, his hands outstretched. "Apologies, huzoor. The boy has been reckless. He is one of ours."

"A Raluhan?"

"Yes, huzoor," Karim bhai admitted. Amir heard a snarl from Hasmin, as if Amir didn't have a right to claim his own kingdom.

There was a tinge of disappointment in Orbalun's face, but he was quick to conceal it. Around him, the other thronekeepers and ministers began to lose patience, though it was hard to say at whom.

"Is this man also a Carrier?" Zariba posed the question first. "Am I to understand there are presently not one but two Carriers in my palace, Orba?"

"Guests." Orbalun smiled. "While my wife and family grieve over the loss of my unborn son, Karim served as an able replacement. Although, I daresay Karim does deserve a place among my retinue even if my entire family were to be available for this feast."

"Ever the champion of the downtrodden," snarled the thronekeeper of Talashshukh, a gaunt-eyed man with a hard, chiseled face and a neatly trimmed mustache who looked more a soldier than a royal.

Orbalun smiled. "My hands are tied, Silmehi. I do what I can."

At that moment, half a dozen chowkidars came streaming out of a door. They came to a skidding halt at the sight of the seven thronekeepers and their ministers, including their own, Rani Zariba.

They quickly shuffled their pikes behind them. "Maharani sahiba." They bowed collectively. "Apologies for barging in like this. We heard a cry for help from the unit." One of them glanced up at the bedraggled figure of Karim bhai at the fore of the royals, and then his eyes met Amir's. Amir identified the chowkidar as the man who had admitted them into the palace.

"You . . ." the chowkidar gasped, snatching everyone's attention toward him. "You're the Jewelmaker's apprentice, aren't you? . . . Maharani . . ." His eyes widened as he addressed Rani Zariba and everyone else in the hallway.

"This man—he comes bearing the Poison from the Jewelmaker."

CHAPTER

11

Be wary of night bazaars. You never realize when your soul is being included as a part of the bargain.

—Ghalil Chitroni, *A Dusk of Peacocks*

For Hasmin, the Jhanakari chowkidar's claim about Amir was a personal affront. That a gatecaste could serve the Jewelmaker was an absurdity. Even in the presence of those who could raise an eyebrow and have Amir whipped, Hasmin could not bury the rising rage.

"A member of the Carnelian Caravan?" Hasmin asked, exasperated. "But that is outrageous, huzoor. This man . . . no, it is not possible!"

The thronekeepers circled Amir and Hasmin. A feeling of naked vulnerability coursed through Amir. He wished he could burrow into a hole like Munivarey's in Illindhi and just slip through.

"Carrier," Orbalun said, "you have a name?"

Amir stood surrounded by glitter and gold. "Yes, huzoor. I'm Amir."

"Are you truly one of the Jewelmaker's?"

Amir swallowed. He glanced at Karim bhai, who, from behind the assembly, was slowly shaking his head. The dilemma fell upon Amir like a coconut from the skies. He was in the presence of the most powerful people in the eight kingdoms, and his closest friend. All of whom would be hunted down by the Uyirsena were he to fail in his task. And of course he was going to fail. He had no idea where Madhyra was. Or what she was planning. Kalay was missing, and he was here, being accused of carrying the very substance he had desperately hunted for all these years.

At least if Harini were here, he'd have managed a flimsy excuse. A pinch of courage, nothing more.

"Yes," he said, deflated. "I am. But I don't carry the Poison with me."

"He lies!" Hasmin shrieked. "Tell the maharaja where you went when you disappeared through the Spice Gate!"

Word in the night bazaar was that the Jewelmaker was a royal alchemist of Vanasi who wished to conceal his identity. That he would have servants and traders from the Bowl, among other homes of the gatecaste, did not escape their thoughts, even if—for people like Hasmin—the idea seemed preposterous. However, if there was one thing they all agreed upon, it was that the Jewelmaker was one of their own. A citizen of the eight kingdoms.

Gates, it must be killing them to think they've been bargaining with bowlers for the Poison all these years.

It was a pinprick of a pleasant thought, one Amir knew would disappear soon enough.

"If you do not have the Poison, where is it?" asked Rani Zariba, ignoring Hasmin's interruption.

Orbalun, however, could not quite dismiss his chief and was curiously eyeing Amir. It would seem Hasmin's words had finally had an impact on the thronekeeper. "We will get to that eventually, Zariba. However, I am intrigued. Senapati Hasmin: Did you see this Carrier use the Spice Gate from Raluha?"

"Y-Yes, huzoor."

"Was it during a scheduled trading exchange?"

"No, huzoor," Hasmin said. "There was no trade scheduled for that day. Or rather, at that hour. I admit there was a trade scheduled for later that evening to Kalanadi."

"So . . ." Orbalun scratched his beard as though he were chewing a particularly pungent preparation of bittergourd. "You crossed the Gates unsupervised, out of turn, and went . . . where?"

Before Amir could gather his thoughts, Hasmin was racing to reply. "Huzoor, I sent a trusted Carrier to each of the seven kingdoms, minutes after this thevidiya disappeared."

"Language, Senapati," Orbalun warned. Amir thought he saw a smirk on Raja Silmehi's face.

"Apologies, huzoor," Hasmin pleaded.

"Continue."

"I have a written admission from the Gate wardens of each kingdom that no Carrier resembling Amir—or anybody at all—had showed up at their respective Gates at that time."

Murmurs spread like ripples through the hallway. The thronekeepers exchanged disbelieving looks, a hint of anxiety creeping into their midst.

Amir wished he could evaporate on the spot. His charade would end now. Hasmin's story had no crack to slip through unless he exposed Illindhi . . . thereby jeopardizing everyone else in the room. Even Karim bhai, standing a few feet away, was shaking his head dejectedly.

"The Carnelian Caravan *is* known to be rather elusive," Rani Zariba said, though her tone indicated she wouldn't believe anything Amir was about to say. She had an ice-cold stare, as though with each word she were puncturing a different part of Amir's body with needles.

"Tut-tut," said Rani Mehreen of Mesht, a diminutive woman with fair, glowing skin, as though she'd been bathing in a pool of milk and saffron since morning. "Been a thronekeeper for thirty-seven years, and I have no bloody idea where they hole up when the sun goes down."

Thirty-seven years as thronekeeper? She looks barely older than you.

"Even so . . ." Rani Zariba said. "We must inves—"

Orbalun cleared his throat, interrupting Zariba's plot. She eyed him with quiet concern.

"This," Orbalun declared, "is now a matter of Raluhan security. I wish to investigate this personally. Senapati Hasmin, you will escort Amir and Karim to my chambers immediately."

A clamor broke out among the thronekeepers.

"Convenient," Rani Asphalekha of Kalanadi said. She was a serpentine woman, decked in a poison-green sari with an emerald crown atop her head. The fall of her sari trailed on the floor for three feet behind her, making Amir wonder how she'd managed to dance with Orbalun in the fields. "Do you wish the Poison for yourself, Orba? Would you so blatantly misuse our laws?"

Orbalun laughed an uproarious laugh. "Asphalekha, meri jaan. Zariba's men have searched the Carrier thoroughly. He carries no vial of the Poison, and even if he were to be a member of the Jewelmaker's caravan, we cannot forsake the Spice Trade's code of conduct for Carriers over a few vials of the Poison. We must follow due process."

Asphalekha, however, was undeterred. She towered over Amir and pinned her gaze to him. "What is it, chokra? Is it spices? Or money? What does the Jewelmaker seek? We have all the wealth."

"I swear I don't have the Poison," Amir replied honestly.

"Then who does?"

"I . . . it's with—"

"Enough," Orbalun snapped. Amir had never thought that the face that had chuckled at being hurled to the ground in a collision was capable of anger, but there was no mirth in Orbalun's voice now. "He is a citizen of Raluha, and I forbid an interrogation in this manner. I assure you, Asphalekha, if he truly does carry the Poison, I will excuse myself of my share. You can have mine and do what you wish with it. You know my word and the weight it carries. Or do you doubt that as well now?"

Orbalun's words cut like a knife through Asphalekha's buttery facade. She appeared defeated but did not admit it openly. Instead, she made a face and avoided meeting Orbalun's eye.

Amir, on the other hand, felt as if he had sprouted a new limb. Had Orbalun just *defended* him? A bowler? True, word in the Bowl was that Orbalun had always been a little soft when it came to Carriers, but Amir had not expected anything less than a punishment and a scandal to erupt out of this mess.

"Now, I must apologize for this ruckus, Maharani Zariba," Orbalun said. "Not every Carrier must be regarded as a doer of evil like Ilangovan. And as a citizen of Raluha, this man stands to be questioned by me and my officials before he bows beneath the Spice Trade's pedestal. Do you disagree?"

A faint smile played on Rani Zariba's lips. "You cannot blame me, Orba, for assuming that all Carriers are cut from the same cloth. The situation with Ilangovan is worsening every day."

"I am aware, Zariba," Orbalun said. "But that is neither here nor there. And if you continue to give credence to the theory that the Jewelmaker is in bed with Ilangovan, or worse, that Ilangovan *is* the Jewelmaker, then I'm afraid I cannot help you. Nor can I encourage the public persecution of this Carrier simply because he is supposedly tethered to our Poison supplier. I must remind you that we still do not have any evidence of that."

Amir's heart swelled at Orbalun's speech. He exchanged hopeful glances with Karim bhai, who shook his head discreetly, as though Amir would be a fool to rest his hopes on the abovefolk.

"It doesn't matter anymore," Zariba said. "Ilangovan has forced my hand, and I will do what I must to safeguard the people of Jhanak, and the Spice Trade."

"Has Ilangovan forced your hand, or has someone else?" Orbalun asked sharply.

"Orba!" Zariba towered over Orbalun in that instant, and everyone around them shrank from the sight. "I pleaded with you to take care of your queen and grieve the death of your son. You insisted you wanted to come for the feast and dine with me. Now, am I to understand that it is for me to suffer insults such as this?"

Maharaja Orbalun did not let his stature dictate his predicament. He let a faint smile play on his lips. "A convenient gesture, Zariba, meri jaan, to keep me away from the happenings of the Jhanakari court. Why, I'm certain everyone here is curious to know the whereabouts of the Halmoran contingent."

"Hear, hear," Asphalekha muttered, just loudly enough for everyone.

Amir swallowed. He continued to stand there like a goat awaiting slaughter to be made into a steaming plate of biryani. So Harini—or her father, Raja Virular—*had* deserted the afsal dina. Or had Madhyra forbade her from attending the feast? What did it matter? The fact was, neither were here. Where could they be?

Orbalun took a deep breath and Zariba stared at him, stunned. "And we shall confer on it tomorrow at the feast, I'm sure," he said smoothly. "But now I must take your leave."

"Orba—"

"Hasmin, take Karim and Amir to my chambers. Now."

Hasmin did not need to be told a third time. He yanked Amir around and dragged him down the hallway. Karim bhai followed them meekly, chewing a cardamom.

Once they were out of earshot, Hasmin's hold on Amir tightened. "The maharaja saved your skin," he spat, aware that Orbalun was following them a few paces behind, flanked by an armed retinue of Jhanakari and Raluhan chowkidars.

Once inside the chamber, they waited for Orbalun. Hasmin paced impatiently, while Amir and Karim bhai squatted to one side against the wall.

"What is going to happen to us?" Amir whispered so Hasmin couldn't hear.

"I don't know," Karim bhai replied. "You *did* break half a dozen laws of the Spice Trade. But Orbalun . . . he's a good man."

Amir's imagination conjured the churning image of the Whorl. Surely they wouldn't punish him under Jhanakari law, would they? It would be Raluhan law, which meant being sent to the jail beneath the Pyramid for a lifetime of darkness. *Which would be worse . . .*

"Karim bhai . . . I . . . you shouldn't be here. I shouldn't have seen you . . . or the maharaja, or anyone else."

"What are you talking about?" Karim bhai leaned closer to Amir and lowered his voice even further. "What happened in Illindhi?"

Amir shook his head. "I can't, bhai." In that moment, he realized how much he sounded like Harini when he last saw her.

What secret did she hide?

Surprise was etched on Karim bhai's face. He looked taken aback for a moment, as though Amir had broken a cardinal rule between them. The next moment, however, he softened.

"Whatever it is, can it get any worse? If you were not supposed to see me . . . but you did. Does it matter anymore? Pulla, you need to let me in."

Amir considered breaking the dam. Letting the words flow. Perhaps sharing the burden wouldn't be such a bad thing. There wasn't a thing in his life that Karim bhai did not know. And yet, the past few days had left Amir adrift. Time had passed in a blur, and Amir couldn't escape the feeling that somehow, everyone and everything had been split from him, a void built in between that couldn't be crossed, each side staring across the chasm and acknowledging the divergence of their fates.

Before he could open his mouth, though, the door opened and Orbalun strode in. He was alone.

Hasmin immediately bowed, while both Karim bhai and Amir stood and folded their hands.

"Huzoor."

"Senapati, close the door."

Hasmin obeyed. Orbalun went and sat on a high-backed chair by the large, arched window, twined his arms behind his head and crossed his legs. He gazed out of the window that overlooked the sea. The tang of the coast sailed in, mingling with sharp fumes of cinnamon that coated even the walls of the palace. It was like the palace itself was a large pastry that ought to be nibbled at, and Amir was glad for the snacks he pilfered just a while ago.

Kalay is still out there. You better pray she hasn't been caught.

After a long, aching silence, Orbalun regarded Amir. "So, you truly did not appear in any of the eight kingdoms when you disappeared from Raluha, is that right?"

Amir glanced at Hasmin, who sported a devious smile, as though he could record the imagery of this conversation in his memory forever.

"That is right, huzoor." Amir bowed even deeper. He could see intricate floral patterns on the carpet.

"Then it is true." Orbalun sighed. "Tell me, Amir. How was Illindhi?"

Amir held his tongue and continued to stare at the patterns on the floor. Gentle daffodils, strung up in rows. With twisted stems that wound around them like dark strings, embedded in velvet. It reminded him of an arrangement of upma kozhukattai that Amma would make once a month, having amassed all their paltry allowances. A lump of rava flour, ginger, mustard, and sesame seeds. Amir could not bring himself to raise his head to reply.

"Huzoor?" he heard Hasmin's gasp.

Beside Amir, Karim bhai stirred. "Maharaja, you know of this place? How?"

"A bit of fortune, really," Orbalun said. "But I must hear it from the Carrier."

Hasmin strode toward Amir to plant a kick. "Answer the maharaja, you vile mongrel. *Saniyaney!*"

"Senapati!" Orbalun warned, and Hasmin stopped his foot inches away from Amir.

Amir was not certain if concealing his purpose would satisfy anyone, least of all himself. This was a path from which there would be no turning back, and it seemed either way might mean the continued pain—if not death—of his family. Swallowing, he looked up. "Yes, huzoor," he said quietly. "I went to Illindhi. I . . . did not see much. I was blindfolded. But huzoor . . . forgive me, how did you—"

Orbalun raised a finger. "A matter of relatively lesser importance. I received a most curious book . . ."

"A *book*?" Amir asked.

"A story, rather. Of a ninth kingdom, and a truly incredible spice called olum, which could be manipulated to evoke the fragrance and taste of any of the spices of the eight kingdoms."

"The book speaks true, then," Amir admitted. "All of it. I saw the spice with my own eyes. I . . . took in its fragrance. It is unlike anything I've ever smelled."

Orbalun smiled. He stood from the chair and began to pace the room. "The question is—why did *I* find the book? Of all the thronekeepers, of all the people in this world . . . it is curious that I must be its recipient. Whoever planted the book went to the effort of infiltrating my own bedchambers and leaving it under my pillow. I have been trying to divine an answer to this and have failed. It has kept my mind occupied when . . . well, when I have not been mourning the death of my child."

So, Madhyra has been in Raluha too.

"I . . . I am sorry, huzoor." Amir went down on his knees and pressed his face to the ground. He knew the moment was not far off when he'd have to tell the maharaja his reason for visiting Illindhi, and the circumstances surrounding it.

He'd have to tell him about Harini.

Miraculously, he felt Orbalun lifting him up. Hard, coarse fingers and an unnatural strength he couldn't place in a man like the maharaja. Beside him Hasmin was aghast.

"You have nothing to apologize for. My healers and I know that my wife failed to deliver a child because of inherent problems in her health and not because the Carriers dispatched to Halmora failed to return with turmeric in their sacks. Yes, we hold store in our traditions. But we must remember not to be swayed by the potency of the stories they are tethered to."

Amir wiped his eyes. "I feel a little unburdened, huzoor. Thank you. But I think I have an answer to your question."

He warily glanced at Hasmin, who egged him on. Orbalun's eyes widened curiously. "Do you, now?"

Amir stared again at the carpet. "The . . . uh, the thronekeeper of Illindhi—a woman named Madhyra. She wishes to leak the secret of Illindhi to the eight kingdoms. I believe she was gathering thronekeepers to her cause. You, huzoor, might have been her first choice. A man in pain, looking for some sort of rationality, or escape."

Orbalun clapped his hands. "I must say, she did sound rather compelling in her book. Which brings me to my next question. If not me, then—ah! It is not a coincidence indeed, that the dignitaries of the Halmoran qila are absent from the afsal dina feast."

Slowly, Amir nodded.

"I would have expected more . . . resilience from Raja Virular."

"It was not Raja Virular, huzoor," said Amir. "Nor Rani Bhagyamma. It is their daughter . . . Harini. It is she Madhyra went to. I believe they conspired to keep Raja Virular and the queen silent on this matter."

"Fascinating, utterly fascinating." Orbalun appeared impressed by the series of incidents.

"Harini, Maharaja . . ." Amir blurted out. "She—she wouldn't do something like this. She—uh, obviously cares for the people of Halmora, but she has never desired the throne."

"You know her well, I suppose." His eyes narrowed, and there was a sudden twinkle in them that Amir had to once more avert his gaze from.

"As well a man thinks he can know another woman, huzoor. Which, it might appear, is not much."

"I should have known," Hasmin spat, "when I saw your name on every Halmoran roster. Whom did you bribe, you thief? Theru porikki! Is it Jhengara? Is this why he's been singing happy tunes? I'll see to him, and I'll see to you, thevidiya, that you don't see a pinch of turmeric for the rest of your life."

Orbalun raised his hand, and Hasmin swallowed the remainder of the words on his tongue. Amir had feared there would be distress, a churn of panic that would force the thronekeeper to summon the others and put an end to this. Instead, Orbalun sank in his chair and began to scratch his beard. "It is heartening to see Carriers mingling with the populace of another kingdom. That there is more to this business of trade than mere spice. Which brings me to my final question, Amir. And I believe you know what that is."

Why did you go to Illindhi?

There would, after all, be no escape from this questioning. It was not

Orbalun's eye he feared meeting in that moment but Hasmin's. There was a strange hunger in the chief of the chowkidar's eyes, a flicker of doubt, as though the initial promise of interrogation had descended into something less terrible, and more in Amir's favor. His lips twitched at the maharaja's question, and nothing but the truth would help him now.

He'd have to tell Orbalun his plan of escape.

And so, he began.

WHEN AMIR FINISHED SPEAKING, THERE WAS A SILENCE SO ABSO-lute, they could hear the distant cries of the seagulls, and the myriad sounds from the docks and the city—the crashing of waves, the bobbing of ships, the creaking of timber, the whoosh of air.

Hasmin walked over to the nearest wall and slammed a fist into it. "I told you, huzoor. I warned you of this creature's plot. Now you have heard it from his mouth. While you have served to protect the people of our great kingdom, it is scum like him who would undermine you. Who would rub your name in the mud and run away to sow chaos and panic along with bandits like Ilangovan. He must be hanged and not a single spice must be embalmed on his rotting corpse. I . . ." Silence was the maharaja's only response, and Hasmin's fervor wavered just a bit. "I obviously await your command, huzoor."

Orbalun was gazing outside. His long hair that fell to his shoulders waved in a sorrowful dance against the wind. Beside Amir, Karim bhai's breathing had gotten shallower. It was one thing to have the ear of the thronekeeper, it was another to predict the outcome of such an account. Amir knew he was alone and that, if he was being realistic, Hasmin's proposal was the only proper outcome.

It was surprising, then, when the thronekeeper of Raluha chided Hasmin. "My command is for you to not harm a single hair on this young man. He brings us valuable information."

Hasmin gasped as if his breath had been violently knocked out of his body. "But huzoor—"

"I understand your anger, Senapati. But do you presume, for certain, to know better?"

Hasmin lowered his head. "No, huzoor. I only meant that this is too bad a crime to be condoned."

"I hear you, Senapati. And I don't necessarily disagree. But right now, the situation demands that Amir help me. And for me to help him." He narrowed his eyes at Amir. "The high priest of Illindhi. Did he say that Madhyra would want to re-create the transformation of olum into the eight spices?"

Amir replied, "Yes, huzoor. Mahrang believed the thronekeepers of the eight kingdoms would not believe her otherwise."

"A valid assumption," Orbalun said. "Madhyra was cunning in mentioning this in her book as well. She detailed a recipe for conversion, and there is one ingredient that is vital and extremely hard to procure."

"Which is?"

"Coriander leaves."

Amir recalled the conversation among the members of the Chairs of Illindhi. Kashyni had cut Madhyra off from acquiring any coriander leaves from their own stores, which meant Madhyra would have to rely on procuring what little coriander grew in the eight kingdoms.

With a rush of fear, Amir understood everything that had transpired in the palace of Halmora.

Coriander was available in only one part of the eight kingdoms.

"The Black Coves!" Amir exclaimed, snatching everyone's attention. "Ilangovan!"

That was why Harini and Madhyra wished to meet with Ilangovan. He controlled the largest—and possibly the only—supply of coriander, and by securing it, they would have everything they required to prove olum's potency to the remaining thronekeepers.

"The Jhanakari chowkidars did not lie when they claimed they had permitted Harini and a companion to enter Jhanak," Orbalun said, untying the knot. "They never arrived in the palace, or to the harvest ritual. It confirms what I thought: Zariba has joined with them, even though she would not outrightly admit it. Ilangovan's menace has plagued her the most. Any negotiation that would mitigate such a threat would benefit her. As a thronekeeper, I can sympathize with her plight."

Karim bhai, who had been silent all this while, said through gritted teeth, "The Black Coves, then."

Hasmin appeared flustered. "I must apologize, huzoor, but I don't understand what is happening. Are we to believe this good-for-nothing and his fancy tale? This is what the bowlers want. To sow discord among us. Given their way, Ilangovan would be the sole ruler of the eight kingdoms."

Orbalun flashed a contagious grin at his senapati. "Hasmin, meri jaan. Trust me when I say I thought the tale no less fanciful when I first read it. But to hear it confirmed by someone who could have had no knowledge of the book? Even if I wanted to, part of me warns against dismissing it outright."

"Do you still have that book, huzoor?"

"No, I burned it after I finished reading. In the wrong hands—even within the palace—it could be put to ill use. I did however preserve a part of it. A particularly curious fragment I found within it aside from the story of Illindhi."

"Pray, tell us what it is, huzoor."

Orbalun was slow to respond. His eyes narrowed at each of them, as though scrutinizing how they would react to his words. Could it get any worse? Amir wondered. Orbalun finally took a deep breath. He went to his trunk, opened it, and began rummaging among its contents. Seconds later, he retrieved a stack of parchment. Dusting off the papers, he stood and showed the stack to his audience. "I found several pages that painted detailed maps of the Outerlands. And of the Immortal Sons who wander their darkness."

Amir watched Karim bhai's face pale. And his own heart skipped a beat, the word Kalay had used echoing in his mind: *Ranagala*. The Outerlands? Impossible, no! This had to be a lie. Yet there was a glint in Orbalun's eyes, a secret Amir knew that he himself had yearned to share all these days.

A glint of truth.

"Huzoor, what are you speaking of?" Hasmin sank to his knees, eyes still on the parchment. Surely he now thought the thronekeeper himself was deranged. That this was all a great conspiracy or a joke.

But Hasmin's disbelief mattered little in the moment. For Amir, the world shifted beneath his feet as the face of his father swam before his eyes. The face of the man who had abandoned Amir and his family. The face of a traitor, of a bowler who was a coward. Amir had known on that day, at least, that only death awaited his father in the Outerlands. And that his absence all these years was evidence of it. That surely nothing could last beyond the impassable chasms, the Whorl, the great mountains that couldn't be scaled, the bogs that couldn't be waded through, the jungles whose branches were poisonous limbs, and the valleys where the air itself was toxic.

Orbalun, however, remained composed, which threw everything Amir thought he knew into chaos. *Could Appa be alive? Does the satisfaction of his death still elude me?*

"I am speaking of a trail that begins at Illindhi and ends at Amarohi," the thronekeeper said, "the kingdom of cloves. And other trails that have not yet been fully charted but nevertheless appear to be hospitable. Where there are treacherous mountains and vales, Madhyra has scribbled 'Immortal Son' beside each of them. It is possible the features of the Outerlands—the dangerous rivers and mountains—themselves are what the Illindhians have, since antiquity, called the Immortal Sons. Our own stories have evolved to give them flavor and life. But that is a different matter. What is important to understand here is that, given the existence of the maps, and their detail, it would appear Madhyra arrived in the eight kingdoms not through the Spice Gate, but via the Outerlands."

Karim bhai exhaled, reaching for the parchment and staring at it. "That's impossible!"

"Huzoor," Hasmin said. "The ministers would—"

"Condemn me?" Orbalun snarled. "Label me a blasphemer? Threaten to oust me? Do you think they don't already desire that? It is the reason why I destroyed the book instead of choosing to hide it in the palace.

"Do not mistake me for an old, gullible fool. I do not believe still that the Outerlands is habitable. Bless the Immortal Sons who watch over our borders and maintain peace between the eight kingdoms. But with all that's going on, I do not wish to dismiss what I do not fully understand. My priority now is to stop Madhyra, Senapati. She cannot be allowed to speak of Illindhi to the other thronekeepers. The danger, as Amir has mentioned, is real. It is the lives of thousands, tens of thousands, of people, across the eight kingdoms. Our gentler curiosities must wait."

Amir could see Hasmin's fists clench, but the chief of the chowkidars inclined his head in a curt nod. "I await your command, huzoor."

Orbalun took a deep breath. "The other thronekeepers will expect me to provide a resolution to this supposed interrogation by tomorrow's feast. Clearly, you are not a merchant of the Jewelmaker, nor do you carry the Poison."

"If Harini and Madhyra are in the islands, I must go there," Amir said, stunned at the force of his own words. "I am certain Harini is with her not of her full volition. I can talk to her. She trusts me."

"You will do as the maharaja commands, rat," Hasmin hissed. "Hold your tongue until then."

Karim bhai stood and folded his hands, ignoring Hasmin's warning. "Huzoor, apologies, but I should go too. I know the fishermen by the docks. There are a few who can lend us their boats."

Orbalun went to the window once more. It was dark outside, and a pale, silvery orb emerged in the sky and moonlight spattered on the sea. A cold gust of air blew through the window, sending a chill down Amir's spine. He and Karim bhai continued to stand with their hands respectfully folded, shivering. Hasmin was eyeing Orbalun eagerly, and perhaps with a hint of suspicion.

"Senapati," the thronekeeper said, "you will go to the Black Coves tonight to stop Madhyra from getting the coriander leaves. And you will be accompanied by Amir and Karim."

"But huzoor, you cannot trust these—"

"This is not up for debate," Orbalun finished. "Do it discreetly. I do not want any Jhanakari guards sneaking into Zariba's chambers and whispering of our ploy. Is that understood?"

Amir did not even hear Hasmin's response. A fearful excitement bubbled in his chest, and a roaring filled his ears. He was going to get Madhyra for his Poison. He was going to see Harini.

And he was going to the Black Coves. To his future home.

CHAPTER
12

The myth of the Immortal Sons must exist for life within the fences to appear more rewarding. It is an imperial concoction, make no mistake.

—NOTES FROM A DIARY RECOVERED FROM
A HANGED PRISONER'S CELL

The docks of Jhanak were not a place of charm and haggling like the bazaar of Vanasi, nor were they decorous like the market of Halmora. Here, tempers flared each second. And everyone ran on a tight timetable with the constant loading and unloading of crates from patamars and urus carrying goods to and from the islands around Jhanak. The air was rife with subtle aromas and a cauldron of recipes. Sailors gathered beside wood fires for their dinner, white hair glowing in the firelight.

Amir's stomach grumbled.

"Pathiri," Karim bhai mused dreamily, looking at their dinners. "And stuffed meat with ghee cooked in coconut oil. Someday, you must try the arikadukka."

"What is that?" Amir asked, quietly jealous of the sailors being able to afford ghee in their meals.

"It's mussels. You stuff them with coconut paste and rice that is steaming with fragrance. The cooks marinate that in a fiery maavu mixed with red chilies, and then fry it till their tongues are satisfied. Gates know they are. At least mine was. And tomorrow at the great afsal dina feast, you may even be fortunate to taste some bananas they stuff with grated coconuts and nuts, which are then fried in vats of ghee. Gates, the ghee these people use! It's a wonder their bellies haven't burst."

"There will be no feasting," Hasmin snarled, and it was all Amir could do to keep from pushing him into the water as they walked toward a promising boat. Karim bhai, meanwhile, had begun to chat up one of the sailors. Part of Amir was nostalgic for the evenings along the docks, among the merchants and sailors and the laborers, when Karim bhai drunk himself down in the taverns while Amir gathered the correspondences that had to be delivered and scoured the wharfs and the granaries, plying the hearts of those to whom the letters were addressed. He spoke their language, he knew their families and their secrets, and above all, he knew the *price* of things. Karim bhai had ensured that. The Spice Trade favored those who could look at an object—big or small—in the bazaar and tell its worth. Jhanak was a crude reminder of that knowledge, of this secret of the Spice Carriers.

Amir's eyes fell upon the sailors, some of whom made a gesture of recognition toward him. They lounged beside the wharfs with their pipes and their mugs, grizzly beards and colorful sarongs, white hair tied up or let loose upon their shoulders. Sailors who'd trade with the Black Coves and the other islands on this side of the Whorl in exchange for coriander leaves.

You will be their merchant in the future. No more just delivering letters. You'll be dealing in spices. Recognize their stances, their smells. Remember their stories.

The sound of gentle rolling waters quieted his mind, although Hasmin eyed the sea nervously. Of course he'd never seen a body of water, let alone something as vast as the ocean. Despite his dominance over Amir and Karim bhai, Hasmin appeared small, defeated in front of the black expanse, and by the ignorance of all that he was surrounded by.

Karim bhai returned from the negotiation looking hopeful. "The Black Coves are the last of the islands before the Whorl. We must cross past eighty isles, so a small boat may not suffice. I got us a dhow-made uru."

Amir raised an eyebrow. "And what did you part with?"

Karim bhai appeared guilty. "A pouch full of jeera. Neither saffron nor cinnamon whets their appetites these days, seeing as they get them in plenty. But cumin, the Meshti kallas have been stingy with."

"Those are not your spices to give away," Hasmin said.

Karim bhai squared up to him. "Then I suggest you take it up with the maharaja, *Senapati*. Remember you're not in Raluha anymore."

Hasmin inched closer, bringing up his pike to attack position. Amir squeezed between them, his hands splayed. "Now, now." He angled his face toward Hasmin, lowering his voice to a whisper. "You don't want to be brawling on Jhanakari wharfs, kaka. A word, and you'd be pinned to the pier with your hands sawed off by these sailors before you can utter the first casteist slur that stains your tongue."

Ah, that feels so good.

Hasmin did not lower his spear at once. But his gaze roved over the sailors, each of them built like an elephant, and he did not find it in himself to question their loyalty toward Amir and Karim bhai should a brawl erupt at that moment. Slowly, he turned away, spat on the ground, and marched toward the uru waiting for them.

"We should feed him to the sharks," Amir suggested once Hasmin was out of earshot.

"The sharks would spit him right back out, pulla. Come, let's go."

Amir ambled down the pier behind Karim bhai, eyes darting from the deck of one resting ship to another; their masts were caught in moonlight, sterns rigged with barrels and coils of ropes. Upon them, the shadows of men huddled beneath a canvas, trying to catch a few hours of sleep. Halfway across the pier, they came across a great ship. Its maroon sails cut the moon and fluttered in the sea breeze. Amir had never seen a ship this large from so close.

Could it be?

The ship of the Condemned. The vessel the prisoners would use to traverse the breadth of the Whorl, never to return. It loomed above him and looked like the darkest tree in the forest had been rudely cut down to build its bulk. The sides were painted a dull black, interspersed with shades of russet. Amir recalled what he had heard of the thick iron chains on the hull used to bind the prisoners, and shivered.

"Don't stare at it," Karim bhai muttered. "It's a curse. Wouldn't wish the Whorl on my worst enemy. Not even that one," he said, subtly jerking his head in Hasmin's direction.

They reached the end of the pier, where in darkness they found the fishing boat. It had a narrow stern and a supply shack on one side beneath the rigging for the sail. The boat was built for four, maybe five people at most. Two oars lay on the benches on each side, along with spools of net, an anchor, and a vat of tack with rods and reels. Amir followed Karim bhai and Hasmin into it with trepidation. The boat rocked on the water. He imagined what it would mean to tumble out over the edge and into the salty depths.

The water was scarier from up close. The endlessness. The darkness. The rivers of Mesht, his nearest point of comparison, were neither deep nor were they wide; the land was always in reach. Besides, Amir had always traversed the rivers of Mesht with twenty other Carriers, and some of the locals. Back in the Bowl, Appa had taught Amir to swim in their narrow kolam—a tank of water not longer than twenty feet, and five feet wide, stinking of unwashed clothes with garbage clinging to the sides.

This, though, was neither the kolam nor the narrow rivers of Mesht. This was the boundless ocean, its depth unknowable. And despite having been on this part of the sea a few times, Amir's fear of the ocean did not abate.

Kabir would love it. This is where he will come every time he's on Carrying duty in Jhanak. To the waters. To the wharfs, to sit and paint, if his fingers are able.

A pang of fear gripped Amir at this thought, and he grabbed on to Hasmin's uniform for balance. Hasmin—who was frightened to his innermost core at the prospect of going deeper into the sea—shook Amir off and pushed him onto the deck. Amir fell with a thump, and pain shot up his elbow. The boat swayed violently.

"Ho," Karim bhai cried. "What was that for?"

"Don't touch me," Hasmin said calmly, even as fear was evident in his eyes. There was an uneasiness on his face as he watched the ripples around the boat. He was wary of the unknown. Ahead, moonlight bobbed on the surface of the sea like a bleeding ghost.

"Now, g-go and grab the oars," Hasmin stammered. "The two of you will work them."

Neither Amir nor Karim bhai complained. They had used the urus enough other times during their spare hours on carrying duty and were no strangers to this vessel. An hour was never enough, however, and they never got farther than a few isles away from Jhanak.

Tonight they would cross nearly eighty of them. Tonight they would be seeing Amir's new home.

Amir untied the mooring rope and pushed the vessel away from the pier's edge, subduing his fear. He watched as the slender support to land wilted away. The feeble firelight from the docks began to dim.

They were under way, toward the dark and empty and endless . . .

Suddenly Amir saw a figure hurtling down the pier. A silhouette that sheared off the dark mounds of taverns and ship hulls and barrels, past huddled shadows against campfires, and emerged closer and closer to their drifting boat.

Before he could say anything to his companions, the figure leaped off the edge of the pier and landed on their boat with a deft roll. The entire boat swayed and shook, and Hasmin, who'd been standing gripping the pole drilled into the hull, teetered and screamed as he lost balance. Amir threw his oar on the bench and caught Hasmin as he fell. Hasmin shrieked and pulled himself off his rescuer.

Ungrateful bastard . . . You should have let the water take him.

There was no time to dwell on that, though, as the figure who had landed on the boat was up on their feet.

Kalay did not appear ruffled in any manner. She looked from a stunned Karim bhai to Hasmin, who had just extricated himself from Amir's arms. She heaved a deep sigh and unsheathed something glinting from her waist and extended it forward.

"You forgot this in the palace," Kalay said, handing Amir his shamshir.

Hasmin pulled himself up, unsheathed his own sword, and sliced it blindly toward Kalay. Kalay pulled her own blade and almost effortlessly swung to parry Hasmin's blow. With her own strike, she clattered the sword out of Hasmin's hand, then held the tip of her scimitar at his throat.

"You fight like my grandfather," she spat. "He did not have hands."

Hasmin splayed his own hands, terror etched on his face. The boat rocked silently in the water.

Amir's eyes widened. "Kalay, let him be. He is with us."

"Evidently," she said, then turned to Karim bhai. "A lot of people are, except me. Mahrang told you to not do anything without my consent, didn't he?"

The boat drifted slowly farther away from land. Amir gulped. He bent down and picked up Hasmin's talwar. "We found out where Madhyra could be. We're going to the Black Coves now. Besides, we couldn't find you. You escaped the guards and I didn't know where you were. Honestly." And having seen her display of athleticism and swordplay moments earlier, he found he meant his words—he truly preferred having her on this particular mission.

Kalay took a deep breath. Despite the movement of the boat, her hand was steady on the sword, whose tip did not shiver an inch as it continued to rest against Hasmin's throat. Finally, she pulled the weapon back and sheathed it. "I'm not letting you out of my sight again," she warned.

"Fine by me," Amir said. "Now, can we all just sit? I don't like standing in the middle of the water this way."

They were silent after that, and the only sound was the incessant creaking as Amir and Karim bhai rowed them deeper into the sea. The waves were gentle at first, and Amir decided he had indeed missed the Jhanakari sea, even if he was still terrified of its depth.

When a gale blew harsh, however, they abandoned their oars and let the boats' sail guide them through the moonlit darkness. Hasmin and Kalay exchanged sharp glances every few minutes. The last thing Amir wanted was a fight between the two of them that would jeopardize everything they were working toward—the *only* thing they were working toward. Orbalun was on his side, and Amir could not have hoped for a stronger supporter. Yet could that translate to Madhyra falling into his lap, let alone his promised vial of the Poison?

One can hope.

When the silence became insufferable, Amir asked Karim bhai quietly, "How's Amma?"

Karim bhai was not one to mince words. They were both witnesses to the world closing in on them at the moment, despite having the power to walk across the eight kingdoms.

"The same. She thinks you're on some secret Carrier business, dispatched by someone from the palace. Now that I think of it, ho, she's not wrong."

Amir smiled. Karim bhai continued: "She's due in a few days, pulla. Calls me home to sing a song for the child in her belly. She's almost certain it's going to be a girl. Wants to name her Velli."

Amir ran the name over his tongue. The sound of silver. Moonlight on the threshold of a home. Quietly, he hoped Amma would give birth in the Black Coves. A good omen, the grandmothers would say.

The surroundings dimmed in his vision. He glanced back, and Jhanak was a pinprick, its last fires extinguishing within the fog that now engulfed the coastal kingdom. Up high, the tallest peaks of the palace melted into darkness, and nothing remained but the sea.

With that came sleep.

When he woke, it was nearly dawn. How long had they been sailing?

Kalay and Hasmin were rowing, their eyes like swords aimed for the other's throat. While the strong winds had abated, Amir found himself getting whipped in the face by a low breeze. All around them were islands, black mounds in their silhouettes, and through them the sea weaved like a river. There was a coldness in the air that forced Amir to hug himself. The moon still hovered overhead, casting a paler light on the ocean.

"Where are we?" he asked, yawning.

Karim bhai stretched his arms. "Close now. Only a few islands on this side of the archipelago remain under Jhanakari control. Where the Black Coves begin, and where they end, nobody knows, but so close to the Whorl, everything is Ilangovan's."

In the distance, Amir spied more hills like mounds upon islands. And . . . were his eyes deceiving him, or did he see a hint of firelight?

Yes!

Hasmin appeared to have not gotten a moment's rest. Having passed the oar to Karim bhai, he now sat beady-eyed, holding the pole running across the sailcloth, looking with suspicion between Kalay and Amir, and occasionally into the distance. He was undoubtedly embarrassed by Kalay overpowering him, and only remained aboard because the maharaja had commanded him.

He clearly didn't intend on liking it.

Amir didn't much like it, either, but as long as Hasmin was with them, there would be one less chowkidar to whip Kabir. It was a feeble comfort.

"Don't get too close to the docks," Hasmin said to Karim bhai. "We must not be seen."

Karim bhai shot him a look that left no doubt which man had been sneaking around for longer than the other had been alive.

Amir, meanwhile, was soaking in the expanse of Ilangovan's world. Here, there was no whiff of Jhanak's cinnamon. Rani Zariba's jurisdiction held no sway, and the sleeping galleys standing like sentries between the islands were a testament to that fact. The more he saw, the more Amir was certain—these were not mere outposts or slapdash settlements—this was a civilization unto itself.

The thought made Amir's heart soar.

They slunk in the dark ripples, whistling between the larger galleys, avoiding several catamarans and patamars moored along the coast of one of the larger islands. A forest lay within that island, dense foliage shrouding the presence of light. And again, deeper through the darkness, the hint of fires. Smoke curling out of treetops. For Amir, this promise of light was a promise of life.

There are people in there. Bowlers. Or rooters. Or the gumgums and the sanders. Whoever they were, the gatecaste of the eight kingdoms, here they are just men and women.

Karim bhai and Kalay steered the boat southward from the forest then veered east, skirting the next island but continuing to linger in the steadily brightening darkness.

The islands were smaller than any mainland kingdom Amir had seen. Only the one with the mountain shrouded in mist ahead appeared to be large enough to accommodate several thousand people. Hastily built bamboo settlements peppered the coastlines, boats anchored around them like wooden necklaces.

Karim bhai must have sensed his wonder. "Sentries and trade check posts," he muttered. "We're fortunate to have clearance." He tapped the side of the boat to gesture to the vague symbols etched on the wood.

It surprised Amir how organized Ilangovan was. All the propaganda of chaos, the lawlessness and violence, seemed to evaporate when faced with this mirror of much of the eight kingdoms' supposed civility.

Would this be where Amir would live the rest of his life? In this scattered archipelago, a night's sail away from Jhanak? Where the memory of Raluha would slowly disintegrate until only the scars on his back and limbs, and the echo of the slurs in his ears, would serve as a reminder of the life he'd leave behind?

It was frighteningly easy to dream. That here, with Ilangovan, he'd begin a new life.

The problem is, it's just as easy for that dream to dissolve.

"A large island ahead," Hasmin called, squinting from beneath the sail through the fog. He checked his compass. "Head north."

While the coasts of the smaller islands appeared deserted but for a few stray boats and broken piers, the larger island ahead funneled out from between rock pillars that jutted out of the sea. The rock pillars framed the entrance to a cove, flanked by high crags, beyond which the island stretched in white dunes dotted with wooden settlements.

Rows of galleys flanked smaller patamars and canoes by the entrance. Large poles were planted into the sands of the cove, and early risers had begun to unspool the coils of rope tying their coracles and catamarans. Birds chirped from somewhere on the island, and there was a sense of placid quietness that Amir had secretly longed for.

"Where is everyone?" asked Karim bhai. "It is nearly first light. Unlike a bowler to be sleeping late."

Kalay ran her fingernails along the edge of her scimitar. "I know Madhyra. If she's here, she must have gathered the people someplace."

"We should go in," Amir suggested. "Two of us are Carriers. They won't deny us entry. We don't have to hide."

After much deliberation, Amir and Karim bhai skirted the cove from the west, then rowed north to enter the island from the more bountiful side of the forest. The fog had begun to thicken. It descended like limping clouds from the mountain that lay at the center of the island, bringing with it a chill that Amir had no intention to fight.

Fogs were ominous in Raluha. A hint of fog rolling down from the Outerlands and across the border meant an Immortal Son's long sigh, laid with curses and spells. Amir was not one for superstition, but today, it nibbled at his gut, forming a thick concoction with the strange elation coursing through his blood.

The sail pulled taut as they edged closer to the shore. Again, nothing but a few abandoned catamarans and canoes to greet them. Fishing nets splayed haphazardly. A torn chappal floating in the shallows, along with empty bottles of arrack. A column of cow dung on the sands like ugly footprints. Coconut shells dried and forgotten.

Remnants of a celebration, perhaps. Perhaps even the Black Coves commemorated the afsal dina.

Where the water was shallow, Karim bhai leaped down and began to drag the uru toward the sands. Amir and Kalay joined him, and Hasmin glared at them as though it was beneath his dignity to perform such a menial task. He seemed perfectly content adding his weight to the vessel as the three of them dragged it to shore.

The sound of birds from the jungle was accompanied by the hollow swirl of the sea breeze. From the east, the first light of day was barely visible through the fog. They were well and truly concealed on this beach.

Gathering their belongings, they breached the tree line and entered the jungle. Hasmin unsheathed his sword and walked ahead of the rest of them, his footsteps cracking the undergrowth. The trees closed around them within seconds, plunging them into darkness once more.

"Coriander grows here," Karim bhai murmured once they couldn't see the coast behind them anymore. "In this forest. Though nobody but Ilangovan's folks know how to harvest it."

"I can't remember its taste," Amir said. "Though I'm certain I've had it in the Bowl."

"Tastes like rarity, pulla," Karim bhai said. "A scent for rare spices. You will find only a few feasts across the eight kingdoms that boast of gravies of brinjal, cauliflower, and rice, and ah—in their midst—a lurking aroma of coriander. There are spicemasters who believe when coriander leaves are consumed, it evokes memories of another spice, of another time. People who eat meals with coriander leaves think they are being smuggled into poppy dens, like an enchantment."

"Coriander is not one of the eight spices of the Mouth," Kalay said grimly. "But it is nevertheless acknowledged in the scriptures as carrying great potency and wonder. It is sacrilegious to think of it as a trip to the poppy den."

"Are you never cheerful?" Amir asked.

"Who said I'm not being cheerful now?" she said, her expression dour.

Amir stared at her as she brushed aside a drooping branch and stepped over a trailing root. She added, "The spices of the Mouth are not the kingdoms' to give away. They are not meant for trade."

Amir sliced the branch with his shamshir in anger. "This has nothing to do with the Mouth, not that you lot tell us much about it anyway. Besides, Ilangovan and his pirates trade the coriander leaves with Jhanak and Vanasi for black pepper and cinnamon *because they have no choice.* If the eight kingdoms treated the gatecaste better, he wouldn't have to do this."

"He is an outlaw," she said flatly, as though there were no two ways about it. Just an absolute fact.

"He is a *new* law," Amir countered, and Karim bhai nodded.

"Nothing but a terrorist and an insurgent," Hasmin declared, stopping in his tracks and looking at Kalay with something other than disgust. "Give you scums a bit of freedom, and one of you will convince the others to forsake your duties and stage a rebellion against the kingdoms. To forget that you are Carriers serving a higher purpose—what you were born to do, what you should be grateful for. You think he's some sort of a hero, don't you?" Hasmin smirked, beginning to sweat as they waded deeper into the jungle. "That he would upend the way of things, what has worked for over thousands of years, by building outposts in the dark of the seas, and being cunning with coriander and thinking he's earned the Mouth's favor. Let me tell you—he is no different from your father."

A flaring sensation crawled up Amir's skin. He didn't wish to stop walking. Beside him, Karim bhai placed a hand on Amir's arm, restraining his urge.

"But I misspeak. Your father was a better man," Hasmin continued, hacking his way through a low-hanging branch. "His brand of cowardice meant, at least, he did not disrespect the Spice Trade. He was true to the

Mouth, allowing himself to be swallowed up by the Outerlands rather than face the shame."

"You know nothing of my father," Amir muttered.

"I know more of him than you think you do; your stink crawls up the slopes of Raluha to our noses and they are all the same rotten smells. You, your father, Ilangovan. All the same. A legacy of dissenting madarchods! What sets you apart is only how you choose to be ungrateful." He took a deep breath. "But it doesn't matter. Today, the eight kingdoms will sit together and find a way to put an end to Ilangovan. His time on these dreadful isles is over. Ah! I dream of the day the scum is caught and sent down the Whorl with rocks tied to his legs."

"You can perhaps send him yourself."

Suddenly, the woods burst open with several shapes hurtling out from the darkness. They were armed with aruvaals, and despite Hasmin and Kalay being quick to raise their blades, they were thumped away from their hands by steel emerging out of the shadows. The clatter echoed across the forest, and the group collectively held its breath.

The next moment, more than twenty people surrounded them. Karim bhai was the first to raise his hands and drop to the floor. Kalay and Hasmin each had the edge of a sword inches away from their throats and reluctantly went to their knees also. Amir remained standing, frozen.

Two of the assaulters made way for a third to enter and stand a couple of feet from Amir. He had a cloth around his mouth, but his eyes were blue and oddly translucent, as though he were seeing not what was in front of him but elsewhere, among the clouds. His hair was thick and fell to his shoulders in ugly curls. A grizzled scar ran along his cheek. Amir ignored the man's ramlike build and instead focused on the hilt of a spiked mace in the man's hand.

"A Carrier," the man spat. He had a raspy voice, as though he'd swallowed a chicken bone during a rather heavy meal.

"We mean no harm," Amir said, dropping his shamshir and raising his hands. "I am a Carrier of Raluha, and this is Karim bhai, also a Carrier."

The man's tongue traced his lower lip as though weighing the merit of Amir's words. His eyes fell on Hasmin. "This one's in uniform, and no mark."

"He was the one who desired to see the Blessed One sent down the Whorl, Sekaran," said the man holding the sword to Hasmin's neck.

"So what if I did?" snarled Hasmin, and spat on the surface of the blade.

At Sekaran's gesture, the man holding the blade twisted the hilt in his hand and rammed the sword hilt-first into Hasmin's gut. The senapati fell, clutching his belly in a fit of coughs. The man wiped the saliva-ridden surface of his blade on Hasmin's head.

Amir joined his hands, suppressing a crude delight at Hasmin's fate. "This chowkidar is with us, and we mean no harm, we promise. We have come searching for a woman . . . or two women. They must have come to the Black Coves. In the hunt for coriander leaves."

This seemed to have caught Sekaran's attention. "How do you know of them? They are the Blessed One's guests."

Amir gulped. "They have come to steal the coriander leaves. Please, you must stop them."

Sekaran lifted his mace and fingered the spiked iron sphere. He glared at Amir. "They're *guests*," he repeated. "Don't think I won't crack a Carrier's skull, but next time, think before you accuse the Blessed One of being shortsighted. Now, tell me the real reason you and your little clump are here."

His gaze sprawled over Kalay and the spit-stained Hasmin before landing on Karim bhai. Amir's pulse soared. He knew he couldn't tell any of his companions Madhyra's true purpose. He felt the Mouth lingering within his head, a haunting he did not wish to begrudge. It was as if he were carrying a deadly plague. He feared lying to the men holding swords, but he also already *had* blades pressed to his neck—and the necks of those whom he loved.

Slowly, Amir shook his head. "Please, I meant what I said earlier. We're here to help, and to warn Ilangovan. You must seek him out and tell him not to trust Madhyra and Harini. They're here for the coriander—"

Even as Amir saw a hint of reluctance—the teeniest bit of consideration seep into Sekaran's face—Kalay ducked beneath the sword aimed at her, lifted her scimitar from the forest floor, and slashed at the man in front of her. The blow cut a gash in his shoulder and he screeched in pain. Kalay wheeled, grabbed Karim bhai, and used his shoulder as leverage to lift herself and plant a reverse kick on another man charging from behind. Her feet caught his shin. His sword clattered out of his hand as he fell back. Kalay used her momentum to round his torso, then caught the falling sword and flicked it at the man striding from between two trees. He caught the flat of the blade on his forehead, and it knocked him down. Kalay ran and jumped on him and pummeled her fist on his face to silence his scream.

"Kalay, watch out!" Amir shouted.

She whirled in his direction but was just a fraction too slow. Sekaran's mace caught her on her shoulder. A resounding crack, and she fell, clutching her arm. Her scream had barely breached the treetops before two men leaped on her to snatch her scimitar, and a third pinned her to the ground. A red stain had developed on her shoulder, a blooming lotus, and a trickle of blood oozed down her arm.

"Stop, please!" Amir cried.

"Bring them in chains," Sekaran said calmly. "Take them to the cages."

Amir did not resist as a pair of hands grabbed him. Hasmin, without a sword, was furious as he struggled with his captors while his hands were bound. Karim bhai alone offered no struggle. He simply stood and extended his arms.

"They're here for the kothamalli, saheb," he told Sekaran, trying to placate him with the more ancient word for coriander leaves. "An old man wouldn't lie."

Sekaran smiled. "You're one of us, kaka, and I respect someone who has traveled from several kingdoms afar to see the Black Coves. But know this: we don't even keep the coriander leaves on this island."

CHAPTER
13

Spice is a terrible vice. But more terrible than spice, or even love, is that hidden realm of desire and yearning, of wanting to cross the Spice Gates and enter the threshold of a strange world. Instead, be grateful for the world given to you within the fences, and to the Mouth that fills your belly. Life is too short to soak in the wonder of a new world.

—ANONYMOUS, *A FENCE FOR MR. RAMADURAI*

Even after walking a couple of miles through the jungle, Amir sensed they were still close to the coast. The tangy brine of the sea ensnared him, and a wetness hung in the air, even as they were bullied by mosquitoes and bugs and the sort of itchiness that was hard to shake off. A perpetual buzz fluttered around his ears, challenged only by the pounding of his heart.

Sekaran marched the group into a clearing at the foot of the mountain, where a host of bamboo and wooden settlements emerged. Stilt houses, sentry towers, stone escarpments replete with canvasing, and delineated pathways gave the appearance of a village. Puddles dotted the lanes. They did not appear to be entering the village; rather, they skirted along the boundary of this place that had not yet fully woken up. It was proper dawn now, and in the distance, Amir spied the first light climbing the mound of a hill, tickling the horizon in strokes of pale vermilion.

The pirates were leading them toward a narrow pathway that meandered into the mountains when Sekaran raised his hand to stop them. At once, the guards halted. Amir noticed Sekaran's eyes were fixated on the town.

"Where is Maricha?" he asked one of his men.

"Probably still shitting." A couple of the men sniggered.

"And Sumati? I don't see the Neck either."

Murmurs stirred among the guards. The two who held Kalay looked confused. Between them, the acolyte of the Uyirsena hung limply, her mouth open, her arm drooping at an angle, now fully stained red from the blow from Sekaran's mace. Hasmin was held by three men. The senapati was visibly distressed, as though every moment spent breathing the air of the gatecaste was a part of his life that he would wish to erase from memory.

"The well's empty," one of the guards said, pointing.

Sekaran's eyes narrowed. "So why the fuck is everyone still sleeping?"

Two of the guards detached from the group and jogged into the village. They peered into houses, opened tent flaps, checked the storage blocks. After a while, they rejoined the group, their faces pale.

"We tried to wake a few of them up, but it's like they went to sleep a few minutes ago. Hard as rocks."

Amir's heart stuttered. "Now would perhaps be a good time to check on that stash of coriander leaves of yours," he suggested. "The one that you said isn't here? Then maybe you will believe us?"

Sekaran grunted, then stomped to within a foot of Amir. He appeared conflicted, and even in the dim light, Amir could tell that he was considering believing this stranger from Raluha.

"Dei," he said through gritted teeth, instead. "This is the last time you open your mouth. Your head is attached to the rest of your body only because you're a Carrier. Don't lose that privilege. I'm not going to warn you again. If I say the coriander leaves are safe, they are safe. Twenty years of harvesting it and keeping it away from the Jhanakari navy, do you think a couple of women can come charming their way onto the island and rip us off?"

These women? Yes.

But Amir said nothing. His heart continued to hammer, as the islands of the Black Coves were not where he'd hoped to meet Harini again. Gates, what would he say if he saw her? Would she be angry at him for what he'd done? He sought answers to countless questions, but above all, he did not wish for Harini to see the Black Coves as a place of chaos and lawlessness. If he somehow pulled this whole thing off, this was to be his new home, and if their hearts were in the right places, then perhaps someday, she would join him.

So many dreams. At what point do I get to wake up in one of them?

Sekaran scratched his beard. He seemed to decide he would take matters in his own hand. "I will go check on the Blessed One," he announced. He disappeared into the village. The buzzing sound of mosquitoes, and the lightening fog—not to mention being surrounded by nervous men with weapons—made for a miserable few minutes. Yet Amir wasn't afraid. He was irritated. Karim bhai, however, simply stood still, muttering a feeble, incomprehensible prayer.

A few minutes later, Sekaran came storming out of the village. His grip on his mace had slackened. "The Blessed One! He is not in his home."

A stunned silence prevailed. Sekaran dropped the mace. "It's . . . It's impossible. He was there after the night's feast . . . Gates, I should never have left."

Before Amir could even form a response in his head, a loud horn shattered the peace of the colony. It blared conch-like from the direction of the cove. A flock of birds breached the tree cover of the jungle and took to the skies.

The silence disappeared and never returned.

Sekaran regained his hold on the mace and lifted his head toward the coves.

"The galleys!"

As the horn persisted, a crowd of guards burst through the jungle, from the path boring into the hillside. Armed with aruvaals and pickaxes, they gathered in the heart of the village, looking flummoxed. Whispers abounded as to why the horn was sounded. A few entered Ilangovan's home—a tall bamboo settlement, the windows concealed by curtains—and emerged with even graver expressions.

A pair of older men approached Sekaran. They wore loose baniyans and sarongs reminiscent of nighttime bowler attire. "What is the meaning of this?" the taller one asked, a hint of trepidation in his voice. "Did you authorize the conch? Where is the Blessed One?"

Sekaran shook his head. "I don't know, anna. He was here until a few hours ago. When the feast was finished, and the guests had retired to their tents. I had posted guards outside his home. Maricha, Sumati, and the Neck."

"And these?" the shorter of the two older men asked, his gaze narrowing at the spicemark on Amir's throat. He stank of garlic. "Who are they?"

"We caught them near the western shore. Two of them are Carriers. The woman's a warrior—she cut up Govardhan and did a number on Kala. That one"—Sekaran pointed at Hasmin—"wants to see our Blessed One go down the Whorl. A chowkidar of Raluha."

Murmurs spread around the gathered crowd. "Hang him!" one of them screamed. "To the vultures, ho!"

The gatecaste thickened around them, and Amir's hope of familiarity began to drain. These were supposed to be his brothers and sisters, his ilk who would accept his family and him when he showed up at their coasts someday. He wanted them to recognize that future in his eyes, in the way he stood in acceptance of what was built here, and what was needed to be done to keep their lives going; untouched by the stain of the abovefolk, of the whips of the chowkidars and the ceaseless demands of the royals.

Which was far from the reception he was receiving right now.

"Please untie us," Amir pleaded with some urgency. "We know who your guests are. We can help!"

Sekaran lifted his mace to strike Amir as a runner came dashing through the bushes. He was a boy of twelve or thirteen, no older than Kabir, certainly, and built like a stick. *"Anna! Anna!"* He screamed. "They've taken—"

The runner stumbled and was on the verge of collapsing when Sekaran caught him.

"Be clear, Maru. What did you see?"

Maru was panting, and each word came out like a puff of air, drowning out his syllables. "Th-The two women . . . th-they . . ."

"Did they take the kothamalli?" Sekaran grabbed Maru by the collar.

The boy's eyes widened as he shook his head frantically. "No. Not the coriander leaves. They've taken *him*, anna. They've taken the Blessed One!"

Amir's knees grew weak, then buckled. A draining sensation swooped down on him.

Madhyra and Harini . . . if they had not sailed to the Black Coves for the coriander leaves, what then? What would they get by abducting Ilangovan? Would they use him to bargain *for* the coriander leaves? Or—or—or, did it really matter? Trapped in chains, Amir cursed his uselessness, especially among people he thought would someday be his family.

Sekaran slapped Maru. "Speak clearly. Taken him where?"

A second conch pierced the skies—a deep, groaning rumble that shook all those who had gathered. This one had a more musical tinge to it, as though it were a particular signal. A look of dread passed among the gatecaste, including Sekaran. Amir could tell the second conch meant something worse.

"They have taken the flagship," Sekaran said grimly. "We must hurry to the docks." He waved frantically at his companions. "Ready the men and women. Raise the sails."

"What about us?" Amir asked. "You cannot leave us here. We can help!" he pleaded again. "Trust me, please. We want to save Ilangovan as much as you do."

"Speak for yourself," Hasmin growled in a low voice.

"You can leave this one in the cages as he so desires," Amir offered in bargain.

Sekaran sighed, shifting his glance from Amir to Kalay. Surely, Kalay had proved her competence. And Karim bhai had been nothing but conciliatory from the time he was apprehended. In fact, Amir could swear some of the gatecaste recognized him, and their whispers were now reaching Sekaran's ears.

"Set them free," Sekaran finally hissed to his companions. "And you . . ." He glared at Amir, tightening his grip on the mace. "You will come with me."

AMIR HAD NEVER IMAGINED THAT HE'D BE SETTING FOOT ON A pirate galley. Even the prospect of a life in the Black Coves did not translate to this possibility in his mind. The great black sails unfurled ahead and above him in a splash of terror. Behind him, Karim bhai, Hasmin, and Kalay stepped off the ladder one after the other with their mouths agape. The hull was packed with the gatecaste running around and preparing the ship to sail. Amir hurried to the railing and gazed out into the sea.

Another large ship rocked ahead on the waters, steadily dimming in size, getting farther and farther with each passing second.

Madhyra and Harini had to be on that vessel. And so was Ilangovan.

From what little Amir could extract from Sekaran and the other gatecaste, who themselves had been attempting to piece together the shattered remnants of the previous night, Madhyra and Harini had managed to give most of the populace of the Black Coves a sleeping poison by spiking their mutton curries. The two women had suspiciously restricted themselves to merely toddy and fish, although those suspicions arrived only with a helping of hindsight. Sekaran and his companions, however, had missed much of the feast owing to repairing nets, and had thus been spared the poisoning. Harini and Madhyra had waited until Sekaran had led his men out on patrol to the western coast—as they did at the break of each dawn—before smuggling an unconscious Ilangovan out.

The rest of the Black Coves had been sleeping like teak logs.

From the coast, Madhyra and Harini had loaded Ilangovan onto a coracle, then rowed to a galley that had been anchored in the bay to the east beside the rest of their pirate seaware. The few gatecaste standing guard and patrolling the coasts had been knocked out by the throne-keeper of Illindhi. But she and Harini had not been alone.

From the onlookers who had witnessed the vessel crossing the mouth of the cove and fanning out into the sea, there were several ponytailed men on board with coarse faces, dressed in golden-brown warrior robes, and holding what were assuredly poison-dipped arrows nocked to their bows.

The Haldiveer of Halmora.

Kalay opined that Madhyra had provided Harini with an entire goblet of the Poison stolen from the caverns of Illindhi. The rajkumari of Halmora had passed that on to a contingent of her Haldiveer.

It certainly answers why there was a rumor in Vanasi about Harini coming into possession of a barrel of the Poison. Bindu was not entirely wrong.

Even now, with all that Amir learned and subsequently surmised, he could not wrap his head around the turn of events. One thing was plain, and Sekaran had confirmed it enough times—Madhyra and Harini had not taken the coriander leaves. In fact, they had not even bothered heading in the direction of the remote island where Sekaran claimed the coriander leaves were tucked away in underground chambers.

All Madhyra and Harini had desired—and had succeeded in—was the abduction of Ilangovan, the Blessed One.

The sobriquet leaves an aftertaste in your mouth, doesn't it?

"They're heading toward Jhanak," Kalay pointed out.

With an impressive lead, no less. An ominous shudder ran along Amir's skin. "If they reach Jhanak and turn Ilangovan over to Rani Zariba, that would be the end of the Black Coves. Your thronekeeper does not understand the implications of what she's doing here."

Kalay scoffed. She appeared to be at ease on the ship for someone who had never left the confines of Illindhi all her life. "The Mouth cares little for these gimmicks in the waters. Nothing will remain if Madhyra spills the knowledge of olum."

Amir chuckled at the apocalyptic seriousness of her words, far more insidious than his own. "Is that it? You would kill her, and—then what? Return to Illindhi to present her head to Mahrang? Are you certain you do not desire to . . . linger around? To see the rest of the eight kingdoms?"

Kalay shot him a look that ought to have burned his irises. "I certainly do not! That is blasphemous."

"Perhaps your eyes were unaware of this blasphemy when they regarded Jhanak and the ocean for the first time," Amir taunted her.

Kalay was livid. "It is a sacrilege to use the Gates for anything but your duty. I drank the Poison to fulfil my oath as an acolyte of the Uyirsena and nothing more. I am not here to . . . indulge some dream to wander. That, I believe, is a vice shared by your people."

"Those who drink the Poison are not my people," Amir countered, losing his grin.

"And yet you seek it nonetheless."

"Not out of choice. Consider it a duty to my mother."

Kalay did not peel her eyes away from Madhyra's ship sailing ahead into the distance. Amir could tell she was not looking at it the way he was. A different urge sat in her belly, manifesting on her face as a pained determination. It was as though Madhyra had reached inside Kalay and wrenched out the core of her soul and Kalay was out here, on this ship, yearning to get it back.

"If it is a duty, then I can trust you to hold your own when we confront Madhyra."

Amir had forgotten about his shamshir almost as soon as Kalay had returned it to him the previous night. Its lightness had not penetrated his mind, and he suddenly found himself aware of its presence upon him.

She suddenly winced, grabbing her hurt shoulder, her breathing intensifying. Amir looked concerned. "Seems like you ought to be worried more about wielding your own blade than me wielding mine. You need a healer. Those were venomous spikes on Sekaran's mace."

Kalay shook her head and blew a stray hair out of her eye. "Nothing I cannot handle. Just get me on that ship. And be ready for battle."

Amir tightened his hold on the shamshir and presented it to Kalay. "I am."

A voice called out, "If I were you, I wouldn't trust a word that comes out of that thevidiya's mouth."

Hasmin spat from where he sat on the floor of the deck, ten feet away, still bound in chains. For threatening to send Ilangovan down the Whorl, Amir doubted Hasmin would see his hands until the end of this ordeal.

Kalay narrowed her eyes at him. "And why should I not?"

"Because he's a bowler," Hasmin replied, as if that should be answer enough. When she didn't say anything, he shrugged as much as the chains would allow. "Not as long as he's got his little rajkumari on that ship, at least. Deserves to go down the Whorl just like the rest of them." Hasmin looked over the breadth of the ship, his lip twitching in disgust.

Amir ripped himself away from the railing and was marching over to plant a kick on Hasmin when Kalay yanked him back. She whipped him around and pushed his shamshir away. "Is she going to be a problem? The Halmoran princess? Or are *you*?"

Amir gulped. "No, of course not. I want to stop Madhyra."

"And what about her?"

"I—uh, I will talk to her. She will not be a problem."

Kalay clicked her tongue. "I do not think there would be time for talk if we have a battle, Amir of the eight kingdoms. Get your shamshir ready. The Mouth commands you to preserve it. And Gates, get a better grip. I could have knocked the blade out of your hand with a thought."

Amir began to speak but stopped. Did he really need to tell her that he had no intention of fighting, let alone the ability? That he would, at the first sign of trouble, run away and let her dance with her scimitar to whatever end was fated for them? That even if he mustered every bone and muscle of his body, he wouldn't last beyond the second blow from even the weakest of the Haldiveer, let alone with a fighter even the Chairs of Illindhi had claimed to be a peerless warrior?

She must have sensed his unrest. "Do not disappoint me," she warned him. "It is a beautiful world you live in." She scanned the horizon, past the lush islands, a momentary sigh escaping her lips, as though a different longing had clawed out of her heart and was corralled by the Mouth. "I do not wish to smear it with your blood."

Then she was gone, one hand on her injured shoulder, marching down the deck to have a word with Sekaran.

Hasmin began to laugh through bloodied teeth. "Ho, I can't wait for this day to end, and for you to be taken back to Raluha and pushed down to the jail. This—madness. Gah!"

"You heard Orbalun," said Amir. "He wants what I want. To stop Madhyra."

"Oh, the maharaja wants it. *For now.* And then, what, you think you will be given a fond farewell—fireworks and spiced rum and the whole charade—as you ferry your family out to this nightmare on the waters? Quit dreaming da, baadu! Even the maharaja is not beyond the law, and after tonight, whether or not you catch this woman, you will be sent down to the bottommost level of the Pyramid, from where you will not be able to hear the screams of your brother as he crawls through the Gate."

Amir kneeled beside Hasmin, stolid and measured. Slowly, he raised a hand and traced a finger down Hasmin's cheek. Hasmin jerked away, dragging himself backward along the deck, scraping against the sides. *"Get your filthy hands off me!"*

"You say these hands are filthy, and yet you have no problem partaking of the spice they carry. You are a hypocrite, Hasmin, just like the rest of you abovefolk. But yes, I may end up cast down even farther than I already am." Amir whispered as the ship crested a wave and fell, a cloud of sea spray raining upon them as his finger did not move from Hasmin's cheek, "If it is to be so, then I will, until that moment, remember how you knelt beneath the boots of the gatecaste on these islands, who bound you with their hands and spared your life, and sent you back to your precious home at their mercies. And I will go down the Pyramid knowing that for every moment for the rest of your life, you will live with that mercy."

Amir pulled his hand away and wiped it against Hasmin's uniform. Slowly, he stood up, exhaled softly, and drifted away, watching the ship close its distance to Madhyra's vessel.

And they were closing. Sekaran appeared determined to catch her. He screamed orders to raise the sails and spar the rigging. He manned the rudder himself. The gatecaste under his command readied ladders, filled their quivers with arrows, and sharpened their swords. Behind their ship, a hundred smaller patamars, coracles, and fishing boats followed, gray and yellow flags fluttering from their gunwales and sterns.

The fog had lightened, and a timorous sun had crept out from beyond the clouds to remind everyone of the time of day. Kalay returned to the gangplank. There was a fury on her face that Amir did not wish to confront anymore. They were close now, both he and Kalay, but how could it matter, when Madhyra seemed to be one step ahead of them at all times?

Until now, until this moment as he leaned over the railing and watched their ship pierce the waves and ride the wind, Amir had never cared for the businesses of the eight kingdoms. Nor any imperial dreams they harbored. He had embraced a simpler—albeit rather illegal—dream of wanting to escape his duty of carrying and flee with his family to the Black Coves. All he had needed was one vial of the Poison.

Simpler dreams from simpler people, however, were easy to shatter. The oppressed could believe only in the moment and hope to tear the fabric that kept them huddled in the Bowl. A single misstep, and the climber could falter. The feet could slip. A traitor could emerge. The weather could change. Any number of obstacles, really. And Amir knew that he was in the midst of climbing this fragile ladder of hope on a slippery wall, on the most tempestuous of nights, surrounded by enemies. Even the promise of love—of his heart, whose fragments lay sheltered in Harini's embrace—could not steady his loose footing. Where he could do little but keep going, hurtling after those who were born with the power to make choices, toward love, toward freedom, but always feeling his feet shaking, so close to slipping, and falling off . . .

How much lower can people fall, those who were already born to fill bottoms and roots? You have a task ahead; do not pity your absence of privilege.

Within an hour, the islands of the Black Coves were distant pinpricks. Only the ocean surrounded them.

"You chase a storm, Amir," said a husky voice. Karim bhai limped toward him across the deck. "Madhyra will not yield."

"I have to try," Amir said. "I don't have a choice, Karim bhai. Not after what I heard and saw in Illindhi." Amir glanced around to be certain none of the gatecaste of the Black Coves were overhearing them. "If I fail, I die. But you see, I don't want to die. It's that simple."

"You won't, pulla. I have faith that you'll see this through. Already in the last few days, I have seen much that I never thought I'd see in someone like you."

"Always the uplifter of us bowlers, aren't you, bhai?"

"It's the truth."

"It is what circumstances have forced me to do." Amir sighed. "But also rather pointless, if we don't have Ilangovan keeping everyone safe."

"He is only a leader. There will be more."

Amir shook his head. "Not like Ilangovan, bhai. Look around you. Look at the fervor these men and women have. They follow him. And without him, I don't know if this dream survives."

"You attribute a lot to him. Ho, he's one of the ideals, but he is also just a gatecaste, pulla."

"And yet there has not been one like him for a long time. I don't know if ever. He's a *beacon*. Most of us . . . we lack the tenacity to stand up to those whips. So far down the Bowl, our necks hurt craning to look up all our lives. There are very few of us who can climb through those cracks. And I mean truly, not in the way some of the bowlers suck up their way to riches and own manors in Raluha and become abovefolk in everything but caste. No, I mean a climb to freedom. Ilangovan did it. And showed us the way, and gave us reason to lose just a touch of fear. He—he is one of the special ones."

"There have always been plenty of special folk in the Bowl, pulla. You just have to look. Sometimes outside the door, sometimes inside."

Amir watched the waves lap against the hull, his mind suddenly impervious to Sekaran's screams and those of his men and women. "I am not one of those, bhai. I can only go so far as to add bodies to this . . . this movement. This little revolution in the waters. I cannot do more."

Karim bhai chuckled. "You make him sound like an Immortal Son of the Mouth, a deity to pray to. Ilangovan's way is not noble, pulla. He only reaffirms what the abovefolk believe about us."

"So what, now the Black Coves are all wrong?" Aware of his raised voice, he glanced back to ensure Sekaran was not eavesdropping upon them.

Karim bhai appeared hurt by the accusation. "I mean that we only look at what is necessary. And that necessity of freedom overpowers our essential moralities. The abovefolk—"

"Fuck the abovefolk, bhai," Amir lashed out, gritting his teeth. "You of all people should understand that. We should not be doing things the way they want it done." He took a breath, calming himself. "You were not there in Munivarey's cavern. Next to that false gate. I heard what he said. About us being considered impure because we pass through the Mouth's feces. Something that is innate in us, which the Poison shields the abovefolk from when they pass through. It . . . we did not choose this. We did not choose to clean the sewers, unclog the abovefolk's toilets, and wet our hands in their shit. We did not ask to be called to clear the carcasses of dead dogs and shepherd their goats on land that ought to be ours. But it happened anyway. We pass through the Gate and bring everyone their spices, and pay for it like it were a crime. Like *we* are inherently a crime, an anomaly that must be exploited without granting us the base human dignities. So yes, bhai. You may have your views gilded by your days in the palace, at Suman-Koti's feet, but I certainly do not care for what happens to the Spice Trade, or what the abovefolk want."

"And yet"—Karim bhai smiled, unaffected by Amir's tirade—"you believe that the Halmoran devadai loves you."

Amir's mouth opened and closed. "I—uh . . . that is different. *She* is different. What is your point? Speak plainly, bhai."

"My point, my dear pulla, is that you ought to be at the Black Coves whether Ilangovan is there or not. He is not the revolution."

"Neither am I!" Amir protested.

"And yet I sense a conflict, not in your desire, but in the way you view the world. You do wish to be with the rajkumari."

Yes, for a million lives.

But right now, he would settle for knowing what she wished. If Harini was on that ship, holding a knife to Ilangovan's throat, what was Amir going to do? Choose his love, or choose the one who he thought would save his family?

Can you even choose?

Karim bhai's smile deepened. "I know your answer, pulla. It is why I trust you to do the right thing by yourself when, sooner or later, you will land on these shores with Noori and Kabir. Right now, we sail to keep that future alive, not to save Ilangovan."

From where Amir stood, Karim bhai looked older, grayer, as if the sea had stolen what little youthfulness endured on his face, and left him frail and on the verge of being carried away by the wind like a piece of parchment with a life's worth of ramblings. Amir knew Karim bhai was struggling to believe, and that each word tumbling out of the old Carrier was said in fear.

The ship crested a wave, and Amir and Karim bhai had to grab the railing.

"Ho, better get used to this." Karim bhai laughed.

Not yet. Not yet.

Sekaran left the rudder to a sailor and began to pace the deck, screaming new instructions. They were gaining on Madhyra's ship. They weaved between the islands peppering the sea, clumps of floating forests, hills teeming with bamboo settlements, and beaches crowded with onlookers watching this chase of vessels that disturbed their quiet morning. And in that tumult of lazy sunlight, it was hard for Amir to say who was loyal to the Jhanakari, and who to Ilangovan and the Black Coves.

"Curse the Gates!" Sekaran's voice boomed on the deck, impatience building. "Unfurl the third sail."

"What happened?" Kalay strode on the deck, worry etched on her face. Ahead, Madhyra's ship was turning west.

Sekaran did not answer her at once. All said and done, neither Madhyra, Harini, nor the Haldiveer of Halmora were sailors. Sekaran, on the other hand, had been bred in these waters. Despite the fair wind driving the sails, he commanded the oarsmen to propel them ahead. Nobody protested what he was doing. Amir watched sweaty hands drag and push the oars in tandem, the fear of losing their Blessed One written plainly on their faces.

At one point, Sekaran brought forth a spyglass and pressed his eye to it in the direction of Madhyra's vessel. He clenched his fist around his mace and roared at the oarsmen for haste. Amir and Karim bhai staggered to the center as the ship roiled against the waves.

"Where are they heading?" Kalay pressed.

Sekaran shot her a glare, and then one at Amir. Slowly, he lowered the spyglass. "It does not make sense. They—they are heading toward the Whorl."

Amir rushed to the railing. From where he stood, he could not differentiate one way or another. But what he could see was that in the distance, the clear light of day had darkened ever so slightly, drawing from some bed of darkness above the canvas of the sky. Karim bhai had begun to murmur a prayer to the Mouth. Kalay, puzzled, made no movement, as though Sekaran's words would right themselves in a while.

But a while passed, and then several whiles, and they did not. Their ship gained on Ilangovan's, but ahead a curtain of gray had begun to descend. The waves became more violent. A hundred boats flanked them on either side or followed from behind. Their impatience rent the air. The intoxication of the previous night peeled away, replaced by the shock of watching their leader being whisked away by two strangers. But as the waters began to get choppier, the other boats fell behind, wary at first, and then almost incapable of navigating.

"They are sailing to their deaths," Karim bhai gasped.

If there was a morning that day, it had disowned this part of the sea. A storm brewed. Sekaran marshaled the sailors and issued more frantic instructions. His uncertainty was the last thing Amir wanted.

Within an hour, the other boats had completely dropped away, leaving only the two great ships on the violent waters. Ahead, the Whorl had materialized, and for the first time, Amir saw it for what it was.

Less than a mile away, the sea ended. Or so it seemed, for it disappeared into the curtain of darkness that was the storm that broiled along the horizon. A wall of thick cloud and rain reaching up to the skies curtained the sea from what lay beyond. Shards of purple lightning crackled inside the blackness, ruling out what little room for life there could be inside that warren of malice. The waves intensified, a lamentation against silence; a wrathful, vengeful tumult that would wring anything to pieces.

The two ships barely survived, and Amir held on for dear life as entire waves of water drained into the ship as it precariously teetered over a crest.

What were Madhyra and Harini doing? This was suicidal.

And then, without warning, Ilangovan's flagship crossed the threshold and disappeared into the Whorl.

Some of the gatecaste let out a gasp. A man wailed, thumping his chest in agony, as though sealing Ilangovan's fate in his mind.

From beside Amir, Kalay gave a determined but calm order: "Follow them."

"I am not putting the lives of honest men and women at risk," said Sekaran. "There is death inside that storm."

Kalay remained unperturbed. "I know Madhyra. She will not have ventured into that without purpose. Follow them." She removed her scimitar and held it to Sekaran's throat. At once, a dozen men unsheathed their weapons and surrounded Kalay. They knew what she was capable of, yet she was wildly outnumbered. Amir backed away, his own shamshir sheathed and unnecessary.

Sekaran hesitated. *Surely not.* He slipped two fingers into his mouth and let out a shrill whistle. The sailors, at once, lowered their weapons and rushed to their stations. The oarsmen were at the ready. With a bellow, Sekaran launched the ship toward the Whorl.

"Brace yourselves!"

Amir grabbed Karim bhai, and together they clung to the mast as the sails fluttered against the thunderstorm luring them into its fold.

Within minutes, the darkness was absolute. Amir, turning back, could glimpse the last vestiges of sunlight coating a faint stretch of the sea at a distance. Oddly, he did not fear this journey. Something in him agreed with Kalay. Madhyra had planned this. But why?

They breached the storm line. A clamorous tangle of rain and wind pelted them, throwing the ship's course into disarray. Amir's very bones juddered under the impact of the curtain, this machination of the Mouth. His ears pounded with the sounds of the Whorl, as though they were sailing through a graveyard of infinite shipwrecks—a wet, malignant desolation. Is this what the Condemned felt? Was this the beginning of their death?

Inside the darkness, the noise of the thunderstorm reached a terrifying crescendo. Ahead, there was no visible sign of Ilangovan's flagship. Amir feared they'd drowned, and his heart ached for even the sight of Harini.

At the heart of the Whorl, Sekaran raised a hand and screamed for the oarsmen and the sailors to halt. The ship continued to teeter and sway, but it did not move forward. The coiling storm tugged and pushed from all sides, but the ship was made of sturdier stuff, enough to withstand whatever it was the Whorl was throwing at them.

Amir could barely hear the exchanges between the sailors. Karim bhai had sunk to the deck, his eyes closed, his face wet with rain, his mouth murmuring prayers incessantly. Kalay was on the edge of the railing, leaning out, squinting through the darkness for a sign of Madhyra and her ship, her braided hair swaying against the lashing storm.

Hasmin, who had not moved from his position, chuckled. "What a bunch of imbeciles!" Brave words, thought Amir, for someone who stank of fear, as palpable as a fresh harvest of cardamoms.

Sekaran, who was less bothered by Kalay holding a sword to his neck than by Hasmin's comment, stepped forward, past Kalay, past his sailors, to where Hasmin lay bound. He bent down and punched the senapati hard on the nose with a soaked knuckle. The chief of the chowkidars promptly crumpled to unconsciousness, rain drooling down his face and seeping into his open mouth.

He had that coming.

Karim bhai, drenched, rose and ambled forward. "This is a fool's hope, Sekaran. We must head back before this place consumes us. Nobody has returned alive from the Whorl."

"You may need to rethink that statement, bhai."

Amir was staring into the black distance, his mouth wide open. For farther ahead, the storm seemed to have an end. And clinging to that precipice between the Whorl and the unknown was Ilangovan's ship. It flickered in and out of the curtain of darkness, trails of lightning coiling around the sails without burning them to crisps. The thunderstorm still lurked like a caged beast, the occasional flash of light casting a shadow as tall as the distance between earth and sky in the shape of a pirate galley, a shimmering sway of sailcloth heralding a doom Amir had come to accept.

Amir wondered what Harini was seeing on the other side. Darkness? A new light that prevented you from returning? And yet, they had already survived their sojourn into the storm. They were not even sailors.

Madhyra knows something the rest of us do not.

It took a moment for Amir, and everyone else on board, to realize that Madhyra's ship was moving once more. And it was now approaching theirs at the heart of the Whorl at a frightening pace. The wind blew southward inside the Whorl, and the flagship careened in their direction, carried by the violent waves that propelled the ship forward. Sekaran, agitated, swept across the deck as though he'd had enough of this madness. He began marshaling his men and women once more, commanding them to turn the ship.

Seconds later, Ilangovan's flagship passed them, a jet of sea spray following in its wake that soaked the deck Amir was standing on. Sekaran promptly gave chase. Amir, Karim bhai, and Kalay held on to whatever they could grab in the darkness, and with each burst of lightning, Amir watched the horror on everyone's faces. Everyone except Kalay, who remained stoic.

She was waiting to board the other ship.

Are you?

Amir's fingers wrapped around the shamshir given to him by Mahrang. He'd never wielded a blade before in his life. And he certainly did not wish to if it came to fighting a battle against Madhyra and the Haldiveer, and certainly not Harini, not when he still needed questions to be answered.

There will *be a better life for you and your family, I promise. Away from the Bowl, away from Raluha.*

Harini's words filled his mind, and it was better that her voice occupied that place than the sonorous, bass-filled, and chaotic symphony of the Whorl that seemed at each moment to be resounding like a death knell.

What had she meant? She had once sat with him on the wet earth outside the Halmoran qila, her fingers intertwined in his, the sound of insects slithering into their ears, their silence absolute, ephemeral, worthy of the few minutes Amir had before he had to scurry back through the labyrinth and back upon the spice trail like an ant gone astray from the march. And she had broken that sacred silence to whisper to him of how she desired to be with him, and in a better place than in the Bowl of Raluha. They hadn't sounded to him like empty words, not then, not now. Yet there ahead was Harini, fighting to reclaim the fading prestige of the turmeric empire, to placate her procession of priests that besieged her in her ancient qila. Amir struggled to reconcile the two images; to think what place it was that she had in mind when she'd expressed lifting Amir's family out of the Bowl. Was she truly yearning for him? Or did her loyalties, ultimately, lie with her parents, and the priests and the people of the qila she was born and raised in?

Gates, he couldn't breathe, not on the dark sea frothing without air! Without light. His emotions collided with the reality unfurling ahead of him and there was only one way to untangle the collision.

As they burst out of the Whorl's curtain, the pallid sky returning with the promise of sunlight, Amir thought something could yet be salvaged from this. He looked to the others. Sekaran wiped the water off his face and seemed to be wearing a mask of rage. And who would blame him? Or any of the other gatecaste who had just experienced a pair of ships hurtling into the Whorl and coming out unscathed? Karim bhai had finally opened his eyes, as though he had not seen the Whorl at all. Hasmin continued lying unconscious on the deck.

As Ilangovan's flagship waded back into the realm of the Black Coves, and then farther toward Jhanak, the smaller boats and catamarans returned. The pirate channel assumed a chaotic string of vessels weaving between the islands. The distance between the two large ships was steadily reducing. Daylight streaked through the clearing clouds, shafting through the sails, throwing every figure on Ilangovan's ship into visibility.

Amir's grip on the shamshir slackened momentarily as he glimpsed Harini then, unmistakable upon the deck. He could have spotted her in a crowded bazaar. Her gown fluttering in the sea breeze, her hair tied in a tight bun, straining to be let free. Beside her stood Madhyra, her sword drawn, both of them facing the approaching mass of wood and sailcloth, and violent screams that'd deafen the deepest fish.

Beyond them both stood Ilangovan.

No, he's not standing.

Dangling like a string of bones, arms and legs splayed and tied in thick knots to the bowsprit, the Blessed One of the Black Coves hung suspended from the prow of the boat and swung like a horse's tail with each crest of the wave.

Was this how he had traversed the Whorl?

Under Sekaran's shrieking command, the ship gained on the stolen vessel with each degree of the sun over the horizon. The sailors readied rope ladders and hooks, donned helms and rubbed the flats of their swords on the wet gunwale. Gritted their teeth despite the sweat raining down their faces at the sight of Ilangovan chained to the stern of his own ship.

As the two ships pulled side by side and the sailors crowded around Amir, he saw Kalay beside him. Her fingers clamped around the railing's larder. Gates, she was the Mouth personified. Eyes fierce with duty, blood congealed on her lip from the blows she'd received earlier from the gatecaste, her cheeks flickering with a grimace of suppressed pain in her shoulder where Sekaran had caught her with his mace. A splash of turmeric in her hair, and seeds of jeera sprinkled on her shoulders, as though she had been drenched in prayer before manifesting upon the deck as an emissary of the Mouth, to complete the mission bestowed upon her by Mahrang and the Uyirsena.

And not for the first time, Amir wondered whether the blade she was wielding was pointed at Madhyra or at Harini. Or at anyone at all who stood in her way.

CHAPTER
14

*Hippocras, clary, and vernage—kindle lust. Suffering
impotence? Look no further than an electuary of ginger,
pepper, galangal, and cinnamon, taken modestly post-dinner.
For a morning ascent, cloves steeped in milk.*

—Found scribbled along the margins of
a courtier's parchment bundle

A cloud of spice erupted around Madhyra's ship, engulfing it in
a dense, colorful mist. The fragrance of cloves and mace filled
the air, and aamchoor and black peppercorns, one scent following the other as though they were being poured into a great cooking
vessel that was the sea. For the first time since the previous evening,
Amir's hunger roared like a beast, and the grip on his shamshir—
already frail and unsure—faltered.

Around him, the raging gatecaste appeared dazed and confused at the
spice-encrusted fog that surrounded them. Nobody moved in that silence
as the two ships broke through the waves running beside each other.

The silence broke when Sekaran slapped the nearest man and yelled
at him to throw the ladder across. The next second, an arrow zipped
through the reddish cloud and clattered into one of the sailors' skulls.

The man staggered like a drunk before tumbling over the railing and into the water.

The sight of death yanked the stunned gatecaste into action. The journey through the Whorl had sapped some of their spirit, but here, on the open sea, against the bright sun, this was their domain. And they had defended it for decades. Immediately, they set about lifting the ladders in fours and fives and hurling them across the waters as Sekaran twisted the rudder to edge closer to Madhyra's ship. When the first ladder fell, the archers fired at once to dissuade Madhyra or the Haldiveer from toppling it back.

Within the blink of an eye, Kalay pushed aside a gatecaste and jumped onto the ladder and sprinted upon it over the water. Amir shrieked, "No, Kalay, wait!" knowing the warning came from a place of fear where if Kalay died, this mission would suddenly be infinitely more difficult to accomplish. But she was already across, her figure a glinting silhouette, nimble against the sun as she raised her scimitar, leaped, and plunged it into the closest Haldiveer as she fell. She dived into their ranks and disappeared into the spice cloud.

The clamor that arose on Madhyra's ship was matched only by a raucous cheer from Sekaran's. More of the sailors, having witnessed Kalay's daring crossing, followed her over the chasm. All of a sudden, Amir found himself on the cusp of a ladder. He did not know what propelled him to climb the railing and hold the shrouds and lean forward to the sea below. He certainly did not know what he was meant to do next, only that standing on the gangplank, watching Harini on the opposite side, and Madhyra, churned something in his stomach, keeping him in place.

So it was not the desire for battle that had him charge across to the other ship. No, it was something far less courageous, perhaps even a trick of fortune or impulse or merely his mind being delusional, but one moment he was standing there on the railing—one foot on the shaky ladder bridge—and the next second, he received a bump from behind and found himself surging forward.

He would have fallen into the water if not for the pure rush of passion that grabbed him in that moment. He teetered, swung to hold the tunic of the man who stank of cloves behind him, but there was an even larger force of gatecaste behind that man who buttressed Amir's fall and wheeled him around once more, then pushed him ahead. A rush of meaningless words of pleading escaped Amir's lips, but there was nobody to listen and nobody to help, only his own stuttering balance on that narrow ledge, and the knowledge that he did not wish to linger and was certain death was waiting to conquer him. So he ran, one step, two, three, and four, leaping and dancing, forgetting in that moment that he was only a bowler of Raluha.

Behind him, he heard Karim bhai scream, but it was quickly drowned in the roar of the sea, of the warriors around him, of the ships that pierced the waves, and of the hundreds of smaller boats and canoes that now flanked them like little ants carrying a large piece of leftover meat through the Bowl.

He closed his eyes and opened them, and he was on the other side, at the edge of the other ship's gangplank. He jumped aboard just as the menacing roar of Ilangovan's loyalists swarmed behind him, accompanied by the clang of steel. They fell upon the meager count of the Haldiveer like a pack of starving Vanasari who'd just been given a plate of mutton kheema, and Amir froze, the thought of violence one thing, its occurrence in front of his eyes—the casual spray of blood, the display of flesh, and the sudden drop in value of human life—clamping his bones, gluing him to the wooden deck floor.

War.

The word rang in his mind as he stumbled, watching the Haldiveer outnumbered by Sekaran and his crew.

Your companions, if you are to come out of this alive. Your procession of butchers.

In his daze, he noticed only one person on the other side unaffected by the swarm of gatecaste. Madhyra fought through the cloud of spice like a trick of the light. She wove the spice around her like a garb, an illusory tapestry whose stark fragrance trapped Ilangovan's men and women in a trance, weakened their strikes, made them falter and stumble. Something silver weaved through the cloud, spilling blood, and when Madhyra emerged—merely feet away from Amir—and raised her sword, Kalay met her, sliding between the two of them and raising her talwar to parry the Illindhian thronekeeper's cut.

Kalay gained her footing and pushed Madhyra deeper into the cloud. Amir followed her, unable to see properly through the haze. Around him, he glimpsed only shapes and heard only disjointed sounds, the spattering of blood and the rush of steel on steel. The creaking of timber and the fall of bodies. The distant roar of more of Ilangovan's men as they scaled Madhyra's ship, which swayed precariously on the waters.

Amir lost Kalay, but he found Harini.

And there goes everything you'd steeled yourself for.

In her tight robe with a warrior's cummerbund, she was backing away, having warded off a blow from a Jhanakari sander, but her weak parry clattered the sword out of her hand. A second gatecaste now stood over her, panting, blood dripping from his lips, and he raised his sword.

Amir pummeled into him at the last moment.

The two of them tumbled onto the deck, a look of surprise on the gate-caste's face as he smelled betrayal. Amir rose and landed a clumsy punch, breaking the man's jaw. Pain reverberated across his hand. He pulled it back and examined it, shivering. Blood coated his knuckles, and a rush of bile screamed up his throat. He wanted nothing more than to look away. Anything but the bloodied jaw of the man lying beneath him would be a welcome sight. But he stood, shook his head, turned, and extended his hands to hold Harini, forgetting completely that one of those hands held his shamshir.

She backed away, nearly falling to the deck.

"You!" she cried as she regained her footing. "Amir, what are you doing here?"

Her eyes widened with terror. Her hair flailed against the breeze, a strange mustard yellow, sprayed in webs of turmeric. She smelled like night's milk, and of Amma's dal. Amir's breath was shallow and he brought the shamshir closer to her, only to find the cloud of spice engulfing them both, breaking them away from the rest of the ship and the battle. Into a cocoon.

"Harini," he gasped. "Um . . . hi? I was afraid one of them had . . ." He inhaled sharply, clutching his chest. "Kalay . . . she—uh, Madhyra . . ." He looked around frantically, but all he saw aside from Harini was the dense cloud of spice, and through it, the smell of the sea, and the innumerable sounds of the gatecaste and the Haldiveer. He gulped, hunting for a breath that had not been released, and found a semblance of it. "Let's get out of here. Please . . ."

"Amir!" Her voice was a ghost, an echo detached from her body. "Gates! You should not be here. Oh, what a fool you are!"

Amir blinked, suddenly aware that he had a weapon that could draw blood out of the person standing in front of him. He pulled his arm back, the daze only slowly retreating, Harini's words occupying the vacancy. His voice regained access to his breath. "And you *should* be here?" He shook his head. "Neither of us should be here! And I am a fool? Harini, I am *done* being in the dark. You missed the afsal dina harvest. And then you were in the coves. And now you have Ilangovan on this ship, tied to the prow. Tell me what is happening—help me understand this madness." He could hear the desperation in his own voice. The need for just a crumb of trust from her.

Harini's eyes almost broke his heart with their denial.

"Amir, I cannot. My hands . . . my hands are tied. I promise. Please believe me." She began to sob, her eyes gazing through the cocoon of spice and out to the sea. She wiped her tears at once. "Gates, you should not be here! The Jhanakari will arrive any moment."

Orbalun had been right. Rani Zariba was in cahoots with Harini.

"You . . . You are ruining everything," Amir retorted, exasperated, looking around the cocoon, wondering if he'd be able to break out of it. "I told you—I don't know how many times now—that I wished to get my family out of Raluha. And you agreed it would be best for them.

For me. You even tried to steal the Poison for me from your father once. And now you're conspiring to apprehend Ilangovan for the sake of—what? *More turmeric?* Since when have you cared about such things?"

"Amir, this is beyond you," Harini replied, a bit more steel in her voice. "Would you believe me if I said *you're* ruining things just as much?"

"Does it matter anymore? I'm here for Madhyra, and so is everyone else. You thought you could just take Ilangovan away and nobody would do anything about it? This is my future, Harini. A future you swore you wished to be a part of. Or was that all a lie?"

Words died on Harini's lips, and she shook her head slightly, her balance tremulous on the deck. "These islands needn't be that future. There can be something better."

Something sharp and agonizing pricked Amir's chest. "Of all the abovefolk, I would never have expected you to tell us what our future must look like. Besides, if not here, then where—the Outerlands?" he chuckled. "I saw what good that did to my father. Please, I beg you, do not insult me. You may be a thronekeeper of Halmora, and I may be a gatecaste bowler, and things may yet be *beyond me* as you claim, but I know the woman I fell in love with. And I wish to know if you are still her."

Harini's hands trembled as she shifted her sword from one hand to the other, then rummaged in her robe's pockets. She pulled out a crumpled piece of parchment—wet and smothered, miraculously still in one piece—and passed it to Amir. With reluctance, he received and opened it, his wet hands causing a corner to peel away. It was one of the first paintings of the Bowl Kabir had made, which Amir had gifted to Harini. She'd liked it, but he didn't imagine she'd have carried it around, least of all here.

"This," she croaked in response as the wind flipped the wet painting and tore it in two, one half floating down the deck and the other clinging to Amir's fingers, "was my reminder of where you lived, and what I had to do to get you out of there. Amir, please . . . whatever you think you know . . . it is not true. I'm only protecting you."

The ship shook violently at that moment, and Harini staggered. Amir grabbed hold of her and straightened her just as a body lurched through the colored smog and landed a foot away from them. Noises pierced the spice cloud, and Amir figured that more people—perhaps even Sekaran—had boarded the galley.

Amir, however, clung to the ghost of Harini's words, and their weight expanded in his chest, releasing him of a burden he'd been carrying since the night in the Halmoran qila. "Harini . . ." he whispered, and the ship teetered once more, forcing Amir to grab tight to a rope wound around a pole for balance. "I know about Madhyra."

"What?" Harini stared at him, holding on to the railing, bewildered, as though Amir should have begun the conversation with this.

"I—uh, long story, ho, but in the last few days, I have been to Illindhi, discovered a cavern full of the Poison, and traveled with an acolyte of the Mouth. I know about the Uyirsena, and—you don't need to protect me from their knowledge. I am already mired in it. The Mouth knows."

"Oh, Amir, what have you done?"

"I've done what I've had to do. But that also means you don't need to hide anything from me," he pressed on. "Tell me. Where have you stashed the coriander leaves to harvest the olum?"

Behind him, another crash resounded, followed by the cracking sound of a slab of timber being uprooted. Amir figured they didn't have much time. The gatecaste were wrecking the ship in their bid to rescue Ilangovan through the spice cloud.

"I don't know what you're talking about," Harini shrieked, to be heard over the crash of waves as the two ships cut across the sea, side by side.

"Why else do you need Ilangovan?" Amir shot back. "What are you giving him to Jhanak for? You need to prove to Zariba the powers of olum, don't you?"

Harini shook her head frantically. "Gates, Amir! You've got it all—"

Suddenly the ship lurched, and the words evaporated on Harini's lips as she slipped and fell toward Amir, who caught her in a tangled embrace of hair and water, a sloppy squelch of bodies that even his grip on the pole couldn't sustain. Together, they were hurled back into the spice cloud as the ship crested the wave and nosed back down toward the water. Amir fell, Harini atop him, and they rolled to a stop amid fragrances of sweet cinnamon and heady saffron. *A memory of home.*

The fragrances retreated and were replaced by a smog of fennel seeds and garlic assailing his senses. And a hint of wild mustard, the earthy scent when crackled in oil before bringing forth a broth of arhar dal, speckled with crunchy jakhiya. The ship was a vast kitchen, and the sea a different world, separated from the ship by an invisible barrier. Madhyra's strange sorcery with spice had intoxicated everyone on the ship.

Amir suddenly felt isolated, clobbered by the spices as though the Mouth itself raged beside him and his battle.

It did ask you for help.

Madhyra.

The whisper of the Mouth was weak, as though he could hear it from as far away as the mountain of Illindhi. He found himself weak in his knees as he came to, the saffron—his reach for home, for his family— dimming in his senses. Of Harini there was no sign. She ought to be in this spice cloud. He sifted through the cloud, calling for her. No response. *You cushioned her fall; she would not be hurt.* He screamed her name twice, until he was in the clear, closer to the prow. He tripped on a body, and then two more, and saw the deck was littered with them— both the Haldiveer and the gatecaste, wrapped in tendrils of spice. Gates, the blood. Slick, wet, diluted by the sea spray, dripping into chipped timber as he crawled through the aroma of garlic and ginger.

He pulled himself up against the railing and let out a long breath, free of the suffocating spice. Free from the rattle of the Mouth's whispers in his head. Ahead, beyond the stern, through the thinning mist, he spied half a dozen Jhanakari ships. They fanned out on the sea in a semicircle, closing in on the two frigates of the Black Coves.

Bulked-up galleys with the Jhanakari flag fluttering from their sterns—an obscene yet sturdy mesh of wood and iron and sailcloth, armed with white-haired archers on their decks, arrows nocked and ready to fire. Amir tasted the tangy brine on his tongue, swallowed it, and stumbled farther toward the prow.

Toward Ilangovan.

The Haldiveer guarding Ilangovan lay unconscious. Ilangovan, however, remained tied to the bowsprit, hair caught in a wild dash of wind, wet with sea spray. He was thin as a bone dipped in kulambu. Gates, even Kabir had more fat than the leader of the Black Coves. Before him, Kalay stood on the gunwale, leaning forward and striking at Madhyra, who parried her blow, then ducked beneath a sweep of Sekaran's mace. The mace caught the netting that held the mast up, trapping it in its web. Sekaran let go of the mace, unsheathed a dagger, and thrust it at Madhyra. She buckled and caved inward, then flipped sideways and bore down upon the now-exhausted pirate. Sekaran growled and stepped away as Kalay leaped again at Madhyra.

Madhyra dodged her and swerved like an uncoiling serpent to swat at Kalay. The blow caught Kalay's face, and she fell, clutching her nose. Madhyra whirled and unleashed a flurry of attacks at Sekaran, who—after repeated retreats—roared and caught Madhyra's sword on his palm—allowing the blood to seep through his skin in dense trickles—before twisting her arm with a snarl.

Madhyra screamed in both pain and anger but did not yield. Rather, she used Sekaran's grip against him, pivoting around him, stepping on his thigh and thrusting up, landing a knee on the underside of his jaw.

Sekaran roared. He let go, clutching his chin as Madhyra jumped, regained her footing, and swung her blade at him. His thighs caught the strike, and he buckled soundlessly. Before Madhyra could finish him off, Kalay dived into their midst, brandishing her talwar and thrusting upward to knock Madhyra's weapon from her hand.

All of this happened in a matter of seconds, precious though they were, as Amir spied the Jhanakari ships inching closer. He clung to his shamshir and hobbled forward, ducking beneath the tack, each step taking him closer to the confrontation between the two Illindhian warriors.

Kalay kicked Madhyra's sword aside. A hint of a smile played on

Madhyra's lips as she nimbly stepped back, her hands raised. "I feared Mahrang would send you, Kalay."

Kalay spat at her feet. "Even the deepest nethers of the Mouth do not deserve you, *Madhyra*."

Madhyra's smile widened. "I much preferred when you called me aunt, cheche."

Amir swallowed all the seawater on his tongue and stared at them. *Aunt and niece.* Madhyra continued, unfazed. "Now, come on, stand tall and fight like I've taught you to. Don't disappoint me when you're here on duty. This is what you were born for."

Kalay blew her hair out of her eyes and straightened. Madhyra was weaponless, but if there was fear in her eyes, Amir couldn't see it. He stood a few feet behind Kalay, his shamshir aloft but wavering in his hands. From the corner of her eye, Madhyra glimpsed him, and he paled as he met her gaze. He looked away, as though to stare into her eyes was to stare into the Mouth's abyss itself.

"You have a few minutes, cheche. Till the ships are here. Then I'm afraid you and I will have to make a farewell."

Kalay was panting, wearing a look of disbelief that Amir shared.

"Why are you doing this?" Kalay cried. "Why did you kill my father?"

"What happened to Fylan was an accident," Madhyra said matter-of-factly, shifting her stance.

"And yet he's dead because of you."

Amir's breath caught in his throat. *A whole family out for each other's heads.* Madhyra didn't seem bothered by the morality of it, whipping around as a pair of men—seeing Sekaran unconscious behind Madhyra—dashed at her. She used their momentum and the stuttering motion of the ship against one before swerving sideways to sidestep the other and topple him overboard. By the time she regained her footing, Kalay was upon her, the edge of her talwar held to Madhyra's throat.

Amir's heart was hammering far up in his throat. *Come on, do it, Kalay.*

A long, droning horn crashed through the air. The Jhanakari ships were announcing their arrival. With only a few hundred meters between them and Ilangovan's pirate galleys, Amir assumed the archers would now be given free rein.

"Too late." Madhyra grinned as she leaned against the railing, Kalay pressing into her. A step back, and Madhyra would topple and fall into the seas. *Could she swim?*

"Answer me," Kalay persisted. "Why?"

The first arrows soared through the air and fell like pelting rain. Amir shielded his head and cowered beneath the shroud netting as the ship thundered with the sounds of shattering timber and pierced flesh. At once, he lost all sense of direction. Panic overcame him.

Gates, where is Harini? He turned to hunt for her, but found once more only the spice cloud occupying the rest of the ship—dissipating, but slowly.

Both Kalay and Madhyra ducked beneath the rafter and emerged on the other side. The Jhanakari ships closed in on Ilangovan, who continued to remain tied to the prow. Kalay pressed her scimitar once again close to Madhyra's throat. She wiped the tears from her eyes with her free hand and took a long, deep breath.

Amir was mere feet behind them. He could sense the anticipation in Kalay's breathing, her itch to overcome her pain and stab Madhyra and end this torment. The Mouth must be whispering in her head, too, he surmised. She was, after all, its acolyte, its vaunted devotee.

Why was Amir, then, so restless? Why was his grip on the shamshir slackening when he ought to be ready to pounce on Madhyra should Kalay fail? Even if he thought himself incapable, even if he had little courage in the face of this—this demand of him from the Chairs of Illindhi—his future and that of his family depended on a stronger grip upon that gilded hilt, so why was he hesitating?

He thought back to Harini's words, as though perhaps he had missed something in them, a hint of what she had meant. His uneasiness had to have a source.

"You ask me why, cheche," Madhyra said, as though in answer to *his* questions, "when you refused to listen to me in the first place."

"Then tell me," Kalay pleaded, her hand betraying a tremor, only for the slightest second. "Tell me why you wish to spread the secret of olum. Is it retribution? Was it one more of that man's fanciful notions? Why did my father have to *die* for all this?"

"As I said, I didn't mean for Fylan's death to happen. And I am sorry," Madhyra said. Amir was surprised at how sincere she sounded. "But you have to understand the path I had set on, cheche."

Kalay laughed in hysterical bursts. "Typical of you, to delay giving me an actual answer." She pressed the tip of the sword into Madhyra's skin, drawing the first trickle of blood. "Not this time. As an acolyte of the Mouth, I cannot let you spread the secret of olum and Illindhi to the eight kingdoms."

"Is this why Mahrang chose you? Or is it the other way round? Did you beg Mahrang to send you under the guise of vengeance?"

"What are you waiting for?" Amir hissed from behind Kalay. "Be done with this!"

Madhyra eyed him briefly, as though he were a bug buzzing irritably near her ears. But it was Kalay who suddenly concerned him. Why was her hand wavering over Madhyra's throat?

She is unsure.

The thronekeeper of Illindhi smiled, confirming Amir's fears. "Ah, cheche, I see you have caught on, the tremble in your hands and the widening of your eyes speak what you have kept hidden from your own heart. You know it, don't you? I did not escape from Illindhi to spread the secret of olum.

"I left so that I could destroy the Spice Gates."

Whatever he had expected, it was nothing close to this. The words burrowed into Amir's heart, then rose to his head and flushed out everything else he'd been thinking of. Harini, the Poison, Ilangovan, a life in the Black Coves . . . Everything came together, kneaded like dough, and then was cast aside into the abyss of blackness to be replaced by the ringing of Madhyra's words, a knell that lasted forever and yet for less than a heartbeat. A thought that had no right to be conceived, let alone germinate and bloom and bask in the sunlight of this world.

For a long moment, there was only silence, a sort of silence that had many sounds to it. The whiz of arrows in the air, the cracking of waves, the crash of water, the break of timber and the flap of sailcloth, the screams of the men and women of Ilangovan, of Halmora, and of the Jhanakari navy. The air was rent with a multitude of sounds in that scallop of silence.

She's lying. She has to be. But—Gates, what would it mean? Gates . . . Gates . . .

Without warning, Kalay pulled back her scimitar and raised it over her head to bring it down, instead of merely driving the blade into her aunt's throat. The monstrosity of Madhyra's claim must have eaten into her flesh and took hold like an abomination, a snakebite that had to be sucked out before it was too late.

What are you doing?

He asked this of himself because Amir wasn't aware of having moved. His mind seemed to remain beneath the rafter even as his body swiveled into action. Kalay's moment of hesitation was sufficient to propel Amir forward. He clattered into her from behind, knocking the talwar from her hand just before it plunged down into Madhyra.

Kalay fell onto the deck, Amir sprawling atop her, her weapon flying out and landing several feet away, at the edge of the ship's prow. She thrust at him with her swordless hand, and Amir's feet slipped on the wet deck as he received his due. Pain shot through his head. *This is what impending death smells like.* He scrambled and turned to Madhyra, but it was too late.

She was already scurrying upon the railing—like a child walking a tightrope in the Bowl—and toward Ilangovan. Using the rope, she swung across to where he was bound. She untied him in a single jerk of the knot and grabbed his tunic.

You're not stopping her from taking Ilangovan. Why are you not stopping her from taking Ilangovan?

Amir remained frozen, the pain of Kalay's punch still radiating. A minute ago, he'd have sprinted with every muscle in his body to prevent Madhyra from untying the Blessed One and handing him over to the Jhanakari. He'd have failed, in all likelihood, but he'd have tried. And now, in this span of a hundred breaths, in this fresh light that illuminated his insides, he remained rooted and watched with a mixture of horror and fascination as Madhyra cast a pitying glance at her niece before she dropped into the water with Ilangovan.

Kalay swore, scrambling toward the edge, only for an arrow to pierce the wooden railing inches from her hand. Amir crawled to the rail from beneath the twanging arrow and peered down into the water. Several Jhanakari boats surrounded Ilangovan's pirate galley, driving back the swarm of the Black Coves' patamars. One of the Jhanakari boats cast a net into the water, and seconds later Madhyra surfaced, holding on to Ilangovan with one arm. She caught the net with the other. The Jhanakari sailors pulled her and Ilangovan onto the fishing vessel. Seconds later, as Amir's heart still leaped and skipped, Harini surfaced beside her. She flailed, and Amir could tell she did not know how to swim. A pair of sailors dived into the water toward her and grabbed her. In a moment, she was on the vessel, coughing in bouts but otherwise alive and unharmed.

Madhyra's words echoed in his head, *thrummed*, and shook his very insides: *So that I could destroy the Spice Gates.*

Destroy

the

Spice Gates—

Wait, wait, wait.

He had to slow down. What did those words even mean? Could such words even mean anything? It was nonsense, ho! Akin to claiming they could erase the sun from the sky or stop the clouds from raining upon their fields.

Yet in that split second, when Madhyra had revealed her purpose, it hadn't mattered to Amir whether the deed was impossible. The mere idea—the fragment of that forbidden thought—had spurred him to an action he would not have taken in his sanest moment. Kalay would have killed Madhyra, of that he was in no doubt, but sparing Madhyra's life, and allowing her to escape—

Wait, wait, wait. Your mind has never worked so fast, it has never perceived a change this drastic in this short a span of time. You're going to hurt yourself. Back off, back off, you're on edge.

His thoughts fell prey to the cacophony around him. Hands on his shoulder. Rough and coarse. A beard on a face, wet and stinking of oil and fish and cinnamon. A gaze that shook him out of his stupor, away from the sight of the Jhanakari ships. Karim bhai slapped him once, twice, and thrice. Amir blinked. The numbness melted, replaced by pain. Overdue and urgent.

"You must jump, pulla."

Amir found his mind had barricaded the entry to any more words. *There simply is no space.* Instead, he looked up in time to glimpse another rain of arrows. Aimed not for the few remaining people on the ship but for the multitude of smaller catamarans and fishing boats. Amir climbed to his feet, holding the railing as screams erupted all around him. Karim bhai was nudging him, but there was nothing ahead but the railing and, beyond—open water.

"Karim bhai, she—she—"

Without warning, Karim bhai toppled him overboard. Wood scraped against his chest, and then air. The Jhanakari galleys and boats, all up-turned, the clouds in his grasp.

The last thing he saw as he fell was Kalay's furious face at the edge of the railing as she watched the boat carrying Madhyra—and Harini—retreat toward the kingdom of Jhanak.

At last, the water took him.

CHAPTER
15

The sound of drums and the blowing conch. The march of
a thousand steps. Rhythmic. A cohesion of violence. At the
vanguard, men and women in iron helms, their breastplates
embossed with the mark of Illindhi. Behind them, the dreaded
legion of pikes, swords, and hammers. A cacophony of steel.
The echo of their cries that brought down debris from the cave's
roof like rain. A promise to end. Their time was coming.
Their time was coming.

—UNKNOWN

Amir woke up on a soft bed, the softest he had ever slept on. Every muscle in his body ached. He wanted to remain lying down, sink into the mattress, and try to piece together the crumbs of his memory, which was hazy and disjointed. A flicker of the oceans, the sway of ships, the smell of spice—nutmeg and anise, a whiff of cardamom, like the rain forests of Mesht—a clash of steel, a fading dream of the Poison, Harini in a robe of azure and gold like sunlight glinting upon a rippled sea, and a lone man tied to the bowsprit of a large galley . . .

Fragments came rushing: they'd taken Ilangovan.

And you *let them take him.*

Amir sat up straight, sweating. His shamshir lay beside him. He'd not lost it this time, or had he? He looked around. The room he was in much resembled the chamber Orbalun had invited them to only a day before. A lifetime ago.

Another fragment arrived without permission, evoking a grimace: falling into the sea from Ilangovan's ship. Less a purposeful leap, more a tumble, as though someone had pushed him from the deck.

More memories began to uncoil like a slow disrobing, revealing the nakedness beneath. A hand reaching out to him as he flailed in the raging water. Not Hasmin, no, he wouldn't, not if Amir was drawing his last breath. But Hasmin was there. As was Kalay. In a larger boat behind them, Orbalun, dhoti flapping in the sea breeze, flanked by a host of Jhanakari soldiers and a smaller Raluhan contingent, with their painted pikes and triumphant expressions. Orbalun, who raised his hands and shouted commands to pluck Amir out of the waters like a bulb of saffron from a field.

Ripe for the Spice Trade. Ripe to be carried through the Gates.

He searched his mind for the fragments that floated like jetsam.

Karim bhai.

Amir's breathing intensified, and he leaped out of bed, eyes roving across his room. Kalay materialized at the edge of his vision. How long had she been there? She stood beside the window, gazing at Jhanak's noxious coast, at the gathering clouds. Her hair was tied loosely, and her eyes appeared heavy, devoid of sleep.

"Did you eat?" he mumbled out of habit.

Slowly, Kalay shook her head. Of course she hadn't. She wouldn't have the appetite for it. His memory returned fully, and the depth of his folly rose to the surface like bile.

It's a miracle she hasn't killed you yet.

"What happened?" Amir asked anyway, as though he still lacked the bare necessities for this conversation.

Kalay scowled. "What *happened*? You have some nerve, Carrier, to ask me this question. What happened is that because of *someone's* ridiculous judgment, Madhyra is here. In this palace."

"My ridiculous judgment? You—you hesitated. I saw it, Kalay. You could not bring yourself to kill her."

"Which meant you attack *her*, not *me*. Gates!"

Amir closed his eyes. A quietness had settled in his mind, a silence he now filled with the memory of the morning.

Why *had* he stopped Kalay from killing Madhyra? He didn't even know if what Madhyra claimed was true. Who even made such claims, besides the deranged individuals who loitered in the paved alleys of Talashshukh, noses steeped in bowls of steamed ginger? Or was it merely that he *wanted* it to be true? An irrational desire at the cusp of desperation. Yes, that had to be it. Not because it was the right thing to do—no. He was fairly certain that until Madhyra had made her absurd claim about destroying the Gates, he'd wanted her dead. *Dead, dead, dead.*

It was bludgeoning, like he was being hammered like a nail from all sides with no respite. The prospect of someone intending to destroy the Spice Gates—how deranged must Madhyra have been? It had to be a lie. Now that he thought of it, she'd been buying time, waiting for the Jhanakari ships to close in. Why, in such dire times, Amir wouldn't put it past himself to have offered such balderdash for a semblance of mercy. For hope.

"But it's impossible," he said at last, finally gaining a sense of clarity.

When Kalay gave a quizzical look, he continued, as though the obvious had eluded her. "The destruction of the Spice Gates. It is physically impossible. Thousands have tried in the past and failed. The Gates cannot be hammered into, nor be crushed by elephants, or even picked at one stone at a time."

"I am aware," Kalay replied coldly.

"Then what is Madhyra even doing here? What does she need Ilangovan for? Or any of the eight kingdoms for that matter? Does she expect to go from Gate to Gate, testing her hammer against stone?"

"I don't know."

"What do you mean you don't know?" Amir retorted. "You're her *niece*. Oh, don't think I did not hear your little exchange on the ship."

Kalay's silence stretched as the sun's rays angled into the chamber, lighting up the marbles. "Surely, she must have a reason to even contemplate this ridiculous notion," Amir prodded on, softening his voice, however. "You are her family. How can—"

"It wouldn't have mattered if you had only let me kill—"

She broke down, and not for the first time Amir saw a part of Kalay detached from the ruggedness of the Uyirsena. The warrior withered like a flower in winter. Her reluctance suddenly made sense, and Amir did not wish to prick her with it again.

She returned to the comforts of the window. Amir thought the conversation to be over. But crossing her arms against her chest, she said, "Despite not being the thronekeeper, my mother always had a hundred things to keep her busy. 'Kalay, I don't have the time right now. Kalay, why don't you take a walk with the other girls, instead? Kalay, learn to play the sitar. Or the sarod. Kalay, you best get some rest.' She thought Illindhi would not run in her absence, and that it was her duty to make sure that Aunt Madhyra never felt the pressure of the crown. Which meant I spent more time with my aunt instead of my own mother. My aunt was everything to me. What I am is because of her. She made me a warrior, a poet, a student, and a priestess. Above all, she told me not to fear the walls we had built for ourselves."

Amir had to blink to be doubly sure that he was still listening to a soldier of the Uyirsena, a ruthless, coldhearted acolyte of the Mouth.

She locked eyes with him, unaffected by his disbelief. "It's not that my mother was a bad person. It's just that she thought doing nothing was the best way I could be safe. Aunt Madhyra thought doing everything was the best way I could be safe. And in between was my father. The man whom my mother said died in your arms in Halmora."

Amir gulped, recalling the blood coating his tunic as Fylan pleaded with him to go to Illindhi. And Kashyni, who sat stone-faced in the pulpit of the Chairs.

"He feared I was getting too close to Madhyra, and that as throne-keeper, she exerted a certain . . . influence on me. And lo, it was thus decided. I would be a priestess of the Mouth, a warrior of the Uyirsena at the age of nine. I was taught to be an acolyte, to fear and worship the Mouth. To watch blood trickle from beneath a man's skin and not flinch. To watch his eyes close and not be surprised when they never opened again. My father took me to the Mouth one day, where the flames rise up from the cavern. He taught me the prayers and taught me what it means to be under the patronage of the Mouth, to swear our food by the taste of olum. I was taught to serve the Mouth and to pray to the Immortal Sons that haunt the Outerlands."

Amir gulped, a shudder running up his spine. "You—You've seen them? The Immortal Sons?"

Kalay shrugged. "I've heard them. Their roars reverberate through Mount Ilom. They don't come close to the city."

"So, they're real?" Orbalun had speculated that the impassable mountains and rivers were the Immortal Sons. In some ways, Amir now preferred that theory to the reality of the beasts Kabir had been painting under Karim bhai's tutoring.

Kalay frowned. "Of course they're real. What kind of a stupid question is that?"

It's the kind of question that comes from having the entire foundation of your world and beliefs upended in the span of a few days.

But Amir didn't say that. Instead, he dragged himself to the past, to the fences around the fields of Raluha staring at the Outerlands at dawn with Appa.

More like being made to walk to the fences. You hated it.

He had. He'd protest and want to go back, and Appa would make him stay anyway—make him stare. Until the drooling mist thinned and the mountains and the forests emerged in the morning light. Until Amir would rage at Appa for being a madman and threaten to scream for the chowkidars to find them.

Perhaps he just wanted you to see how your petty lives stood for nothing in front of the impenetrable Outerlands. To show that nature always won.

"My mother was happy too," Kalay said. "That I finally had a purpose. That I was serving Illindhi in the most honorable way I could. Only one person opposed it."

"Madhyra," Amir whispered.

Kalay nodded. "She had no say in it, though. Even as a thronekeeper. Merely gave a quiet nod on the day I was to be inducted. She blessed me and said this was for the best. I hated her that day. I hated her and I still kept her secrets."

Amir tactfully raised his eyebrows.

"My aunt—she would tell me everything, even during her busiest days of thronekeeping. What she ate, what she planned to wear, who she liked or did not, the gossips of the court, the mysteries of spice, and all about perfumes and oils. She told me her own secrets and asked nothing of me—except to keep an open mind. I knew she despised the Spice Gates. At first, I thought they stopped her, and us, from exploring the wilderness. Our ultimate nature as a people is to wander, she'd say, and I sensed I was listening to seditious talk while we braided each other's hair and played pallankuzhi and danced like wild peacocks in the confines of our chambers. She had been outside the walls. Into the Ranagala. She'd come back with parchments of the maps she'd draw, and made me memorize them. Said as an acolyte of the Uyirsena, it was always useful to know what the Ranagala looked like. I was a child. I believed her. I mugged up the Outerlands. Such talks only worsened with time. She was saying dangerous stuff, and me? I was taught by Mahrang and my father to silence those who spoke in this way. But . . . I couldn't. I . . . I always thought my aunt was just expressing empty desires. Vacant dreams. Things she knew she couldn't change even by being thronekeeper, but that I was some channel, an old archive to store her failures. And so I kept quiet—even after joining the Uyirsena. Nothing of what my aunt told me did I pass to my father. That was my first mistake."

She took a deep breath. "My second mistake was keeping quiet even after she met that wretched man from the Ranagala."

Amir sat up straight. "*What?*"

"A barbarian who pretended to be a merchant and brought for her grapes and nutmegs and white pepper and cardamom, and groundnuts and apples and stole her heart in the process. She decided to marry him. Only, the Chairs would never permit such a union, not even though it was the thronekeeper in question."

His thoughts ran wild. *A man from the Outerlands. Bearing spices.*

"So she ran away," Amir speculated, silencing the throbbing of his head. It didn't feel wise to question Kalay on this at the moment.

"Not for a while," she went on. "Not until Mahrang found out and had the man killed. He brought his head to her, wet and fresh and warm after his death, and warned her to stick to her duties as thronekeeper. That they lay in safeguarding the Mouth. My father remained vigilant. He suspected my aunt to be volatile, hurt, and therefore capable of reckless choices. *Vengeance will be on her mind*, he told me. Bade me keep an eye on her while Mahrang and he fortified the Mouth with more of the Uyirsena. At dusk, each day, he would unfailingly ask me what my aunt had said during the day, what her mood was like, whether she met with any more strangers.

"But nothing happened. She was as quiet as the dark, brooding, dishing out her duties as though she were an automaton serving wine. At some point, I must have thought she'd forgotten all about what happened. I told my father as much. That my aunt could never dream of abandoning the throne. That above all, she held Illindhi closest to her heart. Until one evening, she came and told me that she had forgiven me for having betrayed her secret of her love to Mahrang. I—I couldn't say anything. Except that I hadn't. I couldn't believe that she'd thought that Mahrang found out because I'd told him. I ran to my father, to confess that she did not trust me anymore. By the time we arrived back in her royal chambers, she'd . . . left. Escaped. Turns out, I was the last person she'd spoken to.

"It . . . I never imagined that she'd have abandoned Illindhi. That for love or retribution, she would leave all of this . . . Illindhi . . . me, her faith, and break our secret to the eight kingdoms. Mahrang was certain that's what she was setting out for. The Chairs agreed. My father agreed. It would be catastrophic for the Spice Trade, of course, but it was not the end of the world. We could still stop her. The Uyirsena had stopped Illindhians from toppling the Spice Trade in the past. But this—to destroy the Spice Gates altogether . . . I cannot believe my aunt would—"

Kalay rubbed her eyes and put on a stern face, as though for Amir to catch her teary-eyed was beneath her dignity and pride. Her expression hardened, and she snuffed out any remaining vulnerability.

Not for the first time since that tumultuous morning on the ship, Amir wondered what it'd be like to have no Spice Gates. His mind could not conjure that possibility. What a strange feeling, to attempt to mold his mind this way.

As impossible as the reality of Illindhi had once been, not many days ago. As impossible as a spice that could taste and smell like any other spice. You're ticking off impossibilities by the day, Amir of Raluha.

No more carrying! Freedom from the Bowl. A tomorrow he could not picture in its entirety but merely in these illuminated fragments from a well that had sprung from nowhere. It flooded his senses even as he struggled to shape it and pull it into his reality. Gates, it had to be a dream. What Madhyra had set out to do . . . she would release every bowler from their torment.

But if she didn't . . . if she failed . . .

Of course she will fail. How does one even destroy the Spice Gates?

And more important, why does she even want to do it?

"The Uyirsena," Amir said wearily, clutching the sides of his head and sinking back into his bed, afraid his head would burst into a thousand shards of flesh and he'd need a soft landing for them. "How much longer before they set out?"

"Twelve days."

Kalay's breathing sharpened as she answered him. She was trained for this. Her mind chiseled for this eventuality. He sensed the urgency running in her mind. It was hard to say when she was an acolyte of the Uyirsena and when the niece of Madhyra, dancing in the shadows of the royal chambers of Illindhi. But presently, as she stood by the window, she herself weary from having told her tale, Amir knew she craved that release, the permission that would strip her of any pending affection for her aunt if she had any left anymore. Her mistakes had run their course. There was no room for anything but to prove herself as a warrior of the Uyirsena.

In truth, nothing had changed for Amir either. Madhyra was still out there, and the Uyirsena would come, and they would kill any and all who knew of the Mouth and Illindhi.

And the list of names keeps increasing, doesn't it?

And—if what he believed was true—the Spice Gates would stand as they always had.

Mahrang's voice, and the choices he'd offered Amir, echoed within him. What truly did it matter what Madhyra was doing? A madwoman, nothing more, torn by a failed love, a broken family. An absurd vendetta that Amir—who had nursed absurd dreams long enough to know what could work and what couldn't—brushed off as the ramblings of a wounded soul.

Stopping Kalay from killing Madhyra on the ship had been reckless. A naïve and desperate lunge born out of hope and love.

But then—

Why had Kalay faltered? Was it simply because Madhyra was family?

He regarded Kalay, her gaze locked on the sea, her hair a mess, and he was certain that there were parts of the story she had kept from him. Why was she not as surprised by Madhyra declaring her intention to destroy the Spice Gates as Amir had been? Madhyra *had*, in the past, confessed to Kalay of her dislike for the Gates, but Amir knew plenty of folks who disliked the Gates. The Bowl teemed with them, and if he looked hard enough, even some of the abovefolk were not particularly amenable to fraternizing with the other kingdoms.

And what did she mean that Mahrang and Fylan had fortified the Mouth with more of the Uyirsena?

No, he couldn't ask all these questions at once. Not when Kalay was in this limbo between emotions, traversing the vast realm of vulnerability and duty-bound anger. This fragile connection that hung between Amir and Kalay could be shattered in the blink of an eye, and one more hint of Amir displaying reluctance in carrying out his sacred mission would end with the scimitar meant for Madhyra lodged inside his own chest. He'd run his course of fortune by stopping Kalay from killing Madhyra once. He wouldn't live to see the aftermath of it a second time.

He suddenly realized Kalay was staring back at him. As though she would not let him out of her sight again. He'd proved elusive more than once, and now, he'd actively stopped her from fulfilling her—*their*—mission. She probably thought him volatile and dangerous, and perhaps even doubting the work he was doing.

Gates, but she was also helpless without him. She had to be. Why else would she still be here?

Amir once more took stock of the time they had left, not helped by these bouts of uncertainty. Twelve days. They had twelve days to stop Madhyra.

The door to the chamber opened, and Karim bhai bumbled in, and Amir was glad to not be alone with Kalay anymore. The old Carrier looked haggard and restless, but he was alive. Amir smiled to himself, even as he outwardly displayed a look of pinched annoyance.

"You pushed me off the ship!" Amir said accusingly.

Karim bhai smiled, one eye resting on Kalay, wary of her blade and countenance in equal measure. "I saved your life, pulla. Orbalun could only save the few of us. The other gatecaste, not so fortunate. Sekaran and the others are to be sent to the Whorl. They are now the Condemned."

A weight settled in Amir's stomach, for the people whom he'd met for less than a few minutes, who'd chained him. He'd feared such an outcome. A deeper dread, however, rose to the surface. "What of Ilangovan?"

Karim bhai shook his head. "Imprisoned. He will be presented to the thronekeepers before tonight's feast. Or, that is what Orbalun claims."

Presented . . . for a public execution.

Amir had always yearned for the Poison, for that little vial that would get his mother through the Spice Gate, and into a strange land. But for Ilangovan himself he'd worried little. Until he'd met Harini on that fateful night in the qila of Halmora, he had considered Ilangovan invincible, legendary, a figure cut from the past and immortalized in the Bowl as someone who could never be erased off the coasts of Jhanak, a revolutionary who stood for the gatecastes' cause, who had given them safe haven and a life on their own terms, even if not a life lacking in hardships.

Nothing had changed in his opinion: without Ilangovan, the Black Coves would not endure. He imagined the scores of gatecaste pushed onto the Ship of the Condemned, their limbs chained, their heads shaved, flanked by Jhanakari galleys as they sailed toward the Whorl, where they'd make it through . . . only to be rudderless without Ilangovan on the other side.

He felt disgusted and helpless sitting on this plush bed, surrounded by satin and warmth, and a pleasant view of the sea. This was not the bowler life, even if a corner of their hearts had craved such comforts. No, their life lay in simplicity, garlanded with dignity and respect. And food. Always lots of food. The thought brought a smile to his lips, and he suppressed it, knowing the reality was far from his grasp. And slipping ever further.

The coarse feeling of a noose tightened around his neck. The stomp of the Uyirsena and their fell beasts in the caverns of Mount Ilom echoed in his head. He gulped, fearing how in a matter of seconds he was incapacitated. Not by those closest to him, but by the world itself.

Amir took it in, and there it clashed with a strange suppression of his emotions. He could not rally the anger and the hurt. There went the guardian of his future, in some dank cell guarded by Jhanakari loyalists—possibly to be publicly hanged, or sent to the Whorl—and yet, why were Amir's hands not shaking? Why was he not grabbing Karim bhai by the scruff of his neck and demanding that he do something to save Ilangovan and the Black Coves?

You're letting Madhyra get into your head.

What else was new? Considering how many others—Mahrang, the Mouth, Harini, Hasmin, his mother, Kabir . . . his father—all had taken up residence in his head too.

Karim bhai appeared to have sensed Amir's unrest. "You're thinking of him again."

Amir snapped out of his musings, his anger rushing back, and he was almost glad for it. "Of–Of course I am. How could I not? Ilangovan was my hope. What am I doing all this for? Why else would I be running after a stranger from a ninth kingdom, trying to *kill her*—me, who has never held a knife to a throat—putting everything at stake?"

"You could still have everything you need, pulla. This—chasing after this woman—need not be your burden."

"But it *is*." He swept his gaze over Kalay. "Because I was desperate enough to go to Illindhi for the Poison, I made it my burden. And now it's my family's burden because of my decision. I realize that now. I cannot change it. I'm forced to take this path even if I'm not capable of stopping Madhyra."

"You *had* the chance," Kalay scowled. "And what did you do?"

"Yes, pulla," Karim bhai agreed, deepening Amir's anguish. "Why *did* you stop this one from killing Madhyra?"

Amir wished he could sink farther into his bed. Karim bhai did not hear Madhyra announce she intended to destroy the Spice Gates.

And it gnaws you yet. Grows, feeds. Are you afraid it could be possible? Fool, fool.

With Kalay present, it seemed wiser to hold back. "I . . . killing her did not seem right," he lied. And then, buoyed by the course he was inventing, he attacked Kalay. "How can you even try to do it? She's your aunt. She raised you. She's nothing to me, and yet she's also a human, and I can't let that blood be on my hands. I'm—I'm just not that person. We could have merely stopped her, chained her up. Taken her back to the coves. Pleaded with her—"

Kalay laughed, wiping the tears from her eyes. "You're a funny one.

There is no way to stop my aunt but to kill her. If not by noble means then by treachery. And even that is difficult. She is a warrior without peer. She is a better swordswoman than my father ever was. Or even Mahrang. No one can go up against her and come away victorious. Even the bravest of the Uyirsena stand no chance against her skill."

"You seemed to be able to hold your own."

Kalay chuckled. "Only because I have hope. I am her weakness. She will not kill me. It is why I was chosen by Mahrang."

"I thought he sent you to prove your loyalty to the Uyirsena."

Kalay's lip trembled, and she gripped the window's ledge harder, almost crushing it. "I don't have to prove anything to anyone. Mahrang trusts me completely. As does the Mouth."

Amir was unfazed, though he swallowed at the thought, once more, of the Mouth—a living, breathing entity—capable of judging its acolytes. It irritated him, oddly. "If you say so," he snapped back. "Let me ask you this, though: What if you're wrong? She killed your father. He was as much family as you are. What's to hold her back against you?"

Kalay ground her teeth and looked to Karim bhai to intervene. But Amir knew his friend would have wished to evaporate on the spot rather than meddle in their pointy affairs. "Trust me to know the difference," she said. "My aunt will not kill me."

The seed of doubt had been planted, however, and Amir could not say if it was a good thing. Did Kalay believe Madhyra when she'd said that she hadn't killed Fylan? That it was an accident? Amir only saw the blood on Fylan's chest, not what caused it. It could have been one of the Haldiveer. It could have been Madhyra, or perhaps something between the two, an amalgamation of violent possibilities that had driven Kalay out of her ancient realm and into the bustle of the eight kingdoms. Either way, there was no mistaking her reluctance on the ship, and now—a gradual admission of that possibility budding inside her heart like the slow tilt of a candle wick setting cloth aflame.

She crossed him and strode toward the door. At the entrance, she stopped, and Amir feared she would disavow their tacit truce, their silent dependency on each other. Her gaze flickered momentarily to her talwar hanging from her belt. "Just don't get in my way tonight" was all she said.

She was gone, the door closing behind her, leaving Amir relieved.

"Ho, pulla." Karim bhai sighed in equal relief, sinking against the wall to the floor and removing his headcloth. "You must be a fool, riling her up like that. She fights like a fish dancing in water."

"I wanted her to leave us alone," said Amir. "This was the only way."

"And if she'd decided enough was enough?"

Amir clutched his knee and rubbed gently at the wound. "She wouldn't. She needs me. Without me, she cannot get to Madhyra."

Karim bhai did not appear impressed. "That is some rough talk, pulla. You need a reminder of what we are, and where we are. Already my mind is addled—the kind of things that have come to light. A ninth kingdom, the—the olum, or whatever it is. I pray to the Mouth every minute I am not worrying about your life or my own, and for the first time even sitting in the shadow of the maharaja of Raluha himself has left me feeling . . . nothing. Nasty things are afoot, and we're not built for these abovefolk's concerns, pulla. So get hold of your reckless words before the wrong person hears them and sees the lips they're coming from. This nimble-footed ponnu from Illindhi is trouble in more ways than one, and I wager even filling her belly with biryani is not going to keep her from getting what she wants."

"Her heart's not in it," said Amir plainly. He'd realized it halfway through his argument with Kalay. "Mahrang sent her hoping her vengeance would fuel her rage. He counted on it, but perhaps he did not wager that Kalay would be disillusioned by seeing the eight kingdoms. She's no blind servant anymore. She's Madhyra's niece, after all, and the poison drips through."

Karim bhai shook his head. "Ho, if this Mahrang is what you claim him to be, then I doubt he'd have sent this conflicted soul when the world depended on it, pulla."

"So long as they thought Madhyra wished to spill Illindhi's knowledge to the eight kingdoms, ho, I wager that too. Besides, Mahrang never wanted this, remember? He wanted to send the Uyirsena right away, except I pleaded with him not to. But—"

"But what?"

Amir took a deep breath, the pain retreating to the recesses of his mind. It's what he had wished Kalay out of the room for. He had to tell Karim bhai. He had to tell *someone*. It gnawed at his insides, a scab he had to scratch from his skin before it scarred all over.

"Do you think the Spice Gates can be destroyed?"

Karim bhai was quiet one moment and broke into hysterical laughter the next, tears stemming from his eyes. "Now, what are these foolish thoughts you're running amok in Jhanak with, pulla? You need some sleep. We have been through a lot, and Ilangovan—well, I am sorry for what has happened, but it—"

"Madhyra," Amir interrupted him, "said she wants to destroy the Spice Gates, which is why she set out from Illindhi. Not to spread the secret of olum and shatter the Spice Trade or whatever. Heard it from her own mouth."

Karim bhai continued laughing, but at some point he must have seen Amir's tight-lipped expression, the eyes sunken and true, and the laughter wavered before a frown emerged on that forehead. He opened his mouth, closed it, and opened it again. "Deranged!" he barked. "Of course she's lying. Bless the Mouth and its eternal tongue, pulla, it is nonsense."

"Well, that was my first thought," Amir began defensively.

Karim bhai, however, had no interest in pursuing this conversation. "Nobody can break the Spice Gates. Remember that. Ghajanana with a force of a hundred elephants could not shatter the Gate's weakest pillar in Raluha. They are made of ancient stuff. Not things to trifle with, ho."

"But if she can . . ."

"She is out there manipulating *thronekeepers*. She has the mighty queen of Jhanak in her fold, doing her bidding. Your turmeric princess walks by her side. She nearly convinced Orbalun; though I'd wager it takes more than a well-drawn map to shake him from his beliefs. You're but a Carrier. She is toying with your head, and you'd best believe she is here to sow discord in the Spice Trade and nothing more."

It wasn't that Amir wasn't convinced. He merely wished to understand who—other than him—could conceive of this impossibility. What had he hoped from Karim bhai? Pious, cautious Karim bhai, whose ambitions did not extend beyond the bedecked halls of the Raluhan palace and the bare necessities for his fellow bowlers. What would it take for the old Carrier to imagine with Amir that there could be a life, however loosely defined, without the Spice Gates?

You're just desperate because Ilangovan has been apprehended. You're trying to resurrect a future that has died a thousand deaths, the most recent one also the most irreversible.

He traced his fingers along the ridges of his throat, across the spice-mark branded into his skin since birth, and felt queasy for the first time.

"Just imagine it with me, bhai," Amir pleaded. "Could it be? Can you dream what that life could be like?"

Karim bhai stood and came to sit beside Amir on the bed. He laid a hand on his knee, and Amir could tell there was a flash of pain in the old Carrier's eyes, as though he was revisiting an old wound, a ghost that had only been partly exorcised. "I have imagined it enough, pulla. I have imagined it for years in my youth. Do you know there was a man in the Bowl who once spoke of these wild desires of seeing the Gates toppled and broken?"

Amir sat up straight. "In the Bowl? Who? *You?*"

"Your father."

And while usually the mention of his father caused a flood of anger in Amir, it now formed a puddle of disbelief. "Don't say things simply to defend that man, bhai," Amir shot back. "He abandoned us."

"That doesn't change the fact that he believed the Gates could be brought down. He tried, too, in his own feeble ways. You were too young back then. I wager you only ever remember the trips to the fences."

Amir blinked. "Wh-What did he do? What do you mean, he tried in his own feeble ways?"

237

"Oh, whatever a bowler could muster within the extent of his powers," said Karim bhai, smiling, though not in a mocking way. "Which is not much. Down in the Bowl, he formed what was briefly known as the Tongueless Thieves. A group of ragtag nobodies like your father—all Carriers—who decided the Bowl ought to pretend like the Gates don't exist. And one way to do that was to avoid spice in your food altogether."

"*Ridiculous!*" Amir cried. Although he now wondered if his own moderation toward spices came from his father's reluctance.

"Not really. There were many who found it possible to do. Abstinence became a thing in those days, though it never really carried to the abovefolk. Of course, it became a little violent now and then. Your father and his friends would steal spices from the bowlers who swore by their allowances and flush them down the drains. Set fire to a cart of cardamoms fresh from Mesht in the bazaar one night. Earned your father the moniker Arsalan the Arsonist. Why do you think Hasmin hates him so much, ho? And by consequence, you. More than the other bowlers. It was your father who stole a jar's worth of saffron meant for Hasmin's wife as a gift, and then gloated about it. These prickly, annoying acts of rebellion stirred up the Bowl in those days. What—you thought your father stood up one day and decided to give himself up to the Immortal Sons? No, pulla. He thought the Bowl ought to empty and move to the Outerlands."

Amir's heart skipped a beat. *The day she met the wretched man from the Outerlands.*

Mahrang beheaded him.

"However, the Tongueless Thieves only liked it as long as they were riling up Hasmin, setting fire to spice wagons and stealing from the bowlers' kitchens. The moment your father preached that the true mark of a world without Gates was to escape the clutches of the abovefolk and live in the Outerlands, they stopped listening. Everyone's got a mural of the Immortal Sons etched on their walls, pulla. Frightening images, I don't need to tell you. And you'd find no one as devout as the bowlers about the scriptures. Nobody bought into your father's scheme, least of all you."

"Me?" Amir's jaw slackened. He was finding it suddenly difficult to breathe. Why was everything about his past so hazy, so clouded in anger and hate for the man who had one day disappeared when Amir woke up?

"You." Karim bhai nodded. "Let me tell you this, pulla—nothing mattered to Arsalan more than seeing what was beyond the fence. I know it because I was always with him, we'd be chasing each other's tails across the Bowl, and I knew the flame that burned eternal in his heart compared to my own sputtering embers. Was around that time when a young, dashing Jhanakari sailor named Ilangovan deserted his duty, took a hundred Carriers with him, and pitched tents in the distant islands near the Whorl. Was a scandal, pulla, across the eight kingdoms. In the Bowl, the Tongueless Thieves thought they ought to join him. Many did, though not me—they needed someone in the palace fiddling with the roster work.

"But your father never bothered to. He thought Ilangovan was getting it all wrong, that someday—sooner or later—they'd all be caught by the thronekeepers and drowned. He thought they were not reaching far enough, that they ought to go to the Outerlands. I begged him, pulla, to join Ilangovan. I told him together they could provide haven to every gatecaste man, woman, and child across the eight kingdoms. But no, your father's flame yearned for the dark tempest beyond the fences.

"He almost went, too, except he was forced to marry Noori, and you were born. You were supposed to be like him, pulla. He raised you with that hope. Of raging and dreaming about the Outerlands. I don't think you remember what you told him though."

Amir raised his eyebrows. "What did I tell him?"

"You told him you wanted to become a Carrier. You told him you will never leave Raluha and the Bowl, and that you were dreaming of the day when you'd pass through the Gate for the first time. It's a pity he abandoned you before that day. He'd have then known how right he was."

Amir shook his head. "N-No. I wouldn't have—"

"You were a little thing. Scuttling about in the Bowl, hearing stories from the Carriers about the other kingdoms. Of course you don't remember."

If there was much Amir forgot, he certainly recalled his father's ramblings. Before he had abandoned them, Appa would occasionally walk Amir through the Bowl, across the saffron fields, and beyond the Spice Gate to the great, spiked fences and armed sentries that separated the kingdom from the forbidden Outerlands. He would stare at the jungled fringes and the misty hills without a word and silently nudge Amir, expecting a reaction. He had taught Amir the names of the mountains that surrounded Raluha, the different peaks that jutted out of the horizon like clawed fingers; also the name of the river that was said to run a few miles north, slithering into the forests beyond, where he claimed was the most incredible wilderness Amir could ever imagine. He had painted a picture of grotesque and colorful overgrowths, of canopies of leaves the size of roofs, of wild marshland where strange creatures and monsters bred their offspring, emitting cries that echoed through the hollow jungles and snaked their way out in whispers and hisses. An artistry for storytelling that Kabir inherited.

And Amir . . . had never believed him. How could Appa know all of that?

Karim bhai smiled. "Arsalan thought you were cursed, pulla."

"Cursed?"

"He tried to smuggle you out through the fences a couple of times, but you'd fight back; you'd yell and scream. You'd want to go back to the Bowl. After a while, he stopped, fearing you might get him caught by the guards. But . . . that changed him, your little rebellion. He feared what he and Noori had birthed, and he was . . . I think, he was sad to see his son be so different from him. And when he saw Kabir crawl out of your mother's womb, and he saw the mark on his son's throat, he realized his mistake and he knew that he shouldn't have done what he'd done. That he'd been living a lie, tricking himself that he'd be able to realize his dream through his children while keeping everyone happy.

"Sadly, it doesn't work that way, does it, pulla? You can't keep everyone happy. People like your father, at some point, they tip. All that dread of what lies ahead piles up, over and over, accumulates like a garbage heap, until you can't handle the stink. You just want to leave everything and do what you've always wanted to. And that's what he did."

A wretched man from the Outerlands, a merchant bearing spices.

"Madhyra—she . . . uh, she met a man from the Outerlands, bhai. A *barbarian*. I know it's probably not him, but maybe Appa survived. Maybe this means there can be life in the Outerlands."

Appa survived, and never thought of returning to his family?

Karim bhai, however, was nonplussed. "Your father wasn't the first one to sneak through the fences. There's a reason why they aren't heavily manned by chowkidars, pulla. Many have escaped in the past, and the following morning, at first light, their bones inevitably line up near the fences, as though they're residue of our offerings to the Immortal Sons. Your father's did too. I picked them up."

All these years, Amir had found it difficult to forgive a dead man. Not even the sight of his bones interred behind their home that morning had extinguished the seemingly irreversible hate that blazed in Amir's heart. It was as though Appa had not died but had endured through the wind and the leaves, and in the aroma of spices that hovered above the Bowl.

A heart or a furnace, you keep wondering. Perhaps, it has always been the latter.

Now Amir did not know what to feel. That Appa had dreamed of a world without the Spice Gates seemed to break the cloud of loathing that had mushroomed inside Amir. Maybe, just maybe, he could forgive his father.

"The oppressed are never short of revolutionaries, pulla," Karim bhai continued. "There's always someone with verve and fire, and ideas too large for reality to hold them. Sometimes, you've got to shrink those dreams, fit them into what the world can carry. Ilangovan did that. Your father couldn't. You—you're nearly there, pulla. Don't make a khichdi of this, with absurd notions of destroying the Spice Gates or of life in the Outerlands. You say the Mouth is real, and it lives—*breathes*—beneath that mountain in Illindhi. It doesn't matter, pulla, if it is real or not. Our lives will always be bound by it and its Gates. But ho, within that life, we can demand justice. Our battle is not with the Spice Gates but with the people who determine what it means to pass through those Gates. Our battle is with the hierarchies imposed upon us by the abovefolk. That's what Ilangovan fought, and many others, to different ends, over the decades and centuries that have passed. Ilangovan was only a little older than you are now when he conducted his escape with the sanders of Jhanak. He thought and did what every Carrier of your age thinks of doing but fears to act upon. We are conditioned by the abovefolk to believe that this is all we *can* do—that we are paying for some unknowable sins of our prior births and that there's naught to do but to sail through this—through the Whorl of our lives—and pray that we fare better the next time around. I thought that, too, once upon a time, when I was gallivanting across the Bowl with your father. I still do, on my worst days. But then I remember that the Bowl needs people like me to forsake my dreams so people like you can realize yours. I made a promise to your father that I will keep you alive and safe, and I have done that. I cannot leave Raluha now. Not ever. It's my home, as long as there are pullas like you dreaming of the Black Coves and whatnot."

Karim bhai sighed. It was a deep, resigned sigh, which Amir did not wish to choke with a protest. For there *was* protest on his lips. A bubbling forecast that had begun that morning on Ilangovan's ship, and now culminated at the precipice of his conversation with Karim bhai. More questions needed answering. And he would get them, and he would get them now!

"Bhai"—Amir stood up, suddenly gaining energy in his bones and a sharp clarity in his mind—"I know what I must do."

"You need to stop Madhyra," offered Karim bhai sympathetically.

Amir hesitated. "That, yes. Of course. But before that, I need to talk to Harini."

Karim bhai's mouth remained open. Slowly, it flattened to a smile. "Every hour, I find upon you the contours of Arsalan. Bold, reckless, and full of love for the people he was forbidden from loving. It's like I've been talking to a wall all this while."

"No, bhai," said Amir. "It doesn't matter what you say, or what I think.

But I need to understand what Madhyra is doing in the eight kingdoms, and what this has all been for, for me. Why has Harini chosen to aid Madhyra, and what has she kept hidden from me that she cannot utter? I spoke to her on the ship, bhai—and she . . . she would have told me. She feared the wrath of the Uyirsena on me, too, but that is immaterial now. I walk with one of the acolytes. I am too far deep in, and I would like some light."

"Then you must get ready for tonight."

Amir frowned. "Kalay—she asked me not to get in her way tonight. What did she mean? What is tonight?"

"The reason I had come here in the first place." Karim bhai grinned, revealing betel-stained teeth. "To ask you to get dressed."

He walked to the almirah and opened it, revealing a plethora of colors, nearly blinding to Amir. "Wear your finest kurta. Orbalun has invited us for the afsal dina feast."

"The *feast*?" Amir's jaw dropped. The afsal dina feast had always been reserved only for the highest among the highest, those who never stepped on anything but marble, who traveled in palanquins and wore bejeweled helms and necklaces. What would a pair of bowlers do there? Who would even talk to them? . . .

"Harini will be at the feast," Amir realized suddenly, and added with a hint of dread, "and Madhyra."

He clenched his fists. Harini had dived into the waters, too, and was rescued by the Jhanakari sailors. Of their collusion Amir had little doubt. He was but a gentle bud in a sea of thorns. He couldn't perceive, even if he spent his mind on it, the depth of the machinations of those who were garbed in silk, chewed on cardamom, and rested their bottoms on plush velvet. Harini wouldn't deign to tell him.

And yet, she wished to safeguard you. She kept you in the dark because she feared for your life.

Hope bloomed like the fragrance of ginger at the cusp of a day devoid of tea.

Karim bhai knotted his fingers in front of his chest and his eyes did a dance of mischief. "It would be viciously daring, ho. Orbalun is aware of Madhyra's purpose, and now Madhyra knows he is. But if the words of the servants are true, Rani Zariba plans to parade Ilangovan among the guests, chained and defeated. They will raise a toast to his imprisonment together. And eat the spiciest avial and drink the most peppery rasam you can imagine."

It disgusted him. That the thronekeepers would so obviously love to put on a show like this. An end to Ilangovan's seemingly endless torment of the waters of Jhanak and Vanasi. An end to the hopes of many of the bowlers of Raluha, the sanders of Jhanak, the rooters of Vanasi, the easters of Halmora, the snakers of Kalanadi, the horners of Talashshukh, the oarasi of Mesht, and the reeders of Amarohi—the gatecaste of the eight kingdoms. Songs would be sung of Ilangovan's reign in the taverns by the docks of Jhanak, sure, but Amir did not want poems and eulogies of what *had* been. If possible, Amir wanted Ilangovan alive, and the Poison in hand, and his family safe among the coves.

Do not think of the other possibility. Do not let your mind go down that thorn-laden path.

However, the idea had already taken hold, and he found it impossible to contain its urgency as it laid its eggs, warming to hatch in the recesses of his soul.

CHAPTER

16

*Attempting to replicate the Spice Gate is a worthless exercise,
just as wearing the king's underwear does not make you royal.*

—Ramblings of a court jester who
climbed the Tower of Mesht

That evening, Amir and Karim bhai donned sumptuous, borrowed clothes and examined each other's bodies awkwardly squeezed into them. Karim bhai wore a long, black jibba over a pajama, with little sapphire mirrors on the cotton. Much of it was his own handiwork, and while it was as simple as a broth of dal, there was a certain quality about Karim bhai in this outfit that assured Amir of his fit in the palace. His turban was more glamorous—a dash of maroon cotton wound in a layer and a half—and according to Karim bhai, it lent more prominence to his face.

Kalay, once she had returned from her silent wandering, had slipped into a Jhanakari sari that was familiar in nothing but shades of color, a hint of saffron floating behind strokes of silver and pearl, flowing all the way down to her heels, where zari of fine silver brocade grazed the floor. Her shoulders flattened against a silk blouse, and she tossed her hair over them in a tangle of black and gray. A calm determination bristled on her face, as though she had forgotten both Amir's betrayal on the ship and their conversation in this chamber, and instead preferred to start anew.

Her talwar had been taken away by the chowkidars, but she managed to sneak in a dagger, which she presently pushed beneath her pallu, tucking it between the petticoat and her waist. She had to be careful. The last thing they needed now was another frisking and an eviction from the palace—or worse.

Amir, much to Kalay's impatience, was the last to step out of their guest chamber. He wore a white kurta that fell all the way to the knees, overlapping a peach pajama and new juttis to replace his old, battered chappals that had sunk too much in the dirt of the spice trail. The new shoes pricked the back of his feet so that each step resembled something between a graceful foot forward and an awkward stumble, but as he stood in the mirror and looked back at himself, he grinned, wishing that Amma was there to see him.

Look at your son, all decked up like a prince.

She'd crack her knuckles against her temple and ward off the evil eye.

"Finally," Kalay muttered, spending not more than a heartbeat to look at his attire. And as she walked ahead, Amir wondered if she was glad to be rid of the uniform and armor of the Uyirsena.

Hasmin awaited them, under Orbalun's orders, his impatience spilled on his uniform like drool. Amir had not seen him since the morning on the ship—and was rather disappointed that he'd survived till the evening. A scar along his nose told Amir that Hasmin would not forget the memory of Sekaran's punch anytime soon. As for Amir, he relished that memory every waking minute.

Despite being disarmed of his usual sword, Hasmin was permitted a baton, and his fingers lay curled around it, his frown penetrating Amir's attire.

"Excited for the execution?" He beamed as Amir passed by. "Gates willing, you're next."

Amir itched to respond, but Karim bhai nudged him forward in silence, their heads bowed.

You can wear the swankiest piece of cloth in this palace, but there's little you can do about old habits of servitude.

Each floor of the palace they climbed deepened Amir's worry. Each staircase ended sooner than he expected, bringing the distant music from the great hall above to his ears.

They marched under an impressive stone arch, cracked like the arch of the Spice Gates, flanked by white-haired chowkidars on both sides, their batons and foreheads smeared in turmeric, the ends of their robes emblazoned with the sigil of the Spice Trade.

They were honored at the entrance as companions of Maharaja Orbalun of Raluha. Nobody questioned this deviation from his typical companions, who were either family members or dignified ministers of Raluha's inner circle—the chiefs of silk, honey, steel, and such, who sat on heaps of silver and waited for their turn to impress the maharaja. Orbalun, though, seemed to have abandoned that routine. No Raluhan minister was present. No family member. Karim bhai, Amir, and Kalay were it—this procession of misfits orchestrated by Orbalun on the most auspicious of nights.

Hasmin reminded Amir that he, too, was part of this twisted entourage by pricking him with the tip of his baton. "Stay in the corner, in the shadows," he hissed into Amir's ear. "Do not make a fool of the maharaja for inviting you to be a part of the feast. I don't want to hear so much as a scrape of your feet on this marble."

Nudged by Hasmin, Amir stumbled toward the nearest pillar, but his eyes had already begun to wander the length and breadth of the court hall in search of Harini. Each moving shadow, each flicker of firelight, each stray sound of a footfall or a creaking door pricked him into high alert. His jumpiness annoyed Kalay. She was busy admiring the grandeur on display: the high-strung chandeliers, the floating firelights, the weaving columns of flowers like curtains, the candles scented in cinnamon, the thick sweetness plunging into their senses, the banners wrapped around the mountainous pillars, the pond with lotuses at the heart of the darbar . . . where women garlanded in jasmine sat along the borders of the pond, one foot dipped in water and the other curled beneath their weight, their hands flicking rose petals along the carpet for the arriving guests, their white hair knotted in reeds and seaflower, their bangles brown like cinnamon biscuits. Beyond them was the dais, the throne, and the thronekeeper seated on it: Rani Zariba.

Amir inhaled sharply. It all felt too distant, too precious to touch, to even look at longer than a moment. Gates, he felt dizzy.

"Ah, royalty," said Karim bhai, meanwhile, placing his hands on his waist and a grin on his face.

From the shadows of the pillar they clung to, Amir traced Karim bhai's gaze through a gathering of more than a hundred people—thronekeepers and their spouses, princes, princesses, ministers and their sons and daughters, high guards and their haughty charioteers, old spicemakers and their crooked staffs, the famed alchemists and astronomers of Vanasi, the architects of Talashshukh, the coconut merchants of Mesht, and the silent artists of Amarohi—all of them with their heads held high, turbans and veils tightly wound and pulled, lips thin like a line sketched beneath their noses, words dribbled out of their mouths sparingly, clothes immaculate and jewelry glimmering, reeking of the opulent estates like those along the throne road in Raluha, the abovefolk who, like their ancestors and scions and neighbors, loaded their innermost chambers with trinkets gained by having their fingers deep in the bowl of the Spice Trade.

"I think I'll fall sick," Amir whispered to Karim bhai. "Look at the way they hold their wineglasses." Their fingers were delicately poised around the glass, as though to clasp it tighter would crush not only the glass but also their stature. *Nauseating.* Give Amir some local spiced toddy in a lota any day over this funereal amassing of touch-me-nots.

Yet one thing kept him glued to the court hall.

From the entrance to the pillar where they stood, and everywhere else he imagined, Amir breathed in the aroma of cinnamon floating in the air. In the midst of this embarrassing display of wealth weaved the wild colors of a confectionery—waiters with flour-dusted chins scuttling about with the urgency of those who had managed to smuggle a rosemary delight.

Amir was swept into the past. Sweets transformed this evening into by-lanes to Amir's childhood—to jalebis and balushahis, and Amma's specialties, the pak with ghee; to crusted cheeks and spoiled innocence; to the little desires that composed the symphony of a marriage with delicacies.

Cinnamon was evidence of how a spice, instead of stoking the embers of one's stomach, fiddled with the sweet desires of their minds.

Gates, it was easy to become disoriented! What was Amir even there for? Right! Harini. Madhyra. Ilangovan. His sensibilities scrimmaged in this mystical court hall, ensnared by the lure of cinnamon.

His eyes flickered over the tables that lined the space. *Food.* So much his stomach turned a somersault. Uthappams spiced with milagai podi, banana dalia, sundried fish—what the sanders called karuvadu by the docks—shrined with turmeric and lemon, pumpkin pastries and walnut salads dressed in maple and cinnamon. Gates, he was ravenous! When was the last time he had eaten a proper meal? He did not even remember the food the Illindhians had fed him during his illusory stay among them.

Hasmin tried to wrangle him back, but Amir was already storming across the court hall toward the food-laden tables. Hasmin's hissing threats from behind him melted away on the carpet.

He scooped up what he could get his hands on and shoved them first on to a ceramic plate, heavy and intimidating to hold, and then into his mouth, one dish after the other, manners be damned. The rice was redolent with saffron and cloves, mace and nutmeg rising out of a kootu of meat and drumsticks, salmon cooked and drenched in a kulambu, fillings of spinach, and a counter reserved purely for rabdi and jalebi heaped in an orange pyramid.

Midway through the meal, Karim bhai grabbed Amir's hand and whispered, "Bless the Mouth!"

Amir's darting eyes landed upon a platform beside the dais. Leaning back on a cushion of flayed silk, with a sitar on her lap, was a woman with striking red hair. It fell to her waist like a curtain. Her eyes were closed, lashes a thick purple, her mouth a devious curve. Her fingers twanged the strings of the sitar and music rose in an ascending halo of sound; her head rolled in a rhythmic trance following the notes, and each second of the tune seemed to weaken Amir's knees.

"The mistress of bards, Devayani." Karim bhai spoke dreamily, a croak entering his voice. "She is the Grand Ustad."

Not only the royal singer but also the chief musician among the eight kingdoms. His hands still encrusted in food, Amir drew closer to the stage, and the music enveloped him. Devayani herself only momentarily opened her eyes, lashes rising up like claws to glimpse first Amir and then Karim bhai, where her gaze stood transfixed, and her mouth uttered a single word Amir could make no shape or meaning of. But then her gaze flickered and withdrew to flit over the rest of the assembly of royals and chowkidars.

Kalay, who had been far less fascinated by the food on display than either Amir or Karim bhai, suddenly slunk away. One moment she was beside Amir, frowning at the meen kulambu as though it disagreed with her Illindhian palate, the next she had slipped back into the shadow of a pillar, a different one from the one Hasmin occupied in his pointless vigil.

Amir turned to see the reason for Kalay's departure. Maharaja Orbalun was striding toward the food tables, his hands splayed as wide as his grin, as though he were greeting his oldest friends.

"Welcome, welcome!"

He pulled Amir into a rough embrace, then nearly choked Karim bhai in a ferocious hug. Much of the hall's attention had settled on Orbalun and his companions, including Rani Zariba, who frowned sharply from her throne of lapis lazuli.

"Welcome," Orbalun repeated, louder. "Where are the cup-bearers now? You must be served wine."

"About time," Karim bhai muttered so only Amir could hear. "If that's what it'll take for me to forget this night."

Orbalun wrapped an arm around Amir as the guests began to disperse once more, their attentions returning to their quiet conversations, far beneath the clinking of glass and the clatter of spoons. He could sense everyone's disquiet simmering, their murmurs of Orbalun embracing gate-caste in the heart of the Jhanakari court hall. What were gatecaste even doing here? Had the death of his child worsened Orbalun's sensibilities?

"I hope your stay was comfortable," Orbalun whispered, dragging Amir into his orbit again.

"Y-Yes, huzoor." Amir swallowed, his fears disintegrating.

It was fair to say Orbalun did not believe him. He rested both his hands on Amir's shoulders and narrowed his eyes to focus in on him. "She's here, Amir. Madhyra. She has not shown her face, but there is a lot that is unsaid in this court hall today, and much revolves around the events of this morning, what happened on the seas. It is worth considering that Madhyra may have manipulated more than just Rani Zariba and the rajkumari of Halmora. And as for you—you need not worry about your perceived status as a merchant of the Jewelmaker's Carnelian Caravan. I have managed to throw the thronekeepers off that notion. You are simply a Carrier of Raluha . . ."

Amir had stopped listening to him. Orbalun was the thronekeeper of Raluha: his ruler, the one to whom everyone, except his own queen, bowed and saluted. The one to whom everyone was prepared to submit their lives, and who, in a moment's whip, could overturn their lives if he so desired.

But in that moment, Orbalun was a fat blob of distraction that obstructed Amir's view of Harini.

His heart lurched in his chest as her eyes met his, melting all that Amir had conjured in resistance, springing a thousand leaks in that dam of control. She wore a sari of the ocean blue, the zari woven into the silk brocade, sapphire trinkets stitched to the pallu, her hair a frozen wave of black and brown, eyes the green of curry leaves, staring straight through the back of Orbalun's head and at Amir.

"Maharaja Orbalun," she said, walking toward them, a unique sternness in her voice. "You have not introduced your guests to us."

Amir frowned as neither Orbalun nor Harini spoke about the morning's events. Not even a gesture of recognition. As if they had not been present on the ships at all. It was a matter of discretion, and Amir knew it would continue to remain so.

Orbalun smiled and made way for Harini to join them. She appeared much taller. Gates, he forgot she always had been so tall. Their confrontation on the ship seemed to be a thing of the past, a ghost that had been exorcised. He wanted to apologize, to sneak her away from these ornate halls and into where their memories were made. To ask her myriad questions that nobody else could bear witness to.

"Come, Rajkumari Harini," Orbalun said, interrupting Amir's thoughts. "I daresay *we* haven't met in a while. You were a child when we last saw you at the afsal dina feast of Halmora. And it's a pity . . . the feasts have . . . *evolved*." He glanced around at the court hall and emitted a deep sigh. "How times have changed. Come, meet Amir. He is a Carrier. It has been long since we have honored their likes on the afsal dina. We mustn't forget their contributions to our lives."

If Harini expected lies, she did not show her disappointment at not being given them. "I thought Carriers were not permitted to—"

"Oh, the thronekeeper gets what he wants," Orbalun said with a wave of his hand. "You'll learn soon, I suppose. Or must I say you already have? I have heard of a certain . . . display to come. Congratulations are in order, I suppose, for what you have accomplished this morning that none of us could, over the years. It is almost . . . baffling."

Harini gave a noncommittal shrug. "Things I must do to regain the Spice Trade's favor. The neglect turmeric receives has gone unnoticed for far too long, Maharaja. And my father . . . well, he is not a man to play the games thronekeepers play in court halls and in trade chambers. He is a simple man who prays to the Mouth and eats his food and tries to keep his people happy. But then, such naïveté often does not go unpunished. Surely you know of what I speak?"

Orbalun laughed and clapped his hands. "How can I not, *Maharani* Harini? When it is said my child was stillborn because of a failure to bring back turmeric . . ." His voice was somehow jovial, pointed, *and* sad. He continued, "A failed Bashara, the priests call it. My Carriers came to your fort and returned empty-handed. Amir was one of them, I believe. Weren't you, Amir?"

Amir blinked before nodding vigorously. "Ho-ho, huzoor. I was. No turmeric."

"My condolences." Harini's lip curled, throwing a sidelong glance at Amir, as though still piecing together the parts of this story of how he had managed to squeeze into the most exclusive feast in the eight kingdoms. "But what happened at Halmora that night does not alone reflect what is truly plaguing us, Maharaja. We're a quiet, reserved folk. And if we must resort to glamour and show, you must imagine how desperate we truly are. Halmora is on the verge of collapse because we are unable to bring enough spices to our tables and into our food. It is hard to believe the Spice Trade stands for equity."

Orbalun's lip twitched. "It is noble of you to keep your people happy. But I only hope you are aware of what you are sacrificing in that quest."

"I am sacrificing one man," Harini replied with resolve. "A man who you have claimed in your letters to Rani Zariba 'is a stain that ought to be washed off the coasts of Jhanak.' Am I not merely doing that?"

Amir shot a sharp glance at Orbalun, who lowered his head in silent confirmation that he had indeed said these words. Amir couldn't fault him. Ilangovan *had* menaced the coasts. Much of the Spice Trade was disturbed because Ilangovan would raid the granaries at Jhanak, and oftentimes even those of the other kingdoms. He was after all, a Carrier by birth, and as long as he could persuade a few reluctant chowkidars to allow him access to the Gates, he could go anywhere. Over the years, he had built a strong network of loyalists in the other kingdoms—dens of gatecaste who would aid him in his quest, and even pockets of sympathizers from the upper castes. There had been times when Amir had returned from Jhanak and Kalanadi without a shred of cinnamon or black pepper, and while he was grateful for the reduced burden on his back, there was little recompense back home, where the Bowl bemoaned the absence of their rations. A ripple effect that caused even some of the bowlers to despise Ilangovan, who claimed he was everything a bowler wasn't—a fake messiah who merely pretended to save and serve the gatecaste but was, in reality, selfish and worthy of the punishment that awaited the worst of the Condemned down the Whorl.

Amir had never paid heed to those few who opposed Illangovan. There would always be naysayers, even down in the Bowl.

For once, Amir wished that Orbalun would leave so that he and Harini could speak privately. Instead, their conversations continued even as a procession of Meshti royals climbed the dais to speak to Rani Zariba. She looked resplendent in an emerald gown. A sword hung on the wall behind her, surrounded by a garland of cinnamon sticks, gleaming against the crystal light of the chandeliers. Amir's skin tingled at the sight of it, though he couldn't say why.

Orbalun, meanwhile, did not hold back in his verbal spat with Harini, though both maintained a smile as they assaulted each other's views. "I appreciate your candor, Maharani Harini. But do not for a moment assume that I have ignored the fact that you have brought over two dozen Haldiveer to a peaceful feast. Where did you get the Poison in such quantities to bring such a large contingent to Jhanak?"

Harini brushed a lock of hair from her face. "You think me heartless, Maharaja. I can assure you I am anything but. To answer your question, while the eight kingdoms are miserly about consuming turmeric, the Jewelmaker, fortunately, was not. I was able to save enough over the last year before the Jewelmaker disappeared."

"And you brought nobody else?" Orbalun asked, scratching his beard, narrowing his eyes just a little bit suspiciously.

"My cousin, the wonderful Suhasini, has accompanied me. My mother has been unwell for a while, and Father thought it best to skip the feast this year. Rest assured, you will see them in the years to come."

"A wonderful cousin, Suhasini, ho?" Orbalun gasped mockingly. "And might I see her?"

Harini beamed. "She is with the prisoner. We don't want him slipping away."

Amir stood uncomfortably between them, back hunched, hands folded across his chest, the argument between the two royals now growing tiresome. He'd wanted to talk to Harini, but it was looking increasingly impossible. Behind them, Karim bhai stood a few paces away, his eyes flitting from one royal to the other, as though each of them held a secret he could exploit for his own gain.

Amir desperately looked around the hall for Kalay. He finally spotted her in the shadow of a pillar. Signaling with his eyes as best he could, he tried to communicate where Madhyra was. *Gates, woman, down— down—down in the dungeons.* Kalay, however, either did not grasp his meaning or thought him an idiot, for she shook her head and continued to scan the crowded hall.

Orbalun, however, had decided the time was ripe for whatever he had up his sleeve. He suddenly whirled about and clapped his hands, gaining the attention of everyone in the court hall.

"It's awfully quiet here!" His voice boomed. "Gates know I have had enough mourning for a week. Zariba, mustn't we liven up the most celebrated day of our year a little more?"

Rani Zariba rose from her throne, smiling. "I am always wary of your outlandish ideas, Orba, you know that. And I can see Silmehi here nodding." Chuckles crackled through the crowd. Timid, tamed laughter. "But given that we have more than one reason to celebrate tonight, I am willing to bite. What do you propose?"

Orbalun clapped his hands once more, striding into the center of the hall, dragging Harini with him along the length of the pond. The maidens sitting by the water shied away from his heavy footsteps. "Well, I think it's time we settle the debate of whether Raluha can ever produce a musician worthy of singing in the taverns of Jhanak."

The gaunt-eyed, chiseled Avasdha Silmehi of Talashshukh broke into laughter, his person adorned in livery. Amir had last seen him the previous day, after his collision with Orbalun. "Isn't a feast of the afsal dina where you do not make a fool of yourself, Orba?"

More laughter followed, and Orbalun took it in his stride, marching forward, Harini tagging along like a puppet. He glanced back and flashed a wink at Amir.

"Ladies and gentlemen." Orbalun's voice boomed across the court hall. Rani Zariba stepped off the dais, a curious expression playing on her face. Karim bhai, who with a bowed head, folded hands, and a series of nods had found a few ministers to proffer his courier services to, glanced in Amir's direction rather nonchalantly, as though all this were a plot Amir had not been privy to, although he suddenly had to grasp each and every intricate detail of it. The older man shrugged, disengaged from those ministers, and surreptitiously made his way toward the tables laden with delicacies. As good a time to eat as any.

"Ladies and gentlemen," Orbalun repeated, and Amir wondered in which inglorious direction this was heading. "I am delighted to present to you Karim Ahmed, who has gladly consented to perform beside Jhanak's own Grand Ustad, Devayani."

KARIM BHAI FROZE IN HIS ILL-FATED MARCH TOWARD THE FOOD tables. Sweat beads formed like lumps on his face. It must have been worse under his jibba, glistening into a lake beneath his arms, Amir imagined. He cut an old and solemn figure among the court hall's revelers, his wineglass with barely a sip tasted but already on the verge of being spilled. His eyes were wide, and had rested on Devayani's twirling fingers up until that moment but now slowly ventured to meet the delighted ones of Orbalun, who urged him on toward the dais with frantic gestures.

Devayani, who could well have been Karim bhai's daughter, finished her song on a spiraling crescendo, opened her eyes to Karim bhai approaching her like a prisoner commanded to walk to the gallows.

If this was meant as a distraction, Amir did not see how. Deep down, he was delighted for Karim bhai. A seat beside the Grand Ustad. The Bowl wouldn't hear the end of it for the rest of his life. But on the other hand, if Orbalun had meant this act to serve their purpose in the court hall today, Amir failed to see how. He frantically looked around again for Kalay, but the Illindhian warrior had absconded entirely.

Karim bhai stumbled onto the stage and flopped down on an embroidered diwan beside Devayani and her sitar. As the chatter died out, each footstep Amir took in his new chappals caused a soft clomping sound that seemed to thunder in his ears. Devayani plucked her instrument once more and nodded briefly at Karim bhai. A gentle, hollow tune rose from the sitar and drifted across the court hall. For a moment, it seemed as though Karim bhai was only a privileged spectator who had secured the best seat next to the Grand Ustad. Devayani's fingers sizzled across the sitar, toying with the frets and plucking the strings with ease, a smile forming on her lips as her head began to sway under the allure of the rhythm.

Then, much to Amir's surprise and pride, Karim bhai caught on to the tune, picked up his own rhythm, and in a nasal drone finally began to sing.

All these years, Amir had listened to Karim bhai sing when they lay on their backs on the rooftops of the Bowl's numerous chawls or during the carnivals in the Bowl beside the bonfires where the grandmothers danced. He would sing the oldest songs, the ones his own grandmothers had taught him but were forgotten in the Bowl's rapid progression into the drunk beats of verandah and music of the stairs. His voice, intermingled with the cries of the roosters and the endless tittering of the bowlers, always had a ruffled quality to it. As though it were trying hard to break free of the Bowl's tainted identity. Try as he did, though, the ambient noise would mingle with his voice.

Now those shackles were broken. In tandem with the sitar's bending of the notes, a slow fretting and pulling with its own suppressed hollowness and echo, Karim bhai's voice soared as he conjured the oldest of Raluhan songs—nay, the Bowl's songs—the "Whiff of the Saffron Storm."

It was magical. Even if things went south from here on, Amir knew he could slip through a Gate onto any rocky landing and remind himself of this one little goodness that came of it.

Except for Devayani and Orbalun, however, only a few faces among the crowd exhibited anything resembling approval or pleasure at the performance onstage. While the music engulfed them, Amir imagined the nobles' faces frowning and their lips crunched in scowls. Nobody wanted a gatecaste sharing a stage with an ustad, let alone the Grand Ustad herself. Karim bhai, to them, was one of those they believed were born of the karma of the sins of his past life, one who would scavenge their life away in whatever discarded part of their kingdom that permitted them to languish and endure. Who ought not to touch or be touched.

"Enjoying your moment of glory, are you?" said a voice behind Amir.

Amir turned to see Hasmin had come to stand behind him, his eyes only for the stage, flitting occasionally toward where Orbalun stood, hand in hand with Harini.

They looked at each other in mutual distaste. In two days, Hasmin's own life had been thrown rudely around. He had been forced to fraternize with bowlers, had been chained by the pirates of the Black Coves and then beaten in the face, and now he was watching Karim bhai sit beside the Grand Ustad, singing to his heart's content. How much longer would Hasmin hold all of that within his bosom before the dam broke and, like a vindictive storm, rained down on Amir? Already, Kabir was on the spice trail; how much worse could things get?

Somehow, Amir feared, there was always room in Hasmin's mind to excavate newer, unforeseen, levels of evil. No dearth of pernicious thoughts with which to torment the bowlers. In many ways, Amir decided, it was better to be taken by the Uyirsena than return in failure to Raluha and rejoin the Carriers under Hasmin's regime.

"This should have happened a long time back," Amir muttered, straightening the collar of his kurta and taking a sip of the wine, his eyes gesturing to the stage, where Karim bhai had embarked on a new song.

Hasmin's face scrunched in annoyance, then lightened into a smile. "There is karma, though. Fifty-seven gatecaste apprehended and to be sent to the Whorl at first light tomorrow. Not the fringes we visited, mind you, but all the way, to the part from which there can be no return. And leading them will be your preacher and defiler, Ilangovan. Sentenced to death for a lifetime of piracy. Ha! Sounds sweeter than all the cinnamon in this palace."

Hasmin was unconscious when Madhyra's ship emerged from beyond the Whorl. He does not know. Best let it remain that way.

"Why do you hate us so much?" Amir remembered Karim bhai's story about Hasmin and Appa, and yet it eluded Amir as to how one man could hold this much anger and bigotry as to practically live his life in the quest of another's suffering.

"Hate?" Hasmin chuckled. "No. This is not hate. This is the reality of the Spice Gates; the proper order of things. This is how things have to be because this is how the Mouth intended it to be. You—sifting through the veil—and me—far away from it. It is the way of our life."

"You whip us into a line and ostracize us simply because it *has* to be this way?" Amir asked, finding it difficult to believe the simplicity of Hasmin's dogma.

Hasmin shrugged. "I don't expect you to understand. We all have a role to play in our lives. My duty is to protect; yours is to crawl through the shit and get back spices for us. The maharaja's is to rule. The ancient scriptures have ordained it so. You mistake this order for injustice, for inequality. But is it unequal? Do we get to see the other kingdoms? But no—you bowlers want everything, don't you?"

Amir gritted his teeth, watching Karim bhai wave his hand over his head in a rhythmic incantation and then break into a slower, more melodious section of his song. "We don't want *everything*. We just want more than *nothing*. We want respect and freedom. Is that too much to ask? You've made us dependent on the spices, and you *know* that we'll go through the Spice Gate no matter what. But you've taken much more from us."

"You never had much to begin with. Except the mark."

Hasmin's face twitched as he uttered those words. Amir's heart skipped a beat at the realization. It was the second time the senapati was bringing up Amir's ability to visit the other kingdoms at will. Was Hasmin . . . *envious* of Amir's powers? Of the Mouth-blessed ability to move through the Spice Gates, to cross impossible distances at the blink of an eye—by merely placing one foot ahead of the other? No. He couldn't believe it. And yet, Hasmin's momentary lapse in discretion had told Amir what he had never imagined Hasmin—or any of the abovefolk—could possess. A pinch of yearning for the life Amir had, which, for as long as he could remember, he himself had striven to abandon.

Or at least a part of it. The only good part.

The turmeric is always yellower on the other plate.

Amir suppressed a smile and turned abruptly away. "Yes, we didn't have much to begin with," he said, inhaling sharply. "But you're also wrong. We deserved more in the first place. And it is our right to get it. And I will win that right, and you will watch me, kaka."

And there it was, once more, the gnawing. Each time he thought of the Black Coves in the last several hours, the other, impossible alternative presented itself in his head in fragments.

An illusion, nothing more.

He was frustrated. Ilangovan had been caught, and now Harini was proving elusive to even talk to. Gates, everything was so fragile. His dreams, his hopes, always hanging by a thread, like food on the cusp of going stale. And didn't that sum up the bowlers' lives!

Hasmin was on the verge of responding to Amir in a fit of rage when several things happened in quick succession.

First, the song reached a crescendo, both Karim bhai and Devayani swimming in a trance of their own making.

Like the slow fall of the fragrance of cloves down the throat, the gradual explosion of bitterness in one's mouth, the song ended.

At the same time, the great doors to the court hall groaned open, adding a layer of discord to Karim bhai and the Grand Ustad's song. Through the door marched a dozen Haldiveer, the chains wrapped around their knuckles tethered to a solemn, limping figure straggling between them. Ilangovan was dragged along the carpet, but to Amir, he appeared as though he were floating on air. He was stripped of his clothes but for a checkered lungi. Blood oozed from his face and from lashes on his chest and back, and he did not appear to have the strength to even return the gaze of those who stared at him.

Third, and perhaps what caught Amir's eye more than Ilangovan himself, was who trailed the procession: clad in a magenta sari, her hair in a dark-brown updo, strode Madhyra. Her hands were knotted behind her back, and her gaze swooped over everyone present in a cold, possessive manner, as though the court were a large, spicy golgappa that had to be gobbled at once.

Gates, where was Kalay? Amir's eyes roved over the crowd to where he'd last seen her, but the shadows revealed no warrior of the Uyirsena. If she was hiding, she was thorough about it. Closer to him, Orbalun and Harini both stiffened, different emotions playing in their eyes. Amir's own heart was racing, and he looked from Ilangovan to Madhyra, and back to Ilangovan, his brittle, slashed figure like a tattered cloth hung to dry outside on a stormy day. How much of Amir's future lay enveloped in this moment? When everything he had yearned for was chained and bruised in front of him.

Rani Zariba stood once more from her throne and nimbly stepped down onto the carpet. A curious expression played on her face—was it amusement? The smile was perfunctory, but there also appeared to be a certain withholding, as though she might reveal the weakness that had haunted her all these years, shame for having let this Carrier from Jhanak operate with impunity in her own kingdom.

The guards yanked at the chains. Ilangovan buckled under the press of iron, sinking to his knees in the center of the court hall. Amir grimaced as though the chains snaked around his own limbs. He averted his gaze, instead taking in the rest of the crowd. Every single pair of eyes was upon Ilangovan. Nobody spared a glance for Madhyra, who continued to stand behind the prisoner, her hands folded, her aura diminished by the man in front of her.

Rani Zariba came to stand within two feet of Ilangovan, flanked by her retinue of chowkidars and curious ministers. Her long, white hair, a gossamer sheen interlaced within it, gleamed beneath the cold, crystal light of the court hall. A winter within winter.

Without warning, she brandished her sword—an icicle that appeared as though it had never known warmth. The crowd took a collective breath as she swung it and then lowered the blade, slowly letting the tip rest under Ilangovan's chin, lifting his head ever so slightly.

"At last," she whispered.

"I hope you're satisfied, Rani Zariba," said Harini, extracting herself from Orbalun's shadow. She took the last sip of wine and let the empty glass slip onto the velvet landing of a servant's tray. "It is an old Halmoran tradition to carry a gift to those who host the afsal dina feast. As promised, Maharani, I present to you, Ilangovan, the suleiman of the Black Coves."

Despite their ploy, Amir knew Zariba could still not believe the truth of what she was witnessing. Her icy sword continued to prick Ilangovan's throat, drawing blood before tracing the veins of his neck down to his scarred chest.

Her lip curled before she sighed, almost relieved. "Name your reward, Rajkumari Harini."

This was it, then. This was Harini and Madhyra's big plan. To gather all the thronekeepers under one roof and break the secret of olum and Illindhi to them. Over the years Ilangovan had united them against him, his purpose solely to disrupt the Spice Trade that they held sacred. And Harini had delivered him.

Amir glanced in Orbalun's direction, but the maharaja gently shook his head, forbidding Amir to make a move. Even Karim bhai remained seated on the dais beside Devayani. He shook his head when their eyes met. It was as though all of them had expected Amir to conduct himself in the most reckless manner in that moment.

Do you wonder when you gained this reputation?

Harini adjusted the sapphire pendant around her neck and smiled.

"It's *maharani* now, Rani Zariba. I'm not a rajkumari anymore. Those days"—here, she shot a furtive look beyond Zariba at Madhyra—"are behind me. This here is the first of many steps toward a deeper and more meaningful relationship between Halmora and Jhanak, and with the other kingdoms, too, in time, I would hope. In return, I simply expect a certain amount of extended loyalty for the turmeric we grow with our bare hands back in Halmora."

Amir thought he'd misheard the entire demand. Harini asked for the eight kingdoms to buy more turmeric? Was that all?

"Take a kodamolaga and sit down, woman." It was the thronekeeper of Talashshukh, Silmehi, and Amir had to wonder what the man's fascination was with capsicum. "You don't get to dictate how the Spice Trade works."

"I dictate nothing. I simply observe and make a statement. That said, the rules governing the Spice Trade are a farce, Raja Silmehi," Harini said. "You have taken my father for a fool all these years. That stops now."

Asphalekha, not too much older than Harini but who appeared to possess the vitality of a thronekeeper, stepped forth. She was garbed in the black-gray crow robe of Kalanadi, her hair cropped close to her skull. "Don't blame us for overindulgence. It is well known even in the distant lands of Kalanadi that your own people use up most of the turmeric."

"Ah, here comes the great, serpentine Asphalekha from your seat of privilege. Why, I believe Ilangovan himself was sleeping beside a jar of black pepper when we caught him."

Ilangovan remained barely concerned by the tumult of conversation around him. Amir felt the urge to rush over and dab his wounds but was once more kept in place simply by how insignificant he was in this darbar.

Asphalekha meanwhile glowered at Harini. "I would throw another glance at your accounts before ascending the throne, child." She stressed on that last word in mockery. "It's never wise to curry favors for spice."

Orbalun stepped in, his hands wide in supplication. "Now, now. We're all friends here, Asphalekha, Harini. A big family. The spirit of the Spice

Trade ought to be held true. Maharani Harini, it was gallant of you to have accomplished what you have here. Ilangovan has long menaced these coasts, affecting not merely the trade of cinnamon and black pepper, but of all spices, with each of the eight kingdoms. I imagine Rani Zariba does owe you, but . . ." And here he paused, reflecting on his next words and exhaling softly. "Not with spice. Not with promises of more turmeric. We will revisit our trade contracts; we will gather our merchants from the guilds and demand an explanation for the shortfall in turmeric demand. Jirasandha has agreed to conduct an unbiased investigation into the Vanasari alchemists who have claimed that turmeric is ineffective as medicine and perhaps even toxic. All that said, our foods have always had as much turmeric as we have desired, let me remind you. You cannot impose on us what and how much we must eat, Maharani. It is a tenet of the bazaar, one the Spice Trade obeys unconditionally, the will of the people who orchestrate demand and supply. However," he said, holding up a finger to stave off her protest, "one favor does beget another, and I'm sure the two of you can come to an agreement as to how that can be met."

Harini sighed. There was something about her composure that bothered Amir. Again, why was she negotiating for spices when she had a secret as black as the darkest night to let slip?

"Very well," she said. "I won't pretend I did not expect this. Let's forget the turmeric for now, though we *will* discuss it further, I promise. In its stead, I would like two things, Rani Zariba. The first, the sword hanging behind your throne. And second, I would desire a dozen of your finest merchant ships and galleys that lie on your docks to be written in my name and bearing the colors of Halmora."

Silmehi burst into laughter, although he was not the only one. "Ships? And where do you presume to take those ships? Down the Whorl, I hope not?"

A few titters abounded in the court, but Harini seemed merely amused by the man's bluster.

"Where I take my ships is my business." She conducted herself with a patience Amir had not known her to possess. To him, she'd always been the princess of Halmora who found courtly duties to be awfully draining. Her only political desires rested in wanting to better the lives of the easters forced to live outside the qila to the east of Halmora. Her businesslike countenance both surprised and confused him. Had Madhyra wrought this in her? Or was it always present and Amir had only been too blind in love not to have seen it? "I will want the sword and the ships, and a band of sailors to train the Haldiveer in the ways of sailing. The ships may lie here until I decide what to make of them. But as a reminder, they should be in my name, sporting the seal of Halmora across their hulls."

What would she accomplish commandeering those ships? It had nothing to do with Halmora, or turmeric, or anything at all. And why the sword? What was one Jhanakari blade in the face of the weapons forged in Halmora and sported by the Haldiveer who were famed for the swords they made? What was Harini playing at, asking for such useless rewards? Amir stared at the weapon hooked to the wall behind the throne. Something niggled at the back of his mind. As though the Mouth were whispering once more in an incomprehensible tongue. Gates, as if he didn't have enough concerns already!

What surprised Amir even more was Harini's, and Madhyra's, restraint. Despite the presence of every kingdom's thronekeeper, they had not revealed the secret of olum or Illindhi. Madhyra seemed content to remain in the shadows, lurking behind Ilangovan, orchestrating the ploy but not participating in it.

They had the opportunity to steal the coriander leaves, and instead they'd chosen to take Ilangovan and barter him for a sword and some ships. It didn't make sense. But then, the ways of the Spice Trade never did to Amir. The thronekeepers spoke a language that had always eluded him. What hurt him was not that he could not grasp that tongue. It was that Harini had begun to speak it. And he wished suddenly—more than ever—to unravel the secrets of this abovefolk language, if only to talk to Harini.

If Amir's future was to be the price of this negotiation, then he had to know why.

From the crowd, the murmurs deepened. Silmehi scowled. But before he could protest, Rani Zariba, sensing an intrusion, raised her hand and snuffed out any sounds.

"You have done what none of us could achieve. For that, your demands are reasonable. I will grant your wishes. The sword and the ships are yours, though I wonder how my ancestral weapon can be of use to you. It has hung on this wall for a thousand years."

Harini smiled. "It looks gorgeous."

Zariba hesitated, as though the response were unsatisfactory. But the next moment she dropped her reluctance and returned to her throne. She rounded the Cinnamon Seat and lifted the sword from its hook on the wall. She handled it delicately, as one should an ancestral artifact, without the slightest hint of emotion tethered to it. She presented it to Harini, no questions asked. Amir could sense Zariba's unrest, however. As though she, too, were attempting to unravel the mystery behind Harini's demands.

Harini smiled. "Thank you, Maharani Zariba. You are very kind." Harini passed the sword casually to Madhyra, who hung it at her waist and remained standing behind Ilangovan like a meek servant.

Zariba, immune to flattery, strode past Harini to stand beside Madhyra. She scanned the Illindhian thronekeeper, and Amir had to wonder how much Zariba truly knew of who Madhyra was. His doubts evaporated the next moment. "You have a brave cousin, Harini. Why is it that we have never seen her before?"

Madhyra looked a lot older than Harini. Which had lent little credibility to Harini's lie. When Harini spoke, though, it was with an air of rehearsed confidence. "She has . . . ah, let's just say, she has not been in the good books of my parents. They were too shortsighted to see what Suhasini had to offer and never let her come to the feasts before. Now that I have taken the mantle, though, I've been wise enough to include in my inner circle anyone who would see Halmora return to its glory, and would have their opinions listened to. In fact, without her, we wouldn't have gotten Ilangovan to where he is now. On his knees, in front of you."

Amir knew her words—and their *import*—had landed in everyone's ears. Gates, but it rankled him. Every bone in his body shivered. Even a future in the Black Coves had Harini in it. Despite Karim bhai warning him a thousand times against the entrenched privileges of the abovefolk, Amir had been defiant in his protests that Harini was not like the others. And that she had truly cared for Amir and the other Carriers. And now? Harini appeared no more the young girl who'd wander the gardens of Halmora in the dark with him. Earthworms and daffodils seemed now a thing of the past, a memory that refused to stay tethered to reality. She was now a thronekeeper in all but name. And the more regal she appeared, the further she seemed from the person Amir had once fallen in love with. Like a tender skin shed to reveal a hard seed beneath.

For the briefest moment, Amir thought Harini was looking at him. That she was slowly shaking her head, as though in the most discreet way imaginable she was begging Amir to not lose faith in her. Her words in the Halmoran darbar had to mean something, hadn't they?

When he blinked, her face was not visible anymore. Zariba stood in front of her. She lifted Harini's hands and clasped them in her own. "I bid you welcome to the Spice Trade, Maharani."

Orbalun whistled. A wide grin played on his face. "That has gone on smoothly enough. Now, Zari, are you going to keep me and your guests starving this way? Can't we dispatch Ilangovan to your cells? My eyes keep flitting toward the karuvadu your cooks have prepared. It is, after all, a *feast*."

The mood in the court hall suddenly lightened. Whispers rose to more excited tones as the aroma of food wafted from the now-uncovered vessels.

Zariba clapped her hands and a dozen Jhanakari soldiers jogged toward the center.

"Take him to the dungeons. Station half a dozen chowkidars, but let the cold and darkness be his true guard. Strip him naked and give him not more than a cup of water."

Nobody—not even Orbalun, although he was visibly distressed— questioned Zariba's cruelty. It was her kingdom, and Ilangovan *was* a criminal in their eyes, after all. Amir could only grit his teeth and remain with his head bowed low, as though to raise his gaze would unleash the fury resting on the rim of his tongue.

Madhyra played the role of silent cousin perfectly. Amir found little in her that betrayed the deeper, darker truth simmering beneath. His deliverer of Poison, standing less than ten feet away. All he had to do was make a dash for her and grab her.

And then what?

What could he do in the midst of a circle of thronekeepers who suddenly danced to Harini and Madhyra's tune? A tune more potent than even the Grand Ustad could conjure. He had exhausted any privileges Orbalun had granted him by allowing him and Karim bhai to this feast. He could only stand and watch, knowing even the slightest of misdemeanors would have him arrested, his fate no different from the gatecaste awaiting their punishment in the Whorl. An ironic union with Ilangovan at last.

Even Orbalun had done nothing. Was he playing it safe in front of the other thronekeepers? Besieged by his own ministers in Raluha, a failed Bashara, and a looming end to his bloodline perhaps were all conspiring to silence any courage he wished to muster.

As the people dispersed toward the tables of food or refilled their wineglasses and resumed their composed chatter, Amir began to move in Harini's direction. This was his chance. Gates knew what she and Madhyra had planned after tonight. Kalay was nowhere to be found, and Karim bhai was in thrall of the Grand Ustad. He had to act.

As though sensing Amir's thoughts running errant, Hasmin's shadow fell upon him. Then, the end of the baton.

"Where do you think you're going?"

Amir tried to brush the baton off. Something glinted off Hasmin's waist, a curious instrument that looked like a timepiece dangling from a chain. The baton returned with force. Amir warded it off, his eyes only for Harini, who was getting away. Hasmin, however, decided enough was enough. He whipped Amir around, grabbed his arm, and began to drag him away.

"Wait," Amir whispered, staying within decorum. The Jhanakari chowkidars circled the throne room, quietly content to witness the drama that had unfurled over the last hour. "You don't understand. Let me go! Gah! You—"

Amir looked back to see Orbalun fading into the crowd of royals, oblivious to Amir being dragged away. His heart was racing. He tried to wriggle free of Hasmin's grip, but the chief of the chowkidars would not relent.

They were nearly through the doors when Hasmin stopped. "Maharani," he wheezed.

Harini blocked their path at the doors. She raised an eyebrow at Hasmin. "I must have a word with the Carrier. Let him go."

Hasmin promptly released Amir's arm. He had seen the way Harini had conducted herself in front of the other thronekeepers, and while Hasmin was, in all likelihood, thrice as old as Harini, the memory of her orchestration of Ilangovan's apprehension deterred him from protesting any further.

Amir grimaced as he rubbed the part of his arm clamped by Hasmin. And as he brought his hand down, his fingers grazed the swaying bauble dangling from Hasmin's waist. Irresistibly, he swiped it while Hasmin remained focused on Harini. Pocketing the instrument, Amir smiled innocently at the chief of the chowkidars. "That's two thronekeepers out of eight. You must be writhing inside."

Hasmin shot a look of loathing at Amir, and then a more tamed one at Harini before he retreated to where the other Jhanakari chowkidars stood. Harini took Amir's hand and pulled him into the shadows of one of the pillars, out of the chowkidars' earshot.

Amir's heart galloped in his chest. She smelled of rosemary and sandalwood, and for the first time that evening, Amir could not sense the aroma of cinnamon in the palace.

Before he could open his mouth, however, Harini cast a glance at the royals and ministers crowded around the serving boys and the food tables. She narrowed her eyes at Amir. "How did you know about Madhyra?"

"You are a better flirt than that," Amir replied dryly.

Harini glared. "I am serious, Amir. You need to tell me how you came to know about her, and about Illindhi. That is a secret known to very few. And a dangerous one at that. Perhaps in this court hall, Orbalun is the only one—"

"I am done answering questions, Harini," Amir hissed back, letting himself free of Harini's grasp. "It is time I ask some of my own. Why did you kidnap Ilangovan and hand him over to the Jhanakari? What were you doing in the Whorl? What is it you are planning with Madhyra? Is what she said on the ship true? That she wishes to destroy the Spice Gates? That—that is impossible!"

Harini bit her lip, her gaze once more scanning beyond the pillar for any eavesdroppers. She leaned closer to Amir. "I told Madhyra about you. She asked me if you were going to be a problem, and I said no. So, please Amir, do not get into this. We're starved for time already."

"You're not answering my questions, Harini. Yet, you ask me to trust you. You are not the only one threatened by the Uyirsena, you know. You don't understand—they—Mahrang, I must deliver Madhyra to him, otherwise—"

Harini sucked in a deep breath, and, Gates, she looked beautiful! "Fine, if you want answers, then perhaps Madhyra is a better person to give them to you. But for that, we cannot talk here. Meet us in the perfume market of Talashshukh."

"The—*what*?"

"The perfume market of Talashshukh, don't you know?"

Amir rolled his eyes. "Of course, I know. I got you this perfume that you are wearing from that market. But why there?"

Harini stepped back, suddenly panicking. "I don't have time. I must return."

Amir reached for her hand, merely grazing her fingernails as she slipped away. "Wait, please. Why did you ask for the sword and the ships?" And then, more slowly, realizing the futility of his questions, "Harini, all I'd asked for was one vial of the Poison for Amma. Kabir has already begun carrying, and I just need to—"

"Amir," Harini gritted her teeth, stalling her escape. She returned to within a foot of him, her breath cold and blustery in his ears. "There is going to be no life in the Black Coves, all right? Remove that thought from your head. Tomorrow morning, Rani Zariba will send a fleet to the coves to round up the remaining people taking refuge in those islands. Without Ilangovan and most of his inner circle who were caught this morning, the rest are not going to stand a chance. I have tried talking Zariba out of it, but honestly, I cannot overrule her jurisdiction. It's unfortunate, but it is also an expected consequence. But you—you don't need to go there. Your family, they will have a better place. *We* will have a better place."

"Where is that? You've been saying this for a while, and you've not once told me where this place is." Amir realized how desperate he sounded.

"Come to the perfume market," Harini repeated more urgently. She was already outside the shadow of the pillars, straightening her hair and arranging her face into a gentle smile, donning once more the mantle of the thronekeeper, and Amir thought the illusion of the wet earth of Halmora, riddled with earthworms, was fading from her hands, the dirt receding to be replaced by the sheen of royalty.

And then she was gone, the ghost of his words lingering on his lips and the residue of her fragrance entangling him in an intoxicating embrace.

He stood there behind the pillar for several minutes. The music had resumed; Devayani had strung forth a low, melodious tune that was both calming and celebratory. The sound of clinking glasses and incessant conversations flitted through the music. Life—to the abovefolk—had returned to normalcy in a matter of minutes. They'd go back to their callous, insignificant bickering, and the fact that within a day the Black

Coves would cease to exist would affect them no more than a wrinkle on their perfectly pressed robes and saris.

Slowly, Amir stepped out from behind the pillar and inhaled sharply. Harini was speaking to Rani Zariba while Orbalun was engaged in a conversation with Jirasandha of Vanasi. Amir looked hopelessly once more for Kalay but did not find her. Perhaps she'd gone on the hunt for Madhyra, who was also missing. Perhaps Madhyra was already on her way to the Spice Gate, to travel to Talashshukh. If so, Amir's purpose was clear. If what Harini said was true, then the Black Coves would not last, but he would still have to survive the Uyirsena, and for that, he needed Madhyra. He would tell Karim bhai, and together, they would go to the empire of ginger.

Only, Karim bhai was nowhere to be seen either. Not onstage beside the Grand Ustad, not anywhere in the court hall. The music from Devayani's sitar drifted ominously toward Amir on clouds of cinnamon, carrying in it the portents of trouble.

CHAPTER
17

Of no surprise are people who advocate food without spices.
That is akin to a salamander with a beard breastfeeding a
duckling. The whole idea does not make any sense.

—*A Mutiny of Dogs*, Volume 1

Before Amir left the court hall looking for Karim bhai, he nicked two pieces of patoli from the sweets table—steamed turmeric leaves stuffed with cinnamon, jaggery, and grated coconut. Three years back, on a day of his carrying duty, he'd been offered one by a river merchant in Mesht in exchange for a pinch of saffron. Amir had ever since sought the taste of patoli again on his tongue, and even though he had been to Mesht several times since then, he had never met the river merchant again.

He let its flavor fill his mouth, and he avoided Hasmin's searching gaze as it constantly roved over the people. Bless the crowd of royals, ministers, and their dense attire!

Soon Amir was done eating; the taste of cinnamon rolled down his throat and the woody and smoky flavor of it swelled his chest, drowning out the anxiety Harini's words had inspired. Even though it was unlikely he would see his family anytime soon, he took a third piece of the patoli for them, pocketed it, and prayed it wouldn't get crushed.

He tried to catch Orbalun's eye, but the thronekeeper of Raluha was swarmed by royal ministers and scribes. Too late, he decided. He had to find Karim bhai. And so he slipped away and found an open door used by the serving people, away from the sounds of the court hall.

His first instinct was to retrieve Mahrang's shamshir. Kalay had hidden their weapons in a secluded alcove in their room once she had smuggled them inside. She'd mocked the mediocre security even in high places. She did not trust the Jhanakari to leave her belongings untouched outside the palace. When he got to their hiding spot, however, Amir found neither Kalay's talwar nor the shamshir.

Gates, she was up to no good!

He turned around and nearly ran into the sword he'd been looking for. Kalay stood a foot from him, the curve of his shamshir held to his throat, inches away from death.

"I told you never to let me out of your sight," she snarled, her eyes half in shadow, half in the light of a distant torch.

Amir raised his hands in protest, gulping. "I *looked* for you. Where did you go?"

Her eyes were faint as wisps of firelight, as though forged in the caverns of the Mouth in Illindhi. Her hair was pulled back into a braid, lending prominence to her forehead, the creases converging between her eyes, an anger rooted in serenity. In the darkness of the passageway, Amir feared her for the first time. He glimpsed the Uyirsena in her, heard their echoes in her breath.

A bloodcurdling chill passed through him. He instantly regretted interrogating her.

Slowly, she pulled the blade away, flipped the hilt, and handed the shamshir back to him. Some of the lost warmth returned to his bones. "I visited my aunt's chambers," she said. "To see if she had left anything behind."

"And?" Amir asked, uncomfortable at how close she stood.

Kalay clicked her tongue. "Nothing. She has cleaned it up. Not a trace of her, except her scent. I don't know where—"

"I do."

Kalay cocked her head, frowning. "You spoke to the woman she has been with. The other thronekeeper."

It was not a question. Amir nodded. "Madhyra is going to Talashshukh. To the perfume market."

Kalay paused, as though quietly surprised at Amir's ability to unearth this piece of information. "When?"

"Now, I imagine," said Amir. "I saw her accompany the Jhanakari chowkidars to the dungeons to imprison Ilangovan. There is an exit the guards use for transporting the prisoners to the docks. One of those routes rejoins the spice trail that leads to the Gate. I came here to retrieve my shamshir and meant to follow her."

He, however, did not mention anything about wanting answers from Madhyra. Kalay could not know, he decided. Yet her look of suspicion told him she did not trust him. Not fully, not yet. And at that moment, he was not certain that he trusted himself. He didn't know what he wanted, except that talking to Madhyra seemed to be the best way to start to salvage whatever semblance of a life he could have outside the Bowl. A thousand thoughts and fears rang in his head, circling, pressing, and swirling: the fragrance of Harini, the Black Coves, and the prickling whispers of the Mouth, the god who sought his help.

He rubbed his eyes and regarded Kalay, who appeared to be breathing heavily. Of course, how could he not have seen it?

"You left the court hall because you couldn't control yourself in Madhyra's presence, didn't you?" he blurted.

Kalay blinked. Her hand wavered on the hilt of her sword. Not that she needed much of a grip to oust him. Then she turned without answering, and began to storm down the steps toward the dungeons. "Come, we cannot waste more time," she called.

Amir ran to catch up with her. He could sense the disquiet bubbling within her, an uncontrollable fury mingled with a love that was on the verge of shattering, if it hadn't already. She was hurting, but she was also gaining in strength and faith as a result.

One at the expense of another.

The longer the night rolled, the more Amir feared she was becoming once more a servant of the Mouth. Madhyra had not exposed Illindhi's secret to the eight kingdoms. Which meant only one thing: her desire to destroy the Spice Gates was true, and it seemed to shatter what little ambiguity Kalay nurtured in her heart regarding her aunt. The question remained: Which of the two would end up dead at the hands of the other?

Neither option tasted good on his tongue. He still hadn't apologized to Kalay for stopping her onboard the ship, and now he was certain he ought not to apologize at all. That single thrust and push on Ilangovan's galley—it may well have changed everything. This night—this frantic hunt in the semidarkness, engulfed in the aroma of cinnamon—it wouldn't have been necessary if only Amir had restrained himself, if only he had stayed crouched down and watched Madhyra's murder. He'd have had the Poison now and would have freed Ilangovan. He'd have freed Amma. He'd have freed Kabir from a future of pain.

Yet something nibbled at his heart like an insect biting into a leaf. Was this how Appa had felt all those years ago? Dreaming of a life without the Spice Gates and with no one—not even Karim bhai—willing to join him? A dream to not only save himself and his family but all of the Bowl.

Amir was conflicted, but also a strange elation coursed through him as he imagined the scenario coming to fruition. No more a cycle of failure, father to son. No more an inheritance of shattered dreams.

But how?

It made his heart tremble, and he knew that if he displayed it on the surface, Kalay would not hesitate to kill him as well as her aunt.

He stumbled in the dark after her.

Focus on what is before you. Focus on what you actually might have some control over.

He hardened his resolve, but the anxiety roosting deep inside him called out every few moments, in Kabir's voice.

He was trying.

Eventually the stairs ended and the cold began. The stones closed in.

The voices magnified, one trying to clamber over the other—either in argument or in confusion. Then the voices ceased altogether. Something was not right.

It had taken Kalay and Amir a few minutes to grope their way in silence down the long stairway to the dungeons, their feeble shadows cast by firelight every few turns. The smell of cinnamon still lingered, in faint wisps, boring into his nose. When they rounded a corner, Amir froze in his steps.

Ahead, he counted seven bodies on the cold floor. One after the other, sprawled and unmoving. A splash of white hair on black uniforms. Jhanakari chowkidars. No hint of blood. Just unconscious. Madhyra, he surmised. But why? She had already gotten what she wanted.

On either side were gates to the cells. No prisoners. One of the cells was open, the gate swaying gently. Squatting against the wall beside the gate was Karim bhai. His head was buried in his hands.

Amir rushed to him. "Bhai, what are you doing here?"

Kalay was scanning the area. She took a deep breath. "Where is she?"

Slowly, Karim bhai lifted one feeble hand and pointed to the end of the passageway, where a door rested beneath the weight of the mountain. It was partly open. Kalay needed no further intimation. She unsheathed her sword and raced for the darkness.

"Did she do this?" Amir gasped, shaking Karim bhai's shoulders once Kalay had gone.

You ought to follow Kalay. She might kill Madhyra.

Karim bhai lifted his face and shook his head. There was a sadness etched in those eyes, but also a strange release, as though he had fought against his own belief but for the sake of another.

"Ho, I don't look like I can knock out seven chowkidars, do I?" he said. He turned his head, gesturing to a serving tray lying beside him. Amir picked it up and smelled the crumbs. Jalebis. The royal kind. "Just a small dose of poison. Doesn't really stop their hearts. They'll be up in an hour or so. They couldn't resist when I came down bearing the jalebis. I offered it to them as Rani Zariba's reward to all the chowkidars in the

277

palace tonight. Didn't doubt me for a heartbeat. They'd seen me sing with the Grand Ustad, after all." His face lit up and he grinned, his voice carrying the joyous rhythm he had shared sitting beside Devayani and performing the music of his dreams.

The cell behind Karim bhai was open, and the chains that had once held Ilangovan lay on the floor like serpents coiled into one another. He gazed into Karim bhai's jubilant eyes. "You broke him out."

Karim bhai offered a weak nod. "Ho, I was sitting next to the Grand Ustad when, between songs, I heard Rani Zariba whisper to Mehreen of Mesht of her ploy to send the entire Jhanakari fleet to the Black Coves at dawn and round up the remaining pirates. Nasty one, pulla."

Unbelievable. After everything Karim bhai had told him! Amir was both delighted and furious. "What happened to Ilangovan not being needed to run the Black Coves, ho? What happened to your faith in me?"

Karim bhai grinned once more. "Ho, pulla. You're good, there's no denying that. But you're not *that* good. At least, not yet. Besides, Zariba got Sekaran, too, and several senior sanders—seasoned Carriers all of them, now fated for the Whorl. Ilangovan was one man, ho, but if you take them all out, there's nothing left in the Black Coves, pulla. Not even for you."

"And . . . and Madhyra?" he said breathlessly.

"Ho, she was gone." Karim bhai pointed to the door at the end of the prison. "She had the sword with her, the one Harini got from Zariba."

Amir stood up. He did not understand why Madhyra had wanted Ilangovan imprisoned in the first place. Was it all merely for a sword and a few ships? It didn't add up. And now she was heading to the perfume market of Talashshukh. And Karim bhai, after Amir's desperate pleas, had decided to get his hands dirty. He had done what he had promised Appa.

At that moment, they heard footfalls. From the stairs emerged Hasmin, eyes wide in terror. He scanned the bodies strewn across the prison floor, and then caught Amir and Karim bhai in his gaze.

"You!" he screamed. And Amir instantly knew what the scene must have looked like.

"Listen, kaka." Amir stood, joining his palms in apology. "It is not what it seems."

Karim bhai stood up, too, and pulled Amir behind him. "Go," he muttered. There was a sternness in his voice that Amir did not wish to protest. "Go after her. I'll stop this theru naayi."

Hasmin was advancing with malice in his eyes, the baton in his hand rattling the cell bars. "Thevidiya. You have no idea what you have done."

"Go, pulla," Karim bhai insisted. "I will tell Orbalun of what has happened. He will protect me. Now, run! Stop Madhyra before it is too late."

Amir hesitated. Madhyra might have already traveled through the Gate. Harini with her, possibly. And Kalay . . .

He turned and sprinted across the prison floor. Hasmin began to run, too, but his way was blocked by Karim bhai, who fell upon him with a snarl. The last Amir saw of them was a tangle of bodies, and as he disappeared through the door, he heard the crack of a baton and a piercing cry. He couldn't tell if it belonged to Hasmin or Karim bhai.

The chamber beyond the door was dark—a surveillance room, he surmised. Another door lay at the end of it, and through that into three more chambers one after the other, each identical to the one before. Squeezed between two of them was a Jhanakari chowkidar, unconscious. Amir pulled him aside and pushed open the last door. He must have been at the very base of the palace mountain. He could hear the distant sound of crashing waves. Opening the door, he stepped out into the night.

The moon cast a pale glow on the distant spice trail. He was a couple hundred meters away from the path that wound away from Jhanak's granary and up the trail toward the Spice Gate. To the north, the land extended out of the slope like a bent finger above the sea. Behind him, the mountain and the palace loomed over him, so that he was a speck huddled against it.

His eyes went right to the Gate. A circle of lanterns bobbed around the pillars and arch so that the molten veil swaying beneath appeared like a static orange flame. It looked beautiful. So beautiful. Wielding so much power.

The trail to the Gate was lit by torches hooked to bamboo poles. And against the shadow of their light, Amir glimpsed first Madhyra and Harini running in the distance, and then Kalay hobbling several paces behind them. The injury to her shoulder hadn't healed fully. Of Ilangovan, there was no sign. He'd truly escaped.

Oh, Karim bhai!

Cursing under his breath, Amir followed the three women under the moonlight, fear overtaking his every step. What would he do when he caught up to them? Whose side would he be on? He had to stop Madhyra, for his life depended on it, but he also had a mouthful of questions itching to be answered, answers held close to Madhyra's chest. Kalay would not allow it. If she got so much as a whiff of Amir's reluctance, she wouldn't hesitate to kill him.

When he reached the ridge, Amir glimpsed only silhouettes against the moon and the firelight. Rare were the days that he walked this trail without a sack on his back. Now, more burdened than ever without one, he ran, his breath coming in spurts.

The sound of steel against flesh arrested him in his tracks. He gulped and proceeded slowly up the narrow ridge that stretched to the sea. At the top, a few meters from the Gate, more Jhanakari chowkidars lay flat on the ground, barely stirring. One of them attempted to raise himself up, but he received a boot on his neck and he collapsed immediately. Madhyra wiped blood off her robe and stared at Amir. She frowned as she took heavy breaths.

Kalay stood opposite her, panting also, her talwar raised. Of Harini, there was no sign. She must have already disappeared through the Gate.

"Unsheathe your sword," Kalay instructed Amir. "And stand beside me."

Amir's hands trembled around the shamshir. Madhyra, sensing his hesitation, charged at Kalay. The acolyte of the Uyirsena spat, threw a curse at Amir, and parried her aunt's blow. The two blades danced in flickers of shadow and steel, their feet sidestepping the prone forms of the Jhanakari chowkidars. Kalay was the more agile one, but Madhyra could anticipate every move her niece made, and she was prepared. She made it look effortless, each block, each return, each duck of the head and swerve to avoid blows, each leap and each crouch.

At one point, Amir feared Kalay might overpower her aunt, who'd slipped, her foot sliding backward on the muddy trail up to the Gate. Kalay pounced on Madhyra, only to be met at the last moment by her aunt's sword crossed against the downward blow. Kalay, appearing to fight the pain in her shoulder, pushed down onto Madhyra's blade.

This time, Amir did not need to react. Madhyra allowed her leg to lose more balance, which sent Kalay downward with a jolt. Madhyra swerved at the last moment, so that the crossed swords came crashing to her right. The blade nicked her arm, drawing blood, and she gave a shout. Nevertheless she rose, gaining purchase with her other hand on the ground. Suddenly, she trapped Kalay's head in a lock with her knees, then lifted her sword, flipped it, and slammed the hilt on the back of Kalay's skull.

Kalay fell soundlessly. Madhyra picked herself up, dusted her hands and her robe, and stared at Amir. "Are you Amir of Raluha?" she asked. Slowly, Amir nodded.

"You have followed me from the coves on the ship. Harini told me about you. You're a persistent one, aren't you?"

Her voice was cold, piercing. She had a cocky grin on her face, teeth like a glittering pearl necklace on skin like mottled earth. The grin faded when she glimpsed the shamshir in Amir's hands. Her eyes widened momentarily. "That is a weapon forged in the Mouth. And yet, you do not have the markings of the Uyirsena." Her eyes narrowed, then came to rest on his throat. "You're a Carrier."

"Harini . . . she said I could talk to you in the perfume market of Talashshukh."

"Did she now?" She seemed to consider it, then nodded and smiled. "Then we shall talk there."

She was graceful in parting. Her strides were long and elastic. As the moon bathed her trail in a pearly glow, Madhyra opened a vial of the Poison, swung it down her throat, and ran toward the Gate. With a leap, her hand sprayed a pinch of powdered ginger into the molten, simmering veil beneath the arch. A second later, just as Kalay stirred to her senses, she dived through the Spice Gate.

From behind them, Jhanakari chowkidars were coming up the ridge toward them, their white hair billowing against the sea breeze. *Shit.*

Amir pulled Kalay up. She appeared dazed. "Where . . . Where is she?"

"I tried to stop her," he lied. "But she took the Poison. She's gone to Talashshukh."

Kalay struggled free of Amir's grip, her fists clenched. Slowly, she dug into her pockets to pull out a vial of the Poison and drank it quickly. "What are we waiting for?"

For the second time, Kalay had been bested by her aunt, and the defeat reflected in her eyes, but only partly. The acolyte of the Uyirsena appeared to scream inwardly, but the niece to Madhyra seemed oddly patient, as though some of her own questions needed answering.

Get in line.

Amir stood behind her and smiled, watching the Jhanakari chowkidars close in on them. He rummaged in his pockets until he retrieved the pouch with the peeled ginger skins. He handed half to Kalay, then flung his own portion into the Gate's veil, which shimmered violently, inviting them into its glassy fold. "I hope you like tea," he muttered to her, then stepped through the Gate and gave himself up to the Mouth.

CHAPTER

18

The scriptures do perceive of a time before the Mouth. Or rather, a timelessness of dark and chaos. The emergence of the Mouth, inevitable in its genesis, is rightly taught to children in the gurukuls across the eight kingdoms in the form of fables, some of which are highlighted below.

—*A Critical Analysis of the Archival Records of the Temples of Halmora*

There is no point in dallying, child. She deceives you. Her truth is not yours. Neither is it of this world.

Amir swam inside the Mouth, moving through the air clotted with spices. At one point, where the fragrance was mild, he stopped, gazing into a flickering abyss beneath him. He found he could not raise his head to see what lay above.

She is too strong. I cannot stop her.

Use my devotee. She is able. Together, you can stop this calamity to come.

Amir gritted his teeth, and he found his anger dissipating in heartbeats. I . . . I don't know what to do anymore. Sometimes, I wonder if I have made things worse. That it might be better to go back to how life was, and that this stupid desire for wanting to better it is a fool's hope.

You wander and flail in your thoughts, child. Your mind weakens as it is hammered under the duress of these possibilities. Let it not hold you guilty. For you are not. You are my child, and I will see to it that you remain unpunished. Serve me, and your duty shall be forsaken. Serve me, and the duties demanded of your kin shall be forsaken. Do not dwell in this fear anymo—

THE IMMEDIATE VICINITY OF THE SPICE GATE IN TALASHSHUKH was riddled with more prone chowkidars, these ones in khaki-brown attire smeared with dirt-colored stains in a poor act of camouflage. But it wasn't the unconscious chowkidars Kalay noticed first.

"The sun has not set here." She gaped at the sky beyond the Gate, where dusk had only just begun against the nightfall they had just escaped from Jhanak. A pinkish hue stretched across the sky amid faint strokes of vermilion and blue.

"Karim bhai says Talashshukh is far from Jhanak," Amir replied, proud to be imparting this knowledge to another person. "The sun does not cover all of the eight kingdoms at once."

"Where are we?"

Amir sheathed the shamshir into its scabbard and stuffed it inside his tunic. The Mouth's whispers continued to echo in his head, their meaning lodged and unable to be stirred and shaken away. The Mouth had just told him not only to forsake his duty but also that Kabir could as well.

At the cost of Madhyra.

A bargain. But could he take the Mouth's word for it?

"The old library," he replied absentmindedly to Kalay. "The most ancient building in Talashshukh." They were on the second floor of the library. The Spice Gate stood on the wood-paneled floor of an enormous balcony, the pillars neatly chipped by artisans to form a symmetrical arch unlike the jaded, chaotic arches of Raluha or Vanasi, or the weathered one of Illindhi. The balcony wall behind the Spice Gate was broken, revealing a well-maintained courtyard lined with hydrangea bushes, and a gulmohar tree opposite. Beyond the tree, and on the other side of the walled enclosure of the old library, the streets of Talashshukh bustled with their famed mayhem.

Kalay bent to touch one of the broken ends of the wall. The ruins had not been mended in over a thousand years. Amir never knew why.

They followed the trail of unconscious chowkidars through the old library, between shelves densely crammed with scrolls and books, rounding empty tables and cups of tea hastily abandoned by people who had been undoubtedly spooked by Madhyra and Harini's violent arrival. The smell of wood pulp and musk permeated the library, and Amir—who had walked this trail more times than he cared to remember—found himself oddly enchanted by the prospect of not being on carrying duty.

You're not the only one.

Despite her haste and anger, Kalay paused in her tracks more than once: first to glimpse the dome above, its colored glass reflecting off the rows and rows of shelves and cupboards, and second as she spotted a woman wrapped in a thick blanket poring over a tome beside candlelight at a far-off table. It must have triggered an old memory, Amir supposed, or a desire once promised, but snatched away—for nothing else could evoke silent wonder out of this utterly banal scene.

That should not make you any less wary of her.

The perfume market was not far from the old library. But on the first full evening of the afsal dina, the kingdom of Talashshukh reveled in festivity. A carnival was in progress, the people thronging the streets, dressed in outlandish costumes, and masks, and dancing and singing. Everywhere he looked, he was surrounded by color and music: acrobats, jugglers, animal acts and burlesque pantomimes backed by harps, zithers, trumpets, clarinets, drums, and water organs. There was even a man in the costume of a winged beast who played the flute.

By the time they descended the wide stairs to the crowded main thoroughfare, Amir spotted a column of chowkidars wading through the crowd toward the library. Their khaki uniforms stood out in the midst of the pomp and color. They must have been alerted of unauthorized intruders to the kingdom.

"Hurry," he whispered urgently to Kalay, dragging her into the throng. "Stay close."

He was of half a mind to abandon her, but the prospect of meeting Madhyra had not yet fully resolved in his head. No matter what happened, Mahrang's warning continued to ring in his ears, the slow ticking of time before the Uyirsena stepped through the Spice Gate and laid waste to the eight kingdoms. And if Amir needed to stop Madhyra, he needed Kalay.

Down the street, they slipped into an alley bordered by brick houses three floors high, which seemed to unnerve Kalay. Everything in Talashshukh was grand and tall and crowded. It was, after all, the largest of the eight kingdoms, fattened by the merchants who, over the decades, had learned not to rely on the business of ginger alone but had immersed their cunning hands in perfumes, ceramics, glass, and cotton. Avasdha Silmehi may have ruled with an iron fist, but he knew how to grow a city. He poured the money he earned from the sale of ginger into the business of other products, erecting mills, workshops, and forges. Artisans and craftsmen emerged from every home over the years. In many ways, Amir hated Talashshukh the most, for no other city made him carry on his back as many goods as the ginger empire did.

They squeezed out of the alley into a broad street lined with cobblestones. Wagons, bullock carts, and horse-driven carriages moved without care for who was in their way. People had to cling to the sides of the road to not be trampled by the marauding wheels, or be drawn into shops with polished fronts and topped with colonnades rising into two-floored settlements and flat-topped terraces, where beedi-smoking men and women lounged by their windows and wasted their evenings.

Every third shop sold tea, the wafting aroma of ginger curling around

Amir's head as he suppressed his urge, kept his head low, raised his collar to conceal the spicemark, and walked down the street.

"Not this tea," Amir muttered to Kalay, seeing her being lured to one of the stalls. "The southern Talashshukians boil the milk first and then add the tea leaves, ginger, cardamom, and water. A sacrilege."

It disappointed him that Kalay was not bothered by this travesty as much as he was.

"How are we to find my aunt in this huge place?" She sounded worried.

"You can even find a lost earring in Talashshukh," said Amir, "if you know the right people in the right places."

They reached a central plaza, a large circular area paved in cobblestones, bordered by shops and buildings. Like spokes of a wheel, tributaries branched out of the plaza in twelve directions, each street flanked by stone apartment blocks, and in the distance, larger marble mansions interspersed with columns wrapped in sculptures that evoked the Mouth's lore. At the center of the plaza was a tall statue of the thronekeeper Silmehi, flanked by twin fountains of elephants spouting water out of their trunks. Amir thought the statue to be far more attractive than the man he had seen only hours earlier in the Jhanakari courtroom.

Two dozen turbaned rikshaw pullers cried out to Amir and Kalay, offering to take them to the perfume market.

"Shouldn't we go with them?" Kalay whispered in Amir's ear as he walked past them, impervious to their calls.

"Not if you wish to get swindled. With what they charge, you can buy a fortnight's worth of chai."

"We're running out of time," Kalay reminded him. "If paying a little more means we get to Madhyra before—"

Amir steered her away from a speeding bail-gaadi laden with onions. He lowered his voice, glancing left and right to ensure the people walking past them did not lend an ear to their conversation. "Look, I don't know what you knew of the eight kingdoms before you came here. I don't know what they taught you as an acolyte of the Uyirsena in those caverns, because you seem surprised at every turn we have taken thus far.

Mahrang appointed me to be your guide, so trust me to take you where we need to go."

Kalay scoffed. "Fine. I am merely marveling at the eight kingdoms and their propensity for celebration and growth. They thrive under the blessings of the Mouth. Equitable as they were meant to be."

He knew Kalay was baiting him. He looked again at the statue, the fountains, the cobbled pathways and the shops selling chai and wares, the tall buildings of brick and stone, and the distant spires of Avasdha Silmehi's palace. He saw the people, always busy, always moving, or whiling away their evening as the sun made its way to the western horizon, its vermilion hues mingling with the first lamps and lanterns flickering on. He heard the sound of laughter and drunken revelry.

"No," Amir said flatly, accepting the bait. He grabbed Kalay's arm and dragged her through the crowd once more. Past animated jugglers and snake charmers to the other side of the plaza, where four lanes branched away at different angles. He took the rightmost one, and not too much farther along went down deeper, thinner, darker alleys, then farther onto more branches. At each branch the crowds thinned, until the rich aroma of ginger and lemon and garlic dissipated, and the stench of sewage began to assail the senses. Amir led them into what appeared to be an abandoned building, dilapidated, its boarded windows broken, through ramshackle floors and down a flight of stairs where water dripped incessantly from the roof. Through darkness, darkness, darkness, and finally, into light. Into the light of a hundred fires, into a cavernous underground that would put shame to Munivarey's false gate lair, to a street beneath a street and to homes beneath homes, to a colony beneath colonies. To a festival beneath festivals. The horners of Talashshukh lived in their empire of filth, and Amir led Kalay into their midst, down their thoroughfares of boiling stew, watery rasam and dal, feeble fires born from stubborn firewood, and children playing on winding staircases that led back to the city above. A pale imitation of the afsal dina overhead.

"Look," said Amir, splaying his hands wide. "The children of the Mouth. Your equitable marvels, blessed and sanctified."

KALAY DID NOT SPEAK FOR THE REST OF THE TIME THEY WALKED underground. Her silence cushioned their journey, their footsteps echoing on stone, harmonious with the dripping water. They passed through several tunnels furnished for basic living. Four walls, a lantern, a slab on one side for the kitchen, and a water outlet. Sconces along the walls held torches, beneath which the horners sat in clusters, laughing and talking. Amir waved at a few of the Carriers among the horners he knew and recognized. Some invited him to their homes for tea. He politely refused. They crossed bridges that ran over sludges, then entered another vaulted basement of even more settlements, garlanded in the fragrance of what they had passed. By the time they resurfaced, it had darkened fully, and Kalay's face had paled.

They emerged at the mouth of one of several entrances to the perfume market. And as Amir inhaled, the intoxication rushed into his nose, and swirled his senses. Gates, how long it had been!

"It's easier from down there," he said, breaking the long silence between him and Kalay. "The abovefolk don't take that route, though Gates know it's far quicker than dodging these bail-gaadis and carriages, and stopping for chai every few minutes."

"And why do they not take it?"

Amir blinked at her. "Really?"

Kalay appeared too discomfited to reply. Clearly, she was addled by what she had seen, her reactions slower, just like in the Black Coves when she had seen the band of gatecaste surviving on the bare minimum.

"There are poor even on the streets above," said Kalay. "I saw some shabby tenements earlier."

"Even among the poor, there are hierarchies of caste," Amir explained. "An uppercaste man living in that broken tenement who does not have a single roti to feed his children for the night would still never go to the horners for food, not if the horners showed up with a bowl of payasam at his doorstep . . . Don't look at me like that; these are your scriptures. I thought you would have read them front to back a thousand times."

"The Mouth only advocates equality among its subjects," argued Kalay.

"Be it in Illindhi or in the eight kingdoms. Do not blame the scriptures for the fallibilities of your people."

Does it matter? We bowlers suffer, and blaming the fallibility of the eight kingdoms gets us nowhere.

Amir, however, did not say this aloud. Kalay, he realized, was not easily swayed.

They entered the perfume market beneath purple canvas awnings. The perfumery shops were built of brick, with wide openings into the main thoroughfare of the market. Marble framed doorways and floors of marble and tile welcomed them. Many had colonnades with staircases leading to roofs decorated with ornamental sculptures that worked like open promenades. Hanging streetlamps swayed overhead, guiding them into the labyrinth, the path paved in flagstones.

Perfumes of every kind assaulted his senses. Pepper, spikenard, cinnamon, aloeswood, ambergris, myrrh, balsam, frankincense, lapis lazuli, storax, rose, and many others Amir did not know the names of, but his skin recognized their texture, the way they haunted his nose. A measure of class, each perfume. One bottle cost twenty Carrying duties, perhaps. He had never truly calculated, as they were so expensive.

A man in a white turban sold rose sugar and sharbats. Once again, Amir steered Kalay away and deeper into the maze of fragrances.

"Why do you think Madhyra wished to visit the perfume market?" he asked her, passing a shop selling attar of rose.

Kalay had already begun to take on the smells of the market, of saffron and aloes, and rose along the back of her head. Somewhere in these lanes was Harini too. He had always told her of the perfume market, and to satisfy her deepest desire Amir had fetched for her a perfume of sandalwood and musk at half the price, having pawned an old ring that belonged to his grandmother's grandfather.

And what has she got you in return?

"Kalay, are you listening to me?" he said.

"Yes, I am thinking. This place makes it difficult. My mind is ensnared by these smells. How are you able to think straight?"

"Because I am used to carrying an entire crate of perfumes in these little rock crystal jars that you see on the shelves back to Raluha. But then, I won't lie, it often feels like the first time when you are inside these lanes."

She waded ahead, brushing past similarly dazed customers. At one point, she paused and turned to face Amir, seeming to have conjured an answer. "Is there a shop here that sells kavestha?"

"Kavestha?"

Kalay bit her lip. "It is a perfume with extracts of unadulterated olum. A very strong essence, often of wild places, like forests, mountains, and rivers."

"I don't know about unadulterated olum," replied Amir. "But there is Falaknama's shop that sells chumuri. Karim bhai came back to Raluha one day smelling like he'd slept inside a tree in the rain."

"Yes, that is it!" Kalay grabbed Amir's shoulder.

"But . . ." Amir paused, scratching his head. "Wait, that is exclusively sold by the Carnelian Caravan, and only to Falaknama merely because he can afford it. If it's indeed the Carnelian Caravan, then they're under the thumb of the Jewelmaker, who is—Mahrang. We may be talking about the same thing. But why would Madhyra want chumuri?"

Kalay lowered her voice to a whisper. "The Uyirsena patrollers wear this perfume to be untraceable by the Immortal Sons. Ever since the . . . man from the Outerlands sneaked into Illindhi to meet my aunt, Mahrang and my father decided it was important to keep a closer watch on our walls."

Amir did not stop walking, but his mind was suddenly abuzz. There it was again, a mention of the man from the Outerlands. What was he even doing there? How had he survived? Several memories tumbled into this thought, fueled further by the intoxicating perfumes that surrounded him.

How does Madhyra plan to break the Spice Gates? Why does she need an ancestral sword of Jhanak and a perfume from the market? Or, like the coriander leaves, are these also distractions?

Somehow, Amir knew that the Mouth knew. It was in its nature to know. It had asked for his help against Madhyra each time he passed through the Gate, ridding him finally of the pain of passage as a bribe. Gates, it must be really desperate, more so than Amir himself.

The smell of incense wafted up Amir's nose. A man with a kerchief wrapped around his face yanked him into his shop, spraying a cloud of myrrh on his wrist and lifting Amir's hand to his nose, urging him to sniff. Heady, like sweet licorice. Kalay was beside him one moment, and the next, he was alone. The man offered a price. Amir pushed him away. He stumbled out of the shop, recalling Munivarey saying that the Mouth was tethered to each of the Spice Gates.

How long are its limbs?

"Kalay?" he called out, but there was no answer. He was pushed aside by a woman with braided hair and a turban of silk with tassels. She was another shopkeeper, Amir realized, her hair smelling of fern roots and rhubarb. She offered him two ornamental bottles, one held in each hand, and he breathed in their invisible fumes: srigandha to the left, champakali to the right. The more ancient perfumes of the Spice Trade, their fragrances as old as Talashshukh itself.

He opened his mouth, but his words came out in Orbalun's stentorian voice. *She did not use the Spice Gates. She crossed the Outerlands.*

Amir pushed the woman aside and stumbled ahead. His mind cleared, even if only sufficiently to process what he had uncovered. His heart began to race. The answer came to him in a torrential flood.

Over the heads of a dozen people, Amir saw the board of Falaknama's shop. And beneath it, poring over an array of jeweled containers, their heads bent together—Madhyra and Harini.

Five shops away, on a parallel lane, stood Kalay. Glimpsing her was a matter of fortune, but he knew Kalay had seen her aunt. Her talwar was drawn, and she was slowly creeping closer to Falaknama's shop.

Amir screamed Madhyra's name, but the noise in the perfume market drowned him out, the cacophony of bargains and rejections and pleas and intoxicated brawls smothering his cry.

He would have to push through and pray he got to Madhyra before Kalay. Gates, what a mess!

Amir was closing in on them when a hand wrapped around his wrist and pulled him back.

"Anna!"

Amir froze. He was certain he had imagined the voice, just as he had earlier imagined Munivarey's and Orbalun's. But as he turned to look, he saw the hand on his wrist was real and it was attached to Kabir's body. Kabir, who stood bare-chested with a towel tied around his head. With his other hand, he was balancing a crate of perfumes. Scars ran down his arm and his back, the wounds already dried in the three days he had been on the spice trail. Sweat rolled down his face, but through it all, there was a wide-eyed grin, as though everything was now better, now that Amir was here.

"Anna, you came!"

Amir looked around. Sure enough, there were other Carriers from Raluha scattered around the perfume market, collecting their orders or fulfilling special deliveries. Amir immediately lifted the crate from Kabir's head and relieved him of the burden.

"I . . . of course," he gasped, running his eyes over his brother from head to toe. *This was not supposed to happen. Gates, this was what you'd set out to prevent.*

"Are . . . are you hurt?" he asked Kabir, tracing a finger down one of his wounds. Not even a wince.

Kabir clicked his tongue, winking. "By this? Gah! I have lifted heavier boxes in the Bowl, anna! This is nothing. Dhiru na and Panjavarnam didi both helped me with the sacks earlier. They were very sweet. But"—he frowned, examining Amir in the illusory light of the perfume market— "we are not allowed to wear these fancy kurtas for Carrying, are we? How come you get one? Can you get one for me too? One with mirror beads, like how Karim bhai wears when he sings in the Bowl around the bonfire."

Amir realized he was still wearing the kurta from the afsal dina feast. And the shoes. He smiled, stroking Kabir's hair. "Only if you make a painting of Talashshukh once you're back home."

Kabir's chest fell. "Home, right. Amma asked for you."

The last he had seen his mother was on the night of the bonfire. The following morning, while Amma was cooking, her belly several days away from bursting, Amir had tiptoed out with Karim bhai to the Pyramid to steal the olum back from Hasmin. Gates, it stank of a previous lifetime. "How is she doing? Amma."

Kabir shrugged. "Karim bhai said you were on some errand for Maharaja Orbalun. Is that true? Is that why you are here?"

Shit.

He looked up. Neither Madhyra and Harini nor Kalay were visible anymore. Kabir's arrival had made him forget about them entirely. Falaknama's shop was filled with new customers now. Panic overcame his weary limbs, and he frantically looked around for a sign of any of the women. His head hurt, softened by the aroma of the perfumes, and exacerbated by the thoughts pounding inside like a grindstone.

"Listen to me, Kabir, you must go back to the spice trail. Return to Raluha, all right? Do not leave Dhiru na and Panjavarnam didi." He shifted the crate, gritting his teeth and wishing anything other than this, then placed it back on Kabir's head. *And may this be the last time.*

"Where are you going?" Kabir asked.

"I'll be home soon," he said, and hugged Kabir. "Tell Amma that I will be away for a few more days on this errand, but I will be back. And give a kiss to her for me, will you? Now, go."

Kabir was clearly disappointed, but he turned to leave anyway. Amir had left him in the Bowl alone in the past. But even in Talashshukh, on the night of the afsal dina feast as the kingdom swelled under the weight of the carnival, he trusted Kabir would be fine.

"Kabir," he called after his brother as he walked back through the market. "If Hasmin kaka bothers you, give it back to him, ho?"

Kabir grinned. "I will."

And then he was gone, rejoining the spice trail behind Panjavarnam didi, and Amir's heady daze returned. Kabir would probably tell them about Amir, and that would be fine, as long as they knew he was alive. *For now.*

The line of Carriers thinned until it disappeared. He wondered if any of them had ever thought of a life without the Spice Gates. That the Bowl itself could be erased from their memories. But no, how could they? For one who had lived all their lives in darkness, it was nearly impossible to imagine a world of light.

Wasting no further time, Amir pushed through the bodies to wriggle out of the perfume market. He was certain Madhyra had found the chumuri. He knew what it'd be used for. She was going to destroy the Spice Gates, and Amir knew how.

Talashshukh roared beneath the full moon, the plaza coming to life against the light of a thousand torches. The streets were full of people, and in the distance, floating lanterns rose up in the sky, silhouetted against the stone mansions, and Avasdha Silmehi's white palace.

By the time Amir reached the old library once more, exhaustion pressed his bones, and hunger gnawed at his belly. What wouldn't he give to stop for a few minutes, catch his breath, and have a cup of chai standing beneath the awning of a mandi?

But he plodded on, following in the steps of the Raluhan Carriers and up the flight of stairs to the balcony. He heard voices ahead. He swallowed and unsheathed his shamshir.

Rounding a corner he slipped on the wood-paneled floor beside one of the bookshelves when he saw the scene ahead.

Madhyra and Harini stood beside the Spice Gate. In front of them, a dozen Haldiveer blocked the way, their curved swords held to the throats of the seven Talashshukian guards. It took three Haldiveer to restrain Kalay, who had been disarmed.

"Ah, Amir of Raluha." Madhyra looked up as Amir approached them, his shamshir drawn. "You missed our appointment at the perfume market."

Kalay shot a glare of disbelief at him. She tried to wrestle out of the

Haldiveer's grip, but he was built like a rock pillar, as were they all, his grip on Kalay unforgiving. Amir would be safe from her, at least.

At a nod from Madhyra, the Haldiveer nudged the Talashshukian guards farther into the library, leaving the two thronekeepers and Amir with the Haldiveer who held Kalay. "Tie her up and leave us," Harini instructed her guards. "And ensure nobody else enters the library. Keep your Poisons and cinnamon at the ready. We may have to leave soon."

The Haldiveer obeyed. Kalay was tied in silence. She had even stopped protesting. Her anger had now taken on a sheen of hopelessness, which she divided between Madhyra and Amir. The drunken revelry of the Talashshukian streets reached the library's balcony in muffled whispers.

When the Haldiveer left, Amir raised his shamshir and pointed it at Madhyra. His gaze, however, was on Harini. "You could have told me all of this earlier," he said.

"You've been to Illindhi, Amir. Are you really questioning me as to why I did not involve you?"

Amir scoffed. "That does not give you the right to jeopardize my future. It was a future *we* had imagined together."

"The world often misjudges people who do things for love, Amir." Madhyra smiled. "To suffer their gaze and still do what we do, it takes courage."

Amir's hand quivered. "What you plan to do does not need courage. It requires insanity. Madness! Why do you even desire to break the Spice Gates?"

Madhyra took a deep breath as the moon slunk behind a cloud, darkening the library balcony. It also added a texture of blackness to her shroud of hair. "Because the Spice Gates have taken everything from me. Because we will never be truly human as long as they stand. Because I have seen how a people can be oppressed in the name of the Gates. Because the world is ready to evolve, and for that to happen, the Spice Gates must go. Are these reasons enough? You're a Carrier. I'm disappointed my dreams are not yours."

"You have no right to tell me what my dreams should be. You don't know what it is like to be one of us."

Madhyra raised an eyebrow. "And yet I fight for your cause. For your kind. Do you find that hard to believe?"

Amir shook his head. "No, but it is not your battle to fight. It is mine."

She seemed surprised by this statement, but probably no more than Amir was. With just a touch more respect, she asked, "And what precisely is your battle, Amir of Raluha? What is it that you need?"

Amir took a deep breath, standing there beside Kalay. His fate would not be much different if he opposed her, but Madhyra had spared him so far for a reason. He was not going to let her regret the choice. "I only needed the Poison. I wanted to take my family to the Black Coves and live out the rest of our lives away from the Spice Gates."

Madhyra clicked her tongue. She stepped away from Amir, the moon emerging from behind a cloud once more, spraying light on the balcony. She crouched beside a wriggling Kalay, whose mouth was stuffed with a kerchief. She rummaged through her pockets. Kalay struggled, kicking and moaning, trying to spit the cloth out. When Madhyra rose, in her hand was Kalay's stash of olum.

"No," Amir gasped. But it was too late. Madhyra walked to the edge of the library balcony, to the broken wall, opened the pouch, and emptied its contents upon the garden below.

Kalay's eyes went wide in shock. She did not struggle anymore, but Amir could tell she felt as though Madhyra had sawed off one of her legs. That was all the olum Kalay had. She would not be able to travel back to Illindhi.

The Illindhian queen returned, bending down once more to toy with the cloth stuffed into Kalay's mouth. "You see, cheche, when Mahrang sent you with Amir, I admit I was a little surprised, but then I realized: Mahrang was so confident in having manipulated you into the ways of the Mouth, into the duties of the Uyirsena, that sending you to kill me was his way of not merely insulting me but erasing everything I had worked for. But I know you, cheche, and I know what I have taught you, and I can sense the conflict in your heart as you wander the eight kingdoms, seeing things far differently from what the scriptures taught you in those suffocating caverns of Ilom. But you know what? I don't think you've seen enough."

She opened Kalay's waterskin, which contained the Poison, and emptied its entire contents into Kalay's mouth. It dribbled through the stuffed cloth and down her throat. Kalay kicked at empty air in protest. She wriggled and twisted and turned, but Madhyra cupped her chin and waited for the last drop of Poison to dribble out of the waterskin. When Madhyra was done, she lifted Kalay and, supporting her, led her to the Gate. She unclasped a wooden box clipped to her waist. The aroma of cumin—*jeera*—filled the library. A pinch in Madhyra's fingers, a pinch on the Gate. The veil sizzled, hungry.

And then without warning, Madhyra pushed Kalay through the Gate.

Amir screamed, but no sound came out of his mouth as he watched Kalay disappear. Madhyra turned and, lifting the fold of her belt around her waist, she unclasped a small dark-blue vial. The Poison. She crossed to Amir and extended it to him.

"Go on," she said. "This is what you wanted. Take it."

Amir blinked, his mind still reeling from having watched her push her own niece through the Spice Gate into the strange river empire of Mesht without any Poison to return with. But the moment passed. His free hand seemed to rise of its own accord to receive the vial. In the semidarkness, the Poison appeared darker than the night that surrounded them. He opened the stopper and took a long sniff. Truly the Poison. In his hands.

A feeling of elation surged within his body. His future laid bare, as he liked to call it. Ilangovan had escaped back to the Black Coves, he was certain, and he, Amir, could join him. Harini would come too. It was a delightful image, one that he was not eager to let go of. But then—

Slowly, as though he couldn't believe his own limbs were capable of it, he returned the vial to Madhyra. She frowned.

"It won't matter," Amir said. "Whether I'm in the Black Coves or in

Raluha or anywhere among the eight kingdoms. Mahrang and the Uyirsena will find me. They will find my family and everyone I care about or who knows the secret of Illindhi. The only way I can save my family is if I hand you over to Mahrang."

Madhyra smiled. "I don't think that is an option."

A low breeze whistled past him, carrying not just the aroma of ginger but also the ghost of whispers and the imagined cries of people being slaughtered across the eight kingdoms. "You're risking the lives of thousands. Tens of thousands."

"Nobody needs to die," said Harini. "I thought that much was clear when both Madhyra and I refused to divulge the secret of olum and Illindhi to the thronekeepers at the feast. Be sensible, Amir. We wouldn't be doing this, provoking the ire of a fanatic like Mahrang and his Uyirsena, if we did not think we could pull this off."

"Because of you, over fifty gatecaste are going to be sent to the Whorl tomorrow morning."

Harini rubbed her forehead. "That could have been avoided if you had not come chasing after us, alerting the entire island to our presence."

Madhyra folded Kalay's now-empty pouch and threw it aside. "If you're challenging my actions without understanding what I'm doing, then I must say I'm disappointed at who Mahrang and the Chairs have chosen as their champion."

"I did not want this," Amir argued. "I did not ask for Mahrang to send me here with death haunting my steps." He lowered the shamshir. "And ho, I would have understood if Harini had just told me everything in the qila. Instead, no, I had to piece it all together, hour by hour, incident by incident, watching my dream be crushed at every single turn. Now? I know what you're doing. You have deceived everyone that you're looking for coriander leaves to convert olum into the other spices as evidence of its powers. But you don't care about any of that, do you? You merely wish to lure the Uyirsena out of Illindhi. That is what Fylan meant when he begged Mahrang not to send the army. He discovered your ploy. He knew you wanted the Uyirsena to leave their post in the mountain. To leave their post of"—he took a deep breath—"of guarding the Mouth. Fylan sent me to Illindhi to stop Mahrang from doing it."

Madhyra's smile widened. "Oh—go on. I may have underestimated you, Carrier. Now, why would I do such a thing?"

Amir's heart stuttered within his chest. Egged on by Madhyra, he continued. "If—if the Uyirsena are not guarding their posts, it gives you a straight shot at the Mouth. If you kill the god, the Gates break. Munivarey told me that the Mouth is connected to the Gates, that it *powers* them. And Mahrang, he's going to play right into your hands, ho. When the Uyirsena set out for the eight kingdoms, you will return to Illindhi and finish your task. You got the sword from Rani Zariba—an ancestral blade, which I presume can be used to kill the Mouth. And now you have the chumuri, which will get you safely through the Outerlands."

It all clicked in that moment for Amir. "Gates!" He inhaled sharply, and then, clasping his shamshir tighter, he raised his hands, his senses shattering. "This is absurd! Do you even hear your plan? The Outerlands, the Immortal Sons, killing the Mouth . . . I was wrong to have stopped Kalay killing you on the ship. I admit, at one point I was tempted to know more. After I saw Ilangovan apprehended and sentenced to die, I thought I might even be desperate enough to imagine this ridiculous possibility. But the more I speak of it, the more my head stands to explode. It is not insane, though—insanity I could maybe understand. It is much worse. Gates, I wish I had a word for it."

Madhyra clapped her hands. "If you truly are Amir of Raluha, then I take back my accusation. For, I do have a word for what you're feeling. It is called fatherlike."

The shamshir slipped from Amir's hands and clattered on the wood-paneled floor of the library.

The sounds from the carnival suddenly intensified. A number of instruments were being played on the streets, and the people's cheers and shouts wove through the walls and the bricks and the stones. The moonlight played tricks on his eyes, and he perceived Madhyra as someone translucent and wispy in front of the Spice Gate's veil. Her words were an echo that wrapped around his person, refusing to seep into him, but refusing to leave him either. The echo repeated and repeated, until he remembered only her last words. And when he spoke again, he did not know whether it was a whisper or a shout of anger. "You know my father? He's alive?"

Madhyra's gaze softened. "I'm sorry, Amir. He was one of the bravest men I knew. He died a fortnight ago. I was there."

A wave of sorrow arrived, riding on a juddering bail-gaadi, and with it, a troubled realization that Appa had been alive until recently. And for all these years, he'd never considered returning to Raluha.

Gates, he thought he had already processed this grief. Every day for several months after his father's departure Amir had sneaked his way out of the Bowl to the fences, and squinted into the Outerlands, hoping for Appa to materialize from the forests. But that hope had faded, and Amma and he had resigned themselves to the fact that he would never return. They were convinced the bones they had buried were his. True, Amir had never known his father well. But at his age, what *could* you know? Only that he rambled endlessly about the Outerlands, desperate to whisk Amir and Amma into the folds of the forbidden.

"You think ill of him," said Madhyra.

"Of course I do! He abandoned us. And now you're telling me that he wasn't dead all this while? That he could have come back, and he chose not to?"

"That is not true," said Madhyra. "He did try to return. Know this, Amir. The Mouth prevents a reunion between the Ranagala and the eight kingdoms. Once breached, which in itself is often improbable, there is no going back, not unless you can find a way to overcome the Immortal Sons."

Amir struggled to breathe. No, no. He was done with that part of his life. If he had a father, Amir had scrubbed him off painstakingly over the years. From his skin, from the walls of his home, from the Bowl and the spice trail. To transform that love into a grief peppered with longing and anger, to thread that needle . . . Had Appa really tried to come back to Raluha? Had he spent all these years struggling to tell Amir and his family of the life that lay waiting for them?

Does it matter? He left. And that's what counts.

Gates, Amir hated this feeling, rancid and bitter. He had emptied these emotions into Harini countless times, and now she stared at him as though exhausted, as though she knew what it meant to resurrect this buried grief and have it coursing through his veins all over again.

"Does . . . Does this mean the abovefolk have been lying? To us, to each other? That there cannot be life in the Outerlands?"

"Lying?" Madhyra chuckled. "No, Amir. They have not been lying. Life *is* impossible in the place you call the Outerlands. What I saw with your father was a shadow of it. The terrain is harsh, impassable for large swaths, and above all, the Immortal Sons exist at the whim of the Mouth, watching always. And that is what the Mouth wants. A separation. The continued segregation of the Carriers from the rest. This perception that there cannot be a life in the Ranagala, or beyond the Whorl. That any alternate reality cannot be realized easily, and if realized, cannot be shared. This is why your father could not find a way back to Raluha. Doing so would present an opportunity for the Carriers to abandon their duties— duties that were built on the bones of injustice and stamped into the annals of the scriptures."

Amir shook away his anguish at her words. "But *you* came through," he protested. "You crossed the Outerlands."

"At a great cost. And not without your father's help. Not without the help of many more like him who have battled this oppression for decades, centuries, generations. We both aided each other in a quest that has long simmered in our hearts. He died fighting the Immortal Sons. Killed one too. They call him Serpent's Bane."

Karim bhai had not lied. Appa *had* always imagined a world without the Spice Gates, and he had died in that thorny gap between imagination and reality that had always resisted being brought together.

Amir fell to his knees, clutching his head. "This is all too much."

Madhyra smiled. "Ilangovan felt no different when Harini and I told him the truth in the Black Coves. It is also why he agreed to come with us on his ship. Not because we abducted him but because he was willing to surrender if I showed him the way across the Whorl and what lay on the other side."

Amir vividly recalled Ilangovan's ship disappearing through the storm across the Whorl. Sekaran had refused to believe that they had crossed the barrier.

"I'm going to see this through," she continued. "If you doubt me, follow me in my steps, Amir. Or get out of my way."

From the wooden box Madhyra took a second object. A folded piece of paper that she opened to show him. "This is a map of the Ranagala, one whose copy I had left in the possession of the thronekeeper of Raluha."

Amir nodded. "Maharaja Orbalun showed it to me."

"If you really desire to see the life in these Outerlands, get the map from Orbalun, and follow me. If I succeed in my plan, the Uyirsena never need hurt anyone ever again. The reign of the Mouth must come to an end, Amir, for this to happen. And I shall be its reckoning."

Harini, who had been silent all along, glanced sideways at the thronekeeper of Illindhi. In the days that had passed, the two seemed to have an understanding, and suddenly Amir's presence seemed an intrusion.

"Ilangovan would have returned to the Coves," Madhyra said to Harini. "Zariba might not be amenable to parting with the ships now. But the sword should be enough. It is a worthy bargain."

Harini exhaled softly. "The sword is more important," she agreed. "But I will yet bargain for the deal we made in the spirit of the Spice Trade. For the sake of Halmora."

Without warning, Madhyra embraced Harini, who was taken aback. It took Harini a moment to wrap her hands around Madhyra's back, through her matted and wild hair. "Thank you," Madhyra whispered. "I could not have done this without you."

"There is still much to be done, didi," Harini said, pulling herself free, wiping a tear from her eye. "Now, go. Time is of the essence."

"Wait," Amir blurted out. He picked up both his fallen shamshir and

Kalay's talwar, and raised them foolishly to Madhyra. "What about the Uyirsena? Look, you both might have good intentions, but that will not stop the Uyirsena from laying waste to the eight kingdoms. From killing everyone I've ever talked to in the last few days, if not more. I cannot— I cannot let you go simply because you intend to time it well. What if you fail?"

"I do not have an answer to that," Madhyra replied. "But I'm not going to be stopped by you now, Amir. Not after I've come this far. I trust myself in the efforts I have put forth and the sacrifices I have had to make to accomplish this task."

She didn't give him a moment to recover from her words. The Poison that Amir had returned to her went down her throat. Spraying a fistful of cloves—the spice of Amarohi—Madhyra stepped back and fell into the Gate.

CHAPTER
19

*A long time ago, they would embalm corpses with pepper
and pass it through the Spice Gate with a garland of ginger
and a strip of onion skin, in the hope that the soul would
meet its maker. The only thing the soul met, however, was
a Talashshukian on the other side who robbed the corpse of
its gold and spices, then returned it a naked suckling for the
bereaved family to believe that the Mouth had accepted their
offering.*

—Durbin Kasila, *Anatomy of a Spice Carrier*

Surrounded by a dozen Haldiveer, Amir and Harini stumbled away from the Spice Gate into the tangy sea breeze of Jhanak. The Mouth had once again roared at Amir for having let Madhyra get away. He had provided excuses and apologies. The tingle down his spine now told him that the pain would return with its usual malice the next time. He hoped Kabir had reached home safely.

A shimmer of dawn prevailed in the sky, the first light flirting with the horizon. The islands surrounding Jhanak—like floating peapods from a distance—came alive in that half-light, and Amir wondered if he would ever look at them with the same desire he had until a few hours ago.

Upon that ridge, the Jhanakari chowkidars stood in number, some carrying their still-incapacitated companions back to the mountain fort, others keeping watch over the Gate. At the sight of Harini, they stiffened, bowed, and let her and the Haldiveer pass. Amir trailed them, clinging to Harini's faint shadow, meek, his hands folded.

"Harini," he called after her once they were out of the chowkidars' earshot.

She stopped and gestured to the Haldiveer to go ahead. They stood at the slope that connected the ridge to the spice trail, where Amir had never been allowed to stop in the past.

"You're still angry with me." It was not meant to be a question, but the statement had a singsong quality to it that Amir knew came out stupidly.

In the growing lightness, Harini's face gained a statue-like prominence, her nose ring a relic that he wished to preserve. Her hair had loosened, and her sari, whose emerald had gleamed beneath Rani Zariba's ostentatious court hall lights, now appeared weathered from its immersion in Talashshukh's perfume market. She suddenly looked a lot more like the Harini he knew, and he wished they'd linger on these slopes for a while longer.

"No, I'm not angry with you, Amir. I'm just . . . I'm just tired. The last few days have been overwhelming. And honestly, I didn't expect anything less."

"Ho, no, I understand. I'm sorry. You know, for everything."

Harini climbed the slope to stand within a few feet of Amir. "You don't have to be. You did what you thought would get your family safe. It was not fair of me to demand your trust blindly while giving nothing away."

A golden crease slanted across her face, the breeze nipping the tail of her hair. Gates, he could look at her forever.

But the hours had weighed him down no less than she. His own enervation rose to the fore, thoughts spiraling out from the slowly waning disbelief of everything that had been hammered into him over the past few days.

"Do you believe her? Truly believe her?"

It was a question he knew the answer to. Nothing but a pointless gambit to fortify his own wavering notions. Sometimes the onions had to be fried on a slow fire, Amma would say.

Harini appeared to ruminate on the question for a long time. It was as though the answer were not merely a straightforward yes, but that the yes needed serious qualification. When she spoke, it was with the certitude of a thronekeeper. "For the sake of everything I care about—you, and the people of Halmora—yes, I do believe her."

"You never cared for being a thronekeeper," Amir pointed out, his feeling a bit of pride at being included in the list of things she still cared about.

Harini chuckled. "And it is not a burden I take lightly. I hate wearing this sari. These jewels. I hated walking the marble in Zariba's court, and these charming etiquettes I must follow."

"You do look terrible, ho." Amir managed half a smile.

"Unlike you, who seem to fit into a royal kurta just fine."

For a fleeting moment, Amir forgot entirely about the Spice Gates, the Mouth, the Poison, the Black Coves, Illindhi, and the Uyirsena. The golden hue of sunrise spattered across Harini's face enveloped him into her aura, and everything felt unreal, illusory.

And then it all came rushing back.

"Do you think it can work?" he asked. "I mean, it is—it is *absurd*, ho?"

Harini's smile waned. "Absurd, yes. Impossible? No. Amir, I don't think you understand how significant you have been in my life. When I met you in the qila for the first time, I had been *educated* to treat you differently. From the age of six, they were grooming me to be thronekeeper. Impressing on me the ways of the scriptures, of how each caste must perform its duty, and about how mine was to rule. That I was *born* to do so. And yet it never felt like I was. All I could see was the qila and the endless knotted jungle around it, and everything else in this one color—uniform, but not necessarily . . . alike, you know? And then you came along, and I had to unlearn everything that had been drilled into me. You came with your words from distant kingdoms, with your infinite stories, and you left and came again, and again, and again with newer scars each time, but always with your . . . Gates, your tireless kindness! And I couldn't understand why I was meant to discriminate against you. It felt bizarre, the love I felt for you while being told by my upbringing that you belong outside the qila with the easters, or wherever the gatecaste were supposed to be in any kingdom. And no, Amir, it was not that sense of rebellion in me, or the difference they said existed between us that drew me closer to you. You represented everything I had already felt in the deepest trenches of my heart but was afraid to question because of how bound I was by what was expected of me. It felt so wrong, and yet I would look around me, at the thousands of people in the qila who regarded the easters as less than the dirt they trod on, and I would wonder—surely, so many people cannot be mistaken about one thing. But with you, I could be free. Even on the slopes of the qila, on the mudbank, so close to everything that had imprisoned me, even for a brief moment, you made me feel so free. And I knew that what I wanted for you, I wanted for everyone like you. I went against my parents and the priests to manipulate the treasury and funded the building of new homes for the easters. I tried to convince my father to include the senior-most easter in his inner council, or at least allocate additional land beyond the qila's walls for cultivation. I begged the priests to let the easters inside the temples for the Mouth. I failed more than I succeeded. What was I? Fourteen, fifteen? Who would listen to me? Above all, in that little space of our kingdom, I didn't know what else I *could* do. Even my privilege had its limits. Until . . . Madhyra came along and opened my eyes to what could be truly possible."

Harini took several deep breaths, one hand against her racing heart. Amir stared transfixed at her.

"So don't ask me if it can work, Amir," she pressed on. "Because I don't know if it can. I know what is at stake, but I also know that I *want* this to work. For you, for us."

"Harini . . ." Amir began, but something caught his eye.

The door at the base of the mountain leading into the prison opened, and a column of Jhanakari chowkidars shuffled out, the first light of dawn gleaming against their white hair. Behind them, swaddled in chains, came the long line of gatecaste who had been apprehended at sea by the Jhanakari fleet. At the front of the procession was the enormous form of Sekaran. Bruised and battered, the people of the Black Coves followed the chowkidars down the narrow trail in the shadow of the mountain.

Before the door closed, the last of the prisoners destined for the Whorl staggered outside into the cold morning.

It was Karim bhai.

AMIR RAN DOWN THE SPICE TRAIL TOWARD THE LINE OF PRISONERS. *No, no, no.* The last he had seen of Karim bhai was outside Ilangovan's holding cell, warding off Hasmin. Had the chowkidar gotten to him? Gates, he ought not to have left Karim bhai alone!

Amir slid on the gravel, alerting the Jhanakari chowkidars to his presence. The gatecaste turned in their solemn march to watch his approach. Sekaran wore a cold frown on his face.

"He did nothing wrong!" Amir shouted to no one in particular. Karim bhai shook his head as though he had not expected such idiocy in these early hours of the day.

Three of the chowkidars grabbed Amir and held him back. One of them must have seen the spicemark on Amir's throat and decided he was also one of the Condemned. "Iron this one up and get him in line," he ordered.

"Let him go," a voice commanded from the slopes. Harini had followed Amir down. Flanked by a coterie of the Haldiveer, she glared at the chowkidars until they realized who she was, and what her instructions meant.

"Amir," Harini continued, "you cannot help him here. It is not these guards you must confront. It is Orbalun you must talk to."

"Pulla, don't be a fool," Karim bhai called out, his lips bleeding. "I will be okay. I have always been okay."

"This should not have happened." Amir shook his head, trying to wrestle loose from the chowkidars' grip on his arms. "I will get you free, bhai."

"You will do no such thing," Karim bhai said calmly. "I never felt as satisfied as when I opened the door to Ilangovan's cell. Far more adventurous than nicking royal seals from Suman-koti's chambers, for certain, ho." He chuckled, and much to Amir's surprise, winked in Harini's direction. "And I got to sing alongside the Grand Ustad. And is there a fonder farewell for a man than such a glory?"

Amir's protest flowed in the form of snarling and thrashing. He wanted to scream, but every muscle, every bone in his body was exhausted. The line of the Condemned began to move once more, and before the chowkidars could release Amir per Harini's orders, the chained prisoners had disappeared down the lane that led to the docks.

"Amir . . ." Harini began, her voice soft beside him, but he was already speeding in the shadow of the mountain, burrowing into the palace fort toward Maharaja Orbalun.

THE FRAGRANCE OF CINNAMON RETURNED, SCRATCHING AT AMIR'S empty belly. He had forgotten the taste of his last meal. The sensation of spices was an illusion. A memory of saffron, a mirage of cardamom. Bay leaf in an invisible biryani, the meat not from goats but fragments of the Mouth, bitter to his tongue. His stomach felt distended, and his head thundered with the image of the silhouette of Karim bhai diminishing upon the spice trail under the emerging sun. A new day.

He surrendered both his shamshir and Kalay's talwar to the chowkidars standing guard outside Orbalun's chambers. His chest heaving, words clinging to the rim of his tongue, itching for an outburst, Amir waited for the chowkidar to open the door, then stormed inside.

Maharaja Orbalun stood looking over the balcony at the docks. His shoulders drooped, his hair fell back to his shoulders, wet and unkempt, and he wore not a royal robe but a simple nightgown. He looked like he was ready to abdicate.

"Amir, ah, I am glad to see you are safe," he croaked. Gates, had Orbalun been crying?

Orbalun wiped his eyes and turned, smiling. "Come, my boy. I daresay you look roughened up."

"Maharaja, Karim bhai is being taken to the Whorl. You must stop them from doing this."

Sweat glistened on his palms as he waited for Orbalun to respond. Slowly, the maharaja beckoned Amir to the balcony lined with spider plants and daffodils and karuveppilais. Amir saw Jhanak sprawl beneath him, a rush of the sea breeze moving his hair about. Along the coast, he spied a row of ships anchored to the wharfs. The largest of them, the Ship of the Condemned, stood solemnly apart. The column of prisoners staggered onto a plank and into its holds. Karim bhai was a faint pinprick. Amir was not sure if he was imagining he could see the towel around his head.

His breathing quickened. He turned to Orbalun, who did not appear in the least concerned by Amir's urgency.

"Karim bhai swore if something happened you would get him out," Amir said. His eyes felt moist.

"If he had come to me," Orbalun muttered, "I might have. I might have, I suppose," he repeated, almost absently. Stronger, he said, "Hasmin, however, took Karim straight to Rani Zariba."

A lump settled in Amir's throat. Hasmin had, of course, had enough. The last few days had turned his life around as much as it had Amir's. First, the delay in Halmora, followed by Amir stealing the medallion from Hasmin's office, emptying a pail of shit on his head in the process. Amir and Karim bhai being invited to the afsal dina feast and fraternizing with thronekeepers, being allowed to partake in the same food that Hasmin and the others ate. The gatecaste apprehending him, barreling him onto a ship like loose cargo. Being punched by Sekaran and suffering the ignominy of traveling through the Whorl. Finally, having Karim bhai release Ilangovan back to the Black Coves, a man Hasmin had longed to see plunge down the Whorl—an incessant prayer whispered to the Mouth before every bite of food.

Hasmin had had his fill of being mocked, of tradition being upended. Enough even to cross Orbalun's authority and do what his instincts had craved, not for days or weeks but for years.

"Where is he?" asked Amir.

"Overseeing the loading of the ship," said Orbalun, knowing Amir meant Hasmin. "However, it would not be wise to empty your anger upon the senapati. It would do you little good."

If the accounts of the Jhanakari servants were true, Karim bhai, after Hasmin led him into the holds last night, had received fifty lashes from the guards. It astonished Amir how much bigotry a man could harbor within himself because his faith asked him to. His thoughts strayed beyond wanting to strangle Hasmin. Those days were gone. He didn't think death would absolve Hasmin of the evil he had nurtured in his bones. Or whatever evil masqueraded as duty in his mind.

"Is there nothing you can do?" he asked Maharaja Orbalun.

The thronekeeper of Raluha remained stiff and grim-faced, watching the proceedings below with a tired eye. "I am afraid not. Karim tried to help Ilangovan escape. The truth is absolute."

Amir kicked a pot of the karuveppilai, then set to pacing the length of the balcony. A chill ran down his spine as he contemplated Karim bhai's fate. The Whorl. There would be no coming back. Not like how they all had returned the previous morning. This journey would take them through the curtain and into death. Amir shivered with guilt and turned away from the balcony, as down by the docks, he knew from having seen it before, the Jhanakari chowkidars had begun to announce the names of the Condemned one after the other. A crowd had gathered. Hungover, impassioned, awaiting the judgment and the unmooring of the rope. Some threw tomatoes and eggs at the prisoners and hurled invectives that were gushes of the wind from where Amir stood, but what else could they be?

"You're a thronekeeper," Amir said, stopping just short of grabbing Orbalun's nightgown and yanking him around. "Surely you can bargain for something lesser."

Orbalun shook his head definitively. "I am sorry, Amir. As much as I wish to save Karim, the rules of Jhanak leave no exception. The Condemned are an old, tireless practice, steeped in the culture of Jhanak itself. To leave one person out of the sentence is to undermine the very foundations of this practice. And as deplorable as it is, we must respect the tradition, for there's nothing of our kingdoms left if not our traditions."

Traditions that have always only suited the abovefolk. That have bolstered the weight of the scriptures and fortified your oppression.

Orbalun, for all the goodness of his heart, was not too different from Harini. Buried beneath traditions, unable to escape the Mouth's hold on their lives.

Except Harini is trying.

Amir spat on a plant nearby. "I don't believe this! It's all because of me. I dragged Karim bhai into this. I told him about Madhyra, about everything!"

"Karim did nothing he would not have done of his own accord. In fact, I believe excluding him would have made him act all the more reckless."

"He's a dead man. What could be worse?"

"A dead man who fulfilled what he wished to do. They say those who drown in the Whorl go straight to the bosom of the Mouth. Perhaps Karim will have his sins washed away and he will be reborn as—"

"Abovefolk?" Amir asked sardonically, not realizing he had brazenly interrupted the thronekeeper of Raluha. "Apologies, huzoor, but I believe Karim bhai would want to be reborn as a bowler, although perhaps in a better world, in a fairer world. In a world where he would not be sent down to the Whorl to fulfill the demands of ancient traditions—because he would never have to free a man like Ilangovan, who would never have to exist in the Black Coves in the first place. The world we live in has made all this possible, not because Karim bhai was born a bowler."

Orbalun gazed at the docks, watching the Jhanakari guards wrap the Condemned in thick iron chains, fitting them with oars and instructing them on the way to guide the ships toward the Whorl. The Jhanakari fleet would flank them until they reached the edge of the storm, and from there onward, the Condemned would be on their way alone.

None of the Condemned had ever returned.

Now over five dozen gatecaste would perish. For a strange moment frozen in time, Amir imagined them all in the Outerlands, along with his father, away from the Spice Gates, away from the abovefolk. It was what Harini had wanted. Truth be told, Amir had experienced a pinch of embarrassment during his conversation with her. All these years, he had desired to only free his family, while Harini had yearned to free all of the easters, all of the Bowl.

But then, Amir realized with bitterness, Harini had not exactly climbed out of the Bowl like Amir had. She was not trapped by the limitations of her own imagination as Amir had been. For a bowler to free the entire Bowl—Appa had dreamed this, and even the bowlers had called him deranged and had watched with muted indifference as Amir and Amma had buried his bones in the ground. Or what they thought had been his bones. A bowler did not and could not imagine a world where such freedom could be realized. Madhyra had been right—*I am surprised your dreams are not mine.* His narrow dream of his family safely ensconced in the treacherous Black Coves had been the pinnacle of Amir's expedition to liberation.

A fragile liberation, in hindsight. And now, as he watched Karim bhai sail away in his last hours, the sea breeze whipping his hair, he thought it needn't be.

"All for the crime of—" Amir spat again and then froze. Orbalun's words returned to his mind like a blazing chariot, trampling all other thoughts in its wake. "Maharaja, what did you mean when you said Karim bhai *tried* to free Ilangovan?"

Orbalun frowned. "I had believed you would have heard. Ilangovan did not escape back to the Black Coves, Amir. He surrendered to Zariba's authorities at the docks. He said that he did not wish to abandon his fellow men and women to sail into the Whorl by themselves."

Amir's chest expanded in a triumphant wave, a deluge that battered the walls of misery and doubt that had roosted in Amir's heart from the moment he saw Karim bhai being led to the ship.

In the light of what Madhyra and Harini had told him in Talashshukh about their meeting with Ilangovan . . . "Maharaja," Amir said, gripping the banister, unable to control his fever, an excitement waking from a deep slumber, "can you show me the map of the Outerlands Madhyra had left for you?"

Orbalun slipped into thought, scratching his beard. "I thought I had—ah, I suppose Karim has it. I remember now, he did ask me for it before you left for the Black Coves."

You guessed right. The bastard!

Amir laughed, clapping his hands, an uproarious, untethered cackle that evoked a chuckle from Orbalun, who must have thought Amir deranged. Amir bent down to pick up the pot of karuveppilai he had kicked and spat on, and he kissed the mud and the leaves before placing it back in the row of plants.

"Is there something I have missed, Amir?" Orbalun asked.

Amir shook his head, his laughter taking an age to subside. *Ah, Karim bhai, you conniving old man!* "No, no, Maharaja. But I know what I must do. Madhyra, I must catch up with her. She has entered the Outerlands."

"The Outerlands?" Orbalun sounded more fascinated than worried. "Did you find out what she plans to do? Zariba and the other throne-keepers still believe she is related to Harini. I wonder why she did not break the secret of Illindhi during the feast."

Amir opened his mouth and closed it. It did not feel wise to confess to Orbalun Madhyra's plan to destroy the Spice Gates. After all, Orbalun was a thronekeeper, and there was much that Amir still did not know about him. For now, he would treat him like a benevolent abovefolk.

"No, I do not know what her plan is yet," he lied, and Gates, it felt so easy to lie to Orbalun in the face of the exploding scenarios that tumbled in his mind. "But we have little time until the Uyirsena arrive, and I must get to her. She took the Spice Gate from Talashshukh to Amarohi."

"Reasonable," Orbalun surmised. "If I remember the map, Amarohi was the closest among the eight kingdoms to Illindhi by distance. It was also the only fully charted route. Perhaps she has been forced to retrace her steps." Orbalun inhaled sharply, a sadness overtaking his face. "Amir, I fear for something worse than merely the knowledge of Illindhi pervading the eight kingdoms. Call it a thronekeeper's instinct, or perhaps I have inherited my grandmother's uncanny intuition, but Madhyra's journey, her determination—they seem to elude the outcomes we have been anticipating. Perhaps we have thought about this wrong, or perhaps we are yet to gain all the pieces of the puzzle she has constructed for us. Either way, she has always been one step ahead of us, and we have eleven days before the Uyirsena arrive, by your estimate. I neither have the Poison to send a dozen chowkidars with you nor can I coerce the Raluhan ministers to side with me on this. Powerless as I feel to say this, you are alone in this quest. I will write a letter addressed to Rani Kaivalya of Amarohi, granting you permission to enter her kingdom on a personal errand of mine. But as for the Outerlands themselves, given Karim possesses the map, I cannot help you."

Amir watched the last of the prisoners led in chains up the gangplank and into the holds of the ship. The canvas of its three-part silver sails fluttered against the breeze. All at once, the raucous spectators, audience to the shaming, began to clap and holler. When the sounds reached a zenith, the chowkidars untied the mooring and the ship began to drift away into the sea, surrounded by the Jhanakari fleet.

Amir was not certain if the man standing on the edge of the deck waving a feeble hand in the direction of the mountain castle was Karim bhai. But he liked to think it was, and he gave a subtle wave back.

He turned to Orbalun. "Thank you for the letter, Maharaja," he said. "As for the Outerlands, I know of a way I can make my way into that wilderness." He would regret this. Oh, he would *regret* this. But he also had no choice. "Can you also lend me a vial of the Poison? I wish to carry it to the rain forests of Mesht. I have someone there who can be of help."

CHAPTER

20

*The Spice Trade has not always been equitable. The seven
master alchemists of Vanasi hoped to prove the superiority
of cumin over the other spices, thereby gaining an economic
advantage. However, when their experiments pointed to
saffron's worth eclipsing the others, the thronekeepers ordered
the quest to be silently abandoned.*

—AGUMBA AND ANSARILAL, *THE MYSTICAL VANASARI*

It had begun to drizzle by the time Amir gathered his belongings,
packed food (under Maharaja Orbalun's insistence), carried enough
different spices to travel the eight kingdoms for a fortnight, and
dragged himself to the Spice Gate on Jhanak's wind-lashed ridge.

It had been a week since he'd last been on Carrying duty, and as he
stood by the Gate, his neck wrapped in a shawl to conceal the brand of
the spicemark, a column of Kalanadi Carriers emerged from the Gate.
The week of the afsal dina involved the least amount of trade, since spices
were forbidden to be cultivated. A visible relief painted their faces as they
lumbered down the spice trail toward the go-downs with half-filled sacks
and barrels.

"You don't need to do this, Amir," Harini reasoned with him. She had
insisted on seeing him off. "Let Madhyra complete her task."

"I need to know what my father accomplished," Amir said. "I need to know that his deranged dreams had some truth to them. That this future could be possible. Without that, I cannot let Madhyra do what she's doing, not when the Uyirsena get closer with each hour."

Harini held his hand. "Amir, she's got enough time to—"

Amir yanked his hand away. He instantly regretted it. "Harini, I'm sorry. It's not just that, ho? The Mouth . . ." He closed his eyes and clenched his fists and lowered his voice. He wished he didn't have to speak of this to anyone. "The Mouth *knew* I had let Madhyra slip away in Talashshukh. It threatened that Kabir's Carrying is going to become more painful, to say nothing of mine. Worse, it might even provoke Mahrang to send the Uyirsena earlier. I cannot take that chance. I *need* to be on Madhyra's tail."

Harini appeared to weigh his response. She offered a faint nod. "I understand. But without the map, you will be lost in the Outerlands."

"I am not going to go without the map."

Harini seemed puzzled, but Amir gave her little time to decipher the meaning of his words. He leaped into her arms and wrapped her in his embrace. The smell of sandalwood opened his senses and he thought he could remain there in her grasp for as long as it took the world to set itself right. When he kissed her, he thought the world had already mended.

He pulled back and saw a tear drop from Harini's eye. She smiled. "Don't forget to eat," she said. "And don't pluck mushrooms from the Outerlands. Madhyra told me some of them are poisonous."

"I won't."

The rain started to fall harder. He bade goodbye to Harini, who beckoned the Haldiveer up the ridge for their journey back to Halmora. Their stores of Poison would be exhausted soon enough.

Sprinkling a fistful of powdered jeera into the veil, Amir stepped through the Gate and found himself folding and folding.

YOU HAVE BROKEN YOUR PLEDGE.

Amir knelt in the emptiness between the Gate and the Mouth. If there was guilt, he did not express it. He realized the Mouth had indeed withdrawn the freedom from pain it had earlier bestowed upon Amir. He remained silent, awaiting his due.

My child, my spice-born. Why do you torment me so? You seek to disturb the very customs that sustain you. You fail to understand the tenets of duty, and in that failure you have become tempted. You seek that which is beyond the realm of your responsibilities. Why do you desire, child? Haven't I showered you with the spices that nourish your meal? Haven't I bestowed you with the boon to Pass through me, a blessing that is denied to others? Yet you fail to protect me, knowing that in my absence the world stands to crumble. The balance of life, the Spice Trade, born out of both humanity and me, stands to crumble. Do you wish suffering among your people? Do you wish famine? Starvation? Death? Do you not know what waits and prowls in the beyond, governed by my hands? Or do you know and still act? For evil done in the presence of knowledge is deserving of a punishment higher than evil done veiled by ignorance. I have empowered you with knowledge, my child, my spice-born. You are the best of mine. Do not fail me. Stop her, and reclaim your place as my most faithful.

Amir closed his eyes and waited for the pain. Any moment now—

MESHT WAS AN EMPIRE OF ONE HUNDRED AND EIGHTY-SEVEN rivers, each named after a dish in Mesht's ancient culinary history. They wove through thick rain forests, often meeting, playing, and overlapping before going separate ways, sometimes to meet again but oftentimes, having just met once. Amir had never traversed more than four of those many rivers, and he doubted that today he would exceed that count.

When he stepped out of the Gate, the pain in his limbs reached unprecedented levels, at once drawing him to the ground, his fingernails sinking into the wet earth of the small island upon which the Gate stood. Someone had set fire to his hair, it felt, and the flames seeped into his skull and into the part of his brain that caused his feet to writhe in inexplicable agony. When it ceased, he managed to open his eyes. The shawl around his neck had fallen away.

Canoes and gondolas surrounded the floating mound, guarded by two women smoking their beedis and staring at Amir's predicament with a suspicion he couldn't fault them for.

"Champa didi, it's me," Amir groaned.

One of the women stood up and squinted. "Bite the mace, it is you. Amirawa, today is not a day for Raluha to come in."

"It is not, but I'm looking for someone," said Amir. "A young woman. Who must have come through this Gate several hours ago with her hands bound, and a—"

"A cloth stuffed into her mouth," Champa didi said, with a grin that revealed one lone tooth fighting to stay alive in her mouth. "She floated that way." She gestured to the north, to the first tributary that Amir had noticed when he had stepped out of the Gate. "Feisty one, that. Could fight better without her arms than I've seen most of these Meshti men fight with swords. I hope you're not in her bad books, raja."

Amir puffed out a reluctant breath and shrugged. "Only time will tell."

Shyamala didi, the older of the two women, stepped forth. A strong smell of aloes wafted from her. She was munching on a strip of sugarcane, which she flipped like a sword and pointed at Amir's neck. "Do you know what the Eromba River leads to, raja?" Her voice was raspy, as though embers burned in her throat.

"Does it matter?" asked Amir, even though he knew it must. It must be an answer he did not care for.

Shyamala didi chuckled. "A brave one. Go, and do not forget that I warned you."

A CANOE BORROWED FROM CHAMPA DIDI AND SHYAMALA DIDI, the two guardians of Mesht's Spice Gate, had no strings attached. It was one of the few perks of being a Carrier with a penchant for courtesy, a trait that had eluded even seasoned Carriers. Little escaped the women's surveillance of the rivers, and both had sworn that they had traversed each of the hundred and eighty-seven and come back with fresh tiger skins as evidence of their sojourns. Amir did not need that evidence. He trusted every word they said, seeing how they had helped him out on more than one occasion in delivering discreet items.

The way down the Eromba was not the one the Carriers took. It was a more desolate tributary that Amir quietly cursed Kalay for taking. He did not doubt she had freed herself from her bindings—Gates knew she had more than half a dozen pocketknives hidden in different parts of her attire—but without the Poison, she was helpless to leave Mesht. And if he had not been coming for her, he doubted she'd ever be able to leave this kingdom for the rest of her life.

A mournful gloom lingered above as Amir rowed the canoe down the river in frightful silence. Each plop of water resounded in his ears. Each sound of an insect or a bird or an animal felt like the call for a hunt, a coded communication among the marshland's residents that flesh on the river was ripe for taking. Amir gulped, stayed on alert, and continued to row.

Mesht was a kingdom with few people spread out over a vast marshland and rain forest, and for long stretches, Amir feared he was alone in the entire empire, a relic drifting through a forgotten kingdom. Now and then, he came across ivory traders and teak suppliers who built their sheds and stilted towers on the shores, the depths of the wilderness sagging behind them like a serpentine halo of twisted darkness. Their faces were morose, but they did no harm, except to glance suspiciously as Amir passed them by, a faltering smile his only greeting. He was merely glad for their existence.

Within an hour, he came across Kalay's gondola, moored to one side of the river. Beyond the gondola, a pathway led into the forest, flanked with flags and totems dangling from strings crisscrossing beneath the branches. The gondola stood alone among reeds and floating leaves. The trail into the forest slithered between dense woods. A plank of teak had been shaved and filed into the shape of an arrow, pointing into the darkness.

Could she have gone nowhere else?

He wondered who told her.

Amir waded through the thicket, following the marked path. The undergrowth was soft, and close to his ears the constant buzzing of mosquitoes annoyed him, and he swatted the air with his hands. Within a few minutes, he came into a clearing.

At the center was another Spice Gate, this one a replica of the one he had clawed his way out of earlier. It was larger, also more densely overgrown with shrubs, creepers spiraling up the pillar and twining above the stone in harsh knots. The trees overhead bent to form an arched canopy, the dappled sunlight casting a fractured halo around the temple. A high wall curved around the temple in a semicircle. Its inscriptions eluded Amir's understanding.

More of the scriptures.

Kalay knelt in front of the gate's idol, her nose pressed to the ground, her muttering indecipherable to him. She had broken free of her shackles as he had suspected, and Amir noticed a small chaku placed on the ground beside her.

He did not disturb her at first. He waited. Even in the Bowl, praying to the Mouth had been a sacred act, one that demanded silence and devotion, both of which Kalay had in abundance. And watching her, a strange sense of pity gripped Amir. He wondered if she was apologizing to the Mouth.

Quietly, he slipped out of his chappals and stepped inside the circle of the temple. Kalay stirred from her prayer. "What?" she asked, annoyed.

Amir extended her talwar. "You forgot this."

Kalay stood, rubbed her hands, and pressed them to her eyes. Turning, she received her sword from Amir, then pointed it right back at him. "You have some nerve, coming here."

Amir had expected nothing less. He took a step farther into the temple, evading her sword and circling the Gate's idol. "Madhyra has left for the Outerlands. She is on her way back to Illindhi."

The pillars, he realized, seemed to picture the building of the Spice Gates. Scarlike tentacles branched from a central point on the wall to nine different shapes that represented each of the kingdoms. The central point was a dark clot on the wall—a hideous, miasmic anomaly that Amir could not comprehend. A rancid smell ran up his nose at the very attempt.

"Why are you here?" Kalay asked.

"Because only you know the way through the Outerlands. Madhyra made you memorize the map she had drawn."

Kalay appeared suspicious. "What happened to the one your throne-keeper had?"

"Karim bhai took it. He is being sent to the Whorl."

"He was a good man," she said. "I am sorry to hear."

Amir smiled. "I don't think he's going to die. Death does not come easily to men such as him. Ilangovan is one of the Condemned as well, and he now knows how to cross the Whorl, thanks to your aunt. He will get them all across safely, though I don't know what lurks on the other side."

Kalay opened her mouth and closed it. He knew what she wanted to say: that the Whorl could not be crossed, that it had not been crossed for a thousand years, and that death awaited the Condemned on the other side, even if they could manage it. Instead, she took a deep breath. A drooping of the shoulders. A drawing back of the sword and sheathing it into the scabbard. In front of the temple of the Mouth, Kalay appeared restrained and disciplined.

"I don't trust you, Amir," she said softly. "I don't think I did from the start, even though I supposed you were at one point serious in bringing my aunt to justice. Now I doubt that too. She has swayed your heart like she has swayed many in these eight kingdoms."

"It does not matter whether she has swayed my heart or not," said Amir. "The Mouth wants me to hunt her down, and I am left with no choice. The Uyirsena—your army—stands to conduct their genocide otherwise."

Kalay's scrunched expression told him that she'd have preferred if Amir did this of his own volition, that he saw the wrongness in it, and not because the Mouth was coercing and threatening him into submission.

"The Uyirsena would never kill without reason," said Kalay. "You already know why spreading the knowledge of Illindhi is detrimental to the eight kingdoms."

"My life has been detrimental since the time I was born in the Bowl," said Amir. "I honestly don't care about the Spice Trade."

"Once again, you blame the scriptures of the Mouth, when—"

The undergrowth rustled, and all of a sudden two dozen men and a woman emerged from the thickets behind them, armed with aruvaals and staffs. One of them, Amir realized, was one of the teak traders he had seen while crossing the river on his way to the temple. Their pointed gazes focused on the spicemark on Amir's throat, then lowered to where Amir stood within the circle of the temple. Nobody even looked at Kalay.

"Arre madarchod, how dare you step inside the temple?" one of them shrieked. "Who do you think you are?"

Amir realized his mistake a moment too late. He at once folded his hands. "I apologize, dada. It was a mistake. I came to return an item to this one, and I must have stepped inside the circle unknowingly. I shall leave at once."

His head still lowered, he gestured to Kalay frantically to step out of the temple and follow him back to the swampland and the river. However, the gathered Meshtis—in their attire of silver robes and flowered headdresses—were blocking the way out.

"There's always an apology in the air," the woman said with a smirk. "One apology after another, and you don't really mean it, do you? Even the body of the oarasi floating down the singju did not teach them a lesson. And now you—which part of the eight kingdoms are you from?"

"Raluha," Amir muttered.

"You have a spice trail to follow," a man said. "Instead of sticking to the Pomba River, you dare defile the purity of the Eromba, madarchod?"

"Enough talking," a third man cried. He proceeded ahead, but Kalay had already swept in front of Amir, knocking the advancing man to his stomach with a kick. He convulsed, his eyes widened, and he fell gasping for breath.

"The Mouth does not forbid anyone from entering its temples," she said calmly, addressing the Meshti, a shaft of sunlight glinting off her unsheathed blade. "Now, let us leave in peace."

The natives stared at their fallen companion, who showed no signs of stirring. "What do you know of the Mouth?" countered the woman who had spoken earlier. "You must be an oarasi too. Return to the Singju and stick to what you are supposed to do."

"In that case . . ." Kalay did not smile but merely raised her sword. Amir tried to stop her, but she had already stepped on the fallen Meshti's chest and slashed at one of the three men. They raised their own aruvaals in unison. The clash of steel rang through the forest, louder than the twitter of birds. Everything after that happened in a blur for Amir. Kalay danced like the wind on the wet earth. Her talwar moved far quicker than Amir could trace its trajectory. She swerved and ducked and struck within a heartbeat.

"Don't kill them," Amir pleaded. Kalay scoffed and blew her hair out of her eyes.

Each man who fell clutched his chest, or his feet, or his head, but there was no blood except when Kalay knocked one of their teeth out with a punch. They fell like slender trees being uprooted by a storm, then writhed on the temple floor, raspy moans escaping their mouths.

The last of those who fell was the teak trader, large and beefy. Kalay ducked beneath his attack as he made to strike, then clamped his elbow and twisted it inward. His scream shattered the peaceful twittering of the birds, and they took to the skies in a shimmering breach of the treetops. As he was forced to kneel, Kalay planted her own knee against his chin. Amir heard a dull crack as the man collapsed atop his own companion, who convulsed at the weight slamming upon him.

Only the woman remained. "The Mouth will not forgive you for your sin," she said, her eyes flickering with the curse of one who has been wronged. "May your tongue go spiceless for when you crave its taste the most."

Having said this, she turned and ran, then tripped on a trailing branch and fell face-first on the ground. Amir nearly choked into laughter, but he watched her pick herself up and scamper toward the river.

For a long time, the only sounds came from the moans of the fallen Meshti traders. Kalay stared at the idol of the Gate, her chest heaving, sweat pouring down her face. It was hard to say if she was apologizing or cursing.

"I—uh . . . thank you," said Amir, scratching his head. "It's not unusual, you know."

"Well, it should be," she barked in response. "Nowhere in the scriptures does it state that a low"—she swallowed—"that you are not allowed inside a temple."

Amir smiled. "Sometimes I feel the scriptures you've been fed in the Uyirsena are far from the reality of the eight kingdoms."

"The scriptures are not to blame," Kalay said. She threw a disgusted look at the men writhing on the ground. "These are just idiots. Infidels."

"You'd be surprised at their devotion," said Amir.

She stiffened. "I don't want to talk about this anymore. Now, can we go find my aunt, or what?"

Amir nodded, removing the vial of Poison from inside his robe. "You'll need this. And remember to not speak at all in Amarohi."

AMAROHI. BEAUTIFUL, TREACHEROUS AMAROHI. THE SMELL OF pine wood and cedar, and the cool wind of the hills, the mist trickling around his feet and ensnaring his senses. The whisper of bulbuls jumbled with the grating conversation of a mountain raven.

Nestled in this tenderness, the camphorated aroma of cloves. The winter spice.

Amir found himself unable to open his eyes. A vine of thorns constricted him, piercing his flesh, weaving through his innards like a serpent. He did not know whether he was on a hard surface or soft, whether it was day or night. The mark on his throat pricked; it singed his skin, and he feared it'd burrow through the flesh, revealing the tendons of his neck to anyone who stared at him, and perhaps then this torment would end and he would never be able to travel through the Spice Gates again.

When the pain subsided, after seconds or minutes or hours, Amir opened his eyes. A butterfly lay on the bridge of his nose. When he stirred, it took flight, circling him and then zigzagging away to its freedom. The sloping moor the Spice Gate stood on was wet with dew. A shiver ran down his spine at the sudden burst of cold. Daylight queasily peeked from beyond the clouds of Amarohi's solitude.

Kalay stood a few feet away, her hands on her hips, basking in the ethereal dawn glow. An illusion of felicity on her face. In the blink of an eye it disappeared and she frowned, gesturing for Amir to stand up. He realized she'd been watching him in his pain. What the Mouth was doing to him each time he moved through the Gates, between king-doms. He took solace in the relief on her face when he stood up.

A column of archers was climbing up the hill. A small village squatted at the slope's base, engulfed in a thin fog. Woodfire escaped from chim-neys, and a woman emerged from the woods beyond, pushing a cart laden with fruits and berries. Gates, he did not think he could live in this serenity for longer than an hour. Too tranquil for his liking. In many ways, he missed the chaotic bustle of Raluha and the Bowl.

Amir furnished the letter to the archers, pointing to the curve of the hill looming behind them, gesturing around it. *We need to get around the hill and into the Outerlands. Orbalun's personal errand. We won't go far, just close to the borders. A rare herb. For his queen.*

Kalay appeared surprised at Amir's proficiency with the sign language. He communicated with the archers briskly, They were shaking their heads more than nodding.

In the end, Amir and Kalay would be allowed into the fringes of the Outerlands only if the letter was approved by Rani Kaivalya herself. She had—only late the previous night—returned from the afsal dina feast in Jhanak.

They followed the knot of archers over the hill. The cold breeze nipped at Amir's sleeve, and despite coming out of the heavy-laden air of Mesht, the winds of Amarohi did little to assuage the uncertainty playing in Amir's mind.

As they crested the hill and looked down upon the undulating grassland and the vale in its midst, he finally took in the sights of Amarohi, the kingdom of cloves.

He heard Kalay's sharp intake of breath. Amir imagined she saw it as the Mouth's gift to the eight kingdoms, this dalliance with nature. To the west, where the hill rose higher and steeped into a precipice, a waterfall meandered out of a river winding from the north and gushed down a hundred feet into a pool. White clouds rose up with belches of spray. The pool, bordered by limestone slabs and boulders, split into fragments of brooks, which slid into the vale, where lay the forested town of Amarohi. Beyond the town, the mountain rose again, and upon it, like a weathered, moss-beaten crown, stood the aranmanai of Rani Kaivalya, its turrets spiraling into the clouds, mist engulfing its towers, its windows a gateway into a sepulchral loneliness that Amir did not wish to partake in.

The families of pines and cedars thinned as the hill sloped down into the vale. The wetness of the falls clung to their skin. The slopes had the everlasting appearance of a time just after it finished raining, when the fresh smell of earth unclogged the nose and released the bound spirits of the heart. There was a time when Amir had imagined bringing Amma to Amarohi, a change from the crowded, cluttered Bowl of Raluha. The reeders, the gatecaste tribes that lived in the hills, would accept them, no questions asked. Amir knew the Carriers among the reeders. And

Amma—who had turned fairly quiet after Appa's abandonment—would have fit right in.

Those moments melted and evaporated like butter on a blackened kadai. The reeders were no less alienated, their spices no less limited by the rules of the trade. The sweep of fresh air down from the mountains, carrying the scent of cloves and pines, could only be savored for so long.

The archers came to a wooden cottage at the base of the hill. The guard outpost. From there, a long wooden bridge spanned the river and led into Amarohi.

Wait, one of the archers gestured. From inside the cabin came an old man bearing an eagle on his shoulder. The archer tied Orbalun's letter to the eagle's claws and, patting its mane, sent it flying.

Amir watched as the bird soared above the treetops, silhouetted against the waterfall, before heading for Kaivalya's aranmanai. It disappeared into the clouds.

For quite a while, they waited. Kalay stood by the bridge, staring into the town of Amarohi, her hair whipped by the waterfall's soaking gust. She was restless, and the confusion that had plagued her over the last few days appeared to be plunging her into a guilt that Amir had no recourse to temper. One thing was certain: Amir would not survive a day in the Outerlands without Kalay. Appa may have done it, but Amir was not his father. Nor was he Karim bhai or Ilangovan. Persistence did not always translate to survivability. Determination did not create additional reserves of strength beyond the limit of one's bones and muscles. And if this meant risking Kalay's inflamed temper and an uncanny adherence to her duty to the Mouth, so be it. He'd fight that battle if and when it came.

At some point, Kalay must have lost her patience, for she slammed the bridge's railing and turned to march toward the archers. Amir feared she'd scream at them, and in that process, break Amarohi's only rule.

Her stride, however, was arrested by a deep, piercing shriek from up in the skies.

Amir's heart caught in his throat as he gazed up at the cloud-encrusted aranmanai sitting atop the mountain. No eagle could make that sound, and in all his years of traveling to Amarohi as a Carrier, he had never heard anything like it.

Through the clouds emerged a shape. Bleak, obsidian-scaled, as if a bat had grown to the size of a horse. Its wings spanned twenty feet, punctuated with strokes of gossamer and indigo, and as it descended, Amir caught sight of a beak like an inverted horn. In its talons, something wriggled. The closer the bird-beast came, Amir discerned the victim to be a snake. A python. The bird circled over the town of Amarohi, and for a heartbeat Amir wondered why it was not being punished for its incessant shrieking.

It landed between the bridge and the outpost cottage. The Amarohini archers at once parted as the beast's wings unleashed a final torrent of gust to arrest its acceleration. It forced a rattle out of Amir's teeth, flattening his cheeks. Upon landing, it reared up, threw the serpent into the air, and caught it again in its beak before swallowing it whole.

Amir was certain this was, albeit in no parlance of any of the eight kingdoms, a bird. It had the head of a peacock but ten times as large, and none of its grace. The gossamer streaks on its wings and down its neck throbbed and gleamed.

Kalay was equally mystified. She stood frozen in her tracks, her talwar out, but for the first time he noticed it shuddering in her grasp.

From the bird-beast's back, a figure slid down. Rani Kaivalya was wrapped in a woolen blanket from head to toe. In her hand was the letter Amir had given to the archers.

With a flourish, she gestured to both Amir and Kalay to follow her into the sipahi outhouse.

Amir did not move for a moment. His eyes had returned to the bird-beast, as it devoured the last of the serpent's tail, its beady eyes narrowing at Amir watching it. He immediately averted his gaze and scurried behind Kaivalya. Kalay caught up with him and grabbed his arm in a pincer grip.

"That," she growled in as low a voice as she could manage, "is no ordinary bird. That's an Immortal Son of the Mouth! What in the name of the Gates is it doing inside the eight kingdoms?"

Amir placed a finger on his lips and motioned her inside the cottage. The archers took their weapons and closed the door. Amir, shut out from the shrieking, heard the hammering of his own chest. *An Immortal Son.*

Rani Kaivalya removed her blanket to reveal a crimson sari. She had done away with her crown, making a mess of the top of her head, but this did in no way diminish her regal countenance. During the afsal dina feast, she had watched the proceedings quietly, often whispering to Rani Mehreen of Mesht—inside jokes, he now surmised—and did not involve herself in the arguments between the thronekeepers. In fact, Amir doubted she even recognized him from Jhanak.

"You are the Carrier who attended the feast in Jhanak," she said.

Amir groaned. Her eyes strayed briefly to Kalay. "Don't worry, you can speak inside the confines of this cottage. Or within any four walls of Amarohi. It is the outside we keep sacred for nature."

Amir folded his hands and bowed. "Yes, Maharani."

"Now"—Kaivalya unrolled the letter and glanced over it once more— "Orba wants you both to enter the Outerlands. Why?"

"To pluck some jeevanti, Maharani," said Amir. "The maharaja said the Outerlands bordering Amarohi abound in these."

"Still pining for an heir, is he? Losing two to stillbirth hasn't taught him a lesson, yet. Gates know his ministers have already begun the hunt for a successor outside the royal family. But in some ways, I suppose, it is a good thing. Here I am, struggling with seven sons and two daughters. My succession would be a bloodbath."

Neither Amir nor Kalay replied. "Well," Kaivalya continued. "Be that as it may, it's his business, not mine. Only one bone of contention remains—it is *my* Outerlands you wish to enter."

"The Outerlands belong to the Mouth," Kalay muttered. Amir stiffened by her side. He clenched his hands, hoping she would shut up.

Kaivalya smiled, cocking her head and regarding Kalay head to toe. "That they do. Though I daresay we all permit a certain amount of . . . fluidity, at least close to the borders."

Kalay's breathing had quickened. Before Amir could stop her, she burst out. "That . . . that is an Immortal Son you have lured from the Outerlands. It is a servant of the Mouth. It is a sacrilege to tame such a creature, let alone ride one."

She just had *to.*

Amir bit his lip and rushed into the conversation that was simmering on the verge of explosion. "She . . . uh—apologies, Maharani—she is the daughter of a priest of Raluha. Steeped in the Mouth's scriptures and all that. But . . . *very* knowledgeable about herbs. So, you can understand her . . . sensitivity."

Unlike Amir, Kalay—born and raised in the royal household of Illindhi—did not lower her eyes in front of Maharani Kaivalya. Their gazes were stones scraping against each other, trying to spark a fire. Kalay not negating Amir's lie in itself was a win that he did not wish to sacrifice.

"It is rather queer," Rani Kaivalya said, finally breaking the stale-mate. "The Amarohini watchers swore they spotted another person enter the Outerlands several hours ago. Though, it was too dark to tell; it could have been a deer hopping about in the pale shadows, for all we know. And now you two come bearing Orba's seal requesting entry into the wild. Intriguing." She paused, shifting her gaze from Amir to Kalay. "Fortunately for you, I am not a believer in coincidences. I do, however, nurture a fair bit of skepticism when it comes to odd favors from old friends."

Amir could not have bowed any lower. "We're merely following Maharaja Orbalun's orders, Maharani sahiba."

"Yet . . ." Kaivalya's head inclined ever so slightly toward the cottage's door, beyond which waited the Immortal Son. "Kuka tells me not to trust you."

Amir's glance was brief and frantic. The Immortal Son had sensed him inside the cottage. How? Either way, it was not like he could scamper out of this cottage and run away into the Outerlands. He doubted he'd even reach the bridge across from the cottage.

"But then"—Kaivalya rolled her eyes, snapping the tension in the cottage—"Kuka has always loved the taste of Carriers. He's bound to tempt me to leave you behind. Tell you what . . ." She clapped her hands and exhaled. "You both are free to enter the Outerlands. Stay close to the borders. Head north for less than an hour, and you'll find ample slopes where the jeevanti thrives."

Amir blinked. He looked at Kalay, who continued to regard Rani Kaivalya with the same skepticism the queen had earlier prided herself on. In some imaginary world that tethered their minds together, they would have killed each other a dozen times already.

"We . . . We can go?" he repeated foolishly.

Kaivalya pulled out what appeared to be a wooden whistle from the folds of her sari. "Take this." Amir examined the whistle in his hand. Light as a stick. "It is a call for Kuka. If you face any trouble, don't hesitate to blow, and Kuka will be there within minutes or hours to help. However, I must warn you. You cannot linger in the borders for longer than the day. If you do not return to the village by nightfall, I am afraid I will be forced to send Kuka after you, and not with the intention to help."

Amir hesitated before bundling the whistle into his bag of belongings. Slowly, he nodded.

"Excellent," said Rani Kaivalya. "It is always a pleasure to be owed a favor by Orba in the future."

She extended a hand, but only to Kalay.

Of course.

Kalay quietly offered hers in return.

IT WAS ALMOST TOO INCREDIBLE TO BELIEVE. THAT GOING INTO the Outerlands, and surviving, was possible. It carried the whiff of a tale Karim bhai might have told to the children of the Bowl while sitting around a bonfire. Stories Amir had once despised, given how much they reminded him of Appa. The other children, however, swallowed them up like gulab jamuns.

Even though Amir did not have it in his hand, he knew the map *was* real. It was too complex to be a fabrication of someone's imagination. And as he stood at the border beside Kalay, the sight of the perfectly normal strip of forest spread out before him was overwhelming. Not because of what lay ahead, but because of the realization of what the place, the reality of it, meant to him.

Appa had been alive. And he had tried to come back. Appa had been alive until a fortnight ago. *A fortnight.*

Amir had continually tried to shut out this piece of information from his mind over the last several hours. Truth was, he did not know what he was supposed to do with it. If there was a resurgence of grief, he did not know what it looked like, or how differently it felt in his bones. What he *did* feel, however, was an overt sense of duty. As though, he was in a way responsible and culpable in not believing his father's deranged theories, and that now that those theories held truth, the only way to redeem his impression of his father was to resurrect the dream that had died on the stained steps of the Bowl.

Madhyra could see it. Harini could. And Amir ought to be able to, shouldn't he? Perhaps more so than them.

From high above the clouds that surrounded Kaivalya's aranmanai there came the shriek of the Immortal Son. The Mouth was watching. He shook his head. It was painful to hope. In his life, hope had resulted in nothing but failure, and hope without success hurt more than not hoping at all.

Maybe just this one time.

He'd had the Poison in his hand, and he had handed it back to Madhyra for a reason. The hammering in his chest had convinced him there was yet a part of this future that he had to carve out and sculpt from the scripture-inscribed pillars of the past and the present. The bowler life couldn't just be escaping to the Black Coves. Sure, it was a worthy life, built out of sweat, toil, and thievery. But he had seen that it was a tainted life, a temporary one, and if he could give his family and the Bowl something more, where their dignity and freedom did not come at the cost of a compromised morality, what kind of a bowler was he to not chase after that?

He gazed at the fence, craning his neck. Crows circled the top, where a cabin was built into the sentry, connected to the base by ladders. A pair of Amarohini archers watched him from the cabin, arrows nocked to their bows.

For a long time, Amir stood by the entrance—a path beneath an overhang—staring at the Outerlands. It seemed no different from the wilderness that grew on his side of the fence. A continuation of trees, the tropical humidity oozing through and whistling back, the sound of the birds carrying forth and jingling. Kaivalya had spoken of a tempered fluidity, and he suddenly realized how little he knew of the chicanery running riot in the gilded palaces of the thronekeepers.

If he resisted now, Kalay would not spare him, and she would chase after Madhyra anyway. She did not need him anymore, not now that he had rescued her from the marshland of Mesht. But her eyes were gloomy with a strange sadness, and as she turned back to regard the eight kingdoms, he thought he saw in her a fleeting sigh of longing, and perhaps even pity.

If he persisted with this reckless attempt to fight for the Bowl, he might still not make it alive. But he had come so far. He had traveled to a hidden kingdom, tasted a master spice, spoken to the very Mouth that tormented him as he passed through the Gates. He had sailed on a ship from the Black Coves and fought alongside Ilangovan's pirates. At worst, what could all this add up to, if not to a nightmare of events that could at some point melt into a dream? A dream from which he could awaken to the sound of his mother's cries for breakfast, to the smell of the Bowl's biryani for lunch once a fortnight, to the aroma of the last strands of saffron lingering in his home, to the sound of Kabir's rambles, of a new baby's cries, and the constant chatter of the bowlers as they survived another day at the bottom of Raluha?

"Look," Kalay snapped, "if you don't want to come—"

"I'm going," Amir snapped back. He took a step toward the arch, coated in brambles and ivy, then nodded at the Amarohini archers. If they were suspicious, they did not show it. Taking a deep breath, he stepped into the Outerlands.

CHAPTER
21

Visiting Jhanak and not partaking in its expensive salted
mackerel is akin to making love with your clothes on.
Unless you already have three children, it is not encouraged.

—*Morsels of a Bent Back*, Volume 1

The first hour, they were lively and covered a lot of ground. The food that they packed from Jhanak was divided as per their original rationing plan. Neither of them was a hunter, and there wasn't much in the way of wildlife except a few stray gazelles and a scared fox that shimmied beneath a log and disappeared underground anyway. The forest was endless, and when the trees cracked open to lend them a vision of what lay far ahead, they saw only the conical strip of a mountain, unblemished and pristine.

"How do you know if the direction you're going is the right one?" he asked Kalay at one point.

"It will be easier if you don't ask me too many questions."

"This is my first question."

Kalay scowled. From his pockets, Amir pulled the device he'd stolen from Hasmin in the court hall the previous night at the feast, its glassy face gleaming in sunlight. "Maybe this will help."

Kalay snatched it from him, turning it around in her hand. "Hasmin probably took it for himself from one of the pirates in the Black Coves," he continued. "I thought it was an old timepiece. But it seems more like something that points in specific directions. The black dial that keeps shivering inside, it seems to always be pointed in one direction, no matter where I stand—north."

Kalay did not admit at once that it was a good find. She took her time, squinting at its mechanics. She rotated in place, and with each quarter of a turn, stared at the device, raising it and lowering it. Then she gave a brief nod.

"In Illindhi, they say thieves make good survivors." She did not smile.

A small victory. It made his purpose on this reckless mission a little easier to remember.

Family. The bowlers. Your father.

It did not take away from how out of place he felt. He was not a leader, that much he had always known. Karim bhai might have had his opinions, but Amir knew he was no Ilangovan. Gates, he was not even the leader his father had been in the Bowl. He was adept at stalking and following and mimicking the footsteps of others to perfection. It was such an in-grained trait that, even now, walking through the forest, it was Kalay who led the way. She occasionally zipped ahead in a bid to chase large moths or parrots that flitted from branch to branch. Amir saw flickering signs of the girl who desired to see the realm in all its glory, but those signs quickly disappeared, to be replaced by the hunger she nursed under her training as an acolyte of the Uyirsena. Finding Madhyra was now a rage she wove around her as a cloak, and although it sometimes flapped open, it was usually drawn quite tight.

When several hours had passed, Amir gazed up at the skies. Inside his pockets, his fingers felt the contours of the whistle. "Do you think she'll let him loose? At the end of the day?"

"*It* is not hers to let loose," said Kalay. "The Immortal Sons are not to be tamed."

"You made that clear."

"Yet you seem to voice your doubts aloud."

"I have a tendency to do that. I pray you forgive me," he said sarcastically.

"I think it better that we pray it has not decided to follow us on its own, yes? Unlike my aunt, we do not have the kavestha to conceal our scent from it."

Amir hesitated. "It sensed me, you know." She did not stop walking, encouraging him to say more. "The Mouth knows."

"The Immortal Sons are tethered to the Mouth, just like the Gates are," said Kalay. "They are the Mouth's eyes and ears in the Outerlands, and now, seemingly, in the eight kingdoms too."

Kalay appeared discomfited by the thought of the Mouth invading the eight kingdoms through these creatures that haunted the woods. It did not fit with her understanding of the scriptures. A lot didn't, seeing that she was presently walking through a land that was explicitly forbidden to humans.

And yet.

Amir needed a reminder every now and then that Kalay had as much experience of the Outerlands as Amir. She had the map lodged in her head, but it did not prevent every little sound from making her squeal and jump. He wondered if that's when he saw the real Kalay.

It was a pity she wasn't much of a talker.

THE SILENCE OF THE FOREST WAS A LOT EERIER THAN THE SILENCE of Amarohi. It was a silence wrought of sounds Amir had not been accustomed to. The crush of the undergrowth, the sway of leaves, the haunting echoes of birds and insects, and the spaces between them like a held breath. Amir, born amid the clamor and bustle of Raluha, and the chaos of the Bowl, found the quiet disconcerting. Despite rationally knowing he shouldn't turn back, the itch to return to normalcy was stinging, and Amir yearned to scratch every bit of it until it swelled and blood poured forth in relief. He focused on putting one foot ahead of the other while quietly longing for the sun and a conversation with someone other than the trained assassin stalking ahead.

Amir worried that Kalay had forgotten parts of the map she had been made to memorize. If she could undo the teachings of her aunt and submit herself to the Mouth, what was to say that she still remembered the directions?

Ah, to be lost at the cusp of freedom. Poetic.

Before sundown, they reached the foot of a hairy hill, on whose slopes stood the entry to a cave. Kalay suggested they camp there for the night. It was cold, and Amir was shivering, and he thought his memories were beginning to get corrupted.

As long as Kalay's memories don't.

His eyes never left the cave's opening, as though each trick of the moonlight, each passing sound, was an enemy that had scented Amir's blood. He was used to four walls of brick or mud, not the curve of stone bearing down upon him and needles of cold attacking him like pincers from the cave's opening. Needless to say, he was not convinced of Kalay's idea of halting for the night. The moonlight was perfectly reasonable to trek through. She, however, gave him a stare so hard, Amir cowered and decided to keep his mouth shut.

The cave was not the most appealing of sights. Kalay admitted she had been fortunate to spot it just as the vestiges of the evening light were about to vanish. Just a hole in the wall of the hill, darkness spilling out of its hollowness and rolling down the slope like something viscous and unbreakable.

He had absolutely no desire to be anywhere near the thing, let alone go in.

Kalay shoved him inside.

"Where did you learn how to start a fire?" he asked her an hour later, as Kalay sat hugging her knees against a flame that rose from the wood next to her. He'd been wrong. She *did* have some experience in the Outerlands.

Her shadow bobbed behind her on the cave wall. The firelight had slowly revealed bones scattered on the ground. Animal bones, Kalay assured him, although that did in no way assuage his fear that something out there was causing flesh to transform into bones.

"My aunt taught me," she replied. "When you are nine, every acolyte of the Uyirsena is sent beyond the fences. For a whole night, they have to remain in the wild, close to the borders of course, but in the Outerlands nonetheless. It is a test, one we must pass if we are to be inducted among the ranks. We are expected to survive, though they don't tell us how. My aunt taught me to build a fire, showed me how to hunt a deer or a rabbit, how to cook them over a spit and eat them. I never managed to kill a deer, or a rabbit—that was all my aunt—but I did start a fire that night."

"What about spices?"

"There are no spices in the Outerlands. I remember my mother packed some pepper, cumin, and olum in case I wanted to make a broth. We save the salt for the spirits."

"The spirits?"

"The Immortal Sons come in different forms," she said gravely. "Not all of them can be *seen*. For the unseen, we keep them away with salt. And for the lords of the spirits, we need cardamom, cubeb seeds, gillyflowers, calamite, and sandalwood. *We* don't have all that, of course. So, be wary."

Amir gulped at the thought of an invisible hunter stalking the wild, watching the rim of the cave at that very moment, waiting for him to step out to take a leak.

"Come morning," Kalay continued, "if we survive the Immortal Sons and the cold, we are honored to continue serving the Mouth. That is what I did. That is what every soldier of the Uyirsena did."

"Doesn't sound too difficult," muttered Amir, voice wavering with dumb courage.

"It was the easiest day of my life."

"And you were nine?"

"Eight, actually." Kalay shrugged. "My father and—although against her wishes—Aunt Madhyra thought I was ready."

Amir rolled his eyes at her showing off, but if anything, he decided he could trust her to keep him alive in the Outerlands.

They ate a little salted bread and kept one eye on the entrance to the cave at all times. Before long, sleep came rushing up on Amir. He clicked his fingers in front of his yawning face and slapped his cheeks to stay awake. Sleep would be the end of him. The darkness, the aloneness, the eerie hisses of the night from outside told him that he was just one step and a moment of carelessness away from being whisked off by an Immortal Son, visible or otherwise.

Yet Appa had escaped them. Appa had eluded them and joined a community. Or, at least, that's what Madhyra had said. At this point, Amir had no reason not to believe it. And if Appa could get through, Amir decided he could at least try.

"One of us must keep watch for a few hours," said Kalay.

"Can't be me," Amir said. "I couldn't stop my weasel of a neighbor from stealing turmeric from my kitchen in the middle of the day. Then, of course, Karim bhai would tell me—"

"Fine. I'll take watch," she interrupted, wanting to shut him up. "The Immortal Son that was tamed by the thronekeeper of Amarohi will have realized our deception by now."

Amir did not need a reminder of the way Kuka had swallowed a serpent in a single gulp while watching Amir like a shopkeeper who suspected a visitor of thievery. If that creature was trailing their footsteps—

Will Karim bhai recognize your bones if they turn up arranged in neat rows outside the fences of Raluha?

For the remainder of the night, he drifted in and out of sleep, his body overcoming his fear and desire to stay awake, and at one point, he was certain that both he and Kalay had slept at the same time, and that when he'd woken, Kalay had too, and both had silently thanked whomever they prayed to at their weakest moments for not having been caught off guard. If this was the case on their first night in the Outerlands, Amir wondered how they would survive ten more.

Ten days of this? He shuddered.

For that was how long Kalay confirmed it was to take to travel from Amarohi to Illindhi. Madhyra had been explicit in scribbling on the back of the map the distance she had traveled on each day. Amir recalled seeing it on the map she had left for Orbalun.

And it will be ten days until Mahrang will send out the Uyirsena. A shudder ran down his spine.

Amir could tell that Kalay was thinking about her aunt. When he would wake every so often, he'd see her simply staring outside at the darkness, as though itching for the first light to appear so they could be on their way to catch Madhyra. When dawn came, she shook him awake, they packed without a word and started out in the still-dark morning, scouring the hill for a more straightforward path, one that would expose them to Kuka if it came flying but would reward them with a smoother trail.

The compass quivered to point them over the hill to the other side, forcing them to trudge up the slope. The dawn fog permeated the underbrush, stretching and swirling with gasps of the wind, adding to the sound of garbling birds. Each harsh step further solidified Amir's decision to battle whatever odds the Outerlands would throw at them. While the fear of Kuka and of the other Immortal Sons sat heavy in his bones, the events of the past few days etched in his memory suppressed that fear. The burden of her passion for change had consumed Madhyra, and now it consumed him as it had once consumed Appa. It was an inheritance that had spanned not only generations but also kingdoms.

There was a lingering sense of inevitability about it all, which both disturbed and fascinated Amir, and he feared discussing it with Kalay.

He remembered the sound of her tears from the previous night. What could he say, even if he had wanted to say something? That family was complicated? That he was sorry it had come to this? That his decision to reject Appa's entreaty in the bazaar that day and chase after his idiotic dream of becoming a Carrier had multiplied over and over until it had inevitably led to this day? That, were he to replay the events of two nights ago, he'd once again, in all probability, end up doing nothing but watching Madhyra escape into the Outerlands to destroy the Spice Gates?

Best stay quiet and march on.

The hill's summit welcomed them with a sheet of cold. From there, Amir basked in the sprawl of forest below, speckled with dew-dappled treetops glinting under the sunlight. In the far distance, he spied a narrow river winding through the forest, all the way from the range to the east, sliding westward. Kalay suggested they follow the river's flow before trotting off downhill to avoid further conversation.

Disappointed, but nevertheless determined to get Kalay to open up, Amir followed.

The forest on the other side of the hill was thicker than the one they had just spilled out of. The trees did not have any names Amir recognized, and they bore no fruits or flowers. Certainly no spices. Their bark was twisted and gnarled, and their branches with spidery leaves spiraled to form hypnotic arches overhead, cutting out what little sunlight breached the leaf cover. The silence here was more pressing, forcing echoes from every twig Amir's foot crunched upon, and a loud plop from every step in a puddle.

At least Kuka can't see you now. Small victories.

Kalay muttered a chant to the Mouth for each branch hacked, an apology for each forbidden step. When she spied a heron, she went chasing after it, leaving Amir to fend for himself. Down the trail, he called her back before stopping to erect a small mound in the middle of the forest. Beside the mound, he scribbled Fylan's name and planted a twig. He stood back, nervous at the presumption. But he knew she wouldn't do it herself. It was a feeling that he thought would fester in the days to come, a feeling that he wanted resolved before they got into the heart of the Outerlands.

He shouldn't have been worried. When she came upon the mound, she stared at it. Unblinking. Defiant. As though the mound and the name of her father beside it stood for the shards broken within her. She had not spoken of her relationship with her father as much as Amir had about his. Vengeance hadn't driven her to chase after Madhyra. Her devotion to the Mouth had. But Amir would be a fool to ignore the role her father had played in her life, and how, even if she wouldn't admit it, hearing about the death of her father had fundamentally changed her relationship with Madhyra. When Madhyra had let Kalay go to serve the Uyirsena, her father had taken over. He—and Mahrang—had forged the armor that Kalay now wore around her, reducing her memories of Madhyra's education to little more than snippets and illusions that surfaced like the recollection of a past life.

And as though in acknowledgment of this, she planted her talwar into the mound and began to pray.

A few minutes into her prayer, Amir advised that the dark soul of the Outerlands was not a place to brood and that the spirit of Fylan would prefer they wriggle out of this forest unscathed, or at least alive.

Kalay did not argue. She muttered a few incomprehensible words, one of which Amir presumed was half-hearted gratitude, and then, grabbing her talwar, she stormed ahead between the trees. Amir stood alone, staring at the mound for a while, transfixed, as if wondering whether Fylan would nibble out of it in some form. But then he heard the eerie scratch of twigs behind him and scrambled to catch up after Kalay.

They found the river by evening. Its wavering surface was broken by deeply planted rocks and boulders, and the vestiges of sunlight shimmered over it as it wound ahead toward the ever-looming mountain. Kalay dipped her feet into the water, then waded in, staring at the shallow bed of colored pebbles and silt along the banks. Amir was startled when he heard her leaping out of the water with a fish caught in her bare hands. By the time the sun went down, they'd erected another fire by the bank, and had laid out their beddings.

The warbling of birds increased, as though restless. Embers sparking out of the fire cast strange shadows of them on the banks, and upon the trees that bordered the clearing. Every shifting shadow seemed to carry in it the ghost of a scream, of Kuka as it descended from the mist-wrapped aranmanai of Amarohi.

They sat awhile, counting the days and taking stock of their food until the starlit sky induced a sleep so deep Amir did not bother blanketing himself before he dozed off.

The third day in the Outerlands was slower. The path around the river was uneven, and often they had to delve back into the forest and find a more accessible trail to keep the water in sight. Come afternoon, Kalay, in her ever-restlessness, halted by the banks. She walked to Amir and pointed at the hilt of the shamshir.

"Unsheathe your weapon."

Amir glanced up. "Whatever for?"

"To prepare you for battling Madhyra. I cannot afford you just standing by and watching when we catch up to her the next time. Or, worse, getting in my way. The next time, we stop her for good. Isn't that why you are here?"

Amir admired Kalay's confidence and certainty in confronting Madhyra. He masked his amusement and nodded, but he'd always held a slender control over his emotions, and Kalay saw through his mask.

"You think this is a joke. But you do not understand what is at stake."

"I do. And I do. You think to make me a warrior in nine days?"

"I plan to make you less a liability, plain and simple. So, for the Mouth's sake shut up and do as I say."

With reluctance, Amir drew the shamshir out and held it in front of him like a piece of firewood about to be tossed aside. "Well, what now?"

Kalay did not smile. "I'm going to teach you some basics."

Amir had taken his embarrassment at trying to duel Madhyra for granted and had stowed the memory away in the back of his head. He had seen Raluhan soldiers and patrollers practicing in the barracks or on the open field on training day, and he'd suffered in the realization that he had enjoyed it. The arcing moves, the clang of steel, the deliberate poise—all of it had a poetry that no words could live up to. And then he'd seen the Uyirsena training. And he'd decided that he'd never want to wield a blade again. The stench of death had filled that cavern, and the dripping drool from the beasts that slumbered in the shadows—spawn of the Immortal Sons—had told him what people who had succumbed to the desire of battle had to undergo.

Amir wanted none of that.

In fact, it had been his only gripe against a life with Ilangovan. A world where violence was the solution was not a world worth building upon, and yet, time and again, the eight kingdoms had defied this basic principle and had made him rethink.

When he had received the shamshir from Mahrang, the reality had hit hard. He wanted to decline it, but it hadn't exactly been an option then. As the days passed, he had pondered putting his foot down, for the blade had been nothing but a burden all along. It was only a small recompense that it was lightweight and barely hurt him as he walked.

When he held it now, though, a strange sensation swooped through him. Not of imagining himself as a warrior, or of the revulsion at what warriors symbolized, but of the comfort in gripping it. It felt somewhat as though here in the Outerlands, he was shedding a different weight to accommodate the burden of the blade.

Five minutes later, after finding himself sprawled on the debris of the bank for the third time in a row, scrambling to pick up the sword once more, he figured his excitement was not only premature but also unwarranted.

He rose a fourth time, and charged, only for Kalay to send him down again.

"You're hasty," she snarled. "What's the rush? I'm not going anywhere. Also, you have a *sword*. It's long. You don't need to run to get me so close. Mostly, though, try to remain standing."

Amir spat out some sand, stood up, and scowled. "*Try to remain standing*, right. I have been doing this all wrong."

She scowled back at him and they were at it again. This time, Amir was slower, more deliberate, and waited for Kalay to make her move.

She approached like a bird swooping down on a worm, feinted left, then right, switched her blade between her hands, and caught him in the hip with the flat side of her talwar. All the while Amir had been rooted like a petrified doll.

He fell, clutching his hip in pain, and screamed at her.

"Would you prefer the sharp part? Again," she persisted.

And again they went. Evening snuck upon them, and clouds gathered where there was once a plain, sunny sky. Somewhere around the tenth or twelfth attempt—Amir lost count—he began to predict Kalay's movements. Not that it was of much significance, since prediction had to be followed by useful action, which Amir, given his nonexistent experience with a sword, was never going to achieve this early in his practice. Instead, he simply raised his shamshir in the direction he speculated Kalay would strike him from. Kalay's eyes widened at the last second as their blades met. The momentum of his parry thrust Amir back just as Kalay lost control of her movement. She quickly regained it, however, swerving and then catching Amir on his other hip with the flat of her blade.

He ought to have been minced like a slab of meat at the butcher's by now, but he managed instead a look of gleeful triumph. He was merely grateful to have parried her blow.

"Well," she said, panting, drawing back the talwar and nodding gravely. "That's an improvement. Though it may have prolonged your life only by a second or two."

"Come on, give me some credit."

"I just did."

Amir's breath came hard but steady, and he knew that part of his endurance was a result of a decade of Carrying. He had strong arms, and his back was thick with corded muscles, whipped into obedience and servitude—all of which drove him toward another stuttering practice duel. This time, Kalay stood warily, five strides from him, her bare feet wet as she tickled the pebbles beneath them. Amir, on the other hand, bled from one toe, and from several cuts around his knee.

He steadied his stance, took a deep breath, gripped the hilt of his shamshir tightly, and with needless courage, beckoned Kalay with a curl of his fingers. Kalay shook her head in amusement, and just as she began to charge, she stopped.

She skidded on the pebbles, her face alight first in wonder, then in horror. She was looking not at Amir but beyond him, above him, far above.

Amir wheeled around as if not of his own accord, and he went numb with fear.

For where there had been just clouds, there was now a shape born of those clouds. Amir could think of nothing but the breaking apart of the sky, the tearing of its hide as though to reveal the flesh within.

And reveal it did. A wing emerged, long and scaly, spanning half his vision—dropping down like an anchor. Then another, its twin, just as long, just as incredible to look at, fell through the crack. They were two daggers and yet they were wings and Amir knew that whatever creature it was attached to was trying to break through its abode in the sky.

It wasn't Kuka. It was an Immortal Son five times as large.

Kalay gripped his arm. She was yanking him away from the banks of the river. Couldn't she just let him stand there? He wanted to watch whatever was coming out of the clouds. Watch whatever was eating away the remnants of sunset until only darkness would remain, and when its hollow soul would tear itself free from the membrane of the skies, it would wreak havoc that Amir would not survive and yet would want to watch, watch, watch . . .

He felt tied to this creature somehow, and in that moment of frozen solitude, the Immortal Son's beating heart echoed in Amir's own frozen one.

The darkness became absolute, as though they were back inside the Whorl. Without realizing it, Amir let himself be dragged away from the banks and into the woods as lightning rippled across the skies. A roar—as loud as a thousand elephants, and as vast as to be heard across the nine kingdoms—shattered the silence of the Outerlands . . . and his very soul.

CHAPTER

22

Vishuman was the first royal child to be born with the spicemark. Needless to say, Maharani Guleba's decision to secretly procreate with a gatecaste was not thought all the way through.

—POSTMAN BOWLER, *WHEN FATE HOLDS A ROSE FOR YOU*

What have you done?" Kalay slapped him. Amir was drenched in sweat. He couldn't say if it was from fear or the humidity. A shadow fell on the forest, and the darkness descended upon them in waves. High above, the flapping of wings was accompanied by a strange smell. The smell, in seconds, came alive as saffron.

An ache of longing burned in his heart.

Home.

The aroma hung in the air, and Amir smelled it like he'd smell Amma's lunch from the corner of their home. A vision of spice jars on a dusty shelf, nearly empty, brooding, awaiting the next ration for the Bowl, hungry mouths desiring the allure of saffron. And in the midst of it all, Amma, with her ceaseless quest for abstinence and saving spices until the perfect meal—a meal that would drag every bowler from their wretched corners to their doorstep. A meal that would end with a rasmalai garnished with almonds that Amir would have stolen from the bazaar.

A second roar wrenched Amir from his reverie, and the sweat burned in the imprint of the slap he had just received.

What is happening? What is happening to you?

"I didn't do anything," he said, pushing himself away from Kalay, his heart hammering, his stomach flickering in desire of what he'd left behind. The essence of saffron was so strong, he knew he could kill any-one for a taste of a dish with saffron in it. Was this what it meant to be obsessed with spice? He had thought himself impervious to that feeling. And yet, here in the Outerlands, so far from home, its taste engulfed him.

Amir and Kalay fumbled their way in the wood's darkness to the base of a mound gnarled with creepers. An opening fed into a small space, where Kalay lit a fire. The warmth oozed into Amir's skin, feeding the sweat.

"That," Kalay said, "is one of the older Immortal Sons that patrols the Outerlands, but always close to the Mouth. Close to Illindhi. In our ancient tongue, we call it Kishkinda. It does the bidding of the Mouth and the Mouth alone." She whipped out her talwar and flashed it against Amir's neck. "Tell me the truth."

Amir blinked. "Tell you what?"

"Why you are truly here. The Mouth wouldn't send an Immortal Son so far from its den unless one of our intentions was ill. And it is certainly not mine. What have you not told me?"

Amir's hand shot for his own sword. Kalay calmly watched him. "I will kill you in a heartbeat, Amir. Please, don't take me for a fool. You say you're here because the Mouth threatened you. But I am finding that increasingly hard to believe."

The sound of the river beyond the thickets where they hid drowned the reluctance in Amir's mind. Moonlight spattered on the underbrush, and in its twisted light and in the light of the small fire that burned beneath the mound, Kalay appeared like a reckoning. She was calm, and it terrified Amir. Slowly, he drew his hand away from his shamshir.

Kalay glanced through the treetops at the moving shadows in the skies before fixing her gaze again on Amir. Gates, he knew this conversation would be inevitable. He knew the moment would come when he'd regret rescuing Kalay from Mesht.

She rescued you, in the end.

"It looks like the threat of death at the hands of the Uyirsena has not deterred you," she said. "But I don't know what your intention is. You once wanted the Poison. If that is what you still seek, I will give it to you. Consider it a token of gratitude for getting me out of the kingdom of Mesht. Go back to your lands and let me do my duty."

Amir shook his head. "I don't want the Poison anymore."

"Then I ask again: Why are you here?"

Amir leaned out of the mound and gazed up through the treetops in imitation of Kalay. A gush of air spiraled down, shaking the leaves and choking the branches. A second later, Amir heard the long beat of the wings, a hollow rumble that whipped overhead.

"You've gotten bold, I'll give you that," Kalay said.

"I'm not bold," Amir said, still not taking his eyes off the treetops. "I'm terrified. Just as I was before. This is not what I'd expected."

"Yet you care less about stopping Madhyra. No, do not deny it. You stopped me from killing her on the ship. You let her get away in Jhanak, and then in Talashshukh. Despite all that, I gave you one last chance. I tried to teach you to fight, but I can tell your heart is not in it. I can tell that if Madhyra stands before you, you will step aside once more. So, give me one good reason why I should continue trusting you instead of dropping your corpse over here and continuing on my way."

Not precisely the best conversation to have, huddled beneath a mound on opposite sides of a fire. She was speaking of killing him as plainly as if discussing what to have for dinner that night.

"You won't," he said plainly. "Because your own heart is not in it." Kalay began to protest, but Amir raised his hand to stop her. "If it were, you wouldn't have bothered saving me from the ivory traders. You wouldn't have flinched when Rani Kaivalya offered her hand to you while ignoring me. Don't think I didn't notice that."

"Because I am still wrapping my head around how an entire civilization can so grossly misinterpret the scriptures, it does not mean I want the Gates destroyed."

"Are they truly misinterpreting them?" It was the first time Amir had the nerve to question the Mouth in front of Kalay. She opened her mouth and closed it again, as though the thought had plagued her too. Or perhaps she had, possibly subconsciously, avoided thinking about it.

"You wouldn't understand," he said finally, when words failed her. "I thought you would, at one point. But after Jhanak, I realized what gatecaste amount to in the eyes of the rest of the world, even—perhaps, especially—those of Illindhi. We are tools, to whet your crazy appetites, to keep your precious scriptures sanctified, and nothing more."

"*I* wouldn't understand?" Kalay sounded incredulous. "Any other acolyte or soldier of the Uyirsena would have slit your throat by now. I forgave your mistakes. I made myself patient over the last few days, knowing what was at stake. Knowing you wished to run away from your duty as a Carrier. Knowing you despise the very Mouth that has given you your powers, and to whom I have promised my service and my life."

"You make it seem as if I should be grateful for this power."

"You should be!"

"Your god has left me *cursed*."

Kalay was outraged. "You bear a gift many in Illindhi would kill to possess."

Amir chuckled, then laughed a little louder. He doubted Kalay saw the audacity of her statement. He said, "You can have it! Take it from me, if such an act is possible. I didn't ask to be able to travel through the Spice Gates, nor do I particularly enjoy it, nor—I would wager—does any Carrier. I don't understand why you want this 'gift' anyway. You have caverns full of the Poison in Illindhi. It is painless passage, isn't it? Using the Poison. Neither is it considered *impure*, whatever that means. So spare me these convoluted appeals."

Amir's immediate abnegation appeared to have wounded Kalay. *It is not the pain that she considers, but the fact that* you *were chosen by the*

Mouth. She was agape, as though the meaning of his words had not sunk in fully. She lowered her eyes in contemplation, gaze darting across the forest floor. Slowly, she said, "You need to know what is at stake here."

"I know what's at stake for me, for every gatecaste man, woman, and child across the eight kingdoms. But you don't seem to think that matters much. So go on, tell me, student of Madhyra, Fylan, and Mahrang. Are the stakes simply preserving the great Spice Trade?"

Kalay took a deep breath and ignored his taunts as she spoke. "In the beginning, yes, the Spice Trade was the key to my mission. In the caverns of Ilom, we do not just wield talwars and raise war cries and offer prayers. Gates know, enough people in Illindhi believe that. No. We also learn. The Mouth teaches us the lay of the land, the rules of the nine kingdoms, the sacred duty bestowed upon Illindhi, and how things must be structured for a future to be sustained. The priests in whom the Mouth has instilled the scriptures, the thronekeepers and the warriors who maintain order and equity, the merchants who conduct the Spice Trade, and the velayas who perform the menial tasks. And finally, you—whose duty is to traverse the Spice Gates, the child of the Mouth, the one who has been gifted to see the eight kingdoms while the others must remain confined to where they were born." Amir winced at his implied relationship to the Mouth. Kalay did not notice. "The Mouth deemed these social functions necessary for civilization to flourish. So yes, Amir—the Spice Trade does concern me. But more so than the trade—do you really think there was a world that existed before the Gates? Every part of the realm you see around the nine kingdoms—the balance, the peace, a continuation of life unhindered by corruption—everything is because the Mouth deemed it so. It was creation, and it will be the end. They *are* life, Amir of Raluha. Our philosophies, our education, our values—they all stem from the Mouth. It is not merely a vehicle to carry our prayers and provide blessings at its will. It has always been more; it is the thread that runs across the tapestry that sprawls through the nine kingdoms."

How was she evading the truth? Amir did not give in. "When a million people decide those values and philosophies must include my suffering, then I'm sorry, I do not think it is a case of *misinterpretation*. You saw the Black Coves. You heard the royals in the court of Rani Zariba speak. You saw the city beneath the city of Talashshukh. You heard the ivory traders forbidding me from entering the temple of the Mouth. Do you think they are all misinformed? That eight kingdoms are suffering from some collective delusion?"

Kalay picked up a pebble and stared at its surface. A moment later, she hurled it out of their little cave. It bounced once before rolling beneath a leaf. Her mind seemed washed of the teachings she'd once harbored during the hours she had spent with Madhyra in Illindhi. Here, now, she was purely the acolyte, raised by Mahrang, outsider to the lives of the normal people of the kingdoms.

"Everyone talks about peace, balance, equality," Amir said. "But you know what? I don't see any of it. So spare me your twisted theories of how the Spice Gates have maintained balance and avoided war. It's what the abovefolk like you tell yourself to get a good night's sleep."

Kalay clenched her fists. "That doesn't mean you deny your duty."

Amir laughed. "I have done nothing *but* my duty. I have shown up at the Gates every single day, with a sack on my back, and gone where I was asked to and come back with yet another sack on my back. Where is my due? Where is the Bowl's due? Why does my family get ostracized? Why do we not get the same spices that I work so hard to carry everywhere? Why is my allowance lower than the allowance of a merchant in the bazaar? Why can we not bathe in the public baths? Why are we not allowed to rub shoulders with the abovefolk? Why is our very skin considered polluted? Why must we clean your toilets and wash your shit with our bare hands if we've done our duties? Show me where is the equality and balance you claim."

Kalay looked away and stared into the fire before muttering something incomprehensible. When Amir leaned forward to listen better, she raised her voice to a whisper. "You carry the sins of your previous birth."

"Ha!" Amir clapped his hands. "I can tell from your voice that even you do not fully believe those words. Gah! Born into the gatecaste if I was a sinner in my previous life. Do you even hear yourself? And if it *is* indeed true, you just called being a Carrier a *gift* that you would kill to possess." He shook his head. "I can't bring myself to believe in scriptures that are full of such contradictions."

"Don't you dare insult the scriptures!" Kalay said, her voice rising. She glared at him from across the fire.

"Why not? What do I have to lose? My life? You'd take that anyway. Besides, I don't even know why you've kept me alive these last three days in the Outerlands. I got you out of Mesht; you ought to have just disposed of me once we passed the fences of Amarohi. Even now, knowing the Mouth is sending its Immortal Sons after us, you have not yet killed me. Because I can see how this has all been very bothersome for you. Don't tell me it's gratitude. In the face of the Spice Gates being brought to rubble, what's my little act of rowing a gondola to give you a vial of the Poison? No, Kalay, your hypocrisy is glaring."

She looked at him, agape at his venom.

He was breathing hard, he realized. Softening his tone, he asked, "Do you think we bowlers have not been discriminated against because we're gatecaste?"

Kalay was clearly uncomfortable with the direction this conversation was heading. Cautiously, she delivered each word like they were conceived during the act of speaking, "No, that is not what I think. But breaking the Spice Gates cannot be the solution. You are jeopardizing the lives of millions of people. *Millions*. This is not about you or me, or our beliefs and our problems and our castes. The Mouth reigns over nine kingdoms and all its peoples. Tell me how the Raluhans will react when they wake up one morning and discover that they are never going to get ginger in their tea again."

"Sounds like a regular day in the Bowl," Amir muttered.

"I was giving an example." Kalay grew steadily impatient. "It's more than just ginger, though, isn't it? Lives are dependent on the Spice Trade. And when you deny a livelihood to people, they will rise to rebel. They will crumble as a civilization."

"You don't know that," said Amir. "Besides, what *is* the solution? What can you say or do that will promise us the life we bowlers deserve to live? None of them were clearly happy with the idea of the Black Coves."

"I-I don't know."

Amir pointed a finger at her. "That's right—you don't. Nobody does, or even wants to find out. Things are just perfect the way they are. Carriers trudge through the trail, bringing you your heart's desires. There's never going to be a solution unless we snatch it out from where they cannot be otherwise found. The thronekeepers and their ministers have the perfect story—that there is no life outside the fences and the kingdoms. The Outerlands cannot be entered or crossed. For there is death. There are the Immortal Sons that prowl the wilderness, and there is a Whorl around the sea of Jhanak, impenetrable marshland around Mesht, and deep, black bogs beyond Kalanadi."

"They're not wrong," Kalay protested.

Amir inhaled sharply. "No, they are not, but that is precisely more evidence that the Mouth *wants* things to be the way they have always been. By placing the Immortal Sons in the Outerlands, it has ensured its so-called *children* will always remain ostracized in the eight kingdoms. To me, the Mouth is no different from the abovefolk.

"However, it has failed to account for one thing—our ability to imagine a new life. My father did it. He crossed the fences into the Outerlands and became a part of a community. He was not the first. He won't be the last. He proved the thronekeepers wrong. And if that is not example enough, you can always look closer to home."

Kalay ignored the last part. "So *that's* why you're here. You wish to find your father."

Amir chuckled, surprised at how quickly the pain of knowing his father's story had diminished, to be replaced by something purer, something that he could hold on to for the rest of his life. "My father died trying to get Madhyra through the Outerlands. And you know what? It was probably his bravest act in life."

Here was, Amir imagined, something he shared with Kalay. Two people, wandering the Outerlands, carrying the faint whispers of their fathers. He had restrained himself from building a mound for his father beside Fylan's. He had to know. Kalay looked apologetic, as though she had not expected this commonality.

She dropped her talwar, clutched the sides of her head, and shut her eyes. "I am sorry about your father, but you must realize that this is the consequence of this madness that has consumed you, as it has consumed my aunt."

"I am here because the Mouth has forced me to chase after Madhyra and stop her. Even here, in the place I imagine my people could live freely, I am enslaved to your god."

"Gates, you're impossible," cried Kalay. "At one point, I hoped you would see how not stopping her would bring the Uyirsena down upon your people. I had hoped you had rescued me from Mesht for that reason. Now . . ." She sounded exasperated, and yet, so close to following through on the threat hanging from her lips. "I don't know why I let you come with me."

Amir saw her eye the talwar. She would pick it up, and nothing he could do or say would dissuade her. Perhaps he ought to have created a mound for himself beside Fylan's.

The following moment, however, she sighed, crawled out of their hole, and stormed away.

"Where are you going?" Amir called out.

"I need some air," Kalay shouted back. "Good riddance to you if the Immortal Sons take me out."

Amir rested against a branch that wound like a vein within the mound. His head hurt. He missed Amma. While in any of the eight kingdoms on duty, Amir knew he was always a sprinkle of spice and a leap into the veil away from returning home. But here, in the Outerlands, he was suddenly farther from home than he'd ever been. He felt younger. Unprepared. Alone. Karim bhai had crossed the Whorl and into an unknown realm; Kabir was on the spice trail, carrying crates of perfumes; and Amma, back in Raluha, was about to nurse a newborn. From an unknown father. How would she take it if she knew Appa had tried to return but couldn't? That he had died only a fortnight ago at the hands of a beast like the one that circled the skies?

Gates, his head *hurt*.

And the more the pain seeped in, the more determined he was. The Mouth be cursed, the Bowl had had enough. At one point, he admitted, he did think about what Kalay had said. Destroying the Spice Gates would mean stopping forever the flow of goods from one kingdom to another. The Spice Trade would collapse. There would be no spices except those that were produced in their own respective kingdoms. Was that even fair? Until then, he had thought of nobody but himself and the Bowl all this while. But then he had realized with a stab in his heart—that not all the abovefolk deserved what Madhyra would be imposing on them. Not all of them were like Hasmin, even if a lot of them were. There were folks like Harini, people who strove to build a better life for the bowlers but had always been outmatched, outmaneuvered by those who swore by the scriptures.

By merely standing by and letting Madhyra go, Amir would be snatching the turmeric out of people's milk, cloves from their teeth, ginger from their teas, and pepper from their salves. He imagined a plate of biryani without nutmeg and mace, and even the mere thought of it had sent a rush of bile up his throat. Disgusting! He had to think beyond food, but he hadn't been able to, not then.

The thought now gleamed around him like spilled milk. Harini had been ready. She was prepared to break the world. Worry about the consequences later.

Perhaps Amir could too. In his own way. By resisting the Mouth. By not moving forward after Madhyra but returning to the eight kingdoms. Madhyra would succeed; he had to believe in it. And if—when—she did, nothing else would matter. Not the Mouth, not the Immortal Sons. Not the Uyirsena setting off for their sacred cleansing.

Your bones wish for you to wait. Gates, he was exhausted.

He didn't realize when he fell asleep. The fear of the Immortal Sons—Kishkinda and Kuka—seeped into his flesh, weakening him.

When he woke up, the cold gnawed at his skin. He couldn't say for how long he'd slept, but the edges of the first light crept beneath the tree-tops. He'd slept through the night. Of Kalay, there was no sign. Had she been away all night?

A good time to leave.

He scrambled to pack up his belongings. The fire had died out. He picked up Mahrang's shamshir and crawled out of the hole.

No sooner had he stepped out than Kalay returned. Frantic. *Terrified.* A gust of air followed in her wake, leaves billowing in the wind, clinging to her like she were a pillar on which ivy grew.

"We need to move," she said as she broke into the mound. She kicked the last embers of the fire and placed a roof of leaves to tunnel the smoke. "We made a mistake with the fire. Kishkinda smelled it. It knows we're camped here."

"But how will it—"

The answer came to Amir almost immediately. Following the harsh blowing of the wind, as Amir got to his feet, all at once, a hundred birds shot out of the forest, bursting through the treetops in a cacophonous tumble. They circled the sky over the canopy before swirling around and flying away in the direction of the river.

"Come on," Kalay urged. "We need to get to the river."

Amir wanted to turn around. Leave.

"What? That doesn't make sense. We should stay hidden."

Kalay shook her head, sounding fearful for the first time. "Not unless you wish to be burned to death. We need to be in the open, preferably closer to water."

Amir did not understand what she meant. He glanced back—at the way they had come—but if she was right, then the river was a better option than being charred to death. A double-back could be done later. Quietly, he followed her, engulfed in the rage of the storm. Each moment, the cold deepened, and the leaves continued to billow in the wind, and soon the air was full—an endless swirl of dust, and pebble, and leaf, all of it ensconced in a breeze that smelled starkly of saffron.

Home.

When they breached the tree line and emerged onto the banks, Amir was at first glad to not see any sign of the Immortal Son. There was no sign of daylight, yet he knew that if this had been a normal day, the sun would have risen by now. His eyes were glued to the skies. Far upriver, where the forest was still an infant and the mountains to the east were a scratch mark on the horizon, the skies had turned a shocking gray. They bordered on black, boils of lightning cracking within, sending slivers of white scars across the clouds.

The storm approached with a frightening pace the part of the river where Amir and Kalay had emerged. And within that storm, the Immortal Son, Kishkinda, was cocooned.

The forest and riverbank became a shade darker in a matter of seconds, as though dawn had decided to sleep a while longer and return night to its post. It began to drizzle.

At the same time, a hollow, eerie wind blew toward the river—an echo of a soundless kill or the silent scream of the dead—and it was carrying in its wake a cloud of mud and dust and all the detritus of dropped leaves and scrunched twigs and pebbles that scarred the face and bit the eyes.

The wind blasted against Amir and Kalay. Amir lost his footing. He found the instinct to dig his feet into the wet riverbank and covered his eyes with his wrist. Kalay was already employing a similar strategy. It felt like standing on the edge of the mountain of Illindhi. Such was the wind's ferocity that, before long, Amir was being pushed back toward the river.

From the corner of his eye, Amir glimpsed a great cyclone upon the river, approaching from the east, so close now he could taste the acidic wetness of it, the jolting embrace of the air as it attempted to lift him up into its vortex of cloud and rain and pungent air and the stoppage of time.

Kalay, behind him, was shouting, but Amir barely heard her. Words had lost meaning. How long ago was their training duel? His bag began to slip off his shoulder. He tried to pull it back up over his arm. It slipped again. He gritted his teeth and closed his fist over the strap and held on.

A hand fell on his shoulder. Soft, pebbled, and sandy. Kalay. She grabbed a fistful of his tunic.

The next second he was yanked back. The forest detached from his vision.

His feet left the banks. The Immortal Son swooping down from the east joined with the storm. Amir found himself blown into the river. When he hit the water, the coldness of it crushed him numb. It clogged every pore of his body and froze his muscles. Surely, death was but a few breaths away. But the constant movement, the tumbling underwater, the scrapes and cracks as he brushed against the riverbed as he was being drawn farther down the current kept him from focusing on any one sensation.

When he resurfaced, it was for half a second, and he faced not the river current churning downhill but the wall of lightning-cracked storm that had caught up to them from uphill. He was moving downriver at a blistering pace, the forest falling behind as though he were riding on the back of a very fast wagon. The sky had all but blackened, and Amir's vision beheld nothing but the dazzling spire of wind and dust and death, with those sinewy scars of white light that broke the sky every few seconds. He frantically pulled himself up, but the river was neither letting him drown nor giving him the weight he needed to float. He flailed, submerged, rose up again. The river meandered and fell, and from the corner of his eye, he glimpsed Kalay's bobbing head drifting farther away from him downriver.

The Immortal Son was upon him now, and the darkness was absolute. Through the lightning-embattled storm, the two wings jutted out, streaks of crimson slashed across a tormented sky. Scaly, with gleaming ruby cabochons embedded in its flesh that pulsated with each breath of the storm. If the creature had a head, it was within the embroidered wall of the typhoon, and when Kishkinda roared, its voice broke out of the storm in a vibrating crescendo, casting the river into a tumult.

Amir wanted to control the direction in which he sailed, but the pull of the current was too strong. Water crushed him each time it nudged him toward the banks. Overhead, he saw into the eye of the winged storm, a canvas of treacherous beauty, shades of black scratched on the sky, torn and wrinkled, and air swirling beneath it in a tempest of dust.

The Immortal Son smelled of ash and leaf and saffron.

"Watch out!" he heard Kalay yell before her voice was garbled underwater.

He tried to turn around, but the force of the current and the storm overhead were in complete control of his body.

And so Amir stayed just the way he was when the falls arrived.

His back broke free of the embrace of the river, his legs shot out of the water, and his head, drenched and cold, swiveled upward to gaze right into the storm's heart as he plummeted.

Later, Kalay would say that the drop was fifty feet, but he swore it was much more in that instant. He flailed and flailed until he lost the sense of his own body. When he crashed back into the water, deep deep deep, his breath was sucked out in one fell swoop, and he thought he would never resurface. Down was the only way. His vision dimmed, and for a moment he wondered what it would be to perish in these distant Outerlands, away from everything he knew and called his world, body rotting away and nibbled at by sea carps and mrigals until his remains floated away weeks from now, to be forgotten.

A second later, his back hit hard against the river's floor and he flailed upward in a desperate bid to come up for air. Water choked his lungs and pulled him down and pressed his head. Rain penetrated the surface and attacked him like cold needles.

Standing on the cliff overlooking Jhanak three nights ago, staring at the violent waves and the boats rocking and tethered to their moors, Amir had considered himself fortunate to be among the few bowlers who'd been taught to swim. Appa had been relentless, unforgiving. And when Amma had asked him why, Appa's answer had been simple and prescient—you never know.

Amir pushed the water down and thrust himself up. When he breached the surface, he found Kalay flailing a few feet away. He swam through the current—now gentler, although the Immortal Son persisted above them like a cruel jester, bent on a sadistic end, clinging to the storm as though chained.

Heading underwater once more, Amir wriggled into the gap between Kalay's arm and body and used his strength to push her up. Then, flattening himself as best he could, he began to swim toward the shore.

When his feet touched the bottom of the river, relief flooded through him.

Amir's eyes cleared. The storm had not crossed the waterfall, as if jurisdictionally bound. The Immortal Son was turning around, its wings folding back into the typhoon that dissolved into the rain. The saffron-pinched grayness of dawn dimmed, the scent and memory of home dissipating like dew, and before Amir could take a deep breath, Kishkinda had retreated fully.

Amir coughed and turned around to pick Kalay up, but her eyes were already wide, and she had her talwar out.

The river had dropped from the precipice into a cove of sorts, which opened up into the sea. The sea, though, was not really a sea but a shallow, watery bed of floating wood—a wreckage of a thousand ships accumulated along the coast and as far as the eye could see. The ship closest to them had been cleaved neatly in half as it lay scattered against a bulwark of rocks around the opposite coast. Its wooden remains floated on the river, drifting slowly toward the open ocean.

And on the coast, jumping and waving his hands frantically at Amir, his beard scraggly and unkempt, was Karim bhai.

CHAPTER
23

Besides spices, turquoise, lace, and knickknacks, the Carnelian
Caravan also ferries letters of love between strange encounters.
What food cannot satiate, poems can.

—MUKHTIVEER, *ALONE BY THE WINDOW*

The wreckage sprawled beyond the cove. The trees along the coast swayed against the last vestiges of the storm that had finally given up on destroying Amir and Kalay. It had reduced itself to a gentle morning breeze. Gulls circled over the wooden entrails of the ships, squawking at the jetsam floating around them.

Karim bhai stood beside Amir, one hand on his shoulder, the other juggling a pod of cardamom. A towel lay wrapped around his head and his lungi was torn on one side, exposing gashes on his thigh. He smelled of burned food and cabbage kept out for too long. Yet his raucous laughter rang high into the air.

"You stole Madhyra's map," Amir complained after a moment. "Ilangovan told you about the Whorl, didn't he?"

Amir spied the others from the ship of the Condemned that had set sail from Jhanak three days ago. Sekaran, still dazed, was nursing a wound on his arm. Most of the sanders appeared to have survived the shipwreck as well, and they presently surrounded the bony form of

Ilangovan. The Blessed One looked battered and beaten, as though his body had been used as a board for washing all the clothes in the Bowl. But there was a childish animation to his face as he spoke to his companions, his eyes wandering the breadth of the Outerlands, regarding each leaf, each branch, and each pool of water in fascination, his former reality dwindling in the presence of this strange un-dream. Amir had always regarded Ilangovan as a man of legend and myth, something to be admired and regarded from a distance. Now he looked more like a weak henchman of his own personality. Amir liked him all the more for it.

They all stood huddled beside a now-smothered fire on the coast of the cove, their eyes still on the retreating storm and whatever had throbbed within it.

"The Whorl," Karim bhai announced to a stunned Amir and Kalay, "is a lie. And I stand corrected. Doesn't happen often, ho?"

Kalay had taken a few steps back, her eyes calculating, developing a frown and then settling on something akin to confusion and disbelief. Amir did not engage her.

Karim bhai pointed to the collection of driftwood he had accumulated on the sands. Planks of wood, marble statuettes, a broken chair, a hairy toy, rosewood-inlaid boxes, and jars ideal for housing spice.

Amir whipped Karim bhai around. "There are thousands who have witnessed ships getting sucked into the Whorl from afar. How did you survive?"

Karim bhai ruffled Amir's hair and gave a low sigh. "There is indeed a whirlpool in the ocean around Jhanak, pulla. But to overcome it does not take the mighty power of the Mouth. All it needs is a few good sailors."

And Karim bhai had been sent out with a fair share of them.

"The Condemned do not die in the Whorl," Karim bhai continued, pushing past Amir and Kalay. "At least, not most of them. It is not difficult to cross the Whorl. The death, it would appear, comes after it." He trudged barefoot on the sand, until the grass of the new forest began to grow, leading into a dense copse of trees. From there spread a wider jungle, whose end was yet again far beyond the inkling of Amir's mind. He merely assumed it went a long way. But where the previous forest and its breezes smelled of saffron, here there was a dense aroma of cardamom.

"Where?" asked Amir, already wary of what he knew accompanied the smell of a spice in the Outerlands.

"Come along," Karim bhai said. Kalay followed them like a weak dawn shadow. She did not pretend expertise anymore. Reality was collapsing into her, Amir imagined, and it was not a sight he wished for anyone to endure, to watch someone question their life's beliefs.

All the ships had ended up broken once they had crossed the Whorl, floating in disparate remains on the sea. How *had* Karim bhai survived?

Halfway through the trail into the forest, Amir glimpsed the first bones.

Ah, the answer to life must always rest in death.

Unlike the bones in the cave on his first night in the forest with Kalay, these were unmistakably human. Bile rose up in Amir's chest at the sight of vacant skulls—pale and glossy, coated in leaves and mud, the hollowness staring back at him. They lay strewn on the forest floor. Tatters of clothes spread over ossified limbs.

Human clothes. Human limbs. Is one of them Appa's?

Karim bhai shook his head as though he had read Amir's mind. He did not know, Amir realized. "A little farther."

The trees thickened and then began thinning out. Water continued to drip from the treetops with the remains of the storm. Karim bhai led them down a trail and into a wide opening. There he splayed his hands and stopped just short of saying, *Behold!*

Amir's heart crashed to a halt at the sight in front of him.

"Ammadi!" gasped Kalay, and went to her knees, then kissed the earth, her face strewn with tears.

Spanning the length of the clearing and lying slain on the ground was the largest creature Amir had ever laid eyes on. In fact, Amir wagered it was nearly as long as Kishkinda. This slain one, however, did not sprout wings. It was long, scaly, and sinuous like a serpent, its corpse weaving around the clearing, its tail disappearing into the wilderness.

This is what Appa killed. And was killed by. An exchange of lives. The Mouth's retribution for fighting against its order.

"Must be as large as twelve elephants stitched together," said Amir. The creature's hideous scales were bruised and clawed, its blood long dried. Its body curled around the trees at the periphery, and the ground it was on was charred and cracked, as though someone had set a night's long fire on everything that had grown upon it. The beast's face was buried under one of its limbs, and Amir spotted only a curved horn jutting out of the forehead—emerald once upon a time, he imagined— not unlike the ruby cabochons on the Immortal Son trapped within the storm. The horn was now reduced to something scourged and poisoned. No more gleaming, but dry like a dust-cloaked relic.

Amir glanced at Karim bhai, eyes wide.

"Don't look at me." Karim bhai raised his hands in defense. "It was dead when we got here. Probably why we survived in the first place, if you ask me."

THINGS BEGAN TO FALL INTO PLACE ONCE KARIM BHAI STOKED A fire into life. Amir was curious to meet Ilangovan, but first, he had to contend with Sekaran.

"Why is it that where there's trouble, there's you?" Sekaran grunted, adjusting the shawl around his neck and seating himself on a plank of wood carved out of one of the ships. Amir sensed Sekaran considered himself fortunate for having survived the Whorl, but he was still digesting the reality of the Outerlands, and that he was now a part of it, so far from the Black Coves. It was enough to even reduce the thuglike Sekaran into a mouse, timid and anxious, eyes ever flitting in suspicion. Amir did not blame him. It was life as they'd never known or expected it. They'd been sent to their deaths, and instead had been presented with a reality they'd been told was a myth. Which was worse?

Most of the surviving Condemned remained wary of Kalay. A few still recalled her assault on their numbers in the Black Coves. She'd dropped them like swatted mosquitoes. And then they'd seen her fight on the ship, strike down the Haldiveer, and hold a sword to the woman who had abducted the Blessed One. They knew what she was capable of, and in these Outerlands, she appeared both a blessing and a curse. She smiled at them, even winked at a few as if in mockery.

Ilangovan continued to converse with the other gatecaste. Their whispers told Amir that many wanted to return to the Black Coves, now that they knew the Whorl could be crossed. They had families back in the isles, people who would now be at Rani Zariba's mercy.

"We'll leave nobody behind," Ilangovan assured them. His voice had a glassy, scratchy quality to it. "Sekaran will lead the efforts. Kumbha, Chameli, Bhairavi—you will go with him. But first, we need to rebuild the ship."

"You're putting a lot of hope into the possibility of joining hands with the local community here," said Sekaran. Ilangovan's jaw slackened. Amir's heart skipped a beat at the cadence of those words. *A local community.*

"This place . . . it does not make sense, Blessed One," one of them said.

"It is a nightmare," agreed another. "A spiceless one, no less."

"We must all return to the Black Coves."

Ilangovan nodded, listening to several of them voice their concern. He bit his lip while the complaints and fears poured forth. Then he replied, "This *is* the Black Coves. What we lived in before was an illusion of it. It demanded violence, and we gave it like an offering to the Mouth. Here, this place demands perseverance. A more noble offering."

He lit up a beedi and began to smoke it. Sekaran snatched it from him and smoked it himself. "You're being reckless, Inga." Wisps emerged from his mouth as sunlight angled against his rugged face. "Remember Girima? The coup she attempted to stage when she discovered the Isles for herself? This smells like nothing different. We would be invaders in this strange land; to tame this wild—it is not right. It is not our home."

Amir had not yet fully assimilated the sight of the slain beast in the clearing. Even now, his curious nose could smell the dying flesh beneath the monster's hide and the essence of elaichi oozing out of its skin. He avoided looking into Kalay's eyes. She had retreated to the shadows of the forest, where she lay with her hands wrapped around her knees, deep in contemplation. Seeing the slain Immortal Son had shaken something he'd assumed was unbreakable within her. It was, Amir conjectured, the first sight of the new world Madhyra had promised, and which Kalay had striven to prevent from coming into existence.

"Then, it is simple," said Ilangovan, stealing back the beedi from Sekaran. "We will not be leaders here. We will be what the people of this land want us to be. If there are gatecaste among them, our voices will be heard."

"There are," said Amir, speaking for the first time in the presence of Ilangovan. "My father was one of them."

Karim bhai frowned. "Arsalan died ten years ago, pulla. I picked up his bones at the fences. What are you saying?"

Better late than never. A sharp intake of breath, and Amir watched Karim bhai hold his own. "No, bhai," he began softly. "Appa survived. He lived in these parts of the Outerlands for over ten years, with others from the different kingdoms who had sought a similar life. They could not return because the Immortal Sons prevented them from returning. The serpent you saw slain in the forest—Appa killed it. It was how Madhyra was able to cross over. It was how you survived the Whorl."

While murmurs sparked among the gatecaste, Ilangovan seemed to be mulling over a thought. From the corner of his eye, Amir noticed Kalay listening in on him from afar.

Karim bhai was up on his feet. There was a knowing look in his eye. It was a look of someone with whom you shared secrets. Who understood your minute expressions, the shape of your shoulders and the way the air curled around them. In that instant, Amir knew that Karim bhai knew Appa was dead. He did not say it out loud, nor did he mourn the loss of his old friend, for his own grief had been exhausted as Amir's had. It was a death that had run its course through the Bowl, in the hearts of those who knew Arsalan.

"You know this woman, then." Ilangovan spoke with the beedi in his mouth, and each syllable pushed a wisp of smoke from his mouth.

Amir gave a faint nod, but before he could say more, Kalay's hand was on his shoulder. She dragged him aside, away from the others.

When they were out of earshot, she pushed him against the bark of a tree. "We must get going," she said. "We are wasting time."

"Then go," Amir said. "Look around you. These are my people. You heard Ilangovan. This is the Black Coves now. You don't need me, anyway, do you? You remember the map; go after her if you have the heart to. Kill her if you must, though I doubt you are capable of such an act."

Kalay remained impervious to his tirade. "It does not matter what I am capable of. If you cared about these people, then you would come with me. Every second you remain here—with them—you risk the Mouth sending more of the Immortal Sons."

Amir had not considered that. Along the coast, Karim bhai, Ilangovan, Sekaran, and the others spared a weak glance for him. Was their survival to be undone because Amir had decided to abandon the duty the Mouth had imposed upon him?

"Why do you care?" he asked Kalay. "You have, until now, shown no conscience toward my life, or to those in the eight kingdoms, as long as your precious secret of Illindhi was safe. You are an assassin, bred in an army that conducts genocide on a whim. Why do you suddenly care? I must know."

Kalay sniffed. "Because I would like to see you alive at the end of this."

Amir blinked.

"You're a sore pain, Amir of Raluha, but I cannot deny that you're a man who has been wronged by this world. I do not agree with your solutions, neither will I hesitate to kill my aunt for the sake of preserving the Spice Gates—as you think I will—but I would like to keep you alive if I can. You have shown me much that I was ignorant of, and much more that has gladdened my heart. You may think me heartless, but I am truly grateful to you for the last few days. And if they're your people"—she nodded at the cluster gathered around Ilangovan and Karim bhai—"then perhaps I would like to see them live too. You would be doing them no favors by remaining here. I have seen your heart, and I know what thoughts course through your blood, so make no mistake—the Mouth *will* rally its defenses, and I am one of them. Just . . . *live*. And do not get in my way again."

Amir did not know why he was smiling. She had once again sworn to kill Madhyra and keep the Mouth alive, but he was still smiling. Gates, but it felt good to talk to the real Kalay, Madhyra's niece, and not the wooden doll from the Uyirsena.

He agreed. "It will be dark soon. We will leave tomorrow at first light. Let me say my goodbyes."

That night, Amir offered to share the remainder of his theplas with Karim bhai and the others. They had departed from Jhanak, tied to their fates with only biscuits in a tin can. There had been no need for reserves at the cusp of imminent death. However, once they had crossed the Whorl, the biscuits were gone within hours. They had mixed sawdust with rat droppings and had chewed on the leather of the yardarms of their ships with rattling teeth, fearing scurvy with every cresting wave.

Which meant the simple theplas Amir and Kalay had brought from Jhanak—which could last a whole fortnight—were a divine feast.

They munched in silence, until Karim bhai could hold it in no longer. "I cannot believe that was an Immortal Son, ho."

Some of the gatecaste shuddered at the word, and Amir knew better than to try to assuage their fears. The truth was, he was just as terrified. Escaping from one Immortal Son and finding another dead certainly did not improve his chances of survival in the Outerlands. It was now a question of how foolhardy, how brazen he could be to keep this journey going. What was to come at the end?

On the other hand, Karim bhai was alive. The old Carrier had defied the promised death of the Whorl and was now smoking and laughing in a place he'd once been certain could hold no life.

That ought to count for something.

No, Amir decided. He couldn't turn back now. If the Mouth had determined that Amir ought not to survive the Outerlands, he'd make it his business to defy it. He was tired of being paraded around by the Mouth and Mahrang, a death sentence hovering over his head. He was tired of walking in fear beside Kalay. Floating down the river, drawing water into his lungs, not knowing if he would live or die, a simple fact had shone through—that those were the prices he'd have to pay to claim even the tiniest bit of fairness and dignity in life. To walk into a land of nightmares and face death, if *that* did not give him what he wanted, perhaps nothing would. But he had to try. He had to go all the way and be proved either right or wrong. And perhaps at the end, if he was proved wrong, death would not be so bad. The world would have ceased to hold purpose for him.

But he knew this: Madhyra had traveled from Illindhi to Amarohi. Karim bhai, along with the pirates of the Black Coves, had departed from Jhanak into the unknown and had instead washed up on this strange shore in the heart of nowhere. And this nowhere now was a point on a map that Karim bhai flashed to him. A point from which he could chart a path toward Illindhi, or back to Amarohi, if he so desired.

The thought of returning disgusted Amir more than it captivated him. He couldn't help but think of the centuries of people trapped within fences. Relying on the thin veil of the Gates to whip bowlers like him into carrying sacks of spices across them.

Karim bhai had survived and proved them all wrong.

"Come with us, pulla," said Karim bhai, once Ilangovan had decided how they would split up. Karim bhai would join Ilangovan and a dozen others on an expedition to the place on the map where Madhyra had marked "settlement."

"I can't," said Amir, although Gates, how desperately did he want that! "I must see this through, bhai."

Karim bhai had aged since Amir had left Raluha for Illindhi. A more sunken face, a paleness born out of worry, and more than anything, plain physical exhaustion. There hadn't been a day's rest, and Karim bhai wasn't young anymore. But when he smiled, Amir saw it as the removal of a mask, the shedding of the tight, lined skin revealing a smoothness beneath, as though he had bathed in milk and saffron.

"Then, I'm coming with you."

Amir began to protest. "They need you more than I do. Besides—"

"Besides what, pulla? You fear you'll put my life in danger from the Immortal Sons? Ho, it is terrifying, I'm not going to deny. This snake beyond these trees might be dead, but I can wager on all the saffron hidden behind the walls of my home that there's more out there that's alive. It's the Outerlands, ho. A place sacred for the Mouth, not for tame little lives like us with bellies to fill back home. We are meant for dirt lanes and bamboos and bazaars that sell spices. I don't like this one bit. I'm more useful in the palaces and pockets of shiny abovefolk, where my scheming yields better results than my limbs." Here his eyes narrowed, and he leaned forward. "But if it really is that important, you'll need all the hands you can get. Besides, what are we bowlers here for if not to look out for each other, ho?"

Karim bhai was a pious man. He had grown from hating the Spice Gates to loving them and praying to the Mouth for all the good it had done for him. For every gatecaste he had helped sneak into the Black Coves, he had offered spices and milk to the temple above the Bowl that he was forbidden to enter. It was impossible for him to think of the Mouth as an entity that was corrupt at its soul. What he looked at instead were solutions to individual problems.

Until now. Until he landed on the coasts of the Outerlands and realized he was not dead. A man who experiences such an event changes fundamentally.

"Just don't ask too many questions, pulla," Karim bhai persisted when Amir opened his mouth. "I'm coming, that is all, ho."

And then, without thinking, Amir bumbled ahead and hugged Karim bhai. The man, far from frail, would have fallen back on the sands if Amir had been a little more forceful. Instead, he wrapped his hands around Amir's back and the warmth seeped into his skin.

"Thank you for not dying," Amir whispered.

"Gah! I'm meant to die on the spice trail, pulla. Not at the absurd end of the world like this," Karim bhai replied, pulling himself back. "At first light, we depart."

Amir had made up his mind. Ever since his conversation with Kalay, he knew what he must do. "Before we leave," he said, measuring his words carefully, "do you still have the map of the trail between Amarohi and Illindhi that Orbalun gave you?"

Karim bhai nodded.

"Great," he said, making sure no one else could hear. "Then, I would like your help in stealing Kalay's talwar, and after that, we're going to stop her from getting to Madhyra."

CHAPTER
24

A revolution in the Bowl cannot come to pass until each bowler
revolts against their self first.

—*Morsels of a Bent Back*, Volume I

Once Amir showed Kalay the true path using the map Karim bhai provided, further bolstered by Hasmin's compass, she was quick to uncover Madhyra's tracks. Raw, untamed anger surged within her, and it took Amir nearly an hour of wandering through the wilderness before he could even ask her a question about it.

"Not far," she said. "A day ahead of us, perhaps. The shortcut through the river saved us some time."

"You mean the precarious fall from over fifty feet that would have killed us both if the cove hadn't been deep enough?"

"Most of survival is luck," noted Karim bhai.

Kalay tsked. "We have seven days to stop my aunt. And then, the Uyirsena will be released."

They were slower with Karim bhai in tow, but the old Carrier was a man who could see into the wild and had the natural propensity to evade trouble. Kalay had protested his inclusion at first, but it did not take long for her to accept that Karim bhai instinctually knew more of the Outerlands without ever stepping foot into it than he'd let on. As though he'd bribed the woods to go easy on him.

"The first thing about being in the wild is to admit that you're not the superior creature out here," he said with an air of having planned such a journey all his life. He was oddly calm about their predicament. Amir did not wish to burst his bubble by regaling him with the story of their adventures before they'd reached the cove.

They were at the lower slopes of what appeared to be a ghat, the jungle spreading before them, and to their left, the mountain rose unimpeded, its tallest and most distant peaks piercing the clouds.

"The second thing you need to know," Karm bhai said, "is that we were all wrong about there being no spices out here."

"That is absurd," said Kalay. "There *are* no spices out here."

When Amir opened his mouth, Karim bhai shut it with his finger. "In silence now, turn and witness the wonder that is the black-pepper vine."

Both Amir and Kalay turned. They were surrounded by tall trees rich with leaves, but closer to them, almost concealed in their shadows, were smaller, thinner plants, no higher than seven feet, each like a man garbed in a thick cloak of grass and vines. Karim bhai was ecstatic. "Their tendrils bear clusters of peppercorns. You see those dense but slender spikes? That's where. The peppercorns turn yellowish-red when they mature, like red currants. In Kalanadi, they pick them while they're still unripe. Then they immerse them in boiling water and leave them to dry in the sun. In a few days, the skin of the peppercorn shrivels and blackens, and that's the wrinkly thing you see in a black pepper. It's a climbing vine, remember. Give it some dappled light, some shade, some heat, and some of the wetness of a tropical undergrowth and you have all the conditions required to grow black pepper. When it's hot and dry, the berries cluster and swell, and that's what gives them their pungent, biting flavor. At that point, they're ready for harvest. Among the eight kingdoms, the slopes of Kalanadi alone are ideal for the spice, but here in the Outerlands"—he gasped, gazing around at the infinite stretch of vegetation—"the possibilities are endless."

Amir was more concerned with how Kalay was reacting to Karim bhai. From the corner of his eye, he watched her pay attention to Karim bhai's words, and observed only the minutest change in her demeanor, as though her own beliefs were being challenged and put to the sword with each passing day. However, that did not keep her from forcing Amir and Karim bhai to pick up the pace that day and cover as much ground as possible before sundown.

That night, Amir rolled in disquiet. Nightmares plagued him, and he thought he heard the Mouth hiss to him a warning. He tried to tame his mind, to pretend to be on the hunt for Madhyra like Kalay, but in truth, no matter how hard he tried, he couldn't pretend, and it was deeply nourished in his bones that he was here to see her mission come to fruition and to witness the possibility of a life away from the eight kingdoms. A possibility so rich, so full of truth, cutting through the lies he'd been fed since he was a child, that no threat—not even that of the Uyirsena or the Immortal Sons—could change the way of his heart. He could not cheat himself.

When he woke, thus, he was sweating, the nightmare rumbling out of him like a ghost that desired to torment him even while he was awake.

Still dark.

Karim bhai snored beside him. It was not yet time for their ploy. Kalay, meanwhile, sat outside their cave, hugging her knees. Moonlight garbed her slender figure. Amir doubted she'd gotten a minute of sleep. He went and knelt beside her and looked out from her vantage at the dark silhouettes of the endless jungle and the not-so-distant sea they'd walked away from.

"It's beautiful, isn't it?" Amir said.

"Beautiful," she whispered. "And forbidden."

Amir smiled, stifling a yawn. "The forbidden spices are the tastiest. That's what they'd say of heeng in the Bowl. That the abovefolk secretly desired it, but feared it because it was wrought from our hands."

"You have enough spices in the eight kingdoms. Greed will kill you."

"We're not greedy for spices," Amir said. "We're greedy for a respectable life. If that kills us, so be it."

Kalay remained quiet at that, gazing out. For the first time since stepping into the Outerlands, she let her hair out of its bun, and it fell to her shoulders in thick waves. She looked like a different person. Her desire to see Amir and the gatecaste alive made him wonder if her long marriage to the Mouth was dying and ready to be replaced by the forgotten dalliance with Madhyra's teachings.

You're being reckless. She's no less dangerous.

"My aunt stayed in this cave," Kalay said a moment later.

When they'd climbed into the cave to sleep, there were a few stray twigs and the usual bones they'd found in every cave. But Kalay had been trained to stalk and kill. And if she said Madhyra had visited this cave, Amir was inclined to believe her.

"What will you do if you cannot stop her this time either?" he asked.

Kalay glared at him. "I won't be alive to find out. Either she is stopped, or I die. Those are the only two ways this can go."

"Be honest. Are you doing this because you think Madhyra killed your father?"

Kalay turned her head toward the sound of crickets chirping in the forest below. "I do not carry vengeance in my heart," she said, a stuttering chuckle following. "That is all her."

"For the merchant from the Outerlands?"

"Love makes you do inexplicable things, I suppose."

Amir thought of Harini almost instantaneously. She had been the one who had undertaken this task of destroying the Gates with Madhyra. Whether she did it out of love for Amir or for the people of Halmora, he could not say.

Why can't it be both?

He did not know when he would see Harini next, but taking her for a stroll in the Outerlands did not seem unreasonable to dream of.

"Have you . . . ever loved someone?" Amir asked Kalay. "Or thought of loving?"

Kalay took an age to respond, long enough to fabricate a lie, gloss it with her stoic and staid demeanor, and utter a "no" that showed little compunction.

"I'm doing my duty," she elaborated. "What she did to my father, whether accidental or not, only justifies my purpose, does not define it. My duty defines what I must do. I am married to the Mouth."

Amir was, by now, irritated with the word. "Do you think of nothing beyond duty? There is a life outside of it."

"A purposeless one," Kalay replied. And before he could interrupt her thought, she had raged into a rant. "And am I to blame? Did I ask to be stricken by duty? No. Just like you did not ask to be a Carrier. I wanted to live with my aunt when I was a child. Away from my parents. Away from everyone else. In the great sand palace of Illindhi, in its regal chambers, feasting on apples and pomegranates and singing songs and learning to dance. I wanted to grow to be a courtier, wear expensive clothes, and perhaps one day be eligible to sit on the Chairs. I thought . . . one day . . . I would get to be the next Jewelmaker."

Amir gaped at her. *Surely not.* Almost instantaneously, he realized why.

"So you could visit the eight kingdoms at will. Like Mahrang did, to ply the trade of the Carnelian Caravan."

She nodded. "And more. But I didn't get to do any of that. I was thrust into the caverns of Mount Ilom when I was eight, and I was told to be dutiful to the Mouth instead. So I was, because I was always an obedient daughter. And besides, I was a child, and I saw Mahrang in the caverns, and I thought—well, he could be both: a warrior of the Uyirsena as well as the Jewelmaker. And I continued down that path, because that was what made my life fruitful. My aunt had the chance to make me a different person, and she chose to instead allow Mahrang and my father to take me. Now it's too late. I don't know if I'll ever be the Jewelmaker— I don't think so—but I certainly won't be the person I would have been if I had remained with my aunt."

That was life, Amir thought, always turning back to see the ghosts of the people you could have been.

THE FOLLOWING MORNING, THEY CLAMBERED OUT OF THE CAVE and resumed their journey. They had still not completely lost sight of the sea. The *pichu pichu* humidity clung to his skin. Sweat dripped from his elbows and chin with every step. And with each passing hour, the west became an endless landscape of forest and hills, and of eerie hisses and hollow moans.

Something was watching them. Amir's bones murmured in agreement. The way the trees rustled in the breeze, the way the air smelled not of any spice, but neither of its absence: Amir was certain they weren't alone. The un-silence preyed on him like a meal left unfinished, and he knew that the Mouth would continue to wage war against him.

He kept it to himself, though. It didn't bode well to rain these fears upon Karim bhai and Kalay, though he was certain both of them would dismiss it as a trick of the mind—as though seeing one monster having met its fleshy end wasn't enough.

He glanced at Hasmin's compass every now and then. Viewing it had become a constant reminder of what he had been through. And it wasn't all bad, he told himself. It would be what kept them alive. The comfort helped him fight the crush of his heart.

Kalay was, once again, less forlorn. She still barely spoke, but she did not appear darker than the clouds anymore. A small victory, Amir thought. She was returning home, after all. Or at least walking in its direction. That ought to cheer anyone up. The thought of returning to a place where one could rest their limbs and snore to their heart's content. Where everything appeared safer and closer and nobody wanted to maim you or kill you. It was where even the most poisonous of waters would taste like nectar.

It surprised Amir that he had hated his home so much. That, to him, home was a nasty springboard of thorns and nettles, a tangled briar whose thatches had begun to peel and where rain fell through the roof like acid. And he now longed to discover a new home, with something no other place could offer—the unbinding of his soul.

They had reached the base of the mountain beyond which lay the settlement according to Madhyra's map. The mountain stretched across their line of vision and rose above them like an immense wall, its crags chewed on by the clouds, mist circling beneath them. Amir filled his lungs with the air swooping down. Gates, it was time already.

Your nerves exude their own smell.

Slowly, he exchanged a knowing glance with Karim bhai. He hoped Ilangovan and the other gatecaste would be waiting for them.

The forest fell below as the sun swept westward overhead. Wild goats grazed on the grasses leading up the slope. The higher they climbed, the colder and more alone they became. Twice they had to stop for Karim bhai to rest his legs and to get back the rhythm of his breathing.

Atop one of the hills, they stopped, the mist retreating to reveal a pristine lake in the mountain. Its waters reflected the clouds. It was as though a hundred mirrors were placed horizontally on the surface of the hill, the silver polished every morning. Beyond the lake, the hillocks rose and then fell into the forested valley at whose heart nestled the settlement.

Amir inhaled sharply, the cold air soothing his nerves. A good place to solve a problem. Gates, he could do with a bath.

"Would be good to wash the face and limbs a bit," said Karim bhai, hobbling toward the lakeshore. Kalay and Amir followed, although he was loath to disturb the placidness of the lake.

As Karim bhai performed a hasty ablution, the thickets surrounding the lake rustled, and through the darkness stepped over two dozen shadows.

Kalay unsheathed her talwar at once, but Karim bhai continued washing his face and then began to scrub his arms. Slowly, as if there were still time this act could be reversed, Amir stepped away from Kalay and unsheathed Mahrang's shamshir, his hand shaking as he held it.

From the shadows stepped Ilangovan, followed by his loyal pirates. Sekaran and few others were absent—still making boat repairs, Amir presumed—but Ilangovan had brought enough people to handle Kalay.

They closed in, narrowing the funnel toward the shore where Karim bhai squatted, dripping water down one leg.

"What is the meaning of this?" Kalay asked, one eyebrow raised.

Ilangovan removed a kerchief tied around his face and pressed closer, sword aloft. Kalay recognized Ilangovan for who he was, and—stunned—looked at Amir. Her lip curled at the sight of Mahrang's shamshir wavering in front of his chest. "I'm flattered." She smirked. "Twenty-five of you. Wonderful! When did you decide to do this? Right after I confessed my desire to not see you dead?"

"Around that time," said Amir, licking dew off his lips. "Drop the talwar, Kalay. We're going to just tie you up and take you to the settlement below."

Karim bhai stood up, wiped his face and arms with his towel, and smiled. "Ho, ponnu, we all know you're good with the blade. As for me, I don't even have a chaku, but I trust you to see the sense in this arrangement."

"An arrangement?" Kalay questioned. *Why is she so calm?* She regarded Ilangovan and his men closing in. "I think we're a little late for etiquette, don't you?"

Amir hesitated before stepping forward. Slowly, he lowered the shamshir, as though inviting her to a truce. "I cannot let you go after Madhyra, Kalay."

She smiled perfunctorily. "What happened to believing that I am not capable of killing my aunt?"

"I have decided not to take that chance."

Kalay's mouth straightened. "You know, when Mahrang chose me to accompany you to the eight kingdoms, he told me he was quietly confident of you standing up to Madhyra. I had my doubts, of course. One look at you in Munivarey's cavern, and I could tell that you don't have the mettle of those who draw blood without remorse. But Mahrang made me see sense. He told me what was at stake for you, and that if you could abandon your beliefs, your daydreams, your home, and travel to Illindhi, all for a vial of the Poison, you could—if the need arose—sacrifice your morals for the sake of your family. For the sake of your freedom. You looked like the kind who would go to any end to ensure that the arrival of the Uyirsena could be averted. He trusted you, Amir of Raluha."

Amir's lip curled in response. "I'm afraid being a disappointment to Mahrang is the least of my worries."

Kalay sighed. "I did not lie when I told you earlier that I wished for you to live a long life. For your family, for all your people. I truly cherished your company, Amir of Raluha. You showed me much that I had always dreamed of, even though under fraught circumstances, and even if I may not have admitted it at the time. You are annoying, insufferable, and almost impressively reckless, but I can see now that you were raised in an unjust world, surrounded by people who have misunderstood the realm's philosophy. And for your valiance against that, you have my salute. However, I am sorry. Where you think your journey must end is not right."

Ilangovan laughed. "Tchah! I wonder if I was this brazen when I escaped to the Black Coves, la! When I stood up to Zariba and her mother, and to the Spice Trade. Or must I have looked this stupid?" He twirled his mustache. "These are not odds you can overcome, warrior. Lay down your blade."

Karim bhai limped ahead. "Ponnu, when this pulla here told me about the Outerlands, I laughed in his face. I'm here now. If a stubborn, old man can see the wrong of his ways . . ."

"Please, Kalay," said Amir. "You know you cannot kill all of us. Let this go."

It took an age for Kalay to lower her talwar. Amir admitted he did not think she would. He'd thought her stubbornness a permanent part of her. But perhaps in all this insanity, Kalay could see the festering of her madness, her obsession.

Some would say you are no different. And wouldn't that be as true?

Amir stepped forward to snatch the talwar from her once she sheathed it. She gave a smile he did not expect.

"One thief begets another, Amir of Raluha. You have truly taught me much about the eight kingdoms." She looked to the skies, her stare almost remorseful. "The Uyirsena are not trained to be stupid. I know I cannot kill all of you. But it can."

When she removed the small wooden thing from her pocket, Amir was not certain what it was. When she blew into the narrow slit at one end and a familiar shrill racket soared through the air, Amir tumbled back into the days, falling into the memory of standing outside the guard watch in Amarohi, shadowed against the waterfall, gazing up at the skies, at the cloud-encrusted turrets of the aranmanai of Rani Kaivalya. He did not bother to wonder when Kalay had stolen the whistle from him.

No.

The sound shattered the serenity of the lake. It censured the skies for their silence in the face of the outrage that was being conducted in the Outerlands against the Mouth.

Ilangovan, Karim bhai, and the other gatecaste appeared surprised. Slowly, Ilangovan chuckled. "If you're trying to call for some reinforcements, la, you may perhaps need a reminder that—"

"We need to run!" Amir sounded the warning, his mouth speaking ahead of his raging mind. *Oh, Kalay, what did you do?*

"Grab her sword," one of the men shouted.

Amir reached him first. "No," he repeated. "We need to run! How far is the settlement?"

"What is the matter, pulla?" Karim bhai was the only one who sounded worried. "What is that whistle supposed to mean?"

Amir's heart thundered in his chest. "That," he said hoarsely, "is a call for Kuka, the Immortal Son."

KUKA MUST HAVE BEEN CLOSE BY TO HAVE HEARD THE WHISTLE. Or perhaps it did not matter how far it was, and it could have still heard the call. Amir decided deliberating on these pointless questions was better than letting fear soak into his skin.

Out on the sparsely vegetated slope, they would be easy pickings for the beast. The settlement was their only hope; and even there, Amir feared they were inviting trouble for the otherwise peaceful settlers.

He was not certain during which part of the scramble down the mountain toward the settlement that they lost Kalay. One moment, Ilangovan and the others were dragging her down the slope. The next, a shrieking roar interrupted their escape, and chaos ensued. Kalay must have slipped through their grasp during the commotion. Amir swore he'd been keeping an eye on her, but when he turned back to help Karim bhai leap over a boulder, Kalay had scuttled away.

"What were you doing, carrying something as dangerous as that?" demanded Karim bhai, panting.

"I-I forgot," said Amir, racing behind Ilangovan and the rest. In the tumult of the much larger and more dangerous-looking Kishkinda, the river, the shipwrecked pirates of the Black Coves, and seeing Karim bhai alive, Amir *had* forgotten about the whistle Rani Kaivalya had given him to summon Kuka. No doubt she would have sent Kuka after him and Kalay when they had not returned within that first day.

The Mouth remembers.

Down where the tree line began once more and the forest sprawled as far as the eye could see, Amir glimpsed spirals of woodsmoke and the smell of cloves and cardamom. The promise of a settlement, of *life*, in the Outerlands dimmed in the face of an imminent assault from the Immortal Sons. Amir had hoped for this moment to be cherished, to be seared in his memory as a story he would someday tell Kabir and Amma, how he had discovered their new home.

You'll settle for barely scraping through alive.

The shrill cry jolted him as the twenty-five gatecaste sprinted for their lives. Amir craned his neck to glimpse the sun being blotted out, the shadow of Kuka's wings shimmering on the slope. The shadow thickened as Kuka descended. Ahead, Ilangovan marshaled his men into a knotted ravine that led into the forest and the settlement.

Amir wheeled around. Karim bhai was still fifty feet away, hunkering down, chest heaving.

"Faster!" Amir yelled. Kuka answered his yell with a piercing shriek, its head swiveling downward to regard first Karim bhai up the slope, and then Amir, its eyes narrowing, nostrils snorting, familiarity coursing through its scales.

A second, deeper shriek resounded from the distance. Kuka dived.

With the shamshir in one hand, Amir extended his other for Karim bhai to grab hold of, then he pushed the old Carrier into the ravine. Amir meant to follow, but his foot caught in a tangle of undergrowth, and he tripped sideways, leaning away from the gap. Pain shot up his ankle as he fell. His head smacked against a boulder.

Amir's vision flickered. A distant second shriek alternated with the silence in his head.

He tumbled down the slope. Before the pain in his head consumed his consciousness, he saw in shuddering gasps Kuka swooping down toward him, shadow dark upon the mountain, its wings splayed wide.

CHAPTER
25

Nothing prepares you for the beauty of Amarohi. It is a paradise nestled between waterfalls and a forest encrusted with dew and mist. The branches of trees form arches overhead and their barks form bridges beneath the feet. The air and breaths of those who linger among the woods is rife with cloves. But the moment you open your mouth, you are harried into a cavern, your back whipped and your tongue chopped.

—Ujjvala, *An Encyclopedia for Reckless Carriers*

Amir awakened on a bed of straw, surrounded by a circle of herbs and candles—teakwood and balsam—and the smell of tulsi hanging in the air. *Home*, he feared, thinking he was back in Raluha, and sat up. Sharp pain below his shoulder spiked up and exploded, sending him crashing back down on his bed. He felt a strip of cloth around his head. More strips around his shoulder, taut against the armpit, covering another wound. A greenish tinge on the surface, pus soaking into the cloth. Amir winced as he laid a finger on it.

A flap door opened ahead and Ilangovan strode in. Sunlight outside silhouetted his slender, bony figure, but when the flap closed, Amir's chest tightened.

"Where is Karim bhai?" he asked, raising a hand to block the light. He tried to stand, but Ilangovan bade him to continue lying down.

"Nobody was hurt."

Amir thought he'd misheard. "But the Immortal Son . . . it was right there."

Ilangovan appeared to weigh the response in his head before saying, "It did not harm you, la. Or anyone else. It flew over the settlement and headed north."

Amir breathed out, and pain shot up his shoulder again, and he went slack. When the pain subsided, a jolt of panic took its place.

"It wasn't after me," he choked. "It's gone after Madhyra."

As has Kalay.

Amir sat up, and all of a sudden, the pain seemed to have numbed. It was as if he had tumbled and fallen onto a bed of grass. "I must go after Madhyra."

Ilangovan regarded him with a quiet curiosity. Amir did not think the day would come already where he would be sitting inches away from the legendary pirate, no less in the Outerlands. He'd imagined a glorious entry into the Black Coves, an induction of him and his family to the ranks of the pirates and a drunken reunion with those bowlers who had managed to escape their duty over the years. All of it, however, now bore the taste of a dish on the verge of being spoilt. Amir found it disheartening that Ilangovan was not seeing the same urgency he was. "You should stay here," he said softly. "You have not yet recovered from the fall."

"I'll be fine."

"You've already done enough. Word has reached this settlement of your exploits, of your travel to Illindhi, of your quest for the Poison, and now, of helping Madhyra bring down the Spice Gates. They know you as Arsalan's son. You've done everything you can."

Amir tsked. "Appa would have gone on."

"They cremated your father a fortnight ago. Along with the four hundred and twenty-seven men and women who lost their lives in killing the Immortal Son we saw, and helping Madhyra reach the eight kingdoms. Would you like to see their memorial stone?"

Four hundred and twenty-seven. He ran the number on his tongue over and over, until each count, each number held within it a universe. "No," he said flatly. Gates, he desperately wished to see Appa's name etched on the stone. It would not be anything new, but it would sink in faster, harder, reshaping his grief even more, until the hatred of ten years could dissolve into a love that had been trapped in a limbo between existence and nonexistence.

"No," he repeated. "Not until I have helped Madhyra see this through. Besides, I cannot stay here. The Mouth knows where I am at all points in time. It will send another Immortal Son after me, and I would rather not put this settlement at risk."

He stood and pushed past Ilangovan. This time, the pirate did not stop him. Opening the flap, Amir stepped out into the settlement proper. The bright morning light pierced the tree cover overhead and fell dappled on the forest clearing. When his eyes adjusted, they settled on a village bordered by tall trees. From where he stood, he could see the conical roofs and smoking chimneys of at least a hundred homes. The mountain they had fled from lay behind him. Ahead, rows of bamboo houses stood like sentries, some bricked, some stone-walled. Lanes bustled with people carrying wares. Enormous pots billowed steam while they cooked over a fire.

There was no fence. Nothing crooked and barbed with guards or sentries. Just a retinue of men and women deep in discussion. Among them was Karim bhai. Gates, how seamlessly he fit into all of this. A thread of a different color yet sewing itself into this vibrant tapestry of the Outerlands, a tapestry that Karim bhai had not fully believed in until he'd washed up on the cove.

Amir tore himself away from the yearning to remain in the settlement. He could not, he realized, allow himself to be tempted by this possibility while the threat of Madhyra's failure continued to loom ahead of him. All of a sudden, she was vulnerable.

Amir decided he would not let himself be seen leaving. He had the map Karim bhai had given him. He had Hasmin's compass. Mahrang's shamshir. And an unshakable resolve that burned like a forest fire inside his heart. He looked around and pictured himself here, Harini beside him. And his family. And Karim bhai.

"You would have done well at the Black Coves." Ilangovan stepped out of the tent behind him, hands on hips, a smile dancing on his face.

"We would have been caught sooner or later," Amir replied.

"Not if we did not wish to be," said Ilangovan. "But yes, it was a dance with trouble, la. We flirted with Zariba's ships, and we'd lose a comrade or two. Sometimes ten. Always a difficult conversation to return to the isles and speak to the families. It was easier, instead, to present them with blood in return."

"There would be blood here too," said Amir, glancing around.

Ilangovan shrugged. "Perhaps. But a little less, I would wager. Freedom always exacts a cost, la. Some costs are paid to achieve it. Some persist long after that freedom is achieved. It gives you the illusion that, maybe, this is not freedom at all but a poor substitute. Gnaws at your conscience every time you loot a trading vessel or drown a Jhanakari merchant plying an honest business on the waters because you have mouths to feed back on the isles, mouths craving spice in their dal and sabzi. It is a very selfish act, freedom is. But then, the deeper part of your soul whispers to you that the journey to emancipation justifies its preservation."

Amir chewed over Ilangovan's words. "I don't know," he said at last.

"That's all right. It doesn't mean that you wouldn't have done well in the Black Coves."

Ilangovan smiled. The conversation had run its course. Amir did not say goodbye. He merely walked away, as though heading for a quiet stroll in the woods. He had his bag, his waterskin, and the remainder of the food that would suffice for the next five days. He nearly walked a mile, his pace slackened by the burden of thoughts, when Karim bhai caught up with him. He had a wooden staff in his hand, his stained towel woven around his head, his own bag slinging from his shoulder carrying his survival paraphernalia. He was already out of breath.

"Go back," warned Amir, increasing his pace. "I'm sure you have a lot of explaining to do to the settlers."

"I saw the stone memorial they erected for Arsalan and the others."

That made Amir stop. Gates, again, he did not want to know what it looked like, and whether it truly had his father's name inscribed on it. He did not want to be anywhere near it at the moment.

"I'm coming with you, pulla. When I told you this yesterday, I meant till the end—not to this place in between where I can lie in comfort and await whatever fate is bestowed on me, ho?"

"You will only slow me down," said Amir.

"Nice try. Keep walking. I'm right behind you." Karim bhai caught up with him and laid a hand on his shoulder. "I'll show you some new spices. Curse the tongue of whoever said there aren't any spices in the Outerlands. There's enough here to feed thrice the population of the eight kingdoms. And we haven't even seen all of it."

CHAPTER
26

One nutmeg is good. Two bad. Three deadly.

—UNKNOWN, *THE VIEW FROM THE TREETOP*

I t took them two days of crossing different disparate settlements of the Outerlands. Time was of the essence, and they stopped only to refill their waterskins. Some settlers, it dawned on Amir, had been living there for generations. Their parents and their grandparents had lived in the Outerlands, and some of them did not even remember which of the eight kingdoms they once belonged to, let alone the caste of their birth.

You're doing the right thing.

Mostly, he stuck to observing Karim bhai as the possibilities unfurled in the old Carrier's mind. It was not to say he wasn't taking it well. Spurts of joy and curiosity erupted every few moments—as though with each new discovery, Karim bhai was reconciling the new world with the old.

As for Kalay, there were no tracks Amir could identify. He had neither the skill nor the patience of a hunter or a tracker. He merely followed the map and prayed that they were headed in the right direction. Kalay would not have forgotten.

Gates, the more he thought of her, the more unsettled he felt. A niggle in his stomach. One thing was certain: there would be no pleasantries ex-changed between them if they met again. Nothing Amir carried—either in his soul or in his bag—would atone for the shattering of trust.

Wasn't much to begin with, in your defense.

It didn't matter if, like Kalay, he wanted her to live too. That she could yet claw out of her shell of an acolyte of the Uyirsena and start to become who she'd once wanted to be.

A rich, abovefolk courtier.

Lastly, he kept craning his neck at the skies for a sign of Kuka.

On the third morning since they left from the settlement, Amir and Karim bhai stumbled upon clove trees beyond the river crossing. Ever-greens as high as forty feet, thickly clothed with glossy, aromatic leaves. Karim bhai ran circles around the trees, claiming with delight that this was all he needed to settle down in the Outerlands.

Amir, who couldn't see the clove itself, was confused. Karim bhai nudged him closer. "The clove grows in clusters colored green through yellow, pink, and finally a deep, russet red. You see those buds? They must be harvested before they are overripe. Clove harvesters in Amarohi—they go to the treetops and beat the cloves from the branches with sticks. They're then gathered in nets and hardened and blackened in the tropical sun to look like nails."

They did not stop again until sundown, when Karim bhai's legs couldn't carry him any farther, or he was patently excited to eat the meals they had packed from the settlements. Without Kalay, they felt exposed to the evils that lurked in the darkness, and to Kalay herself, who was probably less than half a day ahead. They were working with a proper map, as compared with Kalay's memory, which—Amir hoped—would give them at least an hour or two on her.

By the fourth morning, the terrain became uneven again, slowing them down. There were two days left until Mahrang's deadline for releasing the Uyirsena. Amir's quest for the Poison seemed as if it were from a different life—settling in the Black Coves, sailing as a pirate beside Ilangovan.

It was still a life better than the one in the Bowl, but it could never be as whole—nor as much a true *life*, free from servitude and scorn—as one in the Outerlands.

When he slept that night, that new life came alive. His new sibling running around, Kabir finding new friends and places and surroundings to paint, and Amma rediscovering her purpose, a facet of her life that had shrunk and withered since Appa abandoned them.

Amir dreamed of a shattered Spice Trade seeking new roots—the old impulse to exchange goods set aside in favor of a new longing to explore the Outerlands. He had thought of what Kalay had said, about Amir's right to destroy the lives of millions of people, and in between his dreams, the weight of those words pulled him down. The dream morphed into a nightmare, ending with him waking up drenched in sweat, Karim bhai watching from the mouth of the cave with worry.

"You shouldn't think so much, pulla."

Amir shook his head. "I can't help it. If you asked me a few days back if I could have imagined anything that happened since the last time I went to Halmora, I would have called it out as a wooden nutmeg."

Karim bhai smiled. "It's what people who seek a better life need to get used to. Even the Black Coves were terrifying for some of the bowlers at first. New truths tend to dislocate the habits of the soul."

"And if we fail?" Amir asked. "Can we live with our failure knowing these new truths and yet not being able to attain them?"

"We won't fail," Karim bhai said. "I have faith in you, pulla. In us."

Amir scoffed. "We're mere ants in a war among elephants, bhai. One stamp will take us out."

Karim bhai smiled. "Not if we can sting them in the foot first."

Amir returned the smile. "If you say so. I won't deny, part of me *is* glad you are here with me, though I'd much prefer you remained back in the settlement. These new truths will stay with me, even if nothing else will."

"You speak like an older man now," Karim bhai said. "I miss the errant Carrier. The reckless boy sneaking off to meet the rajkumari of Halmora."

"I'm still the same, bhai. If things truly change, I would still like to chase after the rajkumari of Halmora."

"Maharani now," Karim bhai corrected.

Yes. A queen. A thronekeeper. He remembered the honeyed sweetness of her lips as she kissed him in the shadow of the Spice Gate in Jhanak, the aroma of sandalwood lurking on her skin, the shikakai in her hair. And above all, her words, her secrets, her tenacious appetite for goodness. She had done what any thronekeeper would have, for the betterment of their people—only she considered her gatecaste just as deserving of a good life as the abovefolk. It was why she had wanted the ships from Rani Zariba. She'd foreseen the end of the Spice Gates and the opening of the Outerlands. The ships meant a head start on trade, of whatever could be traded in the absence of the Spice Gates.

And you had attempted to waylay those plans.

Gates, he loved her. He only hoped the disparate paths they took would one day converge, never again to be parted.

The following day passed in worry and quiet complaints. Deep woods, long stretches on narrow hills, brooks teeming with the kind of fish even the Jhanakari wouldn't know of. The roar of a wild beast in the distance, then the stuttering, dying moan of a gazelle. With only one day to go, Amir wondered if they were even on the right trail. A map could be wrong. Or perhaps, Hasmin's compass had stopped working. He'd be a fool to think he'd figured out the Outerlands within this short journey.

What he *could* do was count the passage of time. Each minute, each hour passed in trepidation. When there was little more than a day left before Mahrang had promised to release the Uyirsena, Amir grew impatient and prodded Karim bhai to increase their pace with a pinch of panic in his voice. The old Carrier, however, was nearing his limits. His initial passion had dwindled. What he overcame with his heart and mind soon slowed the use of his weary limbs.

The mornings and evenings had become colder as they traveled, and a steady mist enveloped them for hours as they skirted a mountain to the east. Every eerie sound in the wilderness sent Amir scurrying for cover. The fear of an Immortal Son lingered with them at each step, and try as he could, he could never shake the image of Kuka swooping down on him as he tumbled down the slope. Nor of Kishkinda, which had descended from the clouds. Nor of the slain serpent. He could sense the Mouth raging. Its anger boiling over. He could afford little deception now, other than to follow in the steps of Kalay and Madhyra.

When night fell, and a full, bulbous moon appeared in the sky, Amir and Karim bhai began to look for a cave in which to stop. Mist coiled around their feet as they plodded through a barren stretch of rocky land. Moonlight bathed their trail, guiding them.

At one point, Karim bhai stopped.

"What is it?" Amir asked, panting. They'd just lumbered up a slope, flanked by boulders on both sides. Karim bhai was leaning against a large rock, his eyes set on the stone.

"This," he muttered.

Amir thrust his torch to where Karim bhai pointed. The firelight fell on a patch of the boulder shaped like a palm.

Blood.

"Wet," Karim bhai said, running his fingers across the handprint. "They're close."

A few hundred meters ahead, they found blood again, this time a sinuous trail of it on their path, blotches on leaves and imprints on mud. Amir and Karim bhai exchanged weary and anxious glances before trudging on. At one point, Amir unsheathed his shamshir. He heard the sound of gushing water from up ahead, steadily increasing until it devoured the night's silence. Fog rolled in, dimming their vision until each step was a chore, a perilous step into the unknown.

When the fog thinned, they appeared to have stumbled onto a clearing. Amir gasped.

Water leaped out from the top of a hill and crashed into a deep, narrow ravine far beneath. Dashing through the ravine was a violent river, its foam cresting and roiling against rocks clinging to the walls of the cliffs on either side.

Ahead, the trail suddenly ended, dropping into the ravine. A bridge—several unstable logs, really—lay across the chasm, and farther ahead, nearly fifty feet away, Amir spied the continuation of their trail. The bridge, Amir supposed, had been built by settlers.

Madhyra knelt in the center of that narrow bridge, heaving and panting, the sword earned from Rani Zariba's ancestry alive in her hand. Her hair was in disarray, and she bled from several parts of her body. A few feet from her, closer to where Amir and Karim bhai stood, Kalay was panting too. She appeared to be in worse shape than her aunt, but there was a fire in her eyes that told Amir that she could go at it all night, and that whatever had to happen, must happen upon this bridge.

Kalay was what stood between Madhyra and her way to Illindhi.

The sound of the waterfall crashing into the river drowned out any sounds the two of them made. Karim bhai caught up to Amir. "Ho, couldn't they find a less perilous place to fight?"

Amri shook his head, and, biting his lip, began to trudge forward, one step at a time.

"Kalay," he called out.

Kalay wheeled around, eyes widening at the sight of Amir and Karim bhai. "You!" she shrieked, but there was also a tinge of surprise, and perhaps, if Amir dissected its timbre more closely, an undercurrent of relief.

She's glad to see you alive, in a way.

"Stay away from this," she said.

Madhyra's head rose and she regarded him. She was just as surprised, but there was a realization dawning on her face that seemed to calm her, even if for an instant. Her shoulders fell ever so slightly.

Your presence is appreciated.

"Pulla, be careful," Karim bhai warned.

Amir reached the edge of the bridge. It was less than five feet wide, great logs lain across and tied using thick ropes at frequent intervals.

The buttresses beneath the logs were likewise nailed into the sides of the ravine, but Amir did not trust them. The railing was patchy and torn, leaving little room for Amir to rely on holding on to anything. A great fog rose from the river below, wrapping him in a wet embrace as he stepped onto the bridge.

The acolyte of the Mouth was less than ten feet away, nursing a twisted knee, when she glared at him, raised her talwar, and screamed, "I said, stay away!"

Amir shook his head. Here was the world once more, telling him he ought to wield a blade when he hated it more than anything else. Coercing him, pushing him beyond his limits, where lay a darkness he couldn't comprehend. His skin fused with the hilt of Mahrang's shamshir. "I-I can't, Kalay. I'm sorry. Madhyra needs to keep going."

Kalay threw him a stunned expression. Blood streaked her elbow and knees, and her breath was ragged. "You fool, don't you realize what you're doing?"

"You know what you saw back there in the Outerlands. You saw the settlement." Amir said, his hands shaking as he clasped his shamshir. "That is my future."

Kalay grunted, struggling to stand. "You're an incorrigible idiot, Amir of Raluha. And it pains me severely to see you dead. But I must do what I must do."

She stood, moaning in pain, and raised her talwar. Beyond her, Madhyra continued to kneel, her energy all but sapped. Kalay took one step toward Amir, whose hands continued to twitch around his shamshir's hilt.

"You're not even holding it right." She chuckled.

Amir's heart galloped as Kalay neared him. Gates, he'd wanted her to live, to survive the Outerlands. And here he was, doubting whether he himself would. And yet, what choice did he have? He had to hold this bridge if Madhyra were to continue her journey. He would be to Madhyra what Karim bhai had been to him.

He remembered that evening by the river when Kalay had taught him to use his shamshir. Everything about it already lay blurred and fragmented in his memory. Within him, the spirit of Ilangovan opened its eyes. He tried to push it back in, urging it to melt, to disappear.

Amir raised his shamshir when Kalay was less than five feet away. Her determined eyes bore into him as she closed the gap. Visions of her fighting on the pirate galley, and later in the marshland of Mesht, flashed in front of him.

"I-I can't do this, Kalay," Amir stuttered. He poked the blade forward into nothing, as if in warning.

"Then head back," she replied calmly, her breathing still slow and heavy. "I have already forgiven you for trying to apprehend me by the lake. Just leave, and we're even."

Amir scrambled to take a step back instead, widening the distance between him and Kalay. When Kalay suddenly thrust her sword at Amir, he yelped and leaped aside, raising his own shamshir in panic.

The blades met. Amir's eyes widened as his grip on the shamshir slackened. Kalay gave him an expression of mock surprise.

He spared a glace for Karim bhai beyond the bridge, and Madhyra ahead of him. He thought of Kabir in those fragile moments as his life lay at the mercy of another, thought of everything he'd hoped to give his brother, first in the Black Coves and now in the Outerlands. He imagined what Velli looked like. A replica of Amma, he hoped.

It didn't matter that he didn't know how to fight. All he had to do was not look down. *Just don't look down.*

Moonlight drenched him, and the cold gripped his bones. He took a step *forward* this time, and swung his shamshir blindly at Kalay. She ducked, and Amir stumbled. She raised her head and sliced at his knees, but his stumble allowed him to drop his shamshir to meet Kalay's thrust. The momentum carried Amir forward more and he rolled beyond Kalay, stopping just short of falling over the edge of the bridge.

His heart beat violently as he gulped a lungful of wet air. He snapped up to see Kalay leap past him with her talwar gleaming against the moonlight.

Any moment now, any moment now.

Impulse dragged Amir sideways as he rolled onto the bridge, yelping as Kalay's blade hacked past his hair by the minutest width.

He scrambled up, groaning in pain, and slashed wildly behind him.

The blade caught flesh.

Amir dropped his shamshir, as if he had not caught Kalay but had buried the blade into his own palm. He stared dumbfounded.

Shit, shit, shit!

Kalay's attempt to stab him on the bridge had trapped her sword between the logs, and in the time she took to pry it free, Amir's wild backward swing had caught her by sheer luck.

Kalay, however, was alive, even though she let out a weak growl, clutching her thigh.

"I-I'm sorry!" Amir stammered. Part of him wanted to rush to her, to see if she was okay. But the other part of him remained rooted, fully aware of what an acolyte of the Uyirsena was capable of until their last breath. He stared at the blood on the shamshir he'd dropped like it were some poison that had been sucked out of him.

"I'm sorry," he repeated.

"No, you're not." Kalay smiled, spitting blood into the waterfall and turning to gaze at him with renewed interest. "You're a fool, but you're certainly not sorry."

She suddenly went down on one knee, planting her talwar on the wooden bridge, panting. Behind him, Madhyra was getting to her feet.

"You don't give up," she said hoarsely, eyeing Amir, her voice barely overpowering the rush of water to reach him. Her knife hand was firm on her hip as she bore the pain of her own battle with Kalay. "It's admirable."

He stood again between aunt and niece. The paleness returned to his face. The corridor of Halmora returned to his mind. The stench, the rain, the blood, the clouds of spices engulfing the palace in a riot of color and flavor. Gates, he'd give anything to end this right now.

Amir turned to Madhyra. "Go on. You must get to Illindhi."

"I cannot go anywhere, Amir," Madhyra said, her voice faltering.

Kalay wiped the perspiration off her forehead. She took three deep breaths and gazed up at the moon. "It's a beautiful night to die."

"Kalay, please—"

She charged at him. A rush of blood to his head propelled him downward as he picked up the shamshir and raised it in time to parry her blow. The first two strikes clanged in front of his face. When he expected a third blow to fall, she instead kicked his knee. Amir buckled, the shamshir slipping from his hands once more.

Kalay knocked the air out of him with a shove. He fell onto the bridge; it shook only just slightly, but in the next moment Kalay towered over him. She raised her talwar as she'd raised it not long ago on the ship to kill Madhyra. There was no malice in her eyes. No hint of violence. She was doing her duty, and duty compelled her to finish Amir like he was a task that couldn't be postponed anymore.

The blade fell. Amir squeezed his eyes shut, but he felt no pain. Instead, as he opened his eyes a tenth of a second later, he found Madhyra's hand in front of his, his reflection in the flat of her blade, her feet inches behind his head.

She'd leaped over him on the narrow bridge, forcing Kalay back with a grunt. Kalay staggered, screaming in pain as she swerved to land on her knees. Madhyra clutched her hip once more. Amir spied a dark blotch underneath her hand. She was bleeding profusely.

Tears streamed down Kalay's face. "Why did you do this to me?"

She cut a solemn figure on the bridge. Kneeling, her head buried in her hands, sobbing uncontrollably. There was a sadness Amir saw in her that fought to overcome her duty, and also anger that came with failure. Amir had never thought Kalay could be this strong and yet look so vulnerable.

Madhyra was calm in response. "As long as the Spice Gates remain standing, there will be no emancipation of those who live outside the walls. Now, come on, cheche. Don't be angry. You know every piece of fiction is rooted in some truth. The settlers have always existed on the edges of our world. Our ancestors have always known it. The thronekeepers have known it. I was a thronekeeper, and yet I was ignorant of it. That was my biggest failure. As a woman to lead her people to better lives, my ignorance was equal to the worst of crimes. All until I met Sukalyan."

The merchant from the Outerlands, bearing spices.

Kalay weakened. Her knees wobbled. Amir, struggling to stand, cast his eyes down at the foam rising up from where the waterfall crashed into the ravine. His mind raged as he processed Madhyra's words. She had loved a gatecaste. She had loved someone from the Outerlands who had been killed by Mahrang, and everything she had done since then was seared in his memory. The thought sent shivers down his spine.

"His reality violated everything I grew up to know and believe to be true. If there's one thing you need to understand about our world, cheche, it is that we will go to great lengths to preserve our identities. We will justify the vilest of crimes in the name of identity. We are creatures bound to the glories of our past, who cannot overcome what we believe to be bright and pure. We build walls to protect that past. Walls! Ha! People on either side of a wall spend eternities wondering what's on the other side. And not because they wish to be on the other side. No. It is only to get a glimpse, to convince everyone that their side of the wall is better. Purer. Nobler. And if someone breaches those walls, we punish them for being the stain on that purity."

The invisible walls surrounding the Bowl shimmered in front of Amir's eyes. *Purity.* Here he was, impure, having passed countless times through the Mouth's feces.

Madhyra continued, now leaning over her sword's hilt. "When I lost Sukalyan, I knew I had no choice but to destroy the Spice Gates. Thousands have tried in the past—each with their own twisted justifications and morals—and have failed. The Spice Gates are made of storms and the earth, and the soul of the nine kingdoms runs through the crevices, binding them to the core. One does not bring them down with hammers and catapults and elephants and giants. They all tried. But none of them knew they were tied to the Mouth." She smiled, her lips coated in blood, her voice growing darker with each word, more prophetic. "None of them knew that to destroy the Spice Gates was not to crack and topple the archway of old stone. It was to undo the god that created it in the first place."

Kalay let go of her talwar. It clattered onto the bridge, its surface wet with the spray from the waterfall. Her mouth quivered. "You could have told me . . ." she whispered. "All those days, *months*, you could have just told me . . ."

Madhyra lowered her head. "I made a mistake. I heeded the words of your father, thinking he would know what is best for your future. Putting you in the ranks of the Uyirsena was not my decision, but my silence to you does make me culpable. Back then, I did not know what a corrupted rank it was, or what we were truly doing in the name of the Mouth. Even when I became thronekeeper, I was blind to the ills that truly plagued our realms. Until Sukalyan . . . until Sukalyan . . ."

"You're wasting time," Amir hissed. "We have only until tomorrow."

Madhyra shook her head. "I'm not going anywhere, Amir, until I tell Kalay the truth of my heart."

Kalay slammed a fist on the bridge, hissing in pain through clenched teeth. "There is no truth except that you lied to me and you betrayed the Mouth and Illindhi." Suddenly, as if the part of the Mouth that breathed within her had suddenly awakened, she picked up the talwar, lifted herself, and limped forward. Her fingers tightened around the hilt and she sliced at Madhyra. The thronekeeper flattened her blade against the blow and, with one foot trailing, invited Kalay to strike further.

"Kalay, please," Amir begged her. "Just hear her out."

Aware of how close he suddenly was to the fight, he scrambled back, past the center of the bridge. Kalay ignored his remark. She gritted her teeth and pounced on Madhyra, swinging first this way then that, feinting and giving her aunt the look that Amir had seen on Ilangovan's pirate galley.

Madhyra was too weak to match Kalay's blows, but what she parried sent her staggering backward.

"You tell me, Kalay, that I do this for vengeance, but it's time you knew the truth."

It was good fortune that Kalay was sapped of all her strength and had no choice but to kneel in the center of the bridge and listen.

Madhyra coughed out more blood. She needed help. What was left of her strength, she put into her voice, her anger transforming, the truth clawing its way out of a shell it had hidden in for too long. "When Fylan was nine years old and sent into the Outerlands to complete his night of vigil, he stumbled ignorantly into the den of an Immortal Son. The Immortal Son would have burned your father alive if not for a young Sukalyan, who was roaming that part of the land, trying to gather firewood. He saved your father's life and sent him back the next morning to Illindhi."

Kalay shook her head. "You're lying."

Madhyra chuckled, coughing up more blood. "I have nothing to lie about anymore. You're here because Fylan survived that night in the wild. Without Sukalyan, you would not have been born, cheche. When I told this to Fylan, he wouldn't believe me, but I think a part of him knew he was wrong. He knew *someone* had saved him that night, and it was a tale he had confessed to no one all those years. I told him I would bring Sukalyan to meet our parents and he could see for himself. He agreed. It was a test as much for him as it was for me."

It was a gentle moment for Kalay's promise to the Mouth to wither. Her shoulders drooped, and she let out a soft breath. Whatever part of Amir had hoped for Kalay to survive the Outerlands returned, albeit tentatively.

Madhyra, though, spoke not just to Kalay but also to Amir. He shared her exhaustion, her desires and desperation, but the truth was all hers. It rolled out of her in waves, and there was no stopping the flow of words. "Even though I was thronekeeper, it was customary to seek the blessings of our parents before we chose our husbands. They ruled Illindhi before. It was only right. It was tradition. And I did this in secrecy, knowing there were many in the court who would disapprove of such a match.

Only Fylan and Kashyni knew. At the least, I had hoped my parents would see beyond their rituals and customs, and into my heart. Into a future where the gatecaste could coexist with us.

"My parents let me bring him to the palace. It was half a victory. They prepared a feast for him—the greatest of spices, sambars, kuzhambus, and meat. And as Sukalyan ate, they embarrassed him. Insulted him. Told him that he was a spiceless gatecaste, less than human, who, within the walls of Illindhi, was no more than a rat that had come to poison their meal. It was an illusion to think he could even talk to, let alone marry, me. They said he had demeaned them, their lineage, and the Mouth. They forced him to spit out the food he thought he had been invited to eat. In front of *me*. I thought I was Illindhi's most powerful woman. I stayed silent and wept, knowing that everything I had believed was wrong. Fylan was quiet too. I think he had recognized Sukalyan from his night in the wild, despite the years. Some faces you don't forget, cheche. And yet he stayed silent. I hated him that night and for several nights since."

If Kalay faulted Madhyra for despising her father, she did not show it. Amir did not want to hear more. He knew what would follow, and he doubted whether he had the stomach for it. Madhyra, however, had no qualms about replaying her past, her voice a tremble in the night.

"And when I thought they'd let Sukalyan go, Mahrang came in and chopped his head off. He cast it into the Mouth as a sacrifice, then had the guards parade me into my chamber."

Amir closed his eyes and the wailing of a thousand gatecaste rang in his head. When he opened them, Madhyra stood erect, one half of her painted in blood.

"That night, I decided that running away to live with the people of the Outerlands would serve no purpose. Being thronekeeper, I could have transformed the laws of the land overnight, imposed a new normal and forced everyone to comply and serve my needs. As the protector of the most ancient of realms among the nine, I could have done that with a flick of my wrist." Amir's mind drifted to Orbalun, and his failure to change the minds of the abovefolk. Madhyra's deepening voice pulled him back.

"Instead, I decided to cause a change more permanent. A change that cannot be undone and one we must live with, knowing it is for the better. You have not lived with the settlers, cheche. I have. Much that I have taught you I have learned from them. And there is even now so much to learn that I fear dying before I do. There is so much to see in these lands, so much to grow and cherish. And we've forbade all of that to satisfy the whims of the Mouth.

"I saw the fear in Mahrang's eyes that night as he took off my lover's head and held it in front of him as though he were staring into the Mouth itself. He feared what could happen if we were to blend with the Outerlands. But Fylan . . . when he confronted me in Halmora, I told him what I was doing. Whether that undid a lifetime of learning with the Uyirsena, I do not know. I hope it did. I begged him to return the turmeric he'd stolen in order to lure me out.

"Unfortunately, there was a mix-up with the Halmoran guards. They mistook his attempt to return the stolen turmeric as an act of aggression and cut him down. Harini apologized to me, but it was . . . too late."

Kalay did not raise her head. Her strength failed her. She swayed where she knelt, as though recovering from a heavy and very unappetizing dinner.

"Three days later," Madhyra continued, her words now softer, "when the Uyirsena did not show up in the eight kingdoms, I sensed Fylan had bought me the time I needed. He was the only man Mahrang was likely to listen to, though even that, not entirely. Mahrang would invariably send the Uyirsena. It was just a matter of time. I knew I still had to act. I still needed a weapon to stab the Mouth with. My own sword was not Mouth-forged. Only two of the eight kingdoms possessed such a weapon—Raluha and Jhanak. They were passed down over generations after their ancestors had recovered those blades during the previous Cleansing. I tried to tempt Orbalun, but he wouldn't budge. Zariba was more . . . malleable. She wanted the pirate's menace to end. But I couldn't do it alone. So I walked into Rajkumari Harini's court. I knew what plagued her. I offered her the gift of truth in return for helping me. Together, we struck a bargain with Zariba. The pirate for the sword and the ships. We knew Ilangovan was elusive. But I promised him the knowledge of crossing the Whorl. I showed him the other side, and with it bought his imprisonment. He was willing to sacrifice his life if it meant I would succeed."

Harini's concealment of the truth did not rankle Amir anymore. He was, on the other hand, even grateful to her for having done what she did.

"And now," Madhyra said, "I'm here. To finish what I started."

Her knees finally buckled. A tear slipped down her cheek. Her glassy eyes regarded Kalay expectantly before her strength evaporated. "I'm sorry, cheche, for what happened to Fylan. But I wanted to tell you the whole truth."

She took a deep breath, planting her own sword into the wood, coughing in bouts. If Kalay came charging now, Madhyra wouldn't be able to defend herself. Of that, Amir was certain. But the expression on Kalay's tearstained face was not one of hate and passion but one of sorrow and fear.

In the vacuum of silence, Amir heard it. A sound that drowned out even the irate waterfall. It came from above, far above. The air thickened with the aroma of ginger and mace, which seeped into his lungs and clogged his pores until he could barely breathe.

Then the clouds broke open, and Kuka swooped down on them, its roar deafening, its sights unmistakably fixed on the three figures on the narrow bridge.

CHAPTER
27

Ancient myths must be preserved for future evils to be justified.

—*A Labyrinth of Dark Corners*, an anthology
comprising writers who claim to have witnessed the
existence of the Immortal Sons

Lightning cracked around Kuka as it dived toward the bridge. Its cry was sharper, piercing Amir's senses until he could discern only a bleak, black shape torn out of the darkness.

"You called it!" screamed Amir.

Kalay was aghast. "On the mountain, I did. Not now. It followed *you*."

"Did you think it wanted me? Then you're an idiot as much as I am, Kalay. It did not harm a single hair on my body. Nor of any of the gate-caste. It went straight for Madhyra—what it perceived as the greatest threat to the Mouth."

The flap of the Immortal Son's wings dispatched a gust of air that spiraled downward. A little heavier, and it'd have blown Amir right off the bridge. Both Madhyra and Kalay clung to their swords dug into the wood. Behind them, Karim bhai scampered to hide behind a boulder, his eyes wide as vadais.

Kuka appeared in a thick plumage of black and green, the emerald signet on its forehead gleaming like a third eye. The stench of mace and ginger intensified as it arced down gracefully, its long, curved beak opening as it aimed for Madhyra. The lightning wove around it like a rope of starlight as it lit up the bridge on the waterfall in descent. Madhyra ducked at the last moment and rolled on the bridge, wincing in pain. Kuka swept and took off again, rising over the rim of the mountain and into the sky and circling over the peak, its spiked tail swaying in the wind.

A moment later, Madhyra clamped Amir's shoulder. "Get off this bridge before it kills you."

"I'm not abandoning you."

There was a faint spark of recognition on Madhyra's face. "I don't mean to the side you came from. I mean the other side of the bridge. Toward Illindhi."

Suddenly, Amir knew what she was asking of him. He took a deep breath and gazed up at the moon. The Immortal Son sailed across it, a monstrous silhouette that veiled the moon entirely for a moment, and then its cry rent the air. It swung downward for a second time.

Amir ran. Behind him, he could feel Kalay sprinting too. As he neared the other side of the bridge, he dived beyond it and landed in thick mud. He braced for Kalay's impact. It never came. As he lifted his head and gazed upon the bridge, Kalay stood towering over Madhyra, her sword aloft as Kuka, the Immortal Son, fell upon them.

Kalay sliced with her talwar, catching Kuka's talon. Nail and lightning met steel. The bird shrieked, flapping violently. The lightning fizzed out of its body momentarily. It landed on the bridge, the whole plank vibrating under tension, and it took flight once more, the lightning sparking on as it soared. Madhyra pushed Kalay aside.

"Leave me alone to deal with this, cheche."

She might as well have instructed the plank of wood, for Kalay clicked her tongue and began to cover her aunt.

Kuka banked treacherously in the air before making a quicker dash toward the bridge. Madhyra stood, one hand pressed to her bleeding hip. When the bird opened its maw and a bolt of lightning issued forth,

Madhyra ducked and rolled. The bolt crackled against the wooden bridge. When she was beneath the bird, she lifted her blade to slash at Kuka's belly. Violet-green blood spilled out in a downpour from the wound, but the beast, using the bridge as leverage, wheeled, and slashed at Madhyra with its free talon, agitated at the violence committed upon it. The lightning-powered nail dug into Madhyra's flesh, and it came away with more than just skin.

Kalay screamed and dived violently between her collapsing aunt and the Immortal Son. She threw her sword like a lance, and it pierced the bird at the heart of its left wing.

Kuka shrieked in pain as it lifted off from the bridge once more. It continued to leak blood, and its ascent was hampered by the talwar that now dangled from its heavy wing. Amir closed his eyes as it nearly crashed into the rim of the waterfall, but it swerved at the last moment, scaling the mountain like a wounded reptile.

Amir watched as Madhyra stumbled. His heart stopped beating for an instant. Even Karim bhai peeked out from his hiding spot.

Madhyra dropped her sword and coughed. She stared at Kalay with a cock of her head, a playful smile fluttering on her lips.

Then she rested her eyes on Amir and fell sideways from the bridge.

Amir screamed, but no sound came out. She grew distant with each passing second, until she looked like a little brown doll that the rising fog swallowed into the dark.

"No, no, no, *no!*" Kalay bellowed, crawling to the edge of the bridge and peering down at the mist. The ravine was dark, and in the dark, Amir knew there was no chance Madhyra could have survived.

His heart shattered into a million pieces. His own bones shook with the impact of Madhyra's fall. It might as well have been he who had fallen, he who had stood facing the Immortal Son and who had failed.

He stood, unable to comprehend what had transpired, only that it had, and he had to act. Not acting would mean death.

Kuka was turning around, and Amir did not know why. Madhyra was dead, and the Mouth had gotten what it had wanted. Yet the Immortal

Son traced a circle in the air, and Amir wondered whether it was coming back for him. Had the Mouth figured it out?

Kuka did not, however, swoop down on him. It aimed instead for Kalay.

The moonlight danced in the reflection on the water as the bird descended. All Amir had to do was watch. It'd be over in a heartbeat. Behind him, the mountain wound into a dark labyrinth of passageways into which the creature wouldn't be able to enter, and he knew he'd be safe.

Yet, as Kuka lifted off the mountain and swerved downward, Amir dashed onto the bridge. He screamed, his shamshir aloft. The Immortal Son, who had not seen Amir until then, raised its beak seconds before it devoured Kalay's head.

Amir slid on the wet bridge. The shadow of the creature loomed over him. He dropped his shamshir, and in a fit of impulse, wrapped his fingers around Kalay's talwar that dangled from the Immortal Son's wing.

His momentum caromed him in the opposite direction. His guts lurched. He was suddenly hanging from the talwar's hilt in midair, the ravine far beneath, inviting him in. Amir shut his eyes and clung to the weapon. The bird screeched as the talwar dug deeper into its body. As it swerved and thrashed in pain, the talwar swerved too, and so did Amir, flailing like a tattered flag in a storm.

Within seconds, the blade cut a line as long as the wing itself, cleaving it in two. When the Immortal Son went to draw its wing back, Amir's heart somersaulted and his body traced a circle in the air. The bird dug its beak into the bridge in a rage, limbs thrashing, biting into the wood and its splinters until the bridge itself threatened to collapse.

Amir screamed in triumph when the wing came apart, but the next moment, he was flung outward. He flew twenty feet into the air, passing over the bridge and the ravine entirely, before crashing on mud and stone. Kalay's violet-coated talwar fell from his hand.

Pain roared in his limbs and his back as he struggled to sit. He was certain his back had broken. Kuka, encased in its now-mortal pain, jerked violently on the bridge before taking off awkwardly. Its talons nearly scratched Kalay as it ascended, missing by a hair. Its body grazed against the stones behind the waterfall as it rose, each flap of its severed wing causing it unspeakable torment. Using its only good wing and digging into the side of the mountain with its talons, the bird-beast finally lifted itself over the mountain and disappeared on the other side, its once-piercing shriek reduced to a whimper.

A gust of relief escaped Amir's lips. Struggling to his feet, he limped onto the bridge to where Kalay lay. Along the way, he picked up Madhyra's dropped sword, the blade she had received from Rani Zariba.

He grimaced in disgust and something nasty chewed his stomach at the sight in front of him.

When the bird had lowered its maw upon Kalay, it had rested one talon not on the bridge but on Kalay's foot. She was shivering. Tendons now lay exposed within a curry of flesh. She gazed into Amir's eyes, her fury and rage tempered into something pitiable. She gripped Amir's arm and managed to sit.

When she stared at the wound below her knee, she clicked her tongue, her breath rattling as she stared at Zariba's ancestral sword in Amir's hand. "Lucky I won't be able to catch you now, ho?"

Amir did not smile. "No, I suppose you won't." Karim bhai scurried over to them, his eyes fixed on the mountain beyond which the Immortal Son had disappeared. He squealed when he saw the wound on Kalay. But upon closer inspection, he scratched his beard. "That doesn't look good," he said. "But she can live."

"I know I can," Kalay replied sternly, as though the alternative were preposterous.

"Shut up, ponnu," Karim bhai sneered. He met Amir's gaze. "I can take her to the closest settlement. Or if she can't limp all the way, I'll fetch someone. Or fashion a cart. We did pass some scraps earlier dumped by the settlers."

Amir nodded, registering the undertones Karim bhai had been employing. He didn't say it out loud, but Amir presumed he had.

"Must I do this?"

There was a gap of silence in which neither Karim bhai nor Kalay said anything. Both seemed to have grasped what Amir had asked, and the question hung in the air amid the stench of burned ginger and mace.

"Only you must do this," Karim bhai finally said.

Amir rubbed his face in exasperated confusion. *Not now, not now, not now.* "But bhai, what right do I have? To make this choice on behalf of others? What right do I have to deny so many their faiths and their means of livelihood? I am taking away from people their god, their habit, their obsession. I'm cutting more ties than I'm trying to knot." He paused and took a deep breath while Karim bhai patiently waited for him to finish. "Kalay was right. Who am I to tell them what they must or must not do? This . . . this has been the order of things, hasn't it? Why should it change?" He smacked himself in the head with his knuckles. "Gates, I was certain a while ago, and now I'm confused again. I shouldn't have asked you. I shouldn't have asked anything at all!"

Karim bhai laid a hand on Amir's shoulder. "Listen to me, pulla. You have the right, ho. You and me, and the people like us, at the bottom of the Bowl. We always have the right to topple what stomps on us and to take that burden off our heads."

"But what's the price?" Amir moaned, recalling Ilangovan's words.

"The price does not matter. The burden off our heads does, pulla. You cannot demand a freer world and refuse to pay the price for it. Look around you. Around us. Look what we have come through. This is right."

Amir cast a glance at the mountains and the distant plains. He thought back to that brief moment in the settlements in the Outerlands, the community, the distance from every whip and spit. He'd seen the life. The breath of fresh air sweeping down from the hills and frolicking through the woods. He had seen the children play and the spices being ground and crushed. He knew he had seen only the good parts of it. He knew trouble lurked in every manner of life. But it did not matter.

Karim bhai pushed him harder. "This will be the way you save Kabir. This will be the way you save everyone who was born with the spicemark

413

in the last few years and is not yet a Carrier. The pain that awaits them—you can snatch it all away."

Karim bhai appeared more convinced than Amir, but his last words bore into Amir's flesh and seared into his innards like a hot brand. He was right. This was how he'd save Kabir. All those children running around the bottom of the Bowl, not knowing that, for a few of them, an eternity of torment awaited, separated from temptation by the walls of privilege.

Finally he thought of Amma. She was why he was here, wasn't she? His little escapade in search of the Poison culminated on this forsaken bridge on the way to the ancient, hidden empire of Illindhi, where the Spice Gates originated and their tireless god lay slumbering beneath the earth. This would be for her.

When he finally nodded in reply to Karim bhai, it was weak, yet Karim bhai stood to embrace him anyway. "Do not think of the eight kingdoms, pulla. They're just people with an obsession for spices. They will live. A new obsession will come their way. This is how the world should have been a long time ago."

Amir looked down at Kalay. There was an inscrutable expression on her face, tumultuous thoughts Amir could only grasp the wispy ends of but without fully understanding the emotions weighing down on her. When she spoke, it was as if the acid the Mouth had left on her tongue and seared into her bones had melted off her skin.

"You should have let the Immortal Son kill me. The Mouth wanted me to pay the price for my failure. My betrayal."

"That'd make me no different from the Mouth," Amir said, already sinking beneath the weight of the burden. "I'd like to think I am in the business of saving lives."

Kalay sniffed. "You couldn't save my aunt."

Amir looked beyond Kalay at the gushing waterfall. He inhaled sharply, as though hoping her spiced fragrance would rush up through the fog and fill the night air. "She'd made up her mind."

"It's my fault," said Kalay. "My aunt, she was safe. She had the scent of the kavestha upon her. But I brought the Immortal Son to her anyway."

Kalay coughed, lifting herself further so she could rest on Karim bhai's knee.

Amir placed a hand on her shoulder. "It's time you finally stop seeing us as those who are paying for the sins of our prior births. You now know what we're capable of. And what we want."

"You still need to get past Mahrang," she whimpered. "And then the Mouth."

Amir smiled. "You think too far ahead. I need to get to Illindhi before that."

"You will," Kalay said. "Less than a day's hike away from here. You will. I . . . when I saw the Immortal Son come down on me . . . I . . ."

"It's okay," said Amir. "Without you, I wouldn't have crossed the Outerlands on the first day. Or on the second. Or the third. You saved me every single day, Kalay. I am not my father. I needed help. Sure, I needed the map, too, but I'd be a fool to not admit I was terrified of charting the Outerlands by myself."

Kalay nodded, but then her body shook in a fit of coughs once more. Karim bhai lifted her and put her arms over his shoulders. She was heavier than a sack of spice, Amir supposed. But for the moment, Karim bhai managed. He was straining, but he was still active, itching to get off of this bridge before Kuka returned. "Go, pulla. Make haste. And"—he grinned, revealing sparkling white teeth—"do it for the Bowl."

CHAPTER
28

*Of much relevance is the age-old argument of whether a great
meal is a consequence of an accomplished cook or the right spice.*

—One Chapati, Two Chapati, Three Chapati, Flour

Time slipped out of its path as Amir squatted on the tall grass at
first light. Illindhi's ivy-covered walls loomed two hundred feet
ahead, dotted with sentries and archers huddled inside. Kalay
had assured Amir that they could see as well as an owl in the dark, and
that even the slightest hint of sound was bound to get them all nailed by
an arrow.

Amir did not desire any arrows in him.

When at first the distant haze of mist had thinned and the searing
peak of Mount Ilom had emerged from the mist, Amir had refused to
believe it. That there was a reward waiting at the end of this journey
had somehow escaped his mind in those feeble moments of bittersweet
agony.

Now, for the first time, he *saw* Illindhi. In all its glory under the
vermilion strokes of dawn. The walls loomed over a hundred feet high,
pillars carved into towers with dome-shaped roofs and cloistered ramparts that shielded everything within from the sight of those outside.

No wonder Madhyra was obsessed with talking about walls.

The stones began to brighten with the first hint of light. Torches were being extinguished. Beyond, Amir barely glimpsed the faint silhouettes of domes and spires and saw-toothed ramparts. Between the high grass and the gates, a wide bridge ran over a moat, flanked by poles bearing saffron flags, leading toward gates as high as thirty feet. Red and buff sandstone, spandrels framed in gray marble, a great tiger in obsidian inlaid into the apex of the arch. Minarets jutting out on either side of the battlements overhead. These sights alone sent a shiver through Amir.

The boundaries of Illindhi had been tiresome to traverse. For the first time since setting out on this journey, an aloneness sat in the core of his chest. A long walk punctuated only by the sound of crickets and birds, and the harmonious crackle of leaves. Not a soul to talk to.

He was, in the end, a Carrier. Seeing this through was his responsibility. He could accept no other path.

One eye trailed the silhouettes on the ramparts at all times. The still largely dark sky afforded him safe passage through the tall grass. Any rustle could be dismissed as a low breeze. All he had to do was remain in the shadows.

It was what he was good at, sneaking.

Failure loomed ever larger with each passing moment, and Amir couldn't ignore it. A single slip could undo days of effort. He could smell his own death lingering around him like burned pepper. It felt as though he were walking toward his own embalming.

The moat wound under the mountain proper. The walls meandered and ended where the slopes began. It loomed ahead, breaking through the clouds, its immensity matched only by what lay beneath it. Memories galloped back of emerging out of the Spice Gate atop the mountain on that frosty morning like a naked child who had to be ushered blindfolded into warmth.

He found the culvert that burrowed into the mountain, as scribbled by Madhyra in the map. He crept through the tunnel, reminded of his sojourn in the Pyramid's toilet. The stench traveled a thousand miles, assaulting his nose even now.

Hasmin's faithful compass pointed Amir eastward in a bid to reach the heart of the tunnel. The mountain started to shudder. The drums had begun to beat. A distant, sonorous sound of clapping echoed through the passages.

The Uyirsena were on the move.

Amir brought out the shamshir and stalked ahead. The tunnels expanded and then forked. Rivulets of caves appeared within each fork, digging farther into the terrain. However, this close to the Mouth, Amir did not need the compass anymore. Nor the guiding sounds of the Uyirsena.

Within him, the pulse of the Mouth throbbed. It seemed to breathe the very air that circulated underground. The fragrances of every spice Amir had come to love and use and taste was loaded in the air. Each time the Mouth unleashed a torrent of saffron cloud—like an orange swirl that could barely be discerned among the russet walls—Amir's breathing rose and fell.

He followed the scent, the aroma, the memory of his home as the spice swirled to form shapes in his mind. Caves collapsed and opened up. Passages appeared where he least expected them to. He was only following the trail of spices. He didn't care if he was ambushed. He'd find a way out. The very idea of failure had all but dissolved in his mind.

At one point, where the cloud of spices hovered above him, and he coughed and sneezed and carried on through the mist, he became faintly aware of growing footfalls. The Uyirsena were nearby.

Not in dozens, but in hundreds. Thousands. It was as if every fallen pebble on the floor rose and grew into a sworn son of Illindhi out to preserve their unbent history.

Their war cries were calls for blood. And those cries were heading in his direction.

When a hand materialized from behind Amir and covered his mouth and lifted him off his feet, everything fell apart.

The shamshir clattered out of his hand. Then a second figure was upon him, crouching to grab his flailing feet and the fallen sword. Together, they carried him backward, strafing sideways into a rough, narrow slope, dark and riddled with stones, the roof closing in, leading away from the central passage of the mountain. It took Amir a moment to understand that any effort to free himself would be counterproductive, and that it was for the best that he lay still and allow his captors to carry him wherever they wished.

It turned out that was not too far. They dropped him on the cave's jagged floor. It took every muscle in Amir's body to work in concert to keep him from screaming his lungs out. The wound beneath his shoulder opened up, staining his tunic, which elicited a sound from one of his captors.

When he stood, the ones who'd carried him blocked the way out, their folded hands a sign of clear disappointment at his behavior.

Of these two Amir had glimpsed nothing but a fraction of their faces, a fleeting sight of their wavy turbans, their puffed cheeks and wriggly posteriors—all of which barely revealed their immortal presence in the mountain of Illindhi.

"It's him again, Sibil-kunj," Makun-kunj said. He was the taller of the two, though Amir knew if he were to look away for a moment and look again, he would have already forgotten who was who.

"You're a mosquito in humid August," Makun-kunj said with a nod. "And you should feel lucky. We saved you from certain trampling."

It was then Amir heard the footfalls of the Uyirsena stomping by the passage he had been stalking just before. The drone, the endless clatter, like the hooves of a stable of horses clomping past, pikes crashing against the earth in concert, their rhythm of hate manifesting in flickering shadows on the walls of the diversion where the two ancient guards stood watch over Amir.

"Thank you," Amir replied. Sweat dripped down his forehead. "Really. I am indebted to you, but right now, you have to let me go."

Makun-kunj and Sibil-kunj exchanged glances. Haste was not a word in their vocabulary. If ever they grasped the concept of time, it was in recounting events of a hundred years past, and right then, Amir was not in a position to sit quietly and listen to a volume of Illindhian infiltrations.

"We will," Makun-kunj said, "if you answer our question."

Sibil-kunj took over. "Now, it's not unknown to even the laziest of upper-level wardens that the Uyirsena have been woken from their slumber. But what stumps me, more than it stumps Makun-kunj, is—"

"That's unfair, Sibil-kunj. We agreed to be on an even footing, at least in presentation."

"Don't get all bitter, now. I had already planned for your moment of advantage in subsequent sentences. If only you had the patience to listen to the other person complete his sent—"

"Will you please get to it?" Amir joined his hands in quivering prayer. He was wasting precious seconds of time here, listening to these two bicker. Once the Uyirsena got to the Spice Gate, there would be no turning back.

Sibil-kunj seemed affronted, but after a moment's thought, proceeded. "As I was saying, what stumped me, *as much as it had* stumped Makun-kunj, was that Fylan was nowhere to be seen leading the army out."

"It defies protocol." Makun-kunj nodded. "The order is simple. The law is broken. The Uyirsena are awakened. The Mouth blesses the Uyirsena, and the captain leads them out. Now, you know us. We don't really ask for much. All we wanted to see was Fylan marching ahead of the troops, his sword aloft, Illindhi's name on his lips. And Sibil-kunj, ever so alert, you have my gratitude for that, should we succeed in our efforts . . . now, Sibil spotted you from a distance and thought to himself and to ourselves: Who was the last person who saw Fylan?"

"That'd be me," Amir said, very well aware of how ponderous this conversation was shaping up to be. He craned his neck to see through the opening. The drone of the Uyirsena continued. He had no choice but to wait.

Without warning, something materialized in his mind. It came in his deepest antipathy for the two men standing in front of him, fawning over their fallen general. The truth could wait yet again.

"Fylan sent me here," Amir scrambled to lie. "A last task before the Uyirsena depart through the Spice Gates."

"Did he, now?" Sibil-kunj asked. His breaths quickened. All around Amir, the ground pulsed beneath his feet, pebbles juddering.

Amir pointed at Mahrang's shamshir. "This, here, is one of Fylan's own swords. He has asked me to bless it with the spit of the Mouth since he himself was too preoccupied to do it."

Makun-kunj's eyes narrowed in suspicion. Sibil-kunj inspected the blade, giving it a closer look in the weak torchlight. "It is a blade of the Mouth, there's no doubt. Slope-forged. Spit congealed along the edges."

"Why would he leave his blade in the hands of another, though, Sibil-kunj?"

Amir sighed, snatching the shamshir back. "Because it is his own sister he had to hunt. A man cannot carry the weight of such a burden on his shoulders as well as manage all his chores by himself. That was the reason he chose a precocious little apprentice in me, so that I could follow and learn from him, and be of use should the need arise."

It worked, one word at a time, Amir crept into their consciousness, lodging in their fragile sensibilities. As much as Amir pitied them, time was of the essence.

The shuddering stopped. Amir whistled in relief. The Uyirsena had left the cave to make their way to the top of Mount Ilom. To the Spice Gate.

He brushed past Makun-kunj and Sibil-kunj. At the entrance, he stopped to regard them. "You will stand guard, won't you?"

"Outside the Mouth?" Makun-kunj asked, his face lighting up in honor. "By our lives."

Sibil-kunj nodded. "Not a soul shall be let through."

Amir did not trust them to that extent, but he trusted them enough to put their heart into it.

They took the path the soldiers had tread upon. The ground had deep depressions, wet and muddy now, the air in that narrow underground cavern reeking of their sweat, enduring as a reminder of their filth. At one point, the Mouth's voice manifested in his head like a thunderous summons, splitting his skull, barraging him with pain.

He began to run, the smell of turmeric lingering in the air, then cumin and ginger, followed by mace and nutmeg. It was like the bazaar came to life along the walls, sprays of spice gathered and dried and fossilized in the stones and the crevices and the harsh terrain of the earth he ran on.

The cave seemed to go on forever. How much farther could the Uyirsena have gotten? It was an army, and they had to climb to the very peak of the mountain.

Light rose and fell. The fading sound of the Uyirsena sharpened the beating of his heart. Behind him, Makun-kunj and Sibil-kunj rushed to catch up.

At one point, the path dropped away, as though into a deep bowel. The cavern's ceiling exploded outward even as the trail hit a steep decline, the air heavier, pungent, black pepper and saffron dense in every pore of the wall.

The Mouth was here. Almost here.

Ahead, the path narrowed again. The roof lowered, and Amir saw a single arched opening in the wall. Inscriptions were on the head of the arch, as though the entrance itself were a replica of the Spice Gate. The flanks were pillars, cracked and bulging, and when Amir touched it, the cold stone of the Spice Gate seeped into his veins.

He waited there to catch his breath. The darkness beyond was total. Not a flicker of candlelight. Just blackness. When the two ancient guardians caught up to him, he borrowed the torch from Sibil-kunj and nodded at them. They positioned themselves one in front of each pillar, their swords close to their chests, heads high.

Taking a deep breath, Amir stepped inside.

MAHRANG WAS SEATED SAGACIOUSLY FACING A DEEP GORGE IN THE earth. The Mouth's floor descended into a shattered and blasted pit, the hole within spouting tongues of flame with bristles of iron and obsidian wrinkling along its scarred sides. It looked like the inside of an enormous tandoor oven.

The monk appeared tired. He seemed to be in penance, sheathing his sword and taking a step forward.

Smoke from the Mouth obscured Mahrang's face, enveloping him in a dense mask of choking mist. It curled out of his turban and wove through his cloak. His blade lay by his side, firelight dancing on it. When he stood, Amir's hands shook. He was never one for courage. All of a sudden, his bladder knocked on its doors.

"Do you know why I gave you that blade?" Mahrang asked.

Amir wiped the sweat off his brow and breathed heavily. He needed to pee and get it over with. He shifted his stance to get a better grip.

Mahrang didn't wait for a response. "The pommel has a latch. It's buried in the hilt's edge so that a simple tap will unlock it. It opens into a little chamber, where there has always been a tiny vial of olum present. Olum enough to spray on the Spice Gate and travel to Illindhi from anywhere in the eight kingdoms."

Well, he should have just told you this when he gave it to you.

Mahrang lifted his own blade and demonstrated. A vial of olum dropped into his palm. He uncorked it, sniffed it, and let its contents drop into the Mouth. A hissing sound scathed the cavern, and Amir's knees wobbled.

Mahrang stood against the opening, right at the rim, cloaked in the shadow of flame. The slightest step backward would be sufficient for him to topple and fall.

When he placed one foot forward, Amir pressed his thumb to the shamshir's hilt. But Mahrang merely lifted his blade, brought it down, and buried the tip into the ground.

The earth reverberated. Amir teetered at the great shudder. The Mouth, in clear annoyance at the disturbance to its surface, cringed and spat out a venomous bolt of flame that spattered onto the cavern's already blackened ceiling in a shrieking hiss.

"You have done well," Mahrang said, leaving his sword buried in the earth and standing straight. "You just saved a thousand lives."

Amir blinked. "D-Did I?"

"You wouldn't be here if Madhyra wasn't gone. I must thank you, as much as it saddens me to carry the news of our thronekeeper's death." His fingers grazed his sword's pommel. "The Uyirsena are attuned to the vibrations in the mountain. I have just communicated to them to halt their march toward the Spice Gate. I am their master. They will listen to me. On the other hand, you . . ."

He ran his hand along the blade's hilt, down to where the steel began. The touch drew blood. "Why don't you tell me about why you're really here, Amir of Raluha?"

Amir was bathed in sweat from the heat rising out of the Mouth. He had hoped to get a better glimpse of the gorge, but Mahrang's question rooted him to his spot. If anything, Amir knew that he had walked right into a trap.

"I don't want to be a Carrier anymore," he said. "I thought I told you that before." There was more where those words came from, but they were being repressed by some inexplicable force, most of it driven by Mahrang's deep, penetrating gaze that could have skinned him alive. The monk appeared nonplussed by the response, however. His voice was deep and flat as always.

"You could have asked. I was willing to indulge you in your desires. There's no need to go to so much trouble."

Amir shook his head, cracks appearing in his psychic dam. "You know better than me that simply asking for what I want has never worked for people like me. Your god down there is a trickster, isn't he? Laughing while he plucks out the lowest of us and brands us with his mark as though he were throwing us a favor."

Mahrang smiled. "We think it generous."

"What difference has it made to you that I have the mark?" Amir asked. "Do you see me as anything more than the rest of my people? Those fortunate enough to not have it?"

A trace of doubt seemed to have crept into Mahrang's expression. He lost the smile, but not his composure. The timbre in his baritone endured. "You have earned our envy. You are empowered to travel through the Spice Gates when nobody else can. Through the very soul of the Mouth. You witness the god every day while even the ones who pray at its feet cannot go any farther than this precipice."

"At what cost?" asked Amir. Mahrang winced, as though allergic to being opposed. But within Amir, the water had now begun to seep through the cracks. The dam was breaking. Crumbling. Rubble. Dust.

He stopped, placed his hands on his hips, and took a deep breath to calm his voice. "Do you know? Only weeks ago, I had to steal olum from Hasmin's constabulary. I waded into his toilet. Do you know who I found there, squatting beside the chamber pot, her hand golden brown and squishy? My neighbor. She is twelve years old, and she was gathering Hasmin's and his loyal men's shit with her bare hands, pushing it into a rusty bowl that she'd carry out to the fences and dump in the waste wedges. Then she'd return and take up the next abovefolk's house, who'd summon her for peanuts. Hasmin never even gave her a cloth, because to spare a cloth for one of the bowlers is to make the cloth itself impure. She knew why I was there. She never uttered a word. But that's what we do. Clean toilets, carry the skins of goats and pigs, wash the ashes off burned pyres, and at the end of it keep our silence. We draw our water from wells whose bottoms hold carcasses of dead animals and birds. That's what we drink—toxic filth—because that's what we are allowed to have. And you . . . you're giving me your envy? How is that even possible?"

Mahrang remained silent, but Amir could tell that his words were getting under his skin, eliciting the slightest of tingles.

"I never asked for much," he continued. "We got by with two meals a day, rice, dal, cabbages and beetroot, carrots if we got lucky at the bazaar. Bland as a white kurta on most days once our rations had finished, like you'd snatched the soul out of a poet. That's what Karim bhai would call our food. That was truth. Can you blame us for wanting to make it a little exciting? Not fancy clothes. Not carriages and wide alleyways.

Not mirrors on our walls and carpets beneath our feet. No, no. All I ever wanted was a good plate of biryani once a fortnight. A pinch of mace, a hint of nutmeg, a little grace of turmeric and saffron, little pools of rose-water, and the tender, marinated meat cooked beneath them all. Curry nourished with chilies and salt, and cardamom crushed and sprinkled. Nobody made curry like Amma did. And you know why nobody made it? Because nobody had the spices for it. We! The great, legendary Spice Carriers, recipients of the envy of big, beefy abovefolks—afforded only a fingernail's worth of saffron or ginger or cloves as a monthly allowance. What do we do with it? Waste it? By the time you get it home, the wind's already carried it off your hands. That's why I steal. Not for anyone else. Only for me and my amma, for my little brother who now carries spice on his back. And let me tell you this—I am the *luckiest* of all the bowlers you'd ever meet."

He stopped pacing and met Mahrang's eye. "Go on, shower me with your envy."

Mahrang seemed to have absorbed all of Amir's tirade, his face twitching in contemplation. "What would your act accomplish now?" he asked after a moment's silence.

Is that all?

Amir chuckled. "The thronekeepers couldn't kill us because we had the brand. And without us, there would be no Spice Trade. None of that silk trail of turbaned merchants nonsense. But without the Spice Gates? We're free. Free to be killed or let ourselves out of that stinking Bowl. We wouldn't spare a single glance backward. There's life in the Outerlands. Good life. With its own problems and chaos, but out there, everyone cleans their own shit, and the water is as pure as the river. Madhyra and I are evidence that the Spice Gates are not needed. And if I can make that journey between the kingdoms, I wager anyone can. The great lie that there's no life beyond the fences needs to stop. Maybe it's time for the abovefolks to get out of their homes and see what it's like to walk with a sack over their shoulders. And if not that, perhaps just walk. I'm tired of carrying everyone's desires on my back and receiving nothing but scorn in return. I, and everyone down in that Bowl, are worth more than that."

Amir clasped the shamshir tighter, a fire raging within him to rival the flames sputtering out of the Mouth. He stood parallel to Mahrang, the heat rushing out of the gorge and slapping against his face in jets of dark smoke. He craned his neck to risk a glance down into the gorge and—nothing. Whatever slumbered beneath was either too deep, or not there at all.

All of a sudden, as though the nothingness itself was his reward, Amir knew what he must do. He chided himself for not coming to this conclusion much sooner. All of this—his rant, his encounter with Mahrang—everything could have been avoided. A part of him had already made up his mind that jumping into the hole was a clean way of accomplishing his task. He had faith enough in his spicemark that he'd emerge unscathed. And if not . . . He stared down the swirling ashes within the Mouth and shuddered, his scared little heart seeming to grow tendrils that crawled out of his body and planted themselves into the earth to prevent him from toppling down.

Amir let out a jet of air, proud of his own timing in discovering the alternative to this death sentence.

"You cannot kill the Mouth, Amir." Mahrang's words echoed across the cavern. "You'd be charred to death before you even reach its beating heart. And furthermore, you must get past me." With that, Mahrang pulled his sword out of the ground, hand steady as a well-laid brick. Firelight gleamed on the blade, and Amir knew that no amount of swordsmanship or luck would be sufficient to overwhelm Mahrang.

He smiled anyway, aware that his heart was fluttering in his chest. "I don't have to get past you. I just have to run faster than you."

Mahrang pivoted sideways to block Amir's path down the gorge into the Mouth.

But Amir dodged the other way, kicking off mud from his heels, dashing toward the exit. Past the archway, where he screamed Fylan's name so that both Makun-kunj and Sibil-kunj shifted sideways in their eternal slumbering gait. Just as Amir passed underneath the arch, they blocked the way for Mahrang.

"Do not let him past you!" Amir shrieked, already hurtling down the caverns.

He only heard a clang of steel, a scream. A crash of bodies. Amir was zipping between ancient pillars, wiping the sweat off his forehead, but he was drenched in it. The heat worked its way out of his body with each stride. Did he have a direction in mind? Hasmin's compass vibrated in his hand, but he was not looking at it any more than he was at his own feet. All of a sudden, the rest of his life seemed an eternity away. Karim bhai, his family, Harini, his Carrying duties—his entire life seemed removed from this singular moment where he ran to set everything right. It didn't matter that his past had brought him to this moment. As long as his strides landed on hard stone and mud, he'd be all right.

The passages twisted and turned, presenting themselves as ominous sculptures. The weight of the mountain sagged over Amir's shoulder, slowing him down, pressing his heels into the earth as though with each step, he grew a little shorter, until, at some point ahead, only his head would be aboveground, the rest flailing in the earth beneath, along with the beast in the Mouth.

Behind and above him, he sensed the thumping, retreating footfalls of the Uyirsena. And beyond that, the sound of Mahrang's ferocious chase.

Cursing, Amir burst forward, and seconds later, tripped himself into a great cavern.

Munivarey was inspecting one of the slither-filled crates when he perked up at Amir's stumbling appearance. He adjusted his glasses. A formal chuckle ensued.

"I was wondering if you'd gotten lost."

The false gate loomed behind Munivarey on the pedestal, a dullness etched between the pillars and beneath the arch. It looked like any other relic of a doorway from where Amir stood, but it was his only hope now.

"There's no time," he gasped, then rushed to the crates. Bending down,

Amir yanked at the cables tethered to the false gate's base and jerked them one after the other into the sockets of the crates. Munivarey watched with an amused expression, his hands on his hips, as though his entire life's work had amounted to this one moment when someone stumbled into his chamber and began to play around with his toys.

The crates at once shuddered to life. The slithering remains of the beast within the Mouth quivered and elongated like limbs of jelly. Black goo spattered on the glass surface as the tentacles were sucked into the tubes. A crack like weak lightning sizzled beneath the arch. Amir did not need any spice this time.

The shamshir in hand, Amir climbed the steps of the pedestal just as Mahrang appeared behind him.

"Stop!" he screamed.

Amir had already placed one foot into the arch.

Munivarey's mirthless laughter echoed through the cavern before ceasing altogether as Amir stepped through the gate without the spices.

His body convulsed and folded. Time stretched and thinned. Space opened up, and elsewhere blinked out of existence, all of it within that thin veil between two stone pillars. Amir's consciousness alone remained while every other part of him succumbed to the fragility of the movement.

He was, once again, zipping through the skies, clouds above, land below, canopies of trees, wide rivers, endless oceans, and tall, circular fences with scores of buildings and palaces and marble towers sulking within. He flitted from Spice Gate to Spice Gate, until the last of them— the Gate upon the small island in the bogged heart of Mesht, the fragrance of jeera and balsam and teak in the air—disappeared too, and he was back within the mountain of Illindhi.

Not in Munivarey's lair, but, as before, within the Mouth itself.

He floated on thin air, like a green pea in water. His first realization was that he was not charred to a crisp like Mahrang had warned him. Instead he was surrounded by inflamed walls, burned shadows, gushing tendrils of smoke. Far beneath, the open maw of something terrible and misbegotten loomed. The Mouth stretched and yawned into a bottomless pit. Its surface was pinpricked and scarred, frosted scales gleaming in firelight, its hide obscuring the mountain walls. If it had eyes, Amir could not see them beyond the lips that were craters soldered into a curve. But even as he floated, he glimpsed a hint of a movement, a forked tongue coiling within the maw, sensing his alien presence above it, sensing the one creature it had tried to torment and constantly shake off in the Outerlands.

It didn't matter. Amir had defied fate and he was here now simply because he'd been pushed and prodded and he'd not backed down. Because he'd refused to surrender, not even when death had hacked through half his door. Even if he survived the Mouth, Mahrang and the Uyirsena would be awaiting him outside Munivarey's false gate, their blades dipped in ghee, edges bent upon his neck.

This—this would be his final act.

The shamshir was as light as ever in his hand. His fingers curled around the hilt. His swordsmanship—or the lack thereof—did not matter. All he had to do was point the sword in the right direction. He took a deep breath, and with a puff of air, he hurled himself down.

Across the spice-tinged throat of the Mouth, walls bloated with burned effigies of the eight spices.

Somehow, having navigated to the Mouth through Munivarey's false gate made him immune to the heat within. It pulsed around him, although nothing could justify why he was left unharmed.

Even when he entered the Mouth's misshapen maw, its stink and its gallons of spice adhered to its gums did not oppress him. It could have all been a dream, a blip of his consciousness. And yet it was real.

My child . . . My broken, precious child. What are you doing?

He thought of Madhyra in those fleeting, flickering moments.

Son of Spice, why must you abandon me so? Do you not see the folly in your actions? Do you not know you will forever be hunted for your sin?

Because there was no way to shut his ears, Amir shut his eyes. His muscles stiffened in reaction to the Mouth's taunts. It was too late to believe anything it said. Wasn't it?

I am your Beginning and your End, and I command you to stop! Vermin of the earth, servant of soil, listen to your Mother. To your Creator. To the one who blessed you and bore you and cradled you while you Passed. Listen to—

The shamshir's steel was imbued with every pulsing energy within the god. Its hide was the beast's, the steel forged from the molten remains of its carapace. Amir opened his eyes and plunged the shamshir into the Mouth's spiced tongue, then twisted it to the hilt.

Nothing happened.

At first.

Then, the earth trembled. A steady thrum reeking of violence, as though the Mouth were vomiting something spoiled. Before the bile of the beast soared up from its belly, Amir, who was screaming beyond his throat's capacity, shot up into the emptiness above the Mouth.

What had folded, unfolded. Where time slipped out and space curved into impossible shapes, they straightened themselves out like a hard-pressed banana leaf refusing to be rolled.

The gate spat Amir out of its abdomen, and he crashed onto Munivarey's pedestal, coughing, gasping for breath.

His hand was free of the blade even as his body reached its limits. His mind, finally unburdened, soared and then descended into the Bowl of Raluha. He wanted nothing more than to walk across the threshold of his home, to the smell of the fading allowance of pepper and saffron, to the pinch of turmeric in the milk and a memory of nutmeg in the biryani, and to lie down on the low cot beside Kabir until the morning came and they'd go chasing the roosters and flying kites in a part of the world far from the marble stain of the abovefolk and their shadows of silks and gold. He wanted nothing more than to finally meet the shining brown eyes of his newborn baby sister.

He went to crawl down the steps of Munivarey's gate but found Mahrang there, kneeling, at the base, his head buried in his hands. He was shivering. Behind him were the huffing, immortal pair of Makun-kunj and Sibil-kunj, hunched beside an astonished Munivarey.

Mahrang staggered to his feet, panting.

No Uyirsena. Just him, the elder monk.

When their gazes met, Amir saw in Mahrang the retribution that awaited his sin. Amir never had much hope, really. That he had come this far itself was a feat he'd have dismissed as impossible a few days ago.

He blinked in utter exhaustion as Mahrang took two giant strides up the steps of the gate, mumbling shlokas to the Mouth.

"What did you do?" Mahrang finally asked Amir.

Amir smiled weakly.

Behind him, the first cracks appeared in Munivarey's false gate. The cracks deepened and widened, like water down the sides of a steaming vessel. The next moment, the gate shattered and fell to rubble. Mahrang leaped sideways to avoid the sundering. Amir, too exhausted to even move a muscle, stood rooted. The pillars fell on either side of him, while the arch crashed ahead onto the stairs.

He stared at the rubble until the dust cleared.

Makun-kunj and Sibil-kunj towered over him on the other side of the debris. Deep grins lined their faces even as their final energies appeared to have been sapped in giving Mahrang chase through Munivarey's endless burrows.

Both of them seemed to be inspecting each other in the dim firelight of the cavern, but neither appeared to see what Amir saw. He ought to have realized they were the Mouth's first Immortal Sons, born to watch over the first Spice Gate. When they sank to their knees together, Amir suppressed the urge to tell them of Fylan's death. Their looks of curious amusement did not dwindle, but when they glanced at Amir, he saw gratitude.

The truth could wait, a third time.

They collapsed on the floor beside him moments later, neither writhing nor in pain. And when they died, Amir knew the Mouth was truly gone.

And so were the Spice Gates.

EPILOGUE

ONE YEAR LATER

Vats of biryani lined the table, steam wafting from their mouths. Amir ignored the other delectable dishes and followed his stomach's grumbles, which ached only for that minced meat and rice swimming in spiced gravy. Amma slapped the back of his head when he lowered his face to take a sniff.

"Wait your turn," she snarled. "Get in line like everyone else."

The line was over fifty people long. Most of them were bowlers from Raluha. Karim bhai stood to one side, singing a song to keep the minds of those in the impatient queue occupied. Even without the presence of the Grand Ustad beside him, Karim bhai held his own, a delicate melody that lured the newest arrivals to the Outerlands into a cocoon of comfort.

One of two people who did not appear comfortable was Kalay. She had a faint limp in her right leg, a relic of Kuka's assault on her from a year ago. She was, however, not alone. Illindhi had ensured its newest member of the royal court would be accompanied by seven others, with whom Kalay had little inclination to converse. Amir decided he would not intrude into her space right away.

Kabir and a couple of other boys from the Bowl served the guests. What little concern he had shown when Amir had announced the end of Carrying seemed to have vanished. The tether to the Mouth was severed. He appeared cheerful, and when he caught Amir staring at him, he grinned, which suggested that all was good despite the turnaround.

It had not been easy setting up the entire congregation near the fences of Illindhi. Over the span of a few months, they had transformed that barren stretch into a settlement, its first houses freshly sunbaked and painted, and yet to be proofed from tigers and other wild beasts. Hasmin, who was the second of the two people far from their comforts, stood guard between the shamiana and the woods. An ever-distrustful eye scanned the horizon, occasionally flitting to the tables of food, where fragrant steam curled out of enormous vessels.

He had not been happy when Orbalun dispatched him to the Outer-lands. The displeasure arrived screaming midway through their long journey from Raluha toward Illindhi, which had included a twelve-day uncomfortable ride on wagons, then a sea voyage ferried by Karim bhai and his new faithful crew from the Black Coves—the same people Hasmin had ensured would be on the ship condemned to drown in the Whorl—but who, instead, had crossed the Whorl, sailed past the bay where they had shipwrecked a year before, and anchored at an uncharted beach four days away from Illindhi. Hasmin, upon seeing Karim bhai not only alive but also in a state of forgiveness, had come to realize the bitter taste of acceptance of this new world.

The journey had been difficult, but Orbalun had promised that con-struction had already begun for paths to be paved from the broken fences of Raluha to where the maps bled dry.

The Spice Trade would be renewed and rewritten. Orbalun had con-veyed as much in a long letter to the other thronekeepers—the Illindhian one addressed to Kashyni—a copy of which now lay crumpled in Amir's pocket. The priority, of course, were the roads and the mapmaking. The existing settlers were enlisted to provide advice on how to best preserve the Outerlands while making it compatible to trade for the nine king-doms. Chaos would reign for another year, or perhaps longer, until the nine kingdoms flourished with wagons of spices and sacks brimming with goods once more. The bazaars would get by with local produce for the time being, and merchants who'd raised themselves upon the spoils of the Spice Gates would bide their time, nurse their disbelief, and mask the loss of their faith. Frustrations would mount, and all who had worshiped the Gates would convene under banners of blasphemy; march the long route to where the candles glimmered in the palaces; and set aflame their invitations to dine. They'd scuffle and raise their voices, and perhaps flash a dagger or two in the glint of moonlight when their hunger would peak and the Raluhan households would realize that it is the longest they had ever gone without cumin in their rice and ginger in their teas and turmeric in their dal.

Amir had been the doer of this great act, and even as he stood among friends and folk who thought well of him, he could still find several eyes that trailed him with a pinch of mistrust, a suspicion that wouldn't fade so much as hover over him as a sentence for being the one to bring down the Spice Gates. Only a select few knew Amir had been responsible for this act. Karim bhai, a perennial gossip, had decided the news to be unworthy of spreading.

Not all bowlers had wanted to leave Raluha, and Orbalun had dispatched chowkidars and ministers to maintain order, all of whom now stood warily in this strange place beyond the fences. And behold their criminal, the one who undid their privileges with the thrust of a blade.

One glance at Kabir grinning on the other side of the biryani table, however, and Amir's worry subsided.

The naysayers and critics would come around. If not today, perhaps in a year or two. Perhaps in ten. For as long as Kabir and his baby sister, Velli, were here, away from the Spice Gates, Amir would wait however long it took for them all to come around.

In his own head, though, reality crumbled and folded and shrunk and powdered into dust. Those minutes spent hovering inside the Mouth had snatched something away from him. Nothing that affected the way he was and spoke and behaved. Not in his daily life, no. But when it was cold and silent and he was alone by the river, or staring up at the top of a clove tree in the Outerlands, his mind dragged him through the false gate in Munivarey's lair to that bottomless chasm where the Mouth had shuddered and died. And the Gates functioned as nothing more than dull archways for children to play with and for stonemasons to chisel at under the orders of the royals to collect keepsakes of the ancient portals and ensconce them in glass cabinets in the homes of the abovefolk.

Amir couldn't say what the Mouth had taken from him, but he was both more and less than what he was before he'd dived into the Spice Gate. Ah, well. He could still smell good food from a distance. On most days, that's all that mattered.

He passed shapes huddled beside a campfire, chins tucked into necks, a warm whisper in the ear, a gentle smile, an inviting look for when the sun went down and the stars sprayed across the skies. The village was life, so what had he expected?

In his dreams the last few days, Harini had been with him, albeit distantly. Orbalun's runners and amateur cartographers had reached Halmora and returned after a forty-day trek through the forests and hills. Halmora was mired in disorder, requiring Harini to tend to her shell-shocked parents and a mob of unruly locals, all of whom had fallen at the feet of the Spice Gate and wept for seven days and seven nights. They'd burned the granaries of turmeric in a fit of rage until they'd realized that they wouldn't be getting any more spices anytime soon.

Harini, though, had foreseen this. She had desired to buy the ships in Jhanak from Rani Zariba to avoid a catastrophe of trade and a fall in morale of her people.

Orbalun had gathered Sekaran and the mercenaries from the pirate coves to patrol the borders and guide their own ships as safely along the Halmoran coast as possible, beyond which, serais and trails were to be laid to the turmeric empire.

Harini was quietly satisfied with the added help.

Amir did not hold Harini's absence against her. Even as he watched couples from the Bowl sneak into the comforts of the Outerlands, his pang of longing subsided to a little niggle in the back of his head, which itched only on the starriest of nights.

They'd see each other someday soon. It was only a matter of surviving the Outerlands and, with the Immortal Sons now tame, and somewhere far away, without the voice of the Mouth to guide them, it was possible.

Two more settlements had already been set up in the Outerlands, one of them headed by Ilangovan. The bony pirate had grown his hair to his waist, tied in hasty pigtails. He had decided that the existing settlements were too far inland and that he—along with Sekaran and the others—were seafarers by nature, and that their lives lay closer to the coast than to the heart of the forests. He did, however, present his thumb's seal to the renewed Spice Trade accords, and for Orbalun and Amir—even if not for thronekeepers like Zariba—that was sufficient.

Kalay strolled toward Amir. A different longing, smothered but now awakened like a single spark in a once-great fire. "Your mother's biryani is truly something," she said.

Amir smiled. "The secret ingredient is stone flower. Kalpasi. And instead of jeera, Amma uses caraway seeds. Now, don't go around telling everyone. It's a family secret."

He couldn't help watching her gait, but Amir never brought up the injury, and certainly not what caused it. "Any news from the emissaries?"

"Just the initial word from those sent to Kalanadi, Vanasi, and Mesht for now," said Kalay. "Talashshukh will come later, as we believe it is the farthest. We are expecting responses in the next month or two."

"And the Immortal Sons are truly gone?" Amir held his breath.

Kalay emitted a low sigh. "I would believe so. They are not dead, and for that, I am grateful. It is not their fault to have been used by the Mouth that way. They are still creatures with a soul, and I would much rather they find solace in whatever part of the world that accepts them, wild or otherwise. And if it is nature's will that they overcome us to establish their dominion, so be it. This is a new world, and we must conform to its new rules."

"It is a new life," Amir agreed, although the prospect of the Immortal Sons returning to reclaim the Mouth's lands chilled his bones. "Full of possibilities."

"You did the right thing."

Amir chortled. "Fancy hearing that from you."

Kalay gripped his arm. "I had my doubts even after you left me with Karim. If I had the strength . . . I-I am not going to lie to you, Amir . . . A part of me—even then—wanted to stop you. A part of me still could not wrap my head around the idea of a life without the Spice Gates. Every pore of my body opposed it until I found myself in my aunt's body, looking through her gaze, and then through yours. That part of me wanted to hold on to my aunt's memory. You were finishing what she had started, and to me, that felt a good enough reason to let it happen, because in many ways, I think she'd have one day wanted me to do this if I hadn't joined the Uyirsena. I'd always trusted her, and what she had done at first, it broke that trust, and I was . . . so angry . . . I know I have taken forever to admit what happened to my father, and by whose hand, but at that moment, it felt right. And I'm glad I saw it through both your eyes."

She let go of his arm and smiled. "Though, to be honest, I did save your skin on multiple occasions. So, if you look at it, we're even."

Amir laughed. "We are indeed. Always good to have a friend to cross the Outerlands with. I only hope your mother did not have too much of a problem with you being here."

"Oh, she's busy with her new title—maharani of Illindhi. No more regent, no more substitute. The last year has been a blur for her. She barely has time to see if I even exist. Which is . . . good, in a way."

"And no more olum," Amir added before his thoughts turned grim. A question that had eluded him until then sprang up from its slumber. "What has happened to Mahrang and the Uyirsena?"

Kalay sighed, casting a glance around to ensure they were alone. They were walking close to the low enclosures, where Hasmin was instructing a squad of chowkidars. At the sight of Kalay, his eyes widened, and he wheeled around, as though his life were much safer in the Outerlands without Kalay being a part of it. Amir permitted him his comforts.

When Kalay spoke, though, it was in a low, grave voice. "The Uyirsena live without a purpose. Mahrang, at least. Some among the Uyirsena have realized that there is life beyond duty . . ." She suddenly frowned and slapped Amir on his arm. "Don't give me that all-knowing smirk. Yes, even I've realized there's a lot beyond duty. But you're lucky they spared your life."

When Amir had met a partially healed Kalay after the breaking of the Spice Gates, they'd avoided speaking of what had happened. It was as if Madhyra, the Mouth, and their journey in the Outerlands had belonged to a different life, a different time. That did not mean Kalay had forgiven him. She merely did not want him dead anymore. It was a tremendous improvement. And Amir began to see in Kalay more and more flashes of the girl who'd stepped out of the Spice Gate upon the narrow ridge in Jhanak and had closed her eyes and spread her hands and inhaled the tangy sea air with an unblemished joy. She would not become the Jewel-maker, but she would not be someone confined by the strictures imposed by the Mouth either. In a way, it hadn't just been the gatecaste who'd come off better after the breaking of the Spice Gates.

"The Uyirsena . . . they must hate me still," Amir said.

"Hate is putting it kindly," Kalay replied. "Mahrang rambles like a madman in his incarceration. He claims the Mouth itself was an Im-mortal Son, just like its servants in the Ranagala. He dreams of finding the others, the ones who've fled; he thinks he can create a new Mouth from among them."

Amir gulped, the thought sending ripples of anxiety through him. "B-But that won't be possible, right?"

"Not as long as Mahrang remains in Illindhi, no. Bah, he's insane, you'd do well not to pay heed to his words. Faith has ruled his life, and he cannot imagine life without it. His acolytes chant shlokas in their cells, awaiting their release."

It was feeble assurance. "I'm glad you're not among them."

"Whether I am or not does not matter," Kalay said gravely. "You need to be careful. It's a new life, Amir, and a promising one, but that doesn't mean it comes without danger. Already there are rumors of cults forming in kingdoms like Talashshukh, although our official trade emissaries haven't reached there yet. It's an unstable world, like a suckling left to crawl in the wild. Anything can befall us."

"Aren't you a cheerful one!" Amir rolled his eyes at her. "Is death all you can think of?"

"Oh, she fears it just like you and me, pulla."

Karim bhai strode toward them, his belly full, a glow on his face that spoke of the meal he had just devoured. In his arms was Velli. There was no spicemark on her neck. She would never see the Gates, even if she would, inevitably, hear a lot about them, and perhaps, in her time, even wonder what they must have been like, for all that was spoken of them, mesmerizing artifacts of stone and storms that could transport people to distant lands in the blink of an eye.

Kalay glared at Karim bhai, her eyebrows twitching, and in some inexplicable way, Amir envied that the two shared a secret from their journey back to the Outerlands settlement that Amir had not been privy to.

He borrowed Velli from Karim bhai and kissed her forehead. "Ho, I'll miss her."

"You'll keep visiting," Kalay told him. "And all this is just for a while, until the network is laid. It's the only thing I'm looking forward to, honestly. Given there's not much for me back home."

"Munivarey being a pest?" Amir inquired.

Kalay blew hair out of her face. "Oh, he's a lot of work. When the Gates broke, there were a few inevitable fires, but we have since forged a formal trail to Amarohi. Munivarey believes he now has a new purpose in life, one that would keep him—and the rest of Illindhi—busy for a decade. He's now inspecting the soils between the two kingdoms. A rather tedious task. But the hope is that the Outerlands can help us cultivate the spices that we couldn't otherwise grow in Illindhi itself. He wants half the city to be digging into the mud."

Amir nursed an itch to be beside Harini, their togetherness mushrooming on the slopes of the Halmoran qila, their hands burrowing into the mud, looking for ants and earthworms.

Karim bhai appeared to have gotten more contemplative since his voyage across the Whorl. He observed the Outerlands with a sage's eye, soaking in the silence, the evergreen vistas, as though he were not entirely certain they should be trampling nature's domain this way, but as long as he was around, he would keep the bowlers within their limits. In fact, Amir counted on it.

"Missing Suman-Koti much?" Amir pinched him.

"He's actually a good man," said Karim bhai. "He's promised to bring his family to the settlement once the trails are laid. But he's been going through a hard time. Addicted to ginger, that one, and after the Gates fell, swore himself off tea entirely. Said he wouldn't have a sip till he got his hands on Talashshukhan ginger and grated it himself into the kettle."

"Ah, to be deprived of spice," Amir said sarcastically. "I wonder how that feels." He rolled his eyes at Karim bhai. "For all his influence, I am surprised he hasn't commanded you to go open a new bazaar or something."

"Actually," Karim bhai said, "Gulbega and I were planning the logistics to lay a new bazaar between Amarohi and Illindhi. And perhaps once that is a roaring success, of which I have little doubt, we can replicate it in other parts of the Outerlands. What is life without a bazaar to haggle our days out in, ho?"

"I was joking. The new world just began, bhai." Amir gently patted Velli's back. "Give it a few days."

"Oh, you don't know humans," Karim bhai countered, grinning. "It's a race. It's always a race. Only, we're now free to run at last."

Velli began to cry. Whether it was at the sight of Kalay or Karim bhai, or whether she truly understood the magnitude of work to be done over the next year, Amir couldn't say. But at that moment, Karim bhai began to sing a song. Faces in the village turned toward him. The men carrying the wood stopped in their tracks to listen. Amma's face broke into a grin; how long had it been since she'd been this happy? And much to Amir's relief, Velli, bobbing on his shoulder, stared fixedly at Karim bhai, her tears drowned in the rhythm of his song.

ONE YEAR FURTHER ON . . .

Harini did not think they'd be able to climb the boulder. It was wet from rain, and every step was precarious. She slipped twice, but Amir was there behind her to steady her footing. When they finally scaled it, they fell flat on the boulder's surface, panting, then broke into laughter.

A shrill breeze blew through the treetops. All around them, the thick, knotted jungle of Halmora spread like a vegetated lake. The boulder pierced the treetops like a mole on the skin of the forest. Far behind them, the Halmoran qila lay engulfed in a thin post-rain mist. Ahead, the jungle sloped upward before joining a series of mountains with no end in sight.

Harini drank a mouthful of water then passed the waterskin to Amir, wiping her mouth. "Do not finish it," she said.

Amir stuck his tongue out, then dodged the waterskin and planted a kiss on her wet cheek. "I won't."

They crawled to the edge of the boulder and perched themselves at the lip, their legs swinging. Harini lay her head on Amir's shoulder, and they watched the sun creep down toward the range of mountains.

"We should have left earlier in the day," said Amir. "We barely have an hour before we must trek back to the qila before night."

"Scared of the dark, are we?"

Amir scratched Harini's head, then planted a second kiss into her hair. Gates, the fragrance of sandalwood and turmeric. And the musk of her skin. And of him, now of him.

You need to stop saying Gates.

"Well, yes," he said. "It's called common sense."

Harini chuckled. "It will be worth it, trust me. They will be here any-time now."

Amir stared at the last vestiges of sunlight falling on the mountain slopes. A dash of vermilion and pink, a bed of orange upon a sea of brown and mottled green.

"Have you thought about what I asked you earlier?" he said. "To visit Tehanu." It had taken them seven months to name the settlement at the edge of Illindhi, where presently Amma, Kabir, and Velli lived, along with a hundred score of bowlers and a fresh batch of five hundred Meshti oarasi.

"I have. But it'll be a while, Amir, I am not going to lie. Halmora is mired in all sorts of problems, and we're solving them one at a time. The priests—they still believe the Mouth exists."

Amir harked back to Munivarey's words. *The scriptures exist to corroborate this spiritual relationship between human and Mouth. They legitimize the social structures in place, this deification of transcendence. Otherwise, it becomes impossible to conduct a religion with . . . an accountable deity.* For the priests of Halmora, the destruction of the Gates was a sign that the Mouth was angry with its devotees; that they had committed a sin that needed retribution. This was merely a test of their devotion. The death of the Mouth itself was unacceptable, an impossibility.

As impossible as the falling of the Gates had once been for you.

"The easters . . ." Amir began. "Have they left?"

"Some have," said Harini. "Not to the west, as you will soon see why. But north leads to the river, which opens to the sea in a journey of a couple of weeks. With Orbalun's support and Sekaran's, we have managed to lay a rudimentary trail. But many easters have remained. They know no home outside of Halmora. They refuse to leave. The Carriers among them keep walking through the Gate, wasting spice, hoping one morning, the Gate will return to normalcy. And the priests encourage such behavior. In fact, I wouldn't be surprised if they're paying the Carriers to remain here. Without the Carriers, the hope for the Gates would be lost. Oh, never mind, Amir, it is a headache I do not wish to share with you at the moment. But I will come to Tehanu, I promise. Soon."

Amir traced a finger down her cheek. "I would love for you to meet Amma. And Kabir and Velli, of course."

And what then?

Amir did not wish to burden her with that question. There was not a future for him that did not have Harini in it, and yet he knew the effort it would take to realize their union. Harini did not think Halmora was beyond saving, and as long as that hope lingered, she would work for its fulfillment.

You could move here.

It was a thought Amir was increasingly inclined toward. Once Orbalun's cartography missions were complete, Amir could come to Halmora, or to a settlement along its fringes. Not for much longer could he contend with merely *visiting* Harini. He desired to live with her, to wake up every morning beside her. He had a responsibility to his family, true, but Amma had already joined the union of farmers in Tehanu. Kabir, unofficially, along with the artists and librarians of Talashshukh, had begun to catalogue the Outerlands into an archive that would be housed in museums across the nine kingdoms. He was not of age to earn money, but he wanted to sketch and paint, and there was little Amir could do to stop him. Either way, Amma and Kabir had already begun their new lives, away from the scorn of the abovefolk, with fulfilling jobs that would help them thrive in the Outerlands. He, Amir, could move on.

He and Harini sat in silence as the sun wound down the remainder of its journey, the sky darkening, the shadows thinning across the jungle.

When the first roar shattered the silence of the forest, Amir stirred, his heart leaping. It was followed by a second roar, and then a third, until the mountains ahead teemed with a series of cries. The darkness was absolute one moment, and the next, a yellowish-red hue began to spread across the base of the mountains. The trees cast shadows upon the slope, darkening each second, as the flaming light bristled out of the jungle.

The tree line was breached, and all at once, two dozen fire-lions fanned out upon the slope, sprinting up the rocks, trampling the shrubs, chasing each other's tails. Flames erupted from their spines like lightning bolts. Their long, thick manes swayed under the evening breeze that fed the flames. Their own farewell to the sun. Poetic, a vigil to the dying light through a promise of preservation of their own.

Harini held Amir's hand, snuggling deeper into the curve of his neck. He decided he would not ask her any more questions. Not tonight. They sat at the rim of the boulder that overlooked the knotted jungle of Halmora and watched the fire-lions in their glowing ember stroll beneath a crescent moon.

A NOTE ON PRONUNCIATIONS

CHARACTERS

Amma: Um-maa

Amir: Ah-mir

Fylan: Fi (like "wifi")-laan

Harini: Hur (like "fur")-i-nee

Hasmin: Huss-min

Ilangovan: Eh-lun-go-vun

Kabir: Ka-beer

Kalay: Ka-leigh

Karim bhai: Ka-reem bhai

Kashyni: Kaa-she-nee

Madhyra: Ma-dhee-ra

Mahrang: Mah-raang

Makun-kunj: Makoon-koonj

Munivarey: Mu-ni-vuh-ray

Orbalun: Or-balloon

Sekaran: Say-karan

Sibil-kunj: Si-bill-koonj

Zariba: Za-ree-ba

PLACES

Amarohi: Am-a-row-hee

Halmora: Hull-mo-ra

Illindhi: Ill-in-dhee

Jhanak: Jha-nuk (like "snuck")

Kalanadi: Kalaa-na-dee

Mesht: Mesh-t

Raluha: Ra-loo-ha

Ranagala: Run-a-guh-la

Talashshukh: Tull-ah-shook

Vanasi: Vun-ah-see

KINGDOMS AND SPICES

KINGDOM	RALUHA	HALMORA
SPICE	Saffron	Turmeric
BRIEF DESCRIPTION OF KINGDOM	The saffron kingdom, built along the sides of a valley, in the shape of a bowl. The saffron fields border the valley across the plains. Amid the fields lies the Spice Gate.	The turmeric kingdom lies in the heart of a forest. It is a fort city believed to be carved out of a single rock. While Halmora is home to priests and cults, fire-lions lurk in the forest beyond.
THRONEKEEPER	Raja Orbalun	Raja Virular
GATECASTES	Bowlers	Easters

Jhanak	Vanasi	Kalanadi
Cinnamon	Nutmeg	Black Pepper
The cinnamon kingdom, built on the largest island of an archipelago. Over a hundred islands surround Jhanak, many among them ruled by pirates.	The nutmeg kingdom, also known as the Empire of Towers. All of Vanasi lives in these nine towers, connected by crisscross bridges and floating markets. Only the rooters live outside the towers, on the ground.	The kingdom of black pepper is surrounded by impassable bogs and marshland. Ruled by the Lekha dynasty for centuries, Kalanadi boasts the most poisonous serpents found in the eight kingdoms.
Rani Zariba	Raja Jirasandha	Rani Asphalekha
Sanders	Rooters	Snakers

KINGDOM	Talashshukh	Mesht
SPICE	Ginger	Cumin
BRIEF DESCRIPTION OF KINGDOM	The ginger empire is the largest city among the eight kingdoms. It is rich in architectural marvels, with grand marble halls, libraries, plazas, and bazaars. The afsal dina celebration in Talashshukh has earned the moniker "the Festival of Madness."	The jeeranadu, the kingdom of cumin, comprises one hundred eighty-seven rivers and at least seven recorded species of elephants. Their famed tortoiseshells are often used as currency to buy Poison from the Jewelmaker's Carnelian Caravan.
THRONEKEEPER	Raja Silmehi	Rani Mehreen
GATECASTES	Horners	Oarasi

Amarohi	Illindhi
Clove	Olum
The kingdom of cloves is one of misty hills and solitude. A place also of silence. Speaking outside the confines of settlements is forbidden. The thronekeeper's palace rests atop the largest peak, shielded by clouds and eagle nests.	The first kingdom, and the heart of the world. Home to the enormous Mount Ilom, beneath which lies the Mouth, the deity that governs the Spice Gates. Illindhi's outer walls are carved in runes, which are said to be incantations from the scriptures.
Rani Kaivalya	Madhyra/Kashyni
Reeders	

ACKNOWLEDGMENTS

My thanks go to my editor, David Pomerico at Harper Voyager, who reminded me to not lose sight of the sense of wonder in this tale. A shout-out to the rest of the team at Harper Voyager, including Rachel Winterbottom, Mireya Chiriboga, Emily Fisher, Deanna Bailey, Rachelle Mandik, Lisa Glover, and Richard Aquan.

Immense gratitude to Naomi Davis and all of BookEnds Literary Agency. Naomi has been a pillar through the development of *The Spice Gate*, with their inexhaustible well of patience, encouragement, and nuggets of publishing knowledge that I hope to carry with me through my writing in the future. I cannot think of better representation than the team at BookEnds, including Jessica Faust, Sophie Sheumaker, James McGowan, and others.

To Omar Gilani, who designed the cover for *The Spice Gate*, and whose jaw-dropping illustrations, paintings, and ideas are always an inspiration. My friends, musketeers, and wonderful writers: Pritesh Patil, Gautam Bhatia, Chaitanya Murali, Lavanya Lakshminarayan, Amal Singh, Samit Basu, Tobi Ogundiran, Aindrila Roy, Kathleen Tan, Suresh Chandrashekhar, and Percy Wadiwala, who have been a part of this journey, some of whom have read this novel more than once, and whose tireless critiques, comments, and oft-underappreciated *being-there-ness* added flavor and taste to *The Spice Gate*.

To Nydhruv Kashyap and Varun Das, who read the earliest drafts of the novel.

Finally, this novel would be incomplete without the support of my family and friends: my grandparents; my parents; my sister, Pavithra

Murthy; my cousins Shrinidhi, Srihari, Sindhu, Bharat, and Swetha; my partner, Sai Kamala; Pavithra Narasimhan, Vysakh Madhavan, Ankush Kunzru, Shruti Ganguly, Sahiba Grover, Harsheen Kaur, Denis Albuquerque, Udit Pandey, Karan Arora, Jigyasa Sharma, Nirav Mehta, Abhishek Rao, Dharna Chauhan, and the late Rajashree Ravi, all of whom have touched this book in more ways than one.

Thank you.

ABOUT THE AUTHOR

PRASHANTH SRIVATSA is a writer of fantasy and science fiction. Prashanth's stories and novelettes have appeared in magazines such as *Asimov's Science Fiction*, the *Magazine of Fantasy & Science Fiction* (*F&SF*), *Beneath Ceaseless Skies*, and *Three-Lobed Burning Eye*, among others. He lives in Bengaluru, India. *The Spice Gate* is his first novel.